CHERNOVS' TOIL AND PEACE

A Novel

RIFET BAHTIJARAGIC

Edited by George Payerle

Translated from the Bosnian by Sanja Garic-Komnenic

Cover Artwork by Bill HOOPES—Painting:
"Mavroona in the Storm of Time", oil on canvas 36 x 48", 2009

PUBLISH AMERICA

PublishAmerica
Baltimore

Hardcover 978-1-4512-7252-9
Softcover 978-1-4512-7253-6
PUBLISHED BY PUBLISHAMERICA, LLLP
www.publishamerica.com
Baltimore

Printed in the United States of America

For Mrs. June with
my respect.

Rifet Bahtijeragić

To anyone liberated from hatred and aggression

And especialy for Mavroona (Popoff) Chernoff,
101 year old Doukhobor lady with hearth full of tolerance
and love, for her sons Michael and Charlie Chernoff;
Also for Doukhobor lady, Sara Grigorievna Kinyakina,
because she gave me a chance to meet contemporary
Canadian Doukhobors on the South of British Columbia
and two their great resurchers and writers Eli A. Popoff
and his son Dmitri.

OTHER BOOKS
By
Rifet Bahtijaragic

Skice za cikluse (Sketches for Cycles), poetry, Sarajevo, former Yugoslavia, 1972

Urija (Barren), poetry, Belgrade, former Yugoslavia, 1982

Krv u ocima (Blood in the Eyes), novel, Wuppertal, Germany, 1996

Bosanski bumerang (Bosnian Boomerang), novel, Tuzla, Bosnia-Herzegovina, 2001

Oci u hladnom nebu (Eyes to the Cold Sky), poetry, bilingual edition,
Tuzla, Bosnia-Herzegovina, 2004

Tragovi (Footprints), poetry and prose, Tuzla, Bosnia-Herzegovina, 2008

Footprints, poetry and essays,
Victoria, British Columbia, Canada, 2008

TRANSLATOR'S COMMENTS

Chernovs' Toil and Peace is an enchanting novel about human resilience. Novelist Rifet Bahtijaragic traces the origins of the Doukhobor teaching and follows the Russian Doukhobors—the clan of the Evstafy Chernovs—through centuries of oppression in Russia to the closing chapters of the novel depicting their arrival in Canada in the late nineteenth century and settlement in the West.

However broad and ambitious the scope of his novel, the author never loses his feeling for individual drama, for ordinary human beings and their destiny in turbulent times. The novel offers a palette of characters defined by their Doukhobor heritage but also by their specific human qualities. The characters live in harmony with nature, with changing seasons, and with the harsh Russian weather. Only the Russian oligarchy is out of harmony with them. The Tsars and the Orthodox Church pose a constant threat to the Doukhobors and their right to choose their own path to God. Persecuted by their own rulers, cursed by righteous in their own country, the Doukhobors are still quintessential Russians. They are Russian peasants, embedded in their tradition, enthralled by old Russian songs, which they bring to the New World. They grieve over the terrible destiny of the last Romanovs, unable to hate even those who symbolize the very oppression they suffered back home.

The characters in this novel of broad ideas and the universal human condition have a surprisingly local flavour. We get to know Leonid the Unfortunate, who looks for his long-ago abducted son among butterflies; Vasily, who can catch a snake by its neck; Lukeriya, the Doukhobor leader who takes Kostuna Chernov to the Caucasus

Mountains to visit the Tartar Little Princess—and we discover a whole world of free people in the Caucasus.

In Canada, the Doukhobors inhabit not only the empty prairies of their new world but also the imaginary spaces of the vast Canadian landscape. They bring their own stories and songs and within a few years they build their settlements, both physical and spiritual. Again Bahtijaragic manages to show the complex history of an entire people by focusing on a few individuals, Misha Chernov and his family. Misha represents the best of the Doukhobors: respect for Doukhobor tradition, informed by recognition of the need to change it. He believes that the Doukhobors in Canada need to become integrated and live not next to but together with the other ethnic groups that form the Canadian mosaic.

The last chapter of the long journey of the Russian-Canadian Doukhobors is the chapter common to all Canadians. Rifet Bahtijaragic, a Canadian Bosnian, speaks to all of us who are part of the long journey of humankind looking for a peaceful place on this planet where we can cherish our traditions and build a new one together with the other people of this great country.

-Sanja Garic-Komnenic

EDITOR'S COMMENTS

This extraordinary book is a fictionalized history of the Doukhobor Movement, from its roots in eighteenth-century Russia to its transplanted evolution in the west of Canada. It was written by a Canadian Bosnian in Central South Slavic, translated by a Bosnian scholar fluent in English, and edited by me, a Canadian Hungarian novelist. With that sort of genealogy, *Chernovs' Toil and Peace* needs a note on its language. The words you hold in your hands are indeed English, for the most part. But it is a fictive Old World English with strong Slavic accents, the flavours of folklore, myth and the kind of imagining called, in recent decades, "magic realism". In his native tongue, Rifet Bahtijaragic is a master stylist and rhetorician. It has been an honour to attempt rendering his talent in a language accessible to anglophones—but I do wish all of us could read Bosnian!

—George Payerle

CONTENTS

INTRODUCTION

Rifet Bahtijaragic has enriched his already prolific creative opus with a new novel titled *Chernovs' Toil and Peace.* With the power of his imagination and creativity, the author has come to grips with a difficult task: to bring his specific light to bear on the 300-year history of the Russian Doukhobors, or the "Christians of the Universal Brotherhood," as they called themselves.

Bahtijaragic does not invent things. He presents a truthful history of the Doukhobors and of their settlement in Canada. At the same time, however, the author's authentic poetic inspiration brings to the actual historical events an empathetic understanding bred from his own personal experience of the Bosnian exile and of immigrant life. The two deeply lived histories blend within the postmodernist texture of this contemporary historical novel. From dusty administrative and historical documents and from the correspondence of Lev Tolstoy and his son Sergey, Doukhobor martyrs miraculously come alive, those hardworking and modest people whose only sin was the desire to live according to their beliefs and habits, considerably different from the canons of the Russian Orthodox Church.

Doukhobors formed their teachings as early as the beginning of the eighteenth century. In many aspects theirs run parallel to the philosophical and religious social beliefs of the great Russian writer Lev Tolstoy, who, together with Sergey, fought for the Doukhobors' cause and protected them with the power of his reputation and authority.

The main ideas of the Doukhobor movement teach that life be organized around God's principles, and that all human beings be regarded as equal, requiring no mediation by Church institutions between man and God. For that reason the Tsar's regime and the Holy

Synod expelled them to faraway, inhospitable regions of Russia—Siberia and the Caucasus. Finally, at the end of the nineteenth century, the Russian tsar Nikolai Romanov the Second decided to allow the unruly Doukhobors to settle in Canada, but without the right to return to their homeland. Around 7,500 people decided to move to Canada, transported there and escorted by Sergey Tolstoy. The new country accepted them warmly, gave them land and the opportunity to make better living conditions for themselves through the hard labour which was part of their birthright. The Canadian government recognized that they would contribute to the development of the true north strong and free.

However, Bahtijaragic's novel is not only a story of the Doukhobors. The book is informed by the life paths of many people expelled both in the past and now from all four corners of the world, who have been forced to look in distant, unfamiliar places for peace and the possibility of a life lived according to their beliefs and insights. The author mentions Jews, Patarenes or "Bogumils," Huguenots, Quakers, Protestants, homosexuals, and all those whose sin is that they are significantly different from others in some respect, usually in their religious, social, ethnic or ideological affiliation.

Over a period of more then two and a half centuries, the author follows the history of the family of the Chernovs, introducing representatives of the successive generations into the story. Through the technique of reversed chronology we first get to know the contemporary Chernovs—Michael and Charlie Chernov and their mother Mavroona, a hundred-year-old lady whose life credo is to love the whole world. Then the author returns to the beginning of the long chain of events that closes in Vancouver. The beginning is in Russia, during the rule of Peter the Great. In a village inn belonging to a woman name Elysaveta, Doctor Evstafy Chernov talks about his tragic war experiences. From a dull rainy day a stranger enters the inn and talks to the gathered crowd about a new Christian teaching. Thus sets root among the gathered people the beginnings of Doukhobor teaching and anti-clerical sentiment, part of the tide of the peasant and workers' movements of social rebellion and unrest which announced the revolutions yet to come.

Evstafy Chernov joined the Doukhobor movement and, afterwards, all his family joined too. The son, Vasily, accepted his father's ideas and continued the Doukhobors' struggle for survival. Vasily's generation was tortured by persecution and, in the time of Catherine the Great, along with the other Doukhbors who would not renounce their beliefs, dispersed across the vast regions of Russia. Then Alexander Romanov the First took the Russian throne; he was a follower of the ideas of the Enlightenment, and he decided to return the expelled Doukhobors to the south of Russia. Thus, the Chernovs again settled in the homeland of their ancestors.

Among the Doukhobors some returned people came forth who believed that the new time required changes in the movement's thinking and way of life, an evolution of traditional Doukhobor teaching. Vasily Chernov and his son Stepan were among the bearers of these ideas. New generations of the Chernovs were born and they continued the struggle of their ancestors. Then we meet the main characters of the novel, Kostuna and his son, Doctor Misha, whose lives the plot of the rest of the novel follows.

The attitude of any immigrants toward their new country is similar, regardless of where people come from. At first, most people, afraid of losing their identity, live in isolation. It is especially typical of the elderly, such as Kostuna Chernov. He is one of those most suspicious of the intentions of the Canadian Government and is afraid that the government wants to quickly erase from their consciousness specifics of their identity and cultural and historical inheritance.

The generation of the middle-aged, where Misha Chernov belongs, has doubts that it is going to be easy to "empty our heads of what we have brought in them…The more others try to bring us closer to them, the more we will find strength to separate from them."

Misha thinks that it is easiest for the young generation, that of his son Petro. They will have a chance to choose. They will be able to accept what to them seems better and wiser in this country compared to what they inherited from their great-grandfathers.

Women are also more adaptable. Kostuna's Pelagiya, when the boat reaches the Canadian shore, already accepts in her heart those people "standing and waving from the shore as if greeting their closest relatives."

We can find almost the same thoughts about the behaviour and feelings of new immigrants in the texts of the contemporary American writer of Bosnian origin, Sasha Hemon. Hemon shares the belief that children are the ones most open to "the new," announced in Bahtijaragic's novel by "the sounds of some strange music coming from the shore".

There are few developed female characters in the novel. They are usually portrayed as good and industrious housewives; they possess the gift of extraordinary vitality, capable of meeting any challenge in order to preserve the family nest. They are loyal, full of understanding and tenderness; they are wives, mothers, sisters and lovers. They represent the light side of life, reliable, merciful, and forgiving. Prominent among them is Misha's first love from his boyhood, later his wife and the mother of their son—Boulisou, a Jewish woman of romantic rapture and strong eroticism.

The author describes their tragic love, stronger than all hatred and prejudice. Boulisou is kidnapped and disfigured by Orthodox priests, the passionate Doukhobors' ancestral adversaries. Misha grieves and in vain tries to find her for many years, as the Bogumil Gorcin in vain searches for his love, Kosara, in the poems of the Bosnian writer Mak Dizdar. Gorcin's Kosara was snatched and disappeared somewhere on "God's routes".

Misha's second love and his loyal life companion is Paroniya, who is educated, strong, remarkable. She helps in healing people, suffers persecution, fights for Doukhobor ideas, and shares their life of exile in Siberia.

The novel presents a whole gallery of characters from the most varied regions, social classes and epochs: common people born in the author's imagination and famous historical characters, Russian tsars and tsarinas, western journalists, representatives of the Canadian authorities, Doukhobor leaders, captains and ships' crews, fantastic beings and mythical heroes. Their thinking, conversations and behaviour allow the reader to grasp all the complexity of the problems of human existence, of ideas, movements and changes happening in the course of two and a half centuries. Especially emphasized is the difference between the Eastern and Western parts of the world, and the border between them, situated by the author at the Strait of Gibraltar.

Taylor, captain of the ship taking the Doukhobors to Canada, and Misha Chernov represent those two—according to them—opposite worlds. Their dialogue reveals a simplified image of the difference— in the East people are victims of their history, they are ruled by emotions, not reason; in the West life is reduced to action and the accumulation of material possessions.

The mythical hero Prometheus underlies almost all the philosophical and scientific-fantastic thoughts and messages Bahtijaragic puts before us. The parallel between the fate of Prometheus and the Golgotha of Doukhobor experience represents the pivotal idea in the novel. Prometheus, like the Doukhobors, is expelled to the Caucasus, punished for his sin of intending for man to be the creator of the most valuable aspects of life and to have the strength to rebel against the rules established religion and government impose by force.

While telling the story of the Doukhobor movement the author reconstructs the ideological and social context of a large part of the world in the time his characters live through. Above their collective destiny rises a mosaic of individual life stories, their individual happiness and sadness depicted in evocative fragments. On that level of story Bahtijaragic creates convincing poetic expression, bringing together the skills of the subtle lyric poet, the folk storyteller, and the versatile epic narrator who has transformed his personal experience and that of war and immigration into a magnificent novel recreating the experience of others.

That is why it is difficult to assign this novel to a genre according to traditional literary distinctions. The classical form of the historical/

social novel is too narrow to include all the life energy, the vast dimensions of time and space contained in Bahtijaragic's work. This novel is mosaic not only in narrative structure, but in its diverse genres, narrative styles and literary techniques.

Based on these features, Bahtijaragic's novel belongs to postmodern literature with all its hybrid literary forms combining fairy tale and myth, the real and the fantastic, philosophical, religious, and political reflections, elements of the detective novel, historical documents and news clips. This type of novel is the reality factory, the place of transformation, suitable for conversion into a film or TV scenario.

Accordingly, there are passages in the novel where the author, with the precision of a historian, gives information about the place of an event, about the participants, real or fictional, and about their ideas and beliefs. Then suddenly, carried by poetic rapture, Bahtijaragic alters the tone of the narrative; subtle lyrical notes stir within him when touched by the beauty of the morning born on the open sea or by the beautiful pattern on the wings of a butterfly. Then he speaks as a poet who, with the whole strength of his reason and heart, desires peace, equality and justice, not only on the entire earth but also in the universe. His novel is a social document in which all is scrutinized according to the moral belief that the topmost ideal is to live according to natural laws and to achieve moral truth. At the same time, the author's messages are abundant in life-happiness and the optimistic belief that people can achieve a full and happy life, deserved simply for being human. Such feeling and atmosphere is most discernible in the scenes abounding in eroticism springing from the depth of human biological instincts. In those moments of coming together the heroes and heroines of the novel are perfectly in tune with the world ruled by natural laws and permanent harmony.

The history of the Doukhobors and their voyage to the new world offers the author an excellent opportunity to reflect on and bring light to basic problems of human existence, the way they appeared in the eighteenth century, and the way they have evolved up to the present time, the twenty-first century. The author's experience and his valuable message to all immigrants is that in the new country one needs to live, reflect on and reform inherited ideas and not find escape in isolation, which equals self-imposed prison. Religious and any other principles cannot be the same through all time periods or in different life conditions. They need to be adjusted to new times and new places of refuge. The author compresses this message into folk wisdom: *When you come to somebody's house, if you want the host to accept you, you need to accept the host.*

With his extraordinary narrative talent Bahtijaragic builds in this novel a beautiful monument to the Doukhobor movement, to the people who, with their enormous vitality, energy, and resilience, were able to survive evil deeds and expulsion, and preserve and bring to their new homeland the best of what their ancestors had left them as inheritance.

Chernovs' Toil and Peace leaves us with the impression of permanent incompleteness and the need for ever fresh understanding, adjusting to historical reality as it changes. Exactly in this openness and the possibility of independent existence for a completed work of art lies the excellence of this novel. As in his books of poetry and in the previous novels, in this latest novel Bahtijaragic perseveres in his desire and search for the salvation of civilization and for the achievement of happiness for humanity. Among the Doukhobors he has found soul mates, brothers and sisters who have through centuries cherished the same idea and hope of world unity and the achievement of omnipresent harmony and cosmic justice, available even to the smallest living creature.

—Mevlida Karadza

FIRST PART

1

In the shop windows on Robson Street I have recently noticed a lot of bizarre and raw metropolitanism, as if Vancouver still did not know how to behave as a winner in the race for the throne as "world's most liveable city". You notice a lack of taste when seeing crumpled clothes on the mannequins in shop windows and a peculiar taste in the colour combinations or arrangements of dinner plates: Old Country Roses, made by the famous Royal Doulton from Stoke-on-Trent, with silverware from some upstart Malaysian manufacturer. I particularly dislike the trivial advertisement of discounts that seem to be more about inciting consumerist fervour than promoting good taste and quality. I wonder how it is possible for people to buy that phoney hype, to accept the tasteless belittling of buyers, and not to finally gain the courage to tell those pseudo-merchants and greenhorn bullies of pedestrians in the most vibrant street of the pearl city of the Pacific: Get lost!

The day that I saw him at the stairs in front of the entrance to the Earls Restaurant on the corner of Robson and Bute, I noticed that those shop windows really annoyed me. I could easily forgive them for the crumpled sleeves of shirts and jackets and for the mismatched colours of the clothes on the mannequins—the disgusting ads about year-round discounts, I could not. But, as the devil wants it, unwittingly, I found myself in a paradoxical situation—the message on the beggar's money box, set in the middle of a big red heart on the sidewalk, was more than refreshing. In bold black marker it was written: You do not need to give me a dollar. Fifty cents is enough. His going along with the trend of the shop windows was forgivable. Even pleasant. His name he told me later. First, I caught myself trying to guess. It seemed to me it could be been Frank. For sure not the legendary sports and broadcasting laureate of this city, Frank A. Griffiths. Nor his son Frank Junior. I do not know why Frank, but something in my subconscious mind was telling me that the man in front of me had that very name. In university I had a classmate called Volich (son-of-a-bull), and to me it was not a surprise that Volich's head looked like a bull's. I almost bit my tongue! The beggar looked like my friend Frank Guidobono when I held out my hand to him to pull him out of a hole covered with snow, two winters ago at the Cypress ski slopes above Vancouver.

He was sitting on a low plastic stool and was looking almost with no interest beyond the plain tin box, which, without its unusual message, would have been left unnoticed by the eyes of the colourful mosaic of shoppers and pedestrians. His face was shaped as if it had been cloaked in fog from which only the tip of his neatly groomed beard could be seen, along with the tip of his round, button-shaped nose and the two burning blue eyes with translucent eyelashes. He looked like Frank soaked in snow. Moreover, they both looked like the snowman that my children used to make in faraway Bosnia. He also reminded me of those winters that used to be common there, when wolves in the mountains would come across a frozen rabbit, and, after some unsuccessful attempts at biting the frozen meat, would leave, not persuaded by the prognosis of the Canadian scientist David Suzuki that global warming would ever warm up the winters in that part of the world.

"Why exactly fifty cents?" I asked.

Surprised, he shifted his gaze from the crowd on the street to my eyes.

"Usually, they don't ask," he tried to explain his surprise. "Either they put something in the box, or they pass by as if I didn't exist…A lot of people don't give to beggars because they want to help improve the beggars' social position. They just want to do their good deed of the day. To gain credit for themselves from the one who is all-seeing and who judges us…Fifty cents is less than a dollar. It is maybe easier for you to give fifty cents. Also, it goes along with all these offers on Robson."

He looked at me curiously, waiting for my reaction.

He followed my gaze toward a dozen magazines on the other side of his box. It must have seemed to him that my look was resting on them. Maybe he was thinking about my likely comment on the several bold titles next to the pictures of naked women on the cover of the magazine on top. Without waiting to hear my impression, he said, while looking away at the women walking on the sidewalk in front of us:

"People are always being enslaved. Nowadays, they are enslaved mostly by the owners and editors of magazines, by TV hosts and movie producers…Here, look at the cover of this magazine." He took the one on top and handed it to me. "Look at these women and the titles of the articles about them. Two of them brag about drastically reducing their body weight in a short time by using weight-loss slimmers manufactured by crafty manipulators of female feelings. The third one claims she rejuvenated her face with plastic surgery, augmented her breasts and bum and became what she has yearned to be since her youth."

He became silent, waiting for my contribution to his protest.

"Everybody is the owner of their own body," I said calmly. "The time has come when people can interfere with destiny. In the past we used to say that one was fated to be fat or another to be ugly…Now people can change that and in a couple of weeks make a skinny person out of a fat one and out of an ugly person they can make a handsome one with just one plastic surgery."

"I do not believe that you so easily accept such a manipulation of the human brain," he commented on my reaction. "In that I see the beginning of chaos in civilization. Such an attack on human genes and the natural order of things will obliterate the visible identity of each individual, his face. People will be able to order one of their legs to be fat and the other slim…Maniacs will be able to change the structure of chromosomes in the archives of the genes, and we will have monster children."

It looked as if this man was reading my thoughts and revealing my feelings. More than that, I was focused on the question of who he could be. He could not be a common beggar on Robson. Our conversation was interrupted by a group of people walking toward us with the obvious intention to visit the man with the box.

It was a group of Filipinos. (I think they were Filipinos since they looked like the people from the Philippines I got to know, who came to Vancouver through Singapore and Hong Kong to maintain the mansions of the rich of this city for low pay.) A little boy separated from the group to venture closer and carefully drop some coins into the box. He moved his lips while doing this, as though praying. He did not even look at the beggar, as if the beggar had nothing to do with the box. Then he ran after the group as they casually walked away, keeping an eye on the boy.

The beggar was looking after the strange donor and was saying something under his breath. He realized I'd noticed his silent comment.

"They must be from Panay Island in the Philippines Archipelago," he explained. "Among them there exists a belief that the one who drops coins into a beggar's box in a foreign village, city or a country, will gain the privilege of asking God for help if he finds himself in trouble. Parents usually grant this honour to their children, believing that in this manner they are buying a special place for their children in the treasury of God's mercy. They always throw metal coins into the box so that God can see and hear their act of mercy."

His comment reminded me of my early youth, when I used to go to town fairs with my grandmother, my father's mother, and she would give me coins to throw at beggars. I wondered how she managed to hide them from me. Sometimes there were more beggars at the fair than she had expected, so, in that case, we had to stay away from the beggar we did not have any more money for.

"I'll buy you dinner at White Spot if you want to eat together. I don't like to eat alone. Especially dinner," I suggested.

He could not hide a wince in his eyes.

"Are you alone too?" he asked, and as if he had exposed himself in front of a too-serious audience, he hastened to say:

"Oh, no! Thank you, sir. I can't...I couldn't!" he refused politely and added, as though owing me an explanation: "I buy food myself. My tastes are also out of the ordinary. In any case, I need to be here till ten tonight. This is my spot and I can't let anyone take it. People leave this Earls place happy and forget about saving. And I spent a long time away from my work today since my curiosity led me to BC Place Stadium. This sudden cold weather has conspired with snow and ice to make a hole in the fabric of the roof, and last night's strong wind tore it wide open so it collapsed onto the huge space of the playing field." The man in front of me had unexpectedly become talkative. He shrugged his shoulders, as if thinking that this might not interest me, but still he added: "When a roof just like this one collapsed in Minnesota in the same way, the owners of our stadium didn't realize that it could happen in this climate too. When it happened, the rumours started that the problem will not be to replace the four hectares of special fabric, but to allay the fear that the same could happen in February 2010. The Winter Olympic Games opening ceremony will take place inside this Stadium at BC Place."

"Strange," I said. "More than strange. That roof is covered with a material made of Teflon and glass fibres and seemed a convincing guarantee of comfort and safety to the millions of people who visited hundreds of games and shows in that sports giant."

The beggar scratched himself behind his ear and looked at the skyscrapers behind which stood the stadium "Nature still rules the earth," he commented. "One storm in Vancouver and a hole in that roof and almost a disaster. BC Place can receive 60,000 spectators. And there have been many important ones... What if the roof had collapsed when Queen Elizabeth was inside? Maybe the media would've blamed it on a terrorist attack. Or when Clinton was there..."

That beggar, still sitting on the stool in front of me, made me wonder. I had believed that such people disregarded common reasoning in life and sank into a very bare-boned attitude toward events at a higher level in society and the environment. This man had walked a mile from the location of his box for the money from pedestrians' pockets. To see a big fallen roof and speculate on its significance.

I put a ten-dollar note in his box. He registered my look with his gaze. I was surprised by the thought that through my eyes he had discovered a path into what he'd wanted to find in me.

"Why ten, sir?" he asked. "I'm only a beggar."

His voice had not changed its colour or intonation. I did not reply. Suddenly his gaze flew towards the intersection of Robson and Burrard. I tried to find out what he'd noticed there, but I could not see anything out of the ordinary.

"Our politicians have recently become subjects for the *Guinness Book of World Records*," he whispered as if talking to himself. "Clark was signing contracts to build fast ferries, and then Campbell was selling them off for 10% of their value. At least, both should've asked the taxpayers who'd paid for those boats what to do with them. Ujjal Dosanjh left the New Democrats to become a minister in Paul Martin's government, and then David Emerson left the Liberals overnight and joined the Conservatives, because the Liberals had handed over the position of Prime Minister to Stephen Harper."

I realized that in front of me was an unusual beggar, somebody who could have come to this street directly from some local political party. Or maybe he was a policeman infiltrated among beggars to investigate an intricate criminal case. Or some scientist who was testing his scientific hypothesis by dressing as a beggar. Or I had so far been greatly ignorant about this class of the human species. Before I made any comment, I accepted that this man was a completely normal individual who, at the least, felt a desire to read the newspapers easily found in the garbage containers from which Vancouver beggars take juice cans and glass bottles to sell at the return depots.

"In one of my poetry books I have a poem called 'Beggar,' and I would like to recite it to you," I said, trying to change the subject of our conversation.

He shifted his gaze from the intersection to his box. I noticed a quiver in his thin eyelashes.

"I'd rather listen to a happy one," he said. "Or, say, one about how Cabinet Minister Emerson switched from the Liberals to the Conservatives overnight so that he could get the minister's seat. I like jokes at their expense."

I caught myself following his train of thought. "Maybe it is the beginning of a new era in our political life, some new definition of dignity and morality for politicians in a society at the borderline of anarchist democracy."

"Maybe. Or it's one more proof of human lust. It seems to me that people are continuing to be aggressive egoists who would, for their own benefit, sell things more sacred than a political party." Thus he concluded his remarks about the politicians, who will, if for nothing else, remain known in Canadian history for that shameful act.

"However, it's nothing new in civilization," I said. "In the region of Tito's Yugoslavia, in the last decades of the 20th century, not long after Tito's death, whole masses of people changed their political convictions overnight and spat at that which they used to swear to."

"I'm not comfortable here either, and I'd go there if there was no other place for me in the world. It seems to me that there they'd throw me a bill, and then change their mind and snatch it from my hands. Maybe they'd even punch me," my snowman said on the frozen sidewalk of Robson Street. "I didn't suppose you'd be a poet. You can read me your poem. My temporary mental absence won't stop those who wish to put coins into my box."

"I know it by heart," I said. "Reading would attract people from this crowd and that is not what I want right now."

He did not react. Noticing his fixed gaze, directed at some imaginary point in his memory, I realized I should start reciting the verses. His focus began to shift outward, at me.

The more of my verses I recited, the more studiously he observed me, not hiding his surprise. After that, in the manner of an experienced critic, he glanced toward the spot across Robson where, by the immense wooden doors of the Thai restaurant, in front of a heap of black bags, another homeless man sat—his closest competition.

"He is my only neighbour on this street," he said, realizing I was following his glance. "All these people who pass like a stream, indifferent to the occasional driftwood that has washed up on their shore, cannot be my neighbours. To them, he and I are just something that has been thrown out from their sort.

I made no comment. For me that beggar on the other side of the street was something else. I believed that all of his possessions were in those black bags.

31

"The poem is impressive," he said pensively.

I felt he was digging through his own life.

"I am glad you're bringing us back among people," he continued his review. "The flood of feeling is unusual in it. The world is growing more and more rough, if I may make that judgement from my position. It's as if you had put yourself in my shoes…but you haven't depicted the causes. Here you are a master of description. That poem is not social criticism. You don't condemn and you offer no solution. You are excellent at depicting the sun perfectly as it shines through the clouds, but you don't say what it represents for this life on earth. You don't say who is to blame for the existence of beggars. Are they a product of social inequality, the rule of unscrupulous lawyers, of exploiters looking at people as if they were gladiators who stay in the arena only as long as they are valuable to the owners of their lives?…Throwing in the mud those who don't have the heart to oppress people, unhappy marriages, the demoralized…A greedy mentality dominating human society.

He stopped and once again fixed his eyes on the homeless man with the long black hair on the other side of the street.

"Who do you think my neighbour is?" the beggar asked, and continued, knowing what my answer would be. "He was a good businessman, got rich trading with the Chinese, had a wife and three kids. He says there wasn't a single night when his kids didn't fall asleep on his chest. Then one day, out of the blue, his wife's lawyer came to him and handed him divorce papers, like lightning out of a clear blue sky. These lawyers analyze families and when they find one they can make money from, they cunningly offer their services, break up a marriage and take everything from the one who loses. What do you think happened to that poor guy?"

"I don't know," I shrugged.

"I know you don't, but you can guess. The same thing that happens to many in this lawful country. Lawyers froze his assets, destroyed his business, got a case ruling which gave 90 percent of his assets to them and his wife, and allowed him to see his children only two hours a month. I hate lawyers more than anything in the world. They rule this country…And, there he is! He told me he was left with no option but to fight for his spot by the Thai restaurant. The remaining 10% he locked in the bank until he decides who to give it to.

"He moved in with some old woman by Skytrain in Burnaby and he shares with her whatever he gets on the street. He uses those bags to claim his couple of square meters by the restaurant."

"If I can judge him by his face, he doesn't look powerless. He could have made a different decision." This opinion slipped from my tongue. I did not mean to talk about Vancouver's societal problems with this man. But I was richer in experience about a different side of life on Robson Street than most people—especially politicians—who find it irrelevant.

I don't know if my comment touched him. It seemed I was talking more to myself. He was, nonetheless, studying my face.

"Maybe you're right," he said, and his face became more shapeless as if he were drowning further into the fog. I realized he was continuing his review of my poem. "We all expect the same from you: to throw us a coin. But each of us is a different story. Some even try to earn your pity. They run across intersections to wash your car windows, they offer to read your palm, to predict your future. I don't even mind if you throw your gift out of arrogance. What's more important to me is that it doesn't miss the box."

He followed his last words with a mysterious smile. There was something about this man that drew me into conversation with him. But it was cold. While I had been walking down Robson Street, I did not feel the cold. Now it was beginning to bite at me. The arthritis in my joints and the painful pressure in my lungs warned me that I had spent more time in Vancouver's wet and chill weather that day than my health allowed. And it was getting darker. Small, sparse snowflakes started falling, but the passersby did not intend to stop their stroll. I almost forgot that it was Saturday afternoon and that in all of downtown Vancouver there was no better place for a stroll than Robson Street, the legendary Robsonstrasse.

"Something strange is happening at my neighbour's corner," my new acquaintance alerted me.

A group of policemen had gathered around the beggar and his bags by the Thai restaurant's huge doors. One of them was talking to the beggar, explaining something while pointing to his black bags. Pedestrians quickly gathered around them, blocking our view of the beggar and his swarm of police.

"I didn't believe they'd do it," the nervous voice of my companion could be heard.

"What?" I asked.

"There is a rumour that the authorities will try to clear Downtown of its beggars, drug dealers and prostitutes. To begin preparing the city for the Olympic Games. It seems they have started with my neighbour."

He got up, clumsily standing on his toes to better see what was happening on the other side of the street, from which we could still hear the voices of the police and the homeless man. Then he looked at me, raising his eyebrows as if to apologize for what was going on there. As if the beggars were guilty of disturbing the peace on Robson.

He stooped down and took his beggar's box and the cardboard on which the big red heart was drawn. He looked again to the other side of the street, trying hard to comprehend the meaning of those voices, and looked at me in confusion.

"Maybe it's not what you think," I said just to say something.

"It is. I am sure it is. I don't dare wait for them to spoil the image of Robson here too. You won't hold it against me. And who knows, maybe they are not even policemen. Maybe they're just wearing police uniforms. You can expect anything nowadays. Many things in the world are disturbing. That damn Pickton killed and butchered fifty prostitutes and until number forty-nine, nobody discovered him. He was on number forty-nine. The fiftieth he killed in his dreams in his jail cell.

It was obvious my interlocutor wanted to leave his beggar's spot, even though as soon as he picked up his box and the cardboard with the picture of the red heart from the sidewalk, nobody would be able to tell he was a beggar. Not by his face nor his clothes. Definitely not by his intelligence.

"Can I help you?" I asked impulsively. "Is there something I can do for you? Come with me! I can help."

He looked at me and in a flash turned his head toward his stool and some things beside it. He quickly took the stool and put it next to a big wooden planter, in which flowers lived until winter came. Only one who knew that the stool was there would be able to find it between the vase and the restaurant wall. Then, from the pile of things he had, he took a paper bag with handles and without a second thought passed it to me.

"If you are offering your help, take this. This is my good friend's manuscript. When this cold spell began in Vancouver he was found dying in a garbage container. I visited him in St. Paul Hospital a few hours before he died. He could hardly move or speak, but managed to give me this manuscript and ask me to show it to a writer. Read it and tell me what you think about the text when you see me. I have been waiting for a long time to come across somebody familiar with literature."

I did not have time to think whether to accept this offer from a man whom I hardly knew well enough to be able to believe him. I took the bag with its contents and asked:

"Where will I find you again?"

"Here. Not even a crazy person would give this place up."

He quickly gathered the rest of his stuff and shoved it in a big greyish backpack.

He threw it over his shoulder and said to me as he was leaving:

"You must have a good heart. Few people would throw such a big bill into a beggar's box. Read the manuscript and get other people to read it. Get it published."

I was afraid that he would disappear among the crowd of pedestrians at the intersection of Robson and Burrard without telling me his name. I shouted:

"What is your name?"

"I'm Frank. My friends in Downtown know me!" He shouted back and disappeared among the people.

I was left surprised. His name really was Frank! How on earth had I guessed that?

He was right about the clearing of Robson Street. I saw a group of policemen approaching, and on the other side of the street they were already pushing Frank's neighbour into a big police van. The policemen approached me and one of them, the bulkiest, with wide shoulders and narrow hips, a fair short-trimmed moustache and ruddy puffy cheeks, asked me authoritatively:

"Where did the homeless man that was sitting here go? We saw that you were standing beside him."

"He's homeless?" I surprised him with my question. "I was talking to an extremely intelligent man…"

"You talked to him? That homeless man is mute. They call him Muty. Since he got here he hasn't said a word to anybody."

I wasn't keen on continuing the conversation with the policeman. I shrugged my shoulders as if I didn't care whether that homeless man was mute or not and I headed toward Bute Street. The policemen did not try to stop me. On the corner of Bute and Robson a tall scrawny teenager was thrusting pieces of paper into the hands of passersby. I got one too and while looking for a garbage bin to put it in, I read what it said: "Will the fate of Tony from *Scarface* befall America too?" I hadn't seen the movie, so the question meant as little to me as the Hippocratic Oath had meant to bloody Dr. Radovan Karadzic.

Two hours later I was reading the manuscript that the homeless man had bestowed on me. The next day at dusk I went to Robson to Frank's working place by the Earls restaurant and waited for him for more than two hours, but he didn't show up. The beggar from across the street didn't come to his spot either. I searched for Frank every day for more than ten days. In vain. I stopped when one day at dusk, the chill having already left Vancouver and gone beyond the first chain of the Coast Mountains, I found another beggar in Frank's corner. He had dirty long, fair hair, pale squinting eyes and a long turned-up nose. He was surprised when I asked him about Frank, for he knew for sure that a person called Frank had never been in that spot, but rather a scrawny Jeremy, whom the police had taken to Saint Paul's hospital about ten days earlier and who, he'd heard, had died that same night on a mobile bed in the hallway of the Emergency clinic before a doctor could see him. His spot was left unoccupied for seven days, according to an unwritten rule of Vancouver's beggars. No Frank or even Muty—as the policeman had called him—had ever been there, he said.

I was left with no option but to pay more serious attention to the manuscript, which that man, who had assumed the name of the Frank the beggar, had bestowed on me. When I again turned the first page of the manuscript, I remembered how the title "In the Storm of Time" had surprised me upon my first reading. "But it is not important," I said to myself, and started reading, this time much more carefully and studiously. Whenever I want to read something that is important to me, I do it at night, when normal people usually go to bed. That night a gentle eastern wind was pushing the rain to Vancouver, so that raindrops were tapping on my window. To me there is nothing more inspirational than the harmony of the sounds produced by raindrops hitting window panes. I am fascinated by the thought of the different wind currents mixing with raindrops, carrying them toward something they eventually hit and thus create a melody I have never heard performed by musicians, neither modern nor classical.

There were a few phone numbers on the title page of the manuscript. There were names next to two of them. One was Michael Chernoff, from Vancouver, and the other, Bruce Chernoff, from Calgary. From the first couple of pages the text frequently referred to that same family name, but I could not find the author's name anywhere. Why not call the Chernoff who lived closer to me? I wanted to explain to him that I held in my hands a manuscript on which his number was written. I dialled the number. I figured it wasn't too late, only 10:15. He answered the phone and I hastily apologized for the comparative lateness of the hour, and told him why I was calling. He was silent for a few moments as if trying to explain to himself what the call was about. When he spoke, there was something in the tone of his voice that permitted one to judge his character.

"You probably have my brother Charlie's manuscript. I don't know how you came across it, but it was stolen from him about fifteen days ago at BC Place during the Doukhobor festival. He brought it to Vancouver to try to find a writer who would produce a book based on it. This text is very important to all of us in our family. You know, my brother hates computers and machines. The manuscript is original. He didn't think someone would steal it, so he didn't make a copy."

We arranged to meet the next morning at around nine for coffee at Thomas Hass in North Vancouver.

When I met Michael there, I immediately recognized in him the Russian I used to describe as a child in the stories I would tell my brothers and sisters at bedtime to entertain them. This Russian from my stories was always a saviour, good-natured and wise. During our conversation, I told him I was a writer. I accepted Michael's suggestion and agreed to consider writing a book based on the manuscript.

Two days after our meeting, I sent him an e-mail saying that in this text about the destiny of the Chernoff family of the Russian Doukhobors, I had found a lot in common with the roots of my family, which emerged into modern times from the destroyed movement of the Bosnian heretics—the Bogomils or Patarens, as they are known around the world. I accepted the challenge.

Michael's reply was swift: "Maybe it would be a good idea for you to meet all those still alive of my Chernoff lineage at my mother's 100th birthday party. If you are not scared of flying in my small jet, you now have an invitation to fly with me in three weeks to Saskatchewan for the celebration."

I did not hesitate. I accepted the invitation.

After meeting the Chernoffs at their gathering in the heart of the Canadian prairies, I was impressed and inspired. This hundred-year-old lady had not lost any of her wisdom and goodness, even though she definitely could not pass as a thirty-year-old woman! I was fascinated by Charlie. He was about twenty years younger than his mother, and I was facing a scientist of many disciplines, among which the science of human goodness dominated. Bruce and his toddler-son Lukas were the real bearers of the family tradition. Michael's daughter, Catherine Anne, and Charlie's daughters, Cheryl Teresa and Carlotta, looked very much like their grandmother Mavroona. Michael's wife, Dorina, could not hide her British roots. Neither could Bruce's wife. An English mother and Egyptian father had given her face a lot of the symbolism found in the past of the pharaohs.

At the end of our visit, we followed the grandmother out of the room. It looked as if she had no trace of arthritis in her legs. They were unable to persuade her not to get into Charlie's car and go to the airport. At the small private airport near Yorkton, this family's two private jet airplanes were waiting for us.

My thoughts wandered off, following Charlie's manuscript into the family's past, where I found them in the Doukhobor communities in the Caucasus, in Russia, more than a century ago, when they held no private property, and when their children were rarely sent to university. In passing, I asked the old lady for her recipe for longevity. Her smile revealed both pride and wisdom.

"So far I haven't followed anybody's recipes. My life was not easy. I worked a lot, loved a lot, and whenever someone tempted me to hate him, I would try to smile widely to show him that I love the whole world. You too are dear to me, although I know neither who you are nor where you come from."

When we hugged the old lady and Charlie to say goodbye, she said to me:

"Brother, I know that when you see my children's and grandchildren's planes you cannot believe that they belong to a family of Doukhobors. What would've become of us had we refused to take in all the good habits of the people we found living in this country when we came here?!"

Through a small window of the plane I studied her face one more time and it revealed satisfaction and triumph.

Michael and Charlie were similar. In Michael's comprehension of life and friendship, the analytic procedure was dominant. But it was easy to read the genetic material of these two brothers from the peculiarities of their faces and from the radiance in their eyes. I got confused when I realized, looking down from the plane at the Canadian flatland covered with snow, that it would be difficult to trace the two of them back into the beginnings of the Doukhobor Movement in Russia, some 300 years ago. It was not difficult to discern the genetic influences of the new world in the features of their faces, dominated by Russian shapes and colours, while Charlie's manuscript began with the description of a bulky, more dark-skinned-than-fair Chernov, his character so typical of the pure-blooded Russians from Tolstoy's and Pasternak's novels.

2

The autumn rains raised the waters of the brook and of the River Isna in the fertile valleys of Tambov's waterways in southern Russia. As the waters swelled and the valleys by the waterways turned into small lakes, everything that lived there and that venerated the blessings of the summer—the birds, rodents, deer and fawns, beasts and humans and their goat and sheep flocks, their herds of cows and horses—all of it retreated up to the plateaus and high plains where the waters could not reach them. Only later, when the cold breath of winter arrived from the North, turned the surfaces of placid waters into a hard shield of ice, and spared only the narrow choppy part of the river's current, would humans and animals occasionally return to the icy shield and bring it to life. In that autumn, in the middle of the 18th century, during the rule of the controversial Russian monarch Peter the Great, common Russian peasants and farmers lived in the Tavrov village of Goreloye. Their way of life was so attached to and entwined with nature that they both loved and respected each other in the way of sailors in a small boat at sea; their lives and all their activities were tied to the laws of nature and its weather conditions. And nature has always announced its tides and sometimes its wrath in a very clear way so that humans, like the plant and animal kingdom, could adjust to its changes in a timely fashion.

All the families in the village, just as those in all other rural communities on the planet, strove to provide for the cold long winter. Like the forests around them, they put away their summer clothing with the first autumn rains, and altered their daily routines. This natural tide, never changing through immeasurable time, brought a wave of conscious changes in the lives of these people. And if one smart-ass dared to challenge this law, nature would slap him so hard that he would quickly learn the lesson and follow the behavioural norm. That tradition in nature and life was defined by such solid laws that all human speculations and philosophies were of lesser importance, sporadic or trivial, like powder or makeup on a human face. The only part of Goreloye that remained immutable was the inn of the old baba Elysaveta Babooshkina. At its frail wooden walls, those waves of seasonal change would stop and become powerless in face of the life inside. Peasants would drop by after daily labour as if coming into sanctuary, looking for relief for their tired bodies and giving themselves to respite and story-telling, to the elixir of vodka and to the drawn-out nostalgic song about something that had been important, now gone and sorely missed.

One day in the middle of the 18th century, while Russia's big cities were warming up under the waves of the European Renaissance in politics, arts, philosophy and ways of life, into Elysaveta's inn there burst a middle-aged soldier, sopping wet from the endless, ever colder rain. He had a long greyish moustache and strands of hair straggled from his soldier's hat. He bore recognizable signs of exhaustion on his neatly shaven face. At a big round table, Evstafy Chernov was telling a group of the village men about his war escapades somewhere in the parts of Finland close to Sweden. He had been serving in the Russian Tsarist Army as a doctor for all soldiers' war calamities, the ailments and wounds of his comrades-in-arms and those of the captured "enemy" who begged for help.

Evstafy was in the midst of trashing statesmen and politicians who proclaim wars, painting word-pictures of suffering beneath all human dignity, when all present turned their heads to see the stranger who had entered the inn. If he were one of them, he would have given some sign, a call or knock, before opening the door. Evstafy felt a current of cold, humid air chill his back. The stranger stopped right by the door, calling God's name as greeting Then, to general surprise, he continued where Evstafy had stopped:

"In war, people kill people. In war people become either beasts who tear apart other people's bodies, or victims of those who like animals maul and kill them. A third group is made up of war profiteers, rulers and politicians, the only ones who benefit from our misery."

He looked at the faces and clothes of those closest to him, looked down at the puddle of water growing at his feet on the floor made of uneven pieces of baked clay set into hard-packed river sand. He shrugged his shoulders by way of apology for having come in carrying so much water. He walked towards the only empty table, stopped as if having remembered something, and added:

"And our church fathers. Believe me, people; for a long time I did not know what they gain from inciting us to kill each other. And all along calling God's name and blessing us and our weapons with holy water. Now I know why. They bless us and sacrifice us on altars to please tsars and to gain their share of power over us. But they call God's name like the worst infidels and blasphemers, they threaten us with God as if we haven't all been created by God's will. Is there a greater blasphemy than inciting God's creatures against each other and being an accomplice in their slaughter?"

The village men did not understand how this stranger could join their conversation as if he had been sitting with them all along, listening to Evstafy's tale about the sorrows of common men. Evstafy understood that the stranger had been standing by the door and listening to their conversation to find out who was inside the inn. He did not blame him, for he would've done the same had he found himself in a similar situation. Perhaps he wouldn't have joined in so spontaneously to reveal his own outlook on social issues, but there was nothing peculiar in the behaviour of the rain-poured stranger. For a moment he likened the worn-out face of the incomer to that of a soldier in Irkutsk whose legs had been severed above the knees by Swedish artillery. The swift intervention of Chernov and his field-hospital crew saved him from the clutches of death. However, this stranger had both legs. Then his memory flew back to a scene when people had run into the hospital tent, screaming for others to clear their path, carrying a stretcher on which lay a middle-aged Cossack with a Swedish saber thrust into his chest. His eyes were the same as those of this tired, probably hungry soldier. But the Cossack had died as soon as the saber was pulled out of his chest. While he was dying, his eyes rolling, searching Evstafy's, he whispered ever more slowly and unintelligibly:

"In my pocket...a letter...Tell them I'm in Siberia...Far...In Si..."
That one had died and Evstafij gathered the soldier's letter contained
information on whom to tell that he was in Siberia. Not that he was
dead, but in Siberia. With a considerable effort, Evstafy forced himself
to cut off further memories of soldiers brought to his hospital tent while
he was stationed for the longest time at places of most fierce fighting.

Curiously, the face of the soldier who had entered the inn a couple
of minutes earlier was like many of the faces Evstafy had encountered
as a physician. Later, thinking about it, he wondered how it was
possible that almost all of the soldiers who had been brought to him
with their legs and arms dismembered, their heads deformed, their
chests and backs slashed, were so alike. Or maybe in his mind he saw
them that way, for they had all been close to death and far from their
dear ones, to whom they wanted to say goodbye at that moment.

Then the old Elysaveta came in, staring at them as if judging. She
scrutinized the stranger and addressed him, businesslike: "Your horse
is tired and, it seems to me, hungry. I'll put him with my horses. Is it
used to horse company?"

"No worries, good woman. My Black rode over half of Russia with
me. He is used to people, so he'll be fine among horses. He does not like
to be stared at but is patient. He eats whatever he's given. If one of your
horses bites him, he will know how to protect himself."

At these words people in the inn burst into spontaneous laughter.

"If something happens to one of us, we have a doctor. The one who
can cure people can cure animals too," added Elysaveta, her eyes gaily
flickering at the village men, their mouths stretched laughing. "Fine,
fine. It is better that way. My horses don't dislike strangers. They are
used to company and quickly accept others. Mashenka! Fetch Mishka
and tell him to tend to the horse!" Babushka Elysaveta shouted this
towards a young woman who was serving the guests, then quickly
disappeared behind the dark doors leading into the house.

The villagers and Doctor Chernov followed the soldier's talk with
surprise and interest and studied his face, trying to fathom his
intentions and identity. The doctor was first to remember that they
should welcome and accommodate the stranger. He signalled the

curious Mashenka, Elysaveta's granddaughter. The girl quickly did Baba's bidding, and came back running not to miss any part of the conversation. She poured hot tea from the samovar, and, helping the stranger to take off his soaking backpack and drenched, washed-out slicker, she asked:

"Where are you from, good man? What's your name?"

"Where am I from? I'd rather you asked me how I got this scar on my lower lip, or how a certain yellow dog pulled me out of the overflowing Neman in Lithuania, or why I laugh my head off whenever somebody mentions the woman's black lacey underpants in the fur hat of the ensign Kooznetsov...I am from every place a little bit. Wherever I was, and I visited so many places that an ordinary man would need three lives to go there, I carried away something of that place that wove itself into my life as if I were born there. When I think of my birthplace, the feelings of happiness and sadness get mixed inside me, so I do not know anymore if I should cry or laugh. Then there are some people who forced themselves into my tiny heart and they keep bloating it, so I am scared it will explode one day and take both me and my memories to infinity. If my homeland was not this planet of ours, then it is for sure our Russia. I have been serving the Tsar and Mother Russia for twenty years, and I have shot at the bodies of whomever I had been sent to fight against.

"At first, I tried to be merciful to those on the other side. I used to shoot past them, thinking I was doing a good thing. Some captain with his face scarred by a saber discovered what I was doing, and shot me in the leg. I saw him shooting at me and drew my saber in defence against my own officer. He threw himself at my feet, wounded though I was, and like a rabid dog shouted: 'If you don't kill them, they'll kill you. They'll kill me. Shoot at them, you piece of shit!'

"From then on I aimed at flesh. Doing that ugly and blasphemous job, I trod across Scandinavia, along the borders of Prussia, Austria and Turkey. I chased the rebellious Kirghiz, and Booryat's Mongolians. You won't believe to what places these soldiers' boots have taken me! I've crushed peasants' riots, peasants like you, at the Ustyoortsk Plain...I've marched through Petersburg, I've been a guard at the

Tsar's Summer Palace…And for all of that I received the great Tsar's honours!" He thrust his hand into the pocket of his faded army coat and took out a few medals on yellow silk ribbons. "I kept these ones. This one is personally from the Tsar. Medals for killing people. These tsars of ours have been teaching us for centuries to kill for their own benefit. Don't you think there shouldn't be any interest higher than human life? We kill while kings write history. A history of bloodshed we commit with our own hands. And then we receive a medal for it."

The stranger turned silent and looked at the soot-stained ceiling of the inn as if brooding over something. Everybody else was quiet, waiting for him to continue. For all of them except Doctor Chernov, this was the first time they had heard such extreme talk. Chernov, on the other hand, shared similar sentiments, and while the stranger was talking, he felt slightly humiliated, for the stranger's words were Chernov's unspoken ones. The stranger had more courage to express what they both had experienced. These villagers were not worriers. They did not see the meaning of life in that, and were not happy when rulers and generals asked them to take up weapons and shoot at people. They did not call for war but war called for them. Every bigger war had taken one of their close ones. However, rulers called for wars but tried to keep their own close ones away from harm.

Mashenka's mother had died from some sudden disease while Mashenka was in her cradle, and when she started walking, her father was called by the Tsar to defend the country from the rebellious Chechans and had never come back. Her mother's mother had grabbed the girl away from some distant cousin, for she had noticed his lustful look as if Masha were soon to share his bed. Elysaveta had raised her, and as soon as she was able to help, she became her babushka's right hand.

While Masha was placing a teapot and a cup on the stranger's table, the youngest among the villagers, the black-eyed Gresha, could not take his eyes off her rosy cheeks and blue eyes.

"Who am I and where from? In the army, after we fought the sailors in Talon, over there on the Baltic, my comrades nicknamed me Gorky, and the commander of our units over there, Colonel Tuzikov, when giving me the medal, addressed me as Tovarish Gorky. From then on everybody called me that name and that is how I was registered in the army records."

Babushka Elysaveta had crept behind the backs of the villagers and was waiting for her chance to address the newcomer. He was first to notice her head wrapped in a dark-coloured scarf, and interrupted his story, signalling to her to talk. "I have nice borscht, and I can put in some boiled smoked pork ribs—if you want it with meat," Baba announced officiously.

"I am used to eating meatless borscht, but if you have boiled smoked ribs, I'll be happy to try that specialty."

"Does anybody else want it?" asked Elysaveta. Nobody replied, so she addressed Evstafy: "Doctor, would you like some? I know your Olya has gone to visit her mother, so maybe there won't be any dinner for you."

"If I hadn't had vodka, maybe. Now, I don't want it. Thanks, Lyska. I can't."

Tovarish Gorky seemed like a composed, levelheaded, and wise man. But if those present could have reached into the cells of his brain, they would have discovered what his face was not showing. While he was talking about how the army had given him a name without caring what he really was, through his memory flashed the images that for years had been suffocating him and making him torture his brain with thoughts of discovering his place among people as he wanted to see it, the place others had once granted him. Even now the face of his Anushka was fresh in his memory, as it had been when, avoiding each other's eyes, they had marvelled at what they had discovered in each other. Then a cold, dark cloud enveloped him: over Anushka's there emerged the face of the youngest brother of General Arhypov—that mighty, insatiable, long-legged Andrey Arhypov, who saw the meaning of life in seducing beautiful young women. Willingly or by force! Gorky clenched his fists, wishing to meet the unscrupulous womanizer in a dark place. The worst was that Arhypov, in order to take Anusha away from him, had used the state and the state's machinery, for which people had been giving their lives on battlefields. True. Andrey had made his brother, the General, call up Gorky to join the army, and, afterwards, he had been sent from one end of the empire to another. Twenty and some years, without a chance to return home. Only from his fellow townsman, Pyotr Alexeyevitch, had he found out what had happened to Anushka. Locked in her mother's house, she had been raising and feeding the two children Arhypov had fathered upon her. And he had abandoned her to take up some job in the diplomatic service of Mother Russia. Nobody noticed the flame in Gorky's eyes when he whispered to himself that, sooner or later, he'd get hold of that Tsar's diplomat and General's brother, tear his penis off and throw it to the dogs.

The villagers had pulled their chairs closer to the table Gorky shared with Doctor Chernov, and urged Mashenka to hastily prepare the food for him and to pour some more of the good Tambov vodka into their glasses.

In the long conversation with Gorky, Evstafy Chernov and the other villagers listened to his eloquent speech against war, against the Tsar's state and the Russian Orthodox Church. Soldier Gorky stirred Chernov's feelings about human freedom, since as a graduate of Saint Petersburg's Medical School, Chernov had been influenced by such ideas while doing his internship in Paris, and also later, through his study of the teachings of the French Enlightenment writers and philosophers gathered at the Paris Academy, especially those of Voltaire and Jean-Jacques Rousseau.

Voices muffled by the sound of the rain that pounded on the shingled roof could be heard approaching the inn. They belonged to three villagers who came in showering water all around them.

The first who entered the inn, the scrawny Dmitry Suvorov, immediately headed toward Evstafy's table, vigorously announcing:

"The priest said that the wedding'd be at the church at noon so that the guests from the Tambov villages could arrive on time. Your brother Kolya will lead them." When he noticed the stranger, Dmitry came to a halt.

"I know, Dmitrooshka. Kolya was going to come see me today, but they decided he'll be the groom's best man, so he has to go with the procession."

Evstafy then addressed Gorky. "You came at the best time. Wait to see our wedding. We're going to drink all of Tambov's vodka and dance so the earth will shake down to Moscow."

The incomer shrugged his shoulders to show he was not sure whether to join them, and then he whispered, as if confiding. "I've decided not to participate in celebrations blessed by priests and recorded by them in their books. Why do the newlyweds need a priest to bind them to spend their lives together?!"

They looked at him curiously, not comprehending the real meaning of his words. Dmitry found the stranger's talk odd, so he asked him:

"What do you mean, tovarish soldier? It is our tradition. It has always been. When we are born, they baptize us in church When we get married, that's where they bless and commend us to God. When we die…"

"I know, I know," Gorky was eager to lead his thought along, "it was the same with me. But, do you think that's what we need? Do we need priests to commend us to God? Aren't we tied so closely to God that we don't need a church and priests to show us the way to Him?"

The villagers were confused. Dmitry did not continue the conversation with the stranger. Evstafy remembered Rousseau's teaching on how the heavy church hierarchy is a great burden on people's backs. He called to mind Erasmus of Rotterdam, who wrote that the higher you go in the church hierarchy, the more lechery, moral decay and God-forsaken canons you find.

"Our priest is from our village. We know him well. The truth is he's lazy, but he is not a bad priest," Evstafy smiled and called Masha, pointing at the newcomers: "Give them some vodka to warm them up. You see how frozen their eyes are."

Dmitry and the other two toasted the villagers with the vodka in their glasses, then retreated a few steps away from the group gathered around the stranger. "He must be that soldier who went through the

Kharkov villages last week talking against the Tsar, the army and church," whispered Dmitry to the other two. They were stealing suspicious glances at the stranger and discreet nods of their heads showed they shared Dmitry's alarm. "I've heard that the army is looking for him and that the Kharkov church has sent a message to the priests to stop him," added the scrawny villager who was taller than the others, with an unobstructed view of the incomer. "Let's listen to what he's saying," suggested Dmitry. Covertly, they sidled back toward the group at the table. In the meantime, Evstafy had moved his chair closer to that of the stranger and asked him in a low voice:

"What is your intention, Tovarish? Are you in touch with some pacifist organization?"

Tovarish turned his head sideway to better see Evstafy's face and looked at him, surprised.

"Why are you asking, Doctor? They've tried to woo me to join different movements. Even in the army. But to me their ideologies are objectionable. Each of them builds institutions, asks for money or asks others to fight for their interests."

"What is your idea? Why are you going from one place to another telling people what you are saying here tonight?"

"People need to be informed. Many don't know what's happening beyond their doorsteps. To many the lives they live seem normal and the only ones possible. Even the evil others do to us. Even how others shove their hands into our pockets. To many it is normal when they call them up to join the army and go to war. Many believe the only truth is what priests and tsars have been repeating forever."

Evstafy felt his forehead start sweating and his peace being shaken.

"But, what is your goal, Tovarish? To rouse people or to ease yourself by letting out what you have been keeping to yourself for years?"

"I don't want to rouse people against anybody." Tovarish was talking more loudly, so the others could hear him. "People need to change their outlook on life. On the meaning of life. We are not born to kill others. And we are not giving birth to our children so they die for others. Nor for others to take their food from them by force. Nor to force thoughts and beliefs into their heads. People should live according to God's teaching. We need to love each other, and not bring evil onto others. To help, not to take away from each other. But also to be free, not slaves. If people decided to be good, the world would change in no time. If I can help at least one person to decide to live as a good man, I'll succeed. And he will bring in another, and another one, and sometime in the future human society could become a society of good people."

The villagers listened quietly. Even Dmitry's group had stopped whispering.

"You do want to stir a movement. Your words are symbols of 'the good'. But human society has institutions that will not like your words. Some will choose the path you are showing, but institutions of power will strike at them. Those who stand by their principles and are strong enough to endure that assault, they will have to go into isolation, into hiding. And it won't be easy for them. If their future generations do live to see the time when human society becomes more humane, it will be an incredible success for your mission."

Tovarish was looking somewhere through Evstafy's face. A mysterious smile appeared on his face and Evstafy did not fail to notice it. Nor did the others gathered around the two of them.

"The only good thing that I experienced in the Army was the story of one Ukrainian man, Panayotov," Gorky continued in a reverent voice enriched by the patina of history. "His roots are Bulgarian but his father and he were born in our country. During our long travels toward politically turbulent parts of this empire, he spoke many times about what was told of an unknown soldier a hundred years ago. He was from the coast of the Black Sea and he was always saying to anyone who would listen that human beings must be organized on the principles of God's rules and that they must erase every single kind of tyranny and hatred from their lives."

That night, voices were heard from Elysaveta's inn and candlelight flickered through the narrow window openings, all until the dawn.

Gorky confessed that he had started his mission to enlighten people in the village of Okhochem, near Kharkov, and that he had already gone to some twenty villages of the Kharkov, Tambov, Voronyesh and Ekaterinoslavsk regions. His goal was to alert people to the terrors that war brings, to the exploitation carried out by the state and the Orthodox Church. To Chernov, these ideas were similar to the new Rationalist philosophy that had engulfed Western Europe. According to its teaching, each individual by the power of his own reason can discern the difference between good and evil, realizing that all people are brothers and sisters and that they, in the process of communicating with God, do not need the church and its costly and heavy hierarchy.

Evstafy was already part of that process of intellectual ferment in the progressive classes of Europe, but he had lacked the courage to directly join them. He foresaw imminent reform in European societies, but was not sure what impact that would have on the common Russian man and what forms it would take in the Russian state. He was afraid of anarchy. He was aware that radical changes in governments and structures of power usually bring periods of lawlessness. And then...The state apparatus and church hierarchy got along very well. The advent of anything new, especially of something that might inspire free thinking among people and rebellion against official ideologies, could be destructive for the followers of the new. Listening to that war-worn Russian soldier, Doctor Chernov became excited. Emotions and stimulated rational thinking got mixed in his mind, and he decided to actively participate in any movement for the betterment of the rights of people and against any exploitation, both material and spiritual, practised for centuries by the Russian Church.

The next day Soldier Gorky went to the nearby village of Nizhny and, afterwards, to many other villages all the way down to the Cossacks of the River Don, where all trace of him disappears from history. Perhaps he went to look for his Anushka, to spend the rest of his life by her and her two children. It didn't matter whose children they were since they were hers too. Or he went to look for a good opportunity for revenge against the scoundrel brother of General Arhypov. Evstafy Chernov did not hear anything more about him.

However, soon after Gorky, among the people of that region, and then in many other parts of Russia and the neighbouring countries, there rose the Doukhobor stance, the stance of the *Dukhobortsy,* the Spirit Fighters, on life, government, and religion. In religion, the Doukhobors adopted a different understanding of the human relationship with God, unlike that preached by the Orthodox Church or by any other official Christian church For those established churches, pandering to rulers and personal interests were more important than cherishing love and friendship among people. In this new belief, the latter should be the fundamental mission of all who want to follow God's commandments. The new movement refused the church hierarchy, the church as an object and priests as mediators between God and people. Its followers considered all people brothers and openly claimed that, since the Tsar himself belonged to the human species, so the rules regulating human relations should apply to him too. The mighty Orthodox Church's reaction was to declare the movement a sect, to anathematize it, and to start a vigorous persecution against any follower of this movement. In the beginning, the state apparatus looked at this phenomenon merely with curiosity. However, the Russian Church soon easily engaged the Russian rulers in its battle against the new belief and stance on life. The support of the unified and powerful church organization suited the rulers. The government decided to persecute Doukhobors when they energetically anathematized war and any activity that leads to killing people.

What happened earlier in the powerful religions of our civilization, and what happened several centuries before with a similar movement of the heretics in the Balkans, was what in the 18th and 19th centuries took place with the Russian Doukhobors. In the midst of all the chaos of civilization, in yet another of its shameful affairs, happened to be the Clan of the Chernovs, starting from the very moment when Evstafy Chernov, on that night in Elysaveta's inn in the village of Goreloye, accepted his part in the movement initiated by the messianic Russian soldier known as Tovarish Gorky. Soon the Army's leaders discharged Evstafy from his duties, and he opened his office for healing people in Tavrov.

At the same time, he began speaking his views publicly, to the dismay of the authorities. When they prohibited him from practising civil medicine, he returned to his village of Goreloye, where he treated Doukhobors.

In the movement that shared the fundamental values of civilization—justice and freedom, and the elimination of aggression or any kind of exploitation from human relations—the Chernovs did not strive for power nor to be close to the powerful, but the generations of their descendants have participated in the dignified evolution of the movement. Owing to its vitality and the climate of Rationalist reform in Europe, the Doukhobor Movement, unlike that of the Bosnian heretics, survived in spite of horrible church and government torture over the past three centuries. The Chernovs did, too.

3

In the south of European Russia, from Tambov to the Azov Sea, in the middle of the 18th century peasants were frightened by the death of Peter the Great, since they believed that there was no one capable of replacing him. When a family loses a member who has raised its name far above its former value, the survivors, as a rule, fear a sudden fall and a worse life. After great rulers, strong currents appear among people, bringing new ideas; from hidden places new leaders emerge, and those who until then have only dreamed of great possibilities start growing wings. Many laws coined and followed in the times of the great ruler start weakening right after the ruler's demise; the masses start stirring up and criticism grows. As before a big storm the sky lights up in areas of imbalanced electric charges, the masses of the people feel anger and a desire for change. Prisons of the human spirit start to open, enslaved giants come out of magic lamps, winds start to turn the pages of holy books, philosophies change their appearance, poets begin new rhymes, painters change their points of view...That is how the Doukhobors were born there in the south, below Moscow.

From fear of unscrupulous people and their institutions, and from anger that the human species is always the source for forces that place man far below the rank that God awarded him, came about the movement of hope for freedom in human life and in man's ties with God.

Not long after the appearance in those parts of Tovarish Gorky and his teaching about the struggle for human dignity, groups of like-minded people started to form in many villages. They were brave, craved freedom and change, and thus encouraged the advancement of the new teaching in various ways.

Then, the news spread that in the village of Nikolskoye, in the district of Ekaterinoslavsk, Sylvan Kolesnikov had turned his home into a centre for teaching the new way of life and the new religion. Those from the neighbouring villages would come to his house on Saturdays, and later spread the news of how they had heard that God lives in every man and that the real Christian teachings are in the New Testament.

The followers of the new teaching, as soon as work in the fields stopped, would go from one region to another and tell people about the new Christian teaching and a more fully human way of life. During one early autumn, when the leaves of the deciduous forests, especially of trees along the river's banks, became colourful in the valley of the Seym River, south of Kursk, Kolesnikov's followers walked from village to village bringing people news. When they arrived at the swampy village of Glyby, positioned at the great bend of the rolling river, the inhabitants greeted them in the way that strangers are usually greeted—with suspicion. The newcomers were impatient and Nikolay Sonkin, one of the bravest among them, without any preamble, asked the gathered people what they thought of the message that the leader of the new movement, Kolesnikov, had sent to them. Among the closest, standing a head taller than the others, was the good-natured Pavloosha Rilkov. The villagers looked around to see who would answer the newcomer's question, and all eyes fixed on Rilkov. He understood that the people wanted him to speak with the newcomers, even though he was not used to giving speeches. He spread his arms, trying to roll up the sleeves of his thick shirt, and by doing this accidentally pushed those next to him closer to the newcomers. Then, without thinking, as if speaking from an empty hay barn, he asked:

"Brother, who is that Kolesnikov of yours?"

Then everybody's head turned towards Sonkin.

"You haven't heard of Sylvan Kolesnikov!? He is the leader of the new people's movement."

"We hadn't heard about him till right now. And, what is his message to us?" Rilkov asked, feigning indifference.

People nodded their heads at him, approving of this burly man's response to the stranger.

"He is inviting all of us to join the movement for a new life which will take the Church and priests off our backs because we don't need them to reach God." Sonkin was trying to sound convincing.

One man in the crowd of villagers started to say something, but he was short and quiet, so even those closest to him couldn't hear. A couple of them grabbed him and raised him above the heads of the others. He quickly made himself comfortable in their arms and shouted, so that he could be heard by everyone:

"I know who Kolesnikov is! He is that kulak whose sister two priests raped, so he wants to raise the people against priests. To take revenge!

"Wait, Nikita…that's not important! Maybe it's not even true," Rilkov called in rebuttal, and those who were holding the short one in the air put him down.

"I like that he wants us to take the Church and priests off our backs. I've had enough of their arrogance and at last somebody's standing up to them," shouted Rilkov and the people were surprised to hear words of rebellion coming from this peaceful giant.

"I like that these new Christians are refusing to pay taxes to anybody," added somebody in the crowd.

"Are the priests fussing about these new ones?" again somebody from the crowd asked.

"The Archbishop himself has already sounded the bells of alarm. They're threatening to use force against the new teaching," Sonkin explained, realizing that this could be important.

"Well, if the priests are fighting back, the teaching must be good for people!" Rilkov shouted. "In that case, my family and I are joining the movement right away."

There was laughter, then many among the men started to publicly approve those words and to declare themselves sympathizers of Kolesnikov and his followers.

The new movement spread quickly. The official Orthodox Church had distanced itself since the beginning, and the priests started closing their church doors against the followers of the new movement.

As if travelling before the hordes of Genghis Khan, the news reached the centres of Church power, and there, strategies for a mighty attack against the novelty were formulated. Meanwhile, the peasants became bolder. The village gates opened and people started communicating more urgently and more audaciously. On its regular travels across Russia's vast lands, the army more frequently avoided the villages of the new movement. And then the news spread that Kolesnikov had died.

The followers of the new movement became dismayed and returned to their villages in fear of harsh measures from state and church. A new leader, Ilarion Pobirokhin, soon appeared. He was more dynamic, more wise and more well-spoken than his predecessor. His charisma livened up the followers of the new movement and their sympathizers. Pobirokhin also introduced new elements to Doukhobor teaching: the truth is not in books but in the human spirit; it is not in the Bible, but in living books, in the memory of people. That was until then the strongest attack on the official Christian religion in the Russian lands. Among the Orthodox oligarchy in the areas where the movement was spreading, the church doors started to open and the drums of alarm started to sound.

Into the hands of the church fathers, Pobirokhin handed a great argument against the Doukhobor Movement—he proclaimed himself the descendant of Jesus Christ.

The teaching's more learned sympathizers shook their heads, indicating their disagreement with this proclamation, considering it naïve at best; the followers shut themselves in their homes and made various comments on the situation.

People considered it normal to follow a leader, but the majority of the followers of the new way did not understand 'following' to mean inflaming fame-thirsty ambitions and creating institutions that would rule over the people. Then, Pobirokhin made a new move: he started to organize the Doukhobor communities according to the new teaching, propagating the new way of life for people, in many aspects opposite to the official way in which Russian people were organized.

The movement developed in the areas where Russia's land was most fertile, where good agriculture and rich harvests lent security and assurance to the development of free thinking among people in their views on religion and the value of work. Except for one leader, the movement did not have institutions of power. The feeling of brotherhood among the people developed very rapidly, as well as the idea of common ownership of production and other material goods. The quick growth of this free spirit created animosity towards state and church authorities and led people to revolutionize their way of life and their beliefs. When the priests, trying to bring those people back to the mother church, asked them where they got the courage to close their doors to the state and religious authorities, the followers of the movement replied without hesitation:

"We are humans. No human being has the right to oppress another, to exert his power over him, and to take away the fruits of his labour. We have sworn to God that we would obey and promote his laws and so we cannot swear to people and promote their laws, for they are different from God's."

The teachings of the new movement were spread across Russia's vast lands and the oppressed saw hope in them. The number of followers grew in all parts of the huge Russian kingdom, which was, as all other kingdoms were, based on this indisputable law: You live within the borders of our kingdom, your mother country, and you enjoy that privilege; therefore, you have to submit yourself to her service and give her everything that she asks from you, even your own life.

From the leaders of the new movement an answer came: "We did not create the borders nor choose the rulers. They should be in our service, not the other way around. As for life, only the Lord is master of people's lives."

This was more than enough to create a centuries-long gap between the new teaching and those authorities who tried to hold people firmly in their grasp.

The Chernovs joined the Doukhobor Movement without official proclamations and a lot of wise talk. Evstavy was a worldly man. His brothers and nephews followed him because they knew he was very educated; he had travelled a lot and was well respected in their region. Their children followed those closest to them by the rule of inertia, as usually happens when new religious teachings and national identifications are being adopted. It suited them that the new way of life warranted boycotting army service and discarding the heavy burden of their duties towards the state and the official church. However, the members of that clan were in no way extremists. They even believed that the values of the new way of life and its simplification of religion did not require mandatory selection of Doukhobor leaders and dignitaries, but they did not protest if some prominent Doukhobor, such as Kolesnikov or Pobirokhin, did proclaim himself leader.

However, when the news reached them that Ilarion Pobirokhin had practically proclaimed himself the new Christ, they were not happy.

They gathered at Evstavy's son Vasily's house in Radionovka, sipped vodka diluted with rosehip juice, nibbled on goat cheese and slices of meat from the host's wife's Lyoobochka's larder and tried to form a common position on the unexpected event. "We don't need this now," Vasily's brother Dmitry resolutely stated. He was a burly and smart young man, astute in his understanding of social affairs. He often quickly reacted to foolishness and was not afraid of verbal confrontations even with men much older than he. "Nobody is so uneducated as to accept Ilarion's self-declared Christhood. Weren't we taught that people are equal and that we are brothers? It seems to me that with this declaration Ilarion has separated himself from that brotherhood."

Dmitry's nephew Igor agreed with his opinion right away: "Not only is that declaration ridiculous, it is also harmful." The scrawny young man, a few years older than Dmitry, was firm. "Now the priests and the state bureaucrats will attack us even more. With this, the great values of our movement have been brought down and our teaching about Christ distorted. Until now folks all over Russia have respected us. Many have admired us. But now…"

"Somebody has to be the leader. Someone has to synchronize the social and religious activities of all our communities. Ilarion is a smart man. Newspapers in Moscow and Petersburg have written about him. I have even heard the Tsarina herself has become interested in him. Maybe Ilarion really did feel some strong spirit within him, something he hadn't felt before." Vasily's brother Nikolay was thinking aloud.

"You don't believe, Nikoshka, in what some granny from Zaporozye was saying: that in her dream she heard a powerful voice saying that Christ himself would appear among the Doukhobortsy and that the whole world would change?" Vasily scolded him.

Some women were also present at the gathering, though they usually let the men talk. Mention of the prophecy by the old Cossack woman, which Ilarion had apparently swallowed, made Lyoobochka angry, and she raised her shrill voice:

"That old woman wanted to appear important and smart and she got the idea to play with Christ. That's why they rewarded her by having somebody beat her up and make her lose the power of speech."

While his aunt spoke, Igor started to sweat and a strange yellow colour appeared in the skin around his eyes. His very prominent Adam's apple started to tremble, more and more severely. His mouth closed then opened as if some inner fear were trying to make him speak against the force of reason. But as soon as Lyoobochka had finished her rant on the words of the old Cossack woman, Igor got up and stretched to encourage himself, as if he stood before a jury whose decision depended on his acting. When he started speaking in his shaky voice, those present immediately realized that the matter was serious.

"Has any of you ever thought that it would be good for all of us to renounce some parts of the new teaching?!"

Everybody's eyes opened wide as if they had suddenly realized that in front of them was somebody they hadn't known well until that moment. Or somebody who was making fun of what was sacred to them. But he was their Igor, until recently a quiet boy with a gentle face and a timid look. It was impossible, they all thought, waiting for Igor to say more. He himself got scared of what he had said, but in those short moments he realized that the ice had been broken and that nobody could bring him back to his previous state.

"I'm serious…kings bow before our Tsarina Katarina the Great, and she is against us. She is sending the army after us and knows that we will not defend ourselves. She knows we don't want to shed anybody's blood. Why then does she want to destroy us?!"

With their eyes wide open the others continued to stare at Igor's resolute face, the lines on his forehead ever more prominent.

"Recently, my friends from Rodnaya have openly reproached me, saying that it is dangerous to be in our company, the Doukhobortsy, and that we'll bring great trouble not only upon ourselves but also upon others. Our neighbours have become afraid. I have heard that some have already decided to move to the other side of the Don, as far from us as they can. Three families from the Nevstrooyev Clan have recently moved out."

Igor was young when he lost his father, when a wave of a dangerous strand of tuberculosis hit a great number of villages between the River Dnieper and the Don. The oldest child of the late Nikolay Vasiliyevitch Chernov had managed to mature quickly from a child to a responsible leader in his family. Igor had thereby gained respect and support amongst the entire Chernov clan. He had accepted the Doukhobor teachings as an inheritance from his parents, but had recently started to question the values of the movement. He undoubtedly enjoyed the communal living, which enabled him to become a member of a family much larger than his own. He believed that the sacred duty of each human being is to resolutely refuse participation in war. However, he came to believe that the Doukhobors should not avoid their financial obligations toward the state, and from the depths of his brain often came the thought that they should in some way initiate at least symbolic relationships with the official church.

Vasily felt he was the most obliged among them to clarify the meaning of what Igor had said.

"If I understood you correctly, you are suggesting that we at least temporarily abandon our activities in the movement. In fact, your words sound more like your own decision to renounce the teachings we live by. If you have become afraid of the persecutions that have been declared I understand you. There is nobody among us who is not afraid of Tsarina Katarina and her power. But you know that there is stronger power and justice above hers. That is God the Almighty. I think our Tsarina knows that too. I myself will never put any human being above our Creator, but still I won't stop you if you want to choose a different way of life, not ours…But I am sure that I belong to the teaching that is dear to God."

Nobody wanted to discuss Igor's proposal. They believed they should give it more thought, sleep on it, and wait until the next morning. Vasily asked Igor that they discuss Igor's reasons in a brotherly manner. He went to the youth and hugged him, but Igor broke away, stretching himself to be taller than Vasily, and in an offended voice, started talking so that all could hear him:

"Uncle Vasya, do you think I am against you? I am not! But when a man finds himself in trouble, he must find a way to get out of the trouble. I agree that one needs to fight for a cause, to choose a more human path in life, but one can't break a wall with his head. I am sure the Tsarina is afraid of the growth of the movement. It means she is afraid that in the state treasury there will be less money because more and more people will start refusing to pay taxes. If we agree to pay, it will be enough for the authorities to stop persecuting us."

"We'll talk about everything, Igrusha." Vasya hugged him again. "You are not alone. We are all together. I also sometimes feel like running away to the mountains to distance myself from that which worries me. But the mountain is not a cure for the soul."

To divert attention from Igor, Vasily addressed those who were vehemently against Ilarion's declaration of direct descent from Christ. "We can't do anything useful now. When something happens it is not in our power to erase it from the time in which it happened. I also have a premonition that Pobirokhin's declaration was not wise and useful for our movement, but we have to wait and see what time will bring. Ilarion is from a kulak's family and it is strange that he even joined our movement. The interests of his social class are different from ours. Maybe he is an exception, but I have not been able to explain to myself why he did that. He is not the first human who has tried to identify himself with Christ or some deity. For us it is strange because our teaching is based on modesty and equality. In this case, Ilarion is no longer of us Doukhobors. He is somebody who has placed himself much higher, who has greatly outgrown his place in mankind. I have always believed that we Doukhobors have found a way to build bridges with the past. That we are so progressive that many other people will follow us, all those who want eternal peace and complete equality among people. Ilarion Pobirokhin is coming to our village one of these days. We'll sit with him and ask for explanations."

At that gathering the Chernovs decided that before the meeting with Ilarion they should invite the other families from the village and come to an agreement about Pobirokhin's declaration and about the rumours that the authorities were making preparations to settle accounts with the Doukhobors.

The next day, right after breakfast, Vasily went to the forest with his sons and other boys from the neighbourhood to cut some tall trunks. He needed lumber for the roof of a storage room that he planned to build between the house and the stable. A couple of grey horses, two years old, full of strength and desire to run down the field, prancing as if in a circus, drew the wooden cart carrying Vasily and the boys. Among them, Vasily's son, Stepan, was neither taller nor more handsome or stronger than the others, but he knew how to catch fish from the river with his hands, and was able to feel when a summer storm was starting to rise from the bosom of the Black Sea.

The sun was already high in the light-blue sky. The pastures in the meadows were in full bloom and the insects were buzzing to and fro in confusion, not knowing which flower was sweeter, and they were humming as though amazed. When Vasily and the boys came past a lake, they saw a flock of wild ducks right by the shore, with their tails up in the air and their heads submerged in the water.

As soon as they crossed a brook at the spot where it was wide and shallow, they heard a hushed singing coming from the direction they were heading.

Then they saw a group of people sitting on outcrops of grey rock up a small hill. They were singing and looking toward the tops of the chain of low mountains far to the east. As the cart drew closer, Vasily realized that those people were the Popovs and Danilovitchs from the neighbouring village of Molohnaya. They did not stop singing even when the horses stopped a few steps away from them. It was an old song brought from the flatlands of Finland by the soldiers of some war in the time of Peter the Great. Vasily liked the last verse of the song, so he readily joined the singing:

And they brought to me
Cold flowers of shining stars
From the north.

"Where are you heading with these weaklings, Vasya?" the oldest among them, Taras Popov, shouted out, stretched full length on the comfort of his rock. He was wearing knee-length shorts and a light hat made of the fur of a grey rabbit.

"To the woods, tovarishes. And these lads are not weaklings. Without them, both I and my kin would be left without timber. What kind of job are you about, lying here?" Vasya teased them, smiling gently.

"It's a shame to work among such beauty," a younger man replied, encouraged by Vasya's smile.

"Despite appearances, we are cutting the grass on the fields by the brook there under the hill," Taras explained. "We got tired of our scythes, having worked since early morning, so we came here to rest." Taras paused. "Is Ilarion 'the Great' coming to visit you as well as us?" he asked, with mild irony.

"Yes, he is," answered Vasya.

"We in our village are not happy about his meddling with Christ. It isn't good for Christ and it isn't good for us."

"We'll see when he comes. We'll talk about it with him," Vasya replied indifferently. "I'm more worried about the news that the army has started to terrorize our folk over toward Kazan."

"We'll soon see what's going on. We should by no means provoke the army to act against us," added the same young man. "Maybe Ilarion is going to find a way to calm down the Tsarina Katarina."

The other reapers were quiet. Vasily's lads did not show that they were in any way frightened by what the adults were talking about. They were paying more attention to a brindled field mouse that one of the youngest among them was holding in his hands. Even the mouse was not afraid of anything. He was sitting quietly in the boy's hands and passing his disinterested gaze from one boy's face to another. One of the boys moved his head closer and started to blow toward the mouse's red snout, and the mouse pushed the pink toes of his hind legs towards the boy as if protecting himself from the wind the boy was making with his blowing.

A few minutes later, the reapers went down the hill towards their fields, and Vasily and his boys followed the dusty trail towards the forest.

Soon afterwards, on one windy day, early in the morning, while the adults were getting out of their houses, stretching and looking at the orange sky towards the east, the news reached them that the village shepherds had found somebody's body in the lake at the foot of Ilovak's Hill. The villagers organized themselves hastily to investigate. One group ran towards the lake. They needed to use boats to bring the drowned man to shore, and saw that he was old Timofey from the clan of the Kalmikovs, who used to cure people with herbs. It was strange that the man was found in the lake far from the shore, with no boat to be seen nearby. The old man did not have enemies in the village, and he was respected in the entire region because everyone believed in the healing power of his herbs. When they dragged him to the shore and turned him on his back, they were surprised to see how big and unusually bulgy his eyes were. He looked startled and hysterically frightened by whatever had happened to him. In keeping with Doukhobor custom, his family members buried him with very modest ceremony.

At that time, great numbers of people in the Russian regions to the north of the frontier with the Ottoman Empire were ever more seriously manifesting their dissatisfaction. From the Caspian regions the priests were informing their parish superiors of open protests by villagers because of the lack of almost any help from the authorities and church for people devastated by a series of earthquakes and floods. Also, the city of Kharkov's independent newspaper published an interview with Ilarion Pobirokhin.

The highest circles of the Russian Orthodox Church were vigorous in their request that the state take measures against followers of the new teaching, derogatorily called *Ikonobortsy* and *Dukhobortsy*. Catherine the Great accepted a deal with the Church, so a team of three members of the State Synod for Matters of Religion was asked to suggest measures aimed at subduing the movement, which, as they presented it to the Tsarina of All Monarchs, was threatening to instigate great social disturbances, even a revolution.

Journalists were given a short statement that the Doukhobor leader, Ilarion Pobirokhin, would be permanently exiled to Siberia for instigating turmoil in the country.

About the same time in 1780, the independent Moscow newspaper *Moskovskie Vedomosti* published the news that along with Pobirokhin, his family would be exiled to Siberia, and that the authorities had given orders to the army to vigorously punish the Doukhobors.

The newspaper announced that news had already arrived from villages south of Tambov and Kharkov about the cruel retribution being meted out to Doukhobors there: How cavalry soldiers cut off their noses and tongues, stamped them with hot irons, impaled them on stakes and persecuted them all over the region. How they took Doukhobor children away, sent them to unknown places, and gave them to Orthodox families, in order to severely punish whole communities, scare them and separate them from each other.

Evstavy's son Vasily refused to show that he was afraid of the announced persecutions. While many were trying to devise a strategy to save themselves and their families, he was working in his field with his wife Lyoobochka and their three children. On the day when news reached them that the army was coming from Kharkov to show the Doukhobors who the mistress of Russia was, they tried to cut as much hay as they could and transport it to the village.

Long before the news reached them, people had started talking about how the great Tsarina was preparing to call to account all those who did not respect the laws of the country and who tried to break its unity, and how the Tsarina showed more interest in throwing festive balls for foreign diplomats and Russian aristocrats who dreamed about nights spent by her naked body than she did in the sufferings of her people.

Ilarion Pobirokhin arrived at the village of Radionovka. The villagers gathered in front of Vasily's spacious house to talk with their leader. They sat under the tall may-trees and started commenting on the news. Some of them were scared and some believed that the blades of the soldiers' sabers would become dull before they reached Radionovka. They were looking at Pobirokhin, expecting many explanations for the situation—the fate of the movement in face of the Tsarina's decision to "settle accounts" with them. Ilarion was aware that many Doukhobors did not like his claim of relationship to Christ and believed this claim had provoked the vigorous reaction from the church and the tsarist regime.

Ilarion looked calm; incredibly, signs of satisfaction were visible on his face. There was no trace of fear that his sentence to exile for life in Siberia would be carried out. His neatly cut overcoat made of black polished leather, and stylish ankle boots made of the same material, suited his above-average height and his refined face. His hands were well kept, telling of a life without peasant work.

As soon as he met with Vasily and the Doukhobors, who all gathered around him, he started enquiring about the case of the former village priest, who had stayed there even when everybody had stopped coming to church.

The priest had disappeared one night. The Doukhobors believed he had left and gone to some church in one of the River Don villages. However, a few days afterwards, Radionovka shepherds brought the news that in the foothills they had seen a man in scruffy clothes who looked like their former priest. The next day some older Doukhobors went to that part of the mountain slopes and found footprints by a cave.

When they came closer to the opening they heard the growling of a bear warning them to stay away. They decided to chase it out by shouting and throwing rocks into the cave. The animal, after making some great noise, calmed down and nothing could be heard anymore from inside. Holding long sabers in their hands, the men got closer to the entrance, shouted and threw rocks at the walls of the cave, but there was no reply from inside. Suddenly, up among the rocks, a few meters away, they saw the bear hurrying towards the mountain heights. The cave had another opening and the animal had decided to give up the fight and distance himself from the people.

In the cave they found clothes, leftover food, an old Bible wrapped in a piece of lamb skin, and cold coals where a fire had burnt. They yelled out, crawled into the dark corridors of the cave, but there was no response. They knew these were the priest's belongings, but the priest was nowhere to be seen. They exited the cave through the opening the bear must have used, but there was not a trace of the priest there. They looked for him on the slopes, they climbed to the top and from there looked as far as their eyes could reach, called him, but there was not a trace of the priest. They returned to their homes at dusk, and during the following days, searched the entire region, but without success. They also informed the nearest church, so the neighbouring villagers searched for him for days, but in vain. The disappearance of that church official remained a mystery for them, while the other priests in the parish as well as the Diocese of Tambov accused the Doukhobors of killing him, and they requested a formal investigation and revenge.

When Vasily and the others explained to Ilarion that in the cave they hadn't found any sign of a struggle between the bear and the man, nor the pieces of a human body, he was thoughtful, and tried to appear saintly. He shook his head, looked at the sky and made a judgement:

"This is a sign from the Almighty. There are no more priests. Bibles need to be wrapped in skin and thrown into caves, and a new life should be lived: the life of village communities of free and equal people, before whom beasts such as bears run away and leave them in peace."

Afterwards they talked about the news of the authorities' cruel repression of the Doukhobors. Ilarion tried to calm the people down, assuring them that in the world of that time, when news travelled quickly, reaching all parts of the country, there could no longer be bloody reprisals from the authorities against people choosing a different way of life, and that movements such as theirs had persuaded the authorities and the populace at large that reason should govern. Finally, God had more openly started to intervene in their relationship with the official church and Russian authorities; He had warned the rulers, bringing a grave illness upon the Tsarina's son, Ilarion emphasized, in order to soften the reprisals against the Doukhobors. And to the Doukhobors he had sent the spirit of Jesus in his, Ilarion's, body, as a message that their new way of life and their religious beliefs had God's protection.

The Doukhobors felt confused but were not willing to challenge Ilarion Pobirokhin. But they did ask him what they should do if the Tsarina's army came to their village.

"Even if they come, it cannot be bad. And even if they start doing evil deeds, we are the just ones and the Lord is with us. We won't raise violent hands against anyone and will bear anything with faith in God and His justice." Pobirokhin was resolute.

A spontaneous discussion erupted about the upcoming encounter with the army.

"These soldiers are also peasants as we are. They won't have the heart to attack the people," a sturdy, bald Mikhail Boolatov was thinking aloud.

"Do not have hope in that, Miha. They are not sending us the weaklings and the goodhearted. All armies obey orders to protect their own skins. Also, there are those in the army who cannot wait to cut off somebody's head, to rape someone's wife or sister, or to plunder... The more evil things they do the better soldiers they think they are," Vasily Chernov spoke up in a dignified voice. "It would be good if we hid at least the women and the children."

The people listened and their faces showed fear and anxiety. They decided to go home and hide the younger women and older children. On that day nobody had lunch in Vasily's village. People tried to hide the valuables that they kept in their houses, as well as some food and cattle. Ilarion Pobirokhin decided to stay at Vasily's until the next morning. However, sooner than they had expected, one older woman who was looking from the attic of her house down the field over which the army would come, started shouting:

"They are coming! They are crossing the stream! One group is coming from beneath the forest above the goat fields!"

The village turned dead quiet. Even the dogs sensed that something ugly was about to happen and they hid under the corn ears and in the bushes by the village, but on the opposite side from the approaching army.

First, a group of officers wearing white uniforms rode in on neatly groomed horses. Vasily, Mikhail and three more villagers greeted them. The officers dismounted the horses and a tall thin one with long moustaches asked who the village leader was.

"We do not have a leader, but the old man Alexey is the oldest. His word is respected here," explained Vasily.

The tall one asked where the old man was.

"He's been ill since the spring arrived. He's lying at home."

"Where is his house?" asked the officer and took off his soldier's hat to wipe the sweat off his brow.

Mikhail pointed at the old man's house with his hand. At the village entrance a big group of soldiers on horseback appeared.

"Where are the other villagers?" the tall one asked more sternly. "Call all the village leaders to gather here! And they better come fast!"

"We don't have leaders in the village. We are all equal here," Mikhail tried to expand on Vasily's explanation. In the officer's hand a quirt suddenly appeared. It snapped in the air and slashed the skin on Mikhail's face. Blood sprang from the wound. Vasily and the others moved a few steps away, and the officers unsheathed their sabers and lifted them above their heads.

"Don't be wise guys, you Doukhobor sons of bitches! I want the whole village to gather here. Right away!" The tall one was now shouting and brandishing his saber above his head.

Vasily wanted to say something, but one officer jumped at him and hit him on the back of his head with the handle of his saber. Vasily fell

71

to the ground. Men, women and children began coming out of their houses. The cavalrymen who had entered the village prodded their horses and trotted closer; the dogs could be heard from behind the houses, the children started screaming, chickens started clucking…and suddenly everything turned into chaos, terrible noise, screams, shouts, swearing, and clanking of metal. People were running all over the place, the horses were rearing high, raising dust from the road…

Abruptly, in that mighty chaos in which the Doukhobors, full of fear, tried to find a way to hide from those sabers, and the soldiers, obeying the officers' orders, tried to control the situation, on the porch of the house of Vasily Chernov there appeared Ilarion Pobirokhin in his leather overcoat and ankle boots. The tall officer spotted him immediately and started shouting at the soldiers and people to quiet down. He unsheathed his saber again and brandished it above his head. But the running and screaming of the people and soldiers did not stop. Suddenly a gunshot was heard, then two more, one after the other. The officers were firing in the air to stop the running.

Then, in that part of the village everything froze. The gunfire paralyzed the people, and the soldiers were staring at the officers. Only a few villagers were still crying and twitching after cavalry sabers had slashed at their backs, arms and legs. One of them had blood pouring in a stream out of the place where his ear used to be even though he tried to stanch the wound with his sweater.

The officers, led by the scrawny tall one, headed towards Vasily Chernov's porch, where Ilarion was standing. The first to approach him was the scrawny one, obviously the commander of this cavalry unit; he stood in front of Ilarion, looked at him searchingly, made a circle around him, and asked in a loud voice:

"And who might you be brave one? Are you the leader of these people?"

Pobirokhin was looking at him without fear in his eyes. He was of the same stature as the officer, but more bulky and looked physically stronger.

"This must be their leader, Pobirokhin. They gave us a description of that man" one of the officers suggested, to help his commander.

The commander made another circle around Ilarion, assessing him from all sides, and then he shouted for everybody to hear:

"Could it be that you are that new Christ who has been telling people that God has sent him to bring justice to people? The one who is taking these poor wretches for a ride and making use of their stupidity for your own seditious schemes?" He was waiting for Ilarion's reply, shifting his gaze from him to the people.

"I am Ilarion Pobirokhin, the representative of these people. It's up to you whether you see a new Christ in me or not. I can tell you that what you are doing here is shameful for us Russians. These people have done nothing to deserve getting attacked with sabers in front of their own houses by their Tsarina's army."

The commander dealt Ilarion a hard slap on the face and shouted:

"Who gave you the right to mention the Tsarina?! You have incited these people against the Tsarina Katarina and our Church and created disorder in our country. You are lucky"—he turned around and shouted at the people—"that we have found this one among you! Now you go back to your homes, and he'll go with us to be brought in front of the Tsarina!"

The people remained standing in the same spot for some time, stunned with disbelief. The soldiers started pushing them to move, and some started backing away. Vasily and a few other Doukhobors approached the officers, trying to say something, but the commander stopped them by firmly grabbing his saber as though to unsheathe it yet again.

"I don't want to hear your speeches!" he shouted, then took Ilarion firmly by the arm. "This one is in the hands of the Tsarina's Army. You go to your homes and pray that your sins be forgiven! The sooner you repent and leave the circle of your cult the happier you will be."

"It is all right, Vasily," said Ilarion. "Don't worry. I am not guilty of anything."

He raised his arms and drew breath to address the people, but the officers jumped at him, tied his hands, ordered a cavalryman to dismount his horse, grabbed Ilarion and threw him on the horse's back. Surprised, the tall horse with the long black mane lowered its back when they threw Ilarion on him; with its eyes wide open the horse turned its head to check what burden they had just dumped on it. When the horse saw the huddled Ilarion, it looked at the soldiers standing nearby, shook its head and a couple times violently blew the air through its wide-open nostrils. If it had been able to use their language to speak, the horse would have made them ashamed and less dignified.

The Tsar's cavalry soon left the village, and right after that the same old woman who had warned them that the army was coming started shouting from the attic window in her squeaky voice:

"They are leaving across the stream up the hill! They're all leaving! And Ilarion is with them!"

After capturing the leader of the Doukhobors and exiling him to Siberia, the authorities again sent the army to the Doukhobor villages and delivered an ultimatum: Renounce your new religion and way of life, or be forced from your homes.

The majority of the Doukhobors stayed loyal to their teachings and were scattered across the regions of the vast Russian Empire. Thousands of horses and ox carts left the Doukhobor villages in the south of Russia and headed towards Transylvania and Poland, the Baltic, the Urals, Siberia...The children of many of them were taken away and given to Orthodox families to raise according to the teachings of the Church. Some accepted the offer to renounce Doukhobor teachings and return to the Russian Church and accept the laws of the state. Those stayed on their properties. Priests returned to the churches in the Doukhobor villages and the church bells were restored. Families from different parts of Russia moved into the Doukhobors' houses and started a new life there. Those people too, for reasons known to the rulers, were being removed from their homes and sent to the southern part of Russia.

The descendants of Evstavy Chernov and his brothers, in that wave that scattered Doukhobors across the vast regions of Russia, were sent to exile far beyond Kazan, towards the Urals. Although broken and silenced, the movement was secretly growing all over Russia, and within the next twenty years it grew even stronger and more appealing.

After the Great Tsarina, Alexander Romanov the First took the throne. The tide of the Tsarina's wrath, which had scattered the Doukhobors across Russia, disappeared in the course of time, and a new tide started to rise. But this tide was favourable for the expelled.

The new Tsar, a monarch with a good heart and an admirer of the ideas of the Enlightenment, decided to return them again to the south of Russia.

4

A group of horsemen were galloping down the western slope of Green Hill toward the broadest part of the River Oskol's flow. However, in that place the river was at its shallowest, abundant with big rocks formed by nature's creative powers. Closer to the main current the rocks were narrower and sharper, and along the river's bank, where the flow of water was slower, lacking the great desire to reach the valley, the rocks were round, covered with traces of moss and lichen. The horsemen stopped at the riverbank looking for the easiest way to get across to the other side. The lead rider, who had all the time scouted ahead of the others, did not by now have patience to look for a better crossing, so he prodded the horse by poking with his heel at its stomach, and the horse leaped into the water between some rocks as far as it could. The others did the same. Passing between the round rocks, the horses obediently dashed forward. But when they reached the strong current, which, fast and forceful, had started eating away the rocks at their softer spots, thinning and sharpening them, the horses felt danger from the sharp rocks and turned their heads away trying to avoid the danger and unexpectedly refused to obey the riders. The first horse stopped with its eyes wide open looking at the current; it gave a snort as if cursing the river and then started moving upstream while the rider was hopelessly trying to calm it down and direct it toward the other bank. The other horses had also gone off the initial path and the horsemen suddenly found themselves in trouble. One of the horses lost its footing and, trying to balance itself, unseated the rider, who fell into the water. The horses were snorting and whinnying, the riders were shouting and cursing, and the river's current was growing louder, crashing with rocks.

Who knows how that crossing would have ended hadn't the first horse come upon a flatter and firmer part of the riverbed, and as fast as it could, the horse ran toward the other bank to leap out of the current. Having seen that, the other horses raced after the first one. The rider who had been unseated was the only one who stayed in the water. He was slowly skipping from one rock to another, taking much more time and effort than the others to get across.

"I didn't know the river had risen," shouted a rider with long fair moustaches, a big woven bag on his back.

"I myself have never crossed the river in this place," added the one who had long black hair and a baggy white shirt, wet after the struggle with the water.

The others were commenting too; then arrived the one who had crossed the river on foot. He took the bag off his back and threw it on the ground. The water was pouring out of it and it seemed as if a little spring had settled inside and was trying to show off its strength.

"Those Doukhobors are cursed people!" shouted the one who had arrived first on this side. "Whenever I come close to them, I lose sleep. Now I got wet in the river, once I got frozen in a snowstorm, and when I was carrying a message from our ataman to their leader Kapustin, I barely escaped being devoured by wolves."

"Why didn't you tell me that before we crossed this water?! If I had known, I wouldn't have prodded my horse into the current," remarked the lad with a prominent forehead and pale blue eyes who had been thrown into the river.

The others started laughing, and the one among them who had managed to keep his fur hat on his head, the water still dripping from his hair down his forehead and bumpy nose and pouring down his arms, shouted:

"We shouldn't go back the same way! We better tell our people in Slavyanska that the Tsar has allowed the expelled Doukhobors to return to their homes; we could then cross this river near Kramatorsk to come back. There are some easy crossings over there."

"What is going to happen with our people who have been living on the land of the expelled for some decades, living in their houses? With our families and cattle we will have to go back across the river," concluded the lad with long black hair. No one replied just then.

When the one who had been unseated threw himself on the back of his still agitated animal, the group prodded their horses into a gentle trot up the hill, behind which lay the big village of Slavyansk. There and in the neighbouring villages, the news about the return of the expelled was received with varied reactions. The families who had moved into the Doukhobors' farms started making plans for departure. Surprisingly, there was but little protest and tension among them. The families of the former Doukhobors, those who under the pressure from the regime of Catherine the Great had accepted reinstatement in the official Russian Orthodox Church to avoid massacre and expulsion, now found themselves in a spiritual dilemma: to return to their own teaching or continue to live under the auspices of the official Church. In general, it was a question of pride, of strength of character and of dignity. Those who now made a decision to stay out of the original Doukhobor teaching would, through generations, carry the blemish of opportunism and would be blamed for shifting with the wind. Those who now decided to return to their Doukhobortsy knew that the others would consider them cowards, proud of their affiliation with the movement only until trouble came, hiding until the danger was over. In fact, these were the times when the tenacious roots of Doukhobortsy were seriously threatened. This was the beginning of the emergence of factions within the movement. In these first serious tests of loyalty to Doukhoborism, the human ego became prominent. The question of private property was very seriously revisited. Those who preferred retaining ownership of what was theirs were assessing their interests in this new critical situation.

Upon hearing the news that Tsar Alexander the First had allowed Doukhobors from all parts of the country to return to their former villages and farms, those who had remained behind gathered in the home of Osep Popov in Ekaterinoslav. They discussed the messages sent to the Tsar by the Doukhobors who had been expelled to the regions between Kazan and the Urals. Among those were the descendants of Evstavy Chernov, Vasily, his son Stepan, Sergey and Nikolay with their families, who had been expelled from this very Ekaterinoslav and nearby villages.

The tall, long-shanked Osep Popov rose and sternly addressed the gathering. "Where did they get the idea to send word to the Tsar that they are not asking to be returned to their former homes because other people live here now? They say children have been born to the people who live here now, these incomers have organized their lives here, and it is only reasonable that what these people have built should continue to belong to them because land is not private property. It belongs to all people and it is for those brought by the winds of destiny to enjoy. They told the Tsar that injustice would be done to these people who had settled on the farms of the expelled Doukhobors if they were to be evicted. They do not want the injustice done to the Doukhobors to now be extended to other people, to those Tartars, who have been given the farms of our expelled Doukhobors." Osep Popov's hat made of rabbit fur slid over his left ear, as it often did. He paused and declared, "This charitableness is suicidal! It is charitableness to the Tartars but not to the expelled Doukhobors."

A few of the gathered people supported his opinion that such behaviour was unwise and that justice would be done if the expelled Doukhobors returned to their homes. Then, the chubby red-faced Andrey Mikhailovitch Kalmikov stood up from a heavy wooden chair and called in rebuttal:

"We were taught to be good people. It means that, first, we would need to ask our Doukhobors, who have survived torture by the authorities, to forgive us for having played the game of converting to the official Church then and of returning to our movement now. Second, it is unfair to remove our newcomers, the Tartars and the Ruthenians, from their present settlements because they were transferred from their farms to these here not at their own wish. They are not to be blamed for the evil done to both us and them. If our brothers from beyond the Kazan have proposed to the Tsar to give them another piece of land in our regions and not to move those settled on

Doukhobor farms, we have nothing to add to that. In that manner they only prove to us and to the entire world that the Doukhobors are just people who consider all humans their brothers."

"Well…" Osep said something under his breath but did not contradict Andrey.

"We need to plan how to welcome the returned," suggested the beardless Ilya, Andrey's son. "It would be good if we could help at least some to find their children who were taken away by the authorities and given to Orthodox families. That would be the best help we could offer to the returned."

Similar discussions were held in many villages in the south of European Russia. In those parts of the world, that spring was one of the most beautiful in the memory of even the oldest people. On many farms cows were giving birth to two calves, mares were foaling twins, foxes and skunks were not stealing chickens from chicken-coops, rivers and brooks were staying in their beds and sunny and rainy days were alternating as it most pleased the sowed fields and the orchards abundant in fruit. People were merry, and as soon as the word spread that the horse carts of the returned had arrived, the melody of the song dear to all was heard:

In our eyes are faraway places.
We were singing when they sent us away.
Our land was foreign to us,
And there they killed our joy.

People were merry. In first encounters between those who had stayed during the expulsion and those who had been expelled there was some restraint, awkward anticipation and tension. Even though the hosts had made preparations to house the returned, they could not anticipate all details. Decades had passed, and although some people had died, new generations had been born. To one house more people came than were expected. To another house came fewer than expected. But in the end most came to believe that good would set everything right.

In the first few days they ate and sang a lot, and the newcomers told tales of their expulsion to other regions of Russia's empire. They arrived in their traditional Doukhobor clothes, clothes of the old Russian South, but a few wore some pieces of clothing from the regions they had been expelled to. The most noticeable were the garments from various parts of Siberia, with their gaudy colours in odd combinations, not common in the territory between the Dnieper and the Volga. From these faraway regions the newcomers brought some new songs, among them some with marked differences of language and tradition. There was much singing.

5

The Chernovs quickly organized their life after returning to the land of their fathers. Houses grew like mushrooms after rain; people started to till uncultivated soil and turn it into fertile land; they planted fruit trees and crossbred the cattle they had brought from the Kazan region. And not only Chernovs. The other Doukhobors had more energy than their friends and family members who had not been expelled, and thus, through the influence of the newcomers, in the entire south of Russia a sudden flourishing of agriculture and crafts took place. Settlements started to change their appearance and houses assumed something of the architecture of cities. A new spirit of rejuvenated life-energy was felt in the entire region and manufacturing became more organized. It stopped serving only people's own needs and now started meeting the needs of the market. The returned Doukhobors brought a strong feeling for more uniform integration of families into the community, a more revolutionary outlook on social relations based on the original practice of the Doukhobortsy but developed during their exile. The returnees also showed more affinity for new technology, especially in crafts and service activities. Above all they showed a strong desire to educate the children of their community. The Chernovs, Popovs and Kalmikovs, immediately upon their return, started to propagate the idea that they should open elementary schools and send children to higher schools in city centres.

The Doukhobor Movement was facing a new strong current that sought revision of some of the traditional characteristics of the *Dukhobortsy* philosophy of life. However, many Doukhobors were suspicious of the talk about novelties, and even started to speak loudly against the negative influence on the movement coming from some of the returned. Division, still mild, was beginning to occur amongst the

Doukhobors. The official Church and the institutions of power started to encourage that schism. In the turbulence caused by the new tide of returned exiles, they saw their chance at bringing the entire Doukhobor philosophy of life and religion slowly back into the official stream.

The aged Vasily Chernov did not express any desire for imposing himself on others, but in his village of Radionovka there was a growing sentiment that he was a self-possessed and wise head of his household, one always capable of finding the right word in a critical situation. He was an excellent carpenter who was also able to carve a wooden owl or falcon that would make all onlookers feel as if they could hear the birds' hooting and screeching. In the shop of Marion Konstantinovitch Gerasimov in Kazan, Vasily and his son Stepan had learned the skill of making stylish furniture. Vasily was of a gentle nature and agreeable appearance, with small freckles on his face, especially under his eyes, and round thin ears. When, in the time after his return, the villagers suggested that he be the leader of the village and the first in contacts and consultations with other Doukhobor leaders, he smiled mysteriously and in the end refused the offer by saying, "I do not like power. I do not like any distinction among our people. We have our Council, our *Sobraniye,* and we do not need leaders. If you need advice on how to make the best beds, then you might ask me, or when it is best to bed out cabbage, then we need to ask advice from Svetlana Kotelnikova…I am scared of leaders, for they often become greedy, cut themselves off from others and look for personal gain. I prefer a simple, uncomplicated way of life."

Years had passed since the return of the Chernovs and the other Doukhobors to their former home. Now nobody bothered them. Their villages had grown, agriculture flourished, and cattle multiplied on their farms. The soil was rich, with its very fertile layer of *chernozem*, the black soil. They succeeded in improving strains of fruit and grain crops to achieve the best quality and abundance. In the eyes of the Doukhobors, the proclamation to allow their return to the regions on the northern shores of the Black Sea, and the offer of material help from the state, considerably contributed to the rectification of the evils formerly done to them. Tsar Alexander I was accepted in the homes of the Doukhobors. They became known in the world; once, even representatives of the British Quakers paid them a visit. After that the Tsar himself visited them. When writing about the Tsar's visit to the Doukhobor villages in the region of the Milky Waters, Russian newspapers reported to the world the Tsar's praise for the Doukhobors' advancements in food production and for their agreeable way of life. The Tsar did not praise their religious distinctiveness, but the Quakers did, which in no time increased the number of their followers in Russia and that of their sympathizers in the world.

Vasily Chernov died on the doorstep of his son Stepan's house. He had lived to a very old age, and when he felt that the end was coming he would visit his son's house more frequently, and more than before he would tell stories to his grandson Vasily, who was already showing a considerable interest in the young girls of the village. On one occasion after having patiently listened to a grandpa's story, the young Vasily addressed Grandfather as an equal:

"Dyedushka, next time talk about girls and how they were the same age as I am now."

"Let me see you better," said Grandpa.

After attentively watching his grandson for some time, Grandpa folded the tips of his moustaches with his hands, smiled and said in a low voice so that he could not be heard by others:

"Well, well...And I thought you were still my little rascal. But I can see you are not anymore. I see you are more interested in girls than in Grandpa's tales. But you better remember, my Vasya, that Grandpa and the stories are soon to leave to a place of no return, while your girls will remain here. Don't forget us, Vasya."

The grandson threw himself into the grandfather's arms, wrestled him down onto the wooden floor and gently pressed Grandpa's grey head against his chest.

Stepan Chernov would often go horseback riding with his son Vasya, across the neighbouring fields and woods and would relate his life experiences to his son. One day while they were fondly watching a flock of pigeons play games high up above the poplar trees along the Little Vorona River, the boy told his father how much he missed the grandfather. Then he also disclosed how much he was fond of their villages and people and how he liked the most to wade in the shallow waters of the rivulet with his companions and to skip over the bushes of black sloe-berries while running wildly across the fields.

"It seems to me that such beauty cannot be found anywhere else in the world. Even if it could, I love ours more than anything else," the son confided to his father.

"Vasya," Stepan addressed him. "Life is beautiful when you feel good, but when you feel life is the most beautiful, be prepared to face some bad things. When you feel you are the happiest person in the world, put an almond kernel in the least tight part of your moccasin, so that you can feel it. It will keep reminding you that it could start pinching seriously and cause painful blisters on your foot. A reminder to be prepared for the bad things in life, the opposite of happiness."

"Maybe you have a point, Father. But when you are telling me this, it seems as if I was reading about it in some book, so that it seems unreal to me. I would prefer to come to my own conclusions through my own experience. I cannot rely on the experience of others when making my own conclusions."

Stepan was astonished. He had not expected such serious thoughts and formal language from his greenhorn son. To console himself, he concluded that children are often smarter than their parents. The present time belongs more to them than to their parents. He felt that he should not attempt to deprive Vasya of his own experience. At the same time, he believed in the value of warnings.

"Personal experience is valuable, but more pleasant if it does not hurt when you are gaining it. I always prefer to learn from the mistakes of others when I can. If you wait to make a mistake so you can learn what is not good or what you need to be wary of, in the best case you will waste time gaining the experience. Look what happened to your companion Rastika when he tried to chase a snake from its pit. He even removed rocks with his bare hands! And the snake bit him. It is good that you cut his wound with a knife to let him bleed, but it was too late.

He had already suffered the pain." Stepan was trying to temper his son's enthusiasm. "For Rastika this was not a pleasant way to learn."

Vasya was quiet; then he nodded his head, accepting his father's correction. However, both of them were thinking how two generations, even when feeling very close to each other, are still different, for time is never static. Each new moment carries a seed of change and it is only normal that fathers and sons do not always hold the same opinion. In the least serious case, difference in age merely creates a different approach to life. When a wind storms through a wood, it is not anymore the same wood as before the wind. If nothing else, what could be noticed by a naked eye is fewer dry branches in the trees and more broken branches and leaves under them.

His pride often prevented the son from admitting that the father was right, but he still took up his father's advice. However, it was not clear to him why he should make a blister on his foot. He told his friends what his father had said and they were surprised and started laughing. They put small round stones in their moccasins, to see what would happen. Almonds and their kernels, which Vasya's father had talked about, they could not get because merchants would bring them from the Krim and Baba Agrafina would buy them all to make her tea to cure backache. The stones proved uncomfortable.

Soon came the time when Vasya understood his father's advice. He suddenly decided to marry Anusha Plotnikov, a young maiden just beginning to bloom. The girl had started to feel something alive moving ever more strongly under her belly button, as if a fish had settled in her belly. She confided in her mother, who looked at her carefully, her face turning red as if she herself had felt something move under her belly button.

"I keep seeing you with that Vasya Chernov. Have you two been doing something?" the mother asked her daughter.

Anushka bent her head, her face blushing. She turned away, ran to the window, put her face against the window frame and started to cry.

Her mother let her cry for some time, then she went to her, made her daughter look at her and said:

"That's from what you have done with Vasya. Now, go quickly and find him and tell him to take you to his father's house. I know his father is not to blame for anything, but that is our custom."

Her mother moved a few steps away and looked at her daughter for a few moments.

"You are still young, Anushka. But you got what you'd been looking for! How are you going to name it if it happens to be a boy?"

"Konstantin!" said Anushka without hesitation. "Konstantin is my favourite name for a boy."

In the early autumn, while the leaves of the deciduous forests and those on the foothills along streams and rivers were still green, through Doukhobor villages there travelled the news that their agile leader, Pobirokhin's heir Kapustin, had started to summon people to a *Sobraniye* and had asked all who were mentally sound and could walk on their own legs to attend. All the members of Stepan's family came. A few thousand Doukhobors—men, women, and older children— gathered in front of the Orphans' Home in the village of Terpeniye. They knew the matter was important and huddled closer together to hear the leader. He shouted so that he could be heard by everybody:

"The Tsar has died!"

The crowd made a spontaneous sigh. There were no cries or tears because those people had been used to troubles.

"His son Nikolay is his heir. Kharkov's newspapers announce that the new Tsar has declared that Doukhobors will either return to the Church or have to leave their beautiful villages in the Milky Waters. Also they will have to swear to the Tsar and the homeland that they will be loyal citizens and that they will respect the Tsar's will and the laws of the country."

Stepan squeezed the hand of his wife Irina. In the same manner, his son Vasya squeezed the hand of his wife Anushka, and looked at his son, Konstantin, whom they had started to call Kostuna when his hair started to grow like grass by the stream and became curly like the wool on their lambs when they start running across the fields. Kostuna looked at the heads of his two smaller brothers. All were quiet, waiting for the leader to speak again.

87

"Yesterday around dusk, some people from Zaporozhye told me that the Tsar was going to expel us to the Caucasus, among the wild tribes, if we did not comply with his Government's demands. They also say that they will force us to do the worst army jobs, and that they will take our papers away, so that we will not be able to move around freely. I do not know where the Zaporozheskiye heard that. Maybe the Cossacks who serve in the Tsar's Guard have brought the news. Maybe some priest has made it up to scare us. But I am sure that the new Tsar has no good intentions towards us. We can expect anything from him."

The people were anxious. They started talking in groups, shouting to each other and making suggestions.

"To the Caucasus…" whispered Vasya to his wife Anushka and to Kostuna.

"There, where the Greek god Zeus expelled and bound the most valiant of the Titans, Prometheus, the creator of humans, because he had not always obeyed the will of the Tsar of Gods and Titans…I would not be surprised, for if that could happen to a god, why not to us!"

"Where did he get that?" thought the chubby, always smiling Irina Popova, Vasya's mother. She was Stepan's second wife.

Stepan's first wife had died unexpectedly. Having felt the child inside her, she got scared and, craving solitude, in the middle of a cold winter she went to a cave above the river and spent a few hours there sitting upon a cold rock and in her thoughts trying to envision the form of her future child. She even managed to picture his healthy rosy cheeks, imagining him running freely across the fields like a young colt which, having broken away from the corral, runs across a field thinking there is nobody as happy as he in the world. When she came home, she took to her bed. She fell ill with dangerous fever, started coughing and vomiting. One night not long after, Stepan felt her breathing stop, and her legs started to stretch in a strange way. The final impulses of her life came from the tiny body of their child inside the already still womb of his mother.

When Stepan married Irina Popova, and when he and Irina noticed that a new life was beginning in her body, they decided to name the boy Vasily, in honour to Stepan's father. There was a belief among the people that if in a family children started to die, the next-born son should be given his grandfather's name to rid the family of the misfortune. It was wise to act according to this folk belief, even if it were a superstition.

"My Vasya has thoughts nobody in the village has. I wonder why he came up with those Greek gods when our Christian tradition does not mention any Prometheus or Zeus. I know that our elders talked about some god Perun from the long-dead past, but they did not mention any of these." Irina was whispering these speculations above Vasya's head while gazing strangely at her husband's face.

Vasya's son Kostuna also did not understand why his father was making a connection between their expulsion to Caucasus and those Greek gods. But it was neither the time nor place to ask him for explanations. It suddenly occurred to him, as when somewhere in the distance sudden lightning in the middle of a calm night announces a coming storm, that the grandson of the merchant Malkin had told them how in the mountains far away to the south there is a fairytale about an eagle that a flock of crows awaits every morning and chases all day long up to the rocky peaks of the mountains, and how at dusk the eagle returns to his nest in the top of the branchy oak tree.

Mother Anushka was trembling and touching the hair of her three sons, passing with her hand from one head to another.

Vasya started to worry about the fate of his family and that of the entire Doukhobor community. More often he looked for solitude in the orchard or in one of the cattle barns and thought about what the best course of action might be. He would come to various conclusions, and in turn each would seem the right solution for dealing with the evil announced by the highest authority in the country. He thought how new rulers, lacking self-confidence and fearing the bad reputation they already have among their people, often resort to threats and force. But threats and force are good neither for such rulers nor for the people. Then, after a few days Vasya would come up with new possibilities and would be ever more doubtful that any solution would work. He respected Kapustin as some sort of leader, a good leader in good times, but felt that Kapustin was not equal to the situation that was coming upon them. He was, in effect, too young to have the wisdom necessary to lead the Doukhobors in these times when a storm was approaching, when the big and powerful were starting to show their grandsires' aversion to the freethinking Doukhobortsy. It would occasionally cross his mind that the family was more important to him than adherence to the movement, and that it would be wise to return to the Orthodox Church and kneel down in front of state rulers. However, such thoughts would immediately make him blush, his breathing would become heavy and he would start feeling pain in his chest. Or, Vasya Chernov would correct himself, maybe they could officially agree to return to the Church, but in reality remain loyal to their Doukhobor teaching. That alternative also did not make him happy, so he decided to let time show him the best course of action.

Time soon showed its impatience; more frequently groups of Orthodox priests, wearing black robes with big shiny crosses hanging down their chests, started to ride their horses through Doukhobor villages. The priests would not stop, but triumph was visible on their faces. Children would see them off by shouting and running after the horses, and on one occasion a stone was thrown from a house at a group of the black horsemen. The horses became scared and dashed out of the village in different directions. Afterwards, fully armed cavalry arrived at the villages. The features of their faces revealed that most of these soldiers had come from somewhere the other side of the Urals.

When the cavalry entered the village, Vasya, with a group of villagers, was shearing sheep in the corral. They stopped working and calmly stared at the soldiers. They knew the soldiers had not come to offer them cakes. Most of the villagers, even the children, disappeared into or behind their houses. The dogs also retreated to a safe distance from the nearest horsemen. Only pigs were left, grunting and picking around the houses, not paying attention to the newcomers. Vasya assumed that the soldiers had come to communicate to them some important proclamation by the authorities; he could not believe that they would start to terrorize people without warning. The soldiers dismounted their horses and rushed into the nearest houses. Soon from the houses were heard curses, men's shouts, women's and children's cries and the sounds of breaking windows, doors and furniture…

Vasya and the other villagers who were in the corral with him rushed out and ran towards their houses. Several gunshots were heard, followed by the mortal cry of the young Boolatov. He shuddered when a bullet hit his back, stopped still, and started pushing his chest forward as if running away from the bullet. With his hands he tried to reach the spot between his shoulders where the bullet had hit him, as if trying to pull the metal out of his body. He screamed a few times and fell to the ground. Vasya and the others ran to him, turned him on his back, but there was no more life in him. Only his lips were slightly trembling as if scared of what had happened to him. The soldiers who were shooting ran to the place where Vasya and his group were kneeling beside Boolatov; they unsheathed their sabers and turned to face the officer who was striding towards them.

"Isn't this one enough for you?" the officer was demanding, his hand pointed at the dead young man, "or do you want more people to perish?"

People started coming out of their houses and approaching the place where the incident had happened. From the crowd came a terrible scream, than a woman's cry. The throng parted to make way for a man and woman followed by two older men who were running toward the place where the youth was lying. They were the Boolatovs: the father, the mother, the grandfather and the uncle. The father knelt by his son's head, and looked straight into his eyes as if trying to find out if the son could see him. The mother fell upon her son's bosom and started kissing his chest, face, hair…Having realized that he was dead, she let out another scream, turned her head towards the soldiers and hissed at them, foam coming out of her mouth:

"Murderers! I thought you came to defend us. God will punish you!"

Again she fell upon her son's body and started kissing him everywhere. After that she started to push her head into the young man's shirt, as if she would like to enter his body. By their manner it seemed that some of the soldiers who stood close felt sympathy for the misfortune that had befallen the family Boolatov. Then out of the crowd of villagers came a group of soldiers dragging children. The children started to scream, and the women started too. And that officer shouted at the top of his voice:

"These ones are going with us. They are going to better families than yours!"

His words were interrupted by the sound of a snapping whip, coming from the place where the soldiers had entered the village. All eyes turned. There, seated on a black ferocious horse reared onto its hind legs, head thrashing against the bit, was a man in dark red clothes. He was snapping the whip above his head. Then he shouted so that all could hear him:

"Murderers! Hangmen! God damn you!

The soldiers pointed their guns at the horseman and started to shoot. He quickly hid behind the horse, the animal darted as if obeying a command, and they both disappeared in the cloud raised by the hooves from the dry, dust-deep road. The soldiers took away a group of village boys and girls.

When the cries and tears subsided, the villagers fell to waiting for any news that their children would be returned, hoping that it had only been a warning from the authorities. Life in the village had suddenly changed. People became ever more afraid. From travelling merchants they tried to find out where their children had been taken.

One day, the deranged Gresha returned from work in the fields and with fear in his eyes said that he had seen that horseman. He had only seen his eyes, glossy and bloodshot like those of a rabid dog. The horseman had told Gresha that the children had been taken away in the manner Turks were taking away healthy children from occupied regions in order to train them to be the best army in the world.

Next summer, in the family of Vasya Chernov some changes occurred that violently shook the whole village. First, Vasya, who had appeared healthy and strong, fell suddenly ill, became weak, and started to wither. He stopped going horseback riding with Kostuna and would more frequently shut himself in a tiny room in the attic. When alone with his son, he would interrogate Kostuna, asking him if he had a girl and if he felt he was ready to start a family. The young man himself had been thinking about that; however, his father's interest surprised him. Later on he realized that his parent had wanted to know if Kostuna was ready to take up the role of the father in the family, for Vasya died suddenly just when the villagers were preparing a feast for St. Ilya's Day. They wanted to celebrate the rich harvest of barley and rye and of the potatoes and beans the fields were abundant in. Mother Anushka with dignity took over the role of the caregiver in the family, but the role of the man of the house she bestowed on her eldest son, Kostuna. Instead of St. Ilya's celebration, the Doukhobors gathered in groups and sang old Russian songs and Christian psalms.

A few years later, the cavalry came to the village again. It seemed to the people that they did not come with evil intentions. With them came the authorized representative of the Kharkov District government, Ivan Gretzky, a refined gentlemen with thin black moustaches, his hair greasy from goose oil. He explained that he was bringing them the Tsar's mercy and the government's offer of the opportunity to swear to be loyal citizens of Mother Russia, to respect the laws of the country, and to pray to God under the jurisdiction of the Orthodox Church. From the crowd of people Evgeny Chubrilov, an old man with long grey hair, stepped spontaneously forward. He expressed what most people felt in their hearts:

"We are grateful to the Tsar for his goodness. With regard to the oath, we only swear to the Lord, our creator. We cannot give an oath to people, for all people are equal. We cannot swear that we would respect everything that the future brings to us because we do not know if it will be good or bad. With regard to the Orthodox Church and its priests, we do not require any mediation between God and us. We can tell you that we are humans and that we won't do any harm to other humans. We believe that is according to God's will."

The representative of the authority said with indifference that he had expected something like that. In front of the whole village he declared that he was giving a free hand to the cavalry commander to move the Doukhobors from their homesteads to the regions between the Caspian and Black Sea. In a cruel manner he declared:

"Those who are willing to accept the Tsar's offer should stay."

6

"I saw with my own eyes and heard with my own ears, Yegrusha. I am telling you…That tall soldier from the Tsar's Guard loosened his tongue and started taking about what the Tsar has in store for the Doukhbors. You don't believe me?! But I heard it with my own ears! I knew that in the bushes above Alex's mill a doe hare had had five kits; I went there every day to see how much they had grown. I chased dogs, cats and foxes as far away from the bushes as I could so that they wouldn't eat the doe and her young." Mikhail was trying to convince his wife, Yegrusha, that he knew something of great consequence. They were resting in the furrow between two lines of cabbage heads. There was no breeze at all. After the rains the weed grass had started pushing forward, taking away the food and water from the cabbage. The two of them determined to square accounts here. They had been pulling up grass all day, the sun was burning, their heads and backs were running with sweat, so they sat in the furrow to take repose and cool down.

"What do the doe hare and her young have to do with the Tsar and the Doukhobors?" asked Yegrusha, just to make him get on with his story so that they could again throw themselves at pulling the grass.

"You are not giving me time to take a breath. This has everything to do with those Doukhobors and the ruler of Russia! I came to see the hare and her young, to check if the biggest one is ready for the soup and the oven, but there in the bushes was that long-legged Tsar's officer, Bulbin, with Marusha's Avdotiya. I hid so that I could see and hear what they were talking about. Probably to show off his importance and his high rank in the Tsar's service, he started to talk:

"'I was on sentry at the palace; I and another one, who came from across the Don and who is closest among us to the Tsar. The Tsar and

95

his Minister of Interior Affairs and the members of the Holy Church Synod were discussing what they should finally do with the Doukhobors. With our ones from Milky Waters. The one who is the most important in the Synod addressed the Tsar boldly, as if he himself was the Tsar and the Tsar was just one of the Synod, and said that the Holy Synod had decided to finally expel that non-baptized sect from that best of Russian soil to a far place where they would grieve over that soil for a long time and where they would disappear without trace. He said that our *chernozem* is not for the Doukhobors! They do not deserve it!

"'The Tsar stared at each of them for a few moments, then looked at his Minister again; the colour of the Tsar's face changed as if it was himself they had decided to expel. The faces of those from the Synod turned red, their foreheads and the backs of their heads started to sweat, and they all looked at the one who had pronounced the declaration to the Tsar, as if scolding him for his determination and hardiness. They became more and more scared that the Tsar would be angry at them for the misfortune they had planned for the Doukhobors. I myself was thinking the same and was expecting that the Tsar would lose his temper and tell them squarely that the Doukhobors are his people and that nobody should dare to settle accounts with his people in such a manner.' "

"But tell me what happened! Why are you beating around the bush?" Yegrusha urged Mikhail. "Did that Tsar's Cossack and Marusha's older daughter do something? You were watching them and enjoying yourself and now you are beating around the bush and talking politics. First tell me about the two of them, Mikhail Ivanovitch, and then you can move on to talking about tsars."

Mikhail was surprised at his wife's interest in the possible love scene in the bushes by Alex's mill and looked her up and down with curiosity. Yegrusha fixed her gaze at him, trying to discover in his eyes the pathway to the images in his head. She felt the rhythm of her breathing become faster and the ever stronger tension inside her was pushing her to attack her husband with nasty words so that she could unveil his secret. Mikhail discovered that in her eyes and, trying to avoid creating problems for himself from the problems of others, he continued to talk:

"Plainly, that soldier was eager to thrust his dirty teeth into Avdotiya's breasts, but she was bolder and faster; she violently pushed him in the chest with her hands, he fell on his back and she stretched herself on top of him like a swamp leech when it sticks itself on the thirsty cow's teat. They cuddled and rolled in those bushes as if they were lying in goose feathers or in astrakhan wool."

"And?..." Yegrusha was impatient.

"What 'and'?" Mikhail provoked her. "When after all that rumble and clatter they were lying on their backs breathing heavily, she told him something, I could not hear what. Bulbin jumped as if a snake had tickled his bum. I got scared that he would discover me, squatting behind the bushes, looking and listening to them," Mikhail continued. "Then as if on the stage, Bulbin started to recite:

"'The Tsar jumped onto his feet, forgetting his dignity and the ache in his back, and shouted so that all could remember his words: "Expel them to the Caucasus! It will best serve them and me! To the Caucasus! There they won't have our churches and crosses to watch with their hostile eyes. And those infidels, the Turks, Azers and Persians, won't raise armies against them and won't treat our people badly because the Doukhobors won't build churches and church bells and won't raise holy crosses to anger them. To the Caucasus with them! To the Caucasus!"

Yegrusha passed her gaze from Mikhail's flushed face to the field, trying to figure out how much of the cabbage was still threatened by the strutting weed. Then she spread her arms, pushed her bosom forward stretching herself and said:

"A filly. They never have enough. And you lash into that soldier as if you were envious of him...Not until a bitch wags her tail do the dogs go after her. The likes of her would lie down with a soldier in any uniform. I wonder how she could have gotten hold of that Bulbin!"

"Wait, Yegrusha! I keep thinking that soldier tricked his way up her skirt. They even go after married women, after those who are still children, after old women..." Anger was noticeable in Mikhail's voice.

"Are you now saying you saw him carrying her to the bushes in ropes, Mikhail?" she teased him. "Her mother is the same. She brought shame upon her husband and family. She pushed Avdotiya's father, that gormless Mitrusha, out of the house and he disappeared somewhere across the Dnieper. As for the Doukhobors, poor people. They won't find such soil anywhere, Mikhailo. See how black it is and full of these thin pink worms. There is no wheat and cabbage in soil where these worms do not go."

"I am not worried about the Doukhobors," Mikhail breathed out. "They work even in their sleep. But, while the long-legged Bulbin was reclining next to that damn broad, he told her that the Tsar will go to war with Turkey, and in those parts, there has never been a war without Caucasus bleeding."

Yegrusha could not even stand seeing roosters fight in her yard, not to mention imagining scenes where people fight, which is what happens in wars. Roosters are extraordinarily violent. She was much more interested in who went after whom to the bushes. If the powerful ones had asked her whether they should send people to the war against some other people, she would have suggested that a corral be built in the field, and that people gather around the corral fence. She would put inside the fence those who start wars, and let them make each other bleed until their appetite for sending people to war subsided. Then the people would take them out of the corral and wash them with icy cold water until the last drop of blood disappeared from their clothes, and the smallest grain of desire for war from their minds. Then, the people would send them among beautiful women to make them feel what life is. But Yegrusha did not want to talk about it with Mikhail. She had once seen him picking a fight with some dandy from the neighbouring village only because he had secretly smiled at her at the wedding of the oldest son of Pyotr Arhypovitch.

7

Kostuna Vasiliyevitch Chernov and Pelagiya Horkov met by the village well. It had been about ten months since Tsar Nikolay the First's definitive declaration to expel the obstinate Doukhobors from the Milky Waters in the south of Russia to the region of the Wet Mountains in the Trans-Caucasus. They had been in love with each other long enough so that he could ask her:

"Yours have decided to accept the demands of the authorities and stay here. Do you want to go with me?"

They had fallen in love the past Christmas when Pelagiya's ex-boyfriend had betrayed her and married Maria Goobanova from a Doukhobor village on the other side of the river. Maria was a spinster. She was of average height, chubby, and had a few smallpox marks on her face. But she was from a rich family. There was rumour that she had given birth out of wedlock, and that her father had taken the child to some village close to Kharkov to be raised by distant cousins. Before he fell in love with Pelagiya, Kostuna had cast an eye on Anastasya, Pelagiya's cousin, who was shy and tried to hide that they had a romantic relationship as if she had been ashamed of Kostuna. He noticed that and it was not difficult for him to pass on his feelings to Pelagiya as soon as she broke up with her unfaithful boyfriend. She was more refined and more open than Anastasya and was in no way trying to hide the fairness of her face under her abundant black braids.

"I will go with you, Kostka, if we get married before you set off to the Caucasus. What other would I go with? Although I will be sorry to be parted from my mother and brother, my father will be glad if I go with you."

When Kostuna and his mother went to visit the Horkovs to make arrangements for the wedding, they received a warm welcome, and after that evening, Kostuna and Pelagiya became husband and wife. According to Doukhobor custom of the time, their wedding was their own affair, sanctioned by their parents, and simply arranged. There was no ceremony, only a group of villagers singing psalms and hymns to a happy life and successful family. On that night Pelagiya moved to the Chernovs. Close to dawn, exhausted of passionate caresses, they agreed, when in the new place, to name the new member of the family Misha, if he happened to be a boy.

In the early spring, as soon as the sun grew stronger, a procession of Doukhobor carts and wagons, followed by cattle, set off from the villages on the north shore of the Azov Sea, across the rising Don, to the faraway Trans-Caucasus, situated along the constantly tenuous border with the Ottoman Empire. These people did not shed tears when leaving their native soil and the land of their fathers because they felt ever more strongly they were leaving their unaccommodating Mother Russia. Kostuna and Pelagiya, with Mother Anushka and Kostuna's two younger brothers, travelled in two horse-drawn wagons. Huddled on the front seats, they said goodbye to their native Radionovka and the Milky Waters.

"There, we will be further away from tsars and governments, and maybe we will be safer," their whispering came out and stayed behind in the Milky Waters.

Those who were leaving let the horses go at their own pace, and those who had decided to stay secretly watched from behind the curtains of their windows.

The Chernovs left their Milky Waters and in one of the Doukhobors' caravans they arrived at the faraway Tbilisi in the Caucasus. When they became used to the eternally white tops of the Caucasian Mountains, the harsh mountain climate and neighbours entirely different from those in their homeland, when they had built their houses, given birth to a new generation of children, the war started: that Russian-Turkish war twenty years before the end of the century, the war in which the Doukhobors had to help the Russian Army but only as transport service for the army's needs. The leader of the Doukhobors at that time, Lukeriya Kalmikova, did not hesitate to refuse the involvement of the Doukhobors in combat, but she proved her cunningness when she offered that her people participate in the transportation of equipment and food for the Tsar's Army. As a reward for their cooperation during the war, Tsar Alexander the Third made it possible for a number of the Doukhobors to move to the newly conquered territories around Kars, at the very new border between their country and Turkey. The climate was more pleasant than that in the bosom of the Caucasian Mountains. Kostuna, his wife Pelagiya, their son Misha and the other Evstavy Chernovs left their hearths again and moved to the Kars District.

8

Paperadicus, stinkingadicus, cabbageadicus…Where is my leg-boy, my rosy butterfly Vladimir. You go everywhere and know everything. Tell me where my blue-eyed son is. They took him away; let theirs be taken, God willing!" Leonid the Unfortunate was walking back and forth across the field along the stream and was whispering to the butterflies lest he scare them. He came across a group of blue ones on the cracked mud of a dried-up pond, jumped gaily and slowly came closer, passing his gaze from one butterfly to another. He carefully lowered his head above the spread wings of the closest ones and whispered: "You all have blue wings; but the other one is different. He also must be somewhere close. That one of mine with a white star."

He realized that his butterfly was not there; he raised his head towards the blue sky, scratched behind his ear, jumped over a group of butterflies (careful not to scare them) and went on searching among the flowers. He had once been a respected teacher in Spasovka, youngest son of the well-known Stepan Dmitriyevitch Ulyanov, who, before the Tambov policemen beat him to death, had been forced to leave his hearth. Leonid Stepanovitch Ulyanov had not cut his hair for eleven years, and his chestnut-coloured mane flowed over his shoulders. Locks of hair criss-crossed down his forehead, creating bars across eyes bloodshot for lack of sleep and from crying when his lunacy for a moment slackened—a lunacy harmful to nobody, not even to himself. Leonid the Unfortunate, the Tartar children from the village had recently started to call him, using it more as endearment than insult or teasing, for in the moments when his mind's activities became strongly devoid of the logical he would start again to cherish the hope that some of these butterflies would take him to the place where his son Vladimir was. Somehow, in his damaged brain he had concluded that Vladimir had turned into a butterfly, a very rare one with a long tail, its wings a pale hue of blue, with one misty-white star on each.

After the unscrupulous but unsuccessful pressure by the Russian Orthodox Church on the Doukhobors to renounce their sectarian beliefs and return to the Mother Church, to accept the Church hierarchy and its paths to God, the rulers of Russia had decided once again to take the case into their own hands. The brother of Tsar Nikolay the First, Grand Duke Konstantin Alexandrovitch, began to apply the earlier proclamation of the Church authorities that Doukhobor children ready for school should be taken from their families and given to families who had proven their loyalty to Tsar and Church. In that way those children could be returned to the bosom of the Fatherland and the following of sectarian beliefs and unlawful ways of living prevented. Leonid's seven-year-old son was among those taken at that time to some faraway Russian region. One month after that, when any trace of Vladimir was lost along with any hope in his return, Leonid's wife Elena jumped into the deep well from which they drew clear water. She refused to take hold of the rope which they threw to her while she was still fighting with death in the deep water, and she drowned. Leonid thrust his head into the darkness of the well trying to make her out in the darkness and shouted:

"Grab the rope, Elena! Grab it, Elyoosha! Please, grab it...I'm ordering you to!" His voice was growing weaker as hope was leaving him. He pulled his head from the well's opening and looked at the gathered people, sadly and suspiciously peeping into the sky, and then, as if he had remembered something, he quickly thrust his head back into the well's damp maw and renewed his shouting:

"Grab the rope, woman! Vladimir will come back! He is alive; he will come back! He will grow up, our Vladimir, and he won't forget us!" Down in the depth there was no more sign of life. Only the dark silence, disturbed by an occasional drop falling from some ledge into the cold water.

"Elyoosha has gone too," declared the giant Yuri Nikolayevitch He gestured with his head somewhere toward the foothills, paying no attention to anybody else. "It is easier for her that way. They have abducted and taken her Vladimir away, and they have expelled my Ivan to Siberia," he whispered, gazing at the distance into which the Doukhobors' children had been disappearing ever more often.

Since that time Leonid had started to wander across the fields and to whisper to butterflies; to sleep in others' cattle barns and to eat what people unobtrusively left behind the barn where he had often been seen. Sometimes he would lie on his back in the field for hours and look at the clouds travelling east. He would pass his stare from one cloud to another, hoping to see Vladimir on one of them.

Leonid's wandering from one butterfly to another was interrupted by the storming of a multitude of horse hooves galloping down the hill along the road to the village. He raised his head towards the sky and there he saw only the hot summer's midday blueness. There was no cloud to be seen. He became afraid of that emptiness, turned his head towards the field and saw horsemen, now at a slow trot, approaching down the road. They seemed to him similar to those who had taken Vladimir away with a group of other children; he went towards them, then stopped as if trying to remember something. Abruptly, with all the might of his heart and legs he dashed toward the road to meet them. When they met, two soldiers in white uniforms and long black leather boots jumped off their horses and grabbed Leonid's arms to prevent the villager from carrying out unpleasant intentions. Their captain, with the golden wreath around his cuffs, stopped the soldiers.

"Let him be! I know him; he is not dangerous."

"Mister officer, ask them," Leonid pointed at the soldiers with his hand, "if any of them has seen my butterfly with blue wings. It ran away from my bosom, and no one knows where it is. I caressed it and it went away, the one with a star on each wing. It's been taken away somewhere…"

"I have. I have seen it. It has gone down the stream toward that lake. Precisely your butterfly with white stars on blue wings."

Leonid stared at captain's big, gently-green eyes, shook his head as if trying to gain control of his own mind and started to move away backwards, saying:

"Thank you, good man. It is my Vladimir. It must be him."

After five or six steps backwards, Leonid stopped, his gaze fixed on one young soldier on horseback. Not knowing what to do, he took a few steps forward, then backward again, not taking his gaze from the soldier with clear blue eyes. He put his shaking hand over his mouth as if afraid of the words stealthily crossing his lips:

"His eyes are like these too. They are like his mother's when I saw her for the first time in Gorelovka at the village gathering. Then they turned white in that damn well. But Vladimir's are brighter and younger…My butterfly with blue wings."

"Who is that Vladimir of his?" asked one of the soldiers who had been holding Leonid by the arm.

"People say he has gone mad and for years he has been looking for that butterfly. Nobody has ever seen a butterfly like that one in the Azov's flatlands. He was hiding while they were gathering the Doukhobors from the villages for the caravan to the Caucasus. And he stayed here in hope that he would find his son. Into these Doukhobor villages they settled the Tartars from the eastern shores of the Caspian Sea. The Tartars have accepted Leonid as one of theirs and they have been helping him to survive. They didn't even take against him when he burned his house, given to some Tartar women with two small children. The villagers helped to rebuild the house and to enlarge it, adding two rooms, which they decided to give to Leonid the Unfortunate, but he has never even peeked through the door." The captain was telling this story to the soldiers standing closest to him. Then while Leonid was moving away, jumping from one butterfly to another, the cavalry unit continued toward the village at a trot.

Leonid lost his mind at a time when in the Tsar's Russia the idea started to take shape that tsars and the Church are part of the people and not representatives of an unreachable God. It happened at the middle of the nineteenth century, the century in which across Western Europe the fires of social rebellion were spread by the winds of storming masses of people in their struggle for human dignity. Russia lagged behind Western Europe in the enthusiasm of the masses of people for changes in civilization, in the same way as, at the end of winter, the blowing of warm spring winds start later to reach the freezing regions of Russia's

North. However, that warming announcing change, which people had dreamed about for centuries, was being felt in the works of great Russian writers, in their lives and their enlightening role among the masses of the people. After the Middle Ages, during which people suffered terrible crimes from those who had put themselves above God, and in his name cut off any form of freedom, people started shifting from one movement to another and changing their character. The cages in which the rulers and the Church were keeping people became ever tighter, and the pressure was growing from the inside outward.

9

One year after the Russian-Turkish War, Lukeriya Kalmikova, the famous Doukhobor leader, was visiting the villages of her people in the Kars region. Being aware of her fame among the Doukhobors, but also among the representatives of the Tsar and the Orthodox Church, Lukeriya made an effort to see each Doukhobor family in the Trans-Caucasus as often as she could and to participate in all important events in Doukhobor villages. When she met with Kostuna Chernov in the village of Pokrovka, she suddenly asked him if he would go with her for a couple of weeks to the highest mountaintops of the Caucasus to meet with the Tartars' Little Princess. Kostuna was surprised that Lukeriya wanted to travel with him, and she, having noticed his surprise, explained that she had learned how the Tartar tribes extremely appreciated Kostuna's having hired Tartar workers to help with farming during the summer.

"I'll go with you, Lushechka, if you explain to me why you didn't invite Peter Vasiliyevitch to go with you. It is well known that Verigin is learning from you what kind of leader we need. He also knows that you are especially devoted to him." Kostuna was being gently provocative.

Lukeriya avoided the conversation about Verigin. She explained her belief that the Doukhobors in the Trans-Caucasus had to have good relations with the Tartar tribes if they wanted to have a peaceful and free life. On that journey, she added, they would need a wise fellow-traveller who would know how to dull the sharp edges of the Tartars' hotheaded mentality.

Long before her proposed departure, Lukeriya had sent a message for the Little Princess to the closest mountain range in the Caucasus—the Kazbek. She had sent it through a Tartar merchant who had built strong commerce routes between the Armenian and Tartar tribes. "I am delighted to accept your proposition to meet with you in the mountains of the Kazbek," was Lukeriya's message to the legendary Tartar woman, about whom stories were told not only in the regions of the Caucasus but in all the four corners of the world. Rumour had it that lucky was one who won her favour, and that the Tsar himself had met with her several times to ask her help in sorting out the problems on the borders with the Ottoman Empire and Persia while continuing to keep whatever control she could over the numerous Caucasian peoples. The Tartar tribes of that part of the world were feared by peoples who did not know how to cooperate with them, but at the same time, the Tartar tribes were the cohesive force in that nightmare of peoples, cultures and languages. Although they did not have official executive authority, the Tartars in that part of the world in the second half of the 19th century respected the Little Princess as their advisor and judge in internecine conflicts

Kostuna did not hesitate much in accepting Lukeriya's proposal because a meeting with the mystical Princess for him meant much more than an exceptional life adventure. Although the summer farmwork would ordinarily have required Kostuna's presence in the village, the Chernovs supported him in his intention to go to the slopes of the Kazbek to bring them new stories about the Tartar woman. Despite the fact that each hand was needed during the summer work in the fields, the *Starosna,* the Council of the Elders, gave permission to Kostuna to leave with Lukeriya. When Lukeriya came to pick him up, Kostuna was surprised to see that one of his fellow-travellers, the one sitting proud and dignified on the polished ox-leather saddle atop a fierce young horse, was Peter Verigin in person. The shiny black hair on the horse's chest and between its legs was slathered in the foam of hard riding. "So," Kostuna thought, having noticed a mysterious smile on Lukeriya's lips, "she couldn't go without him."

Kostuna himself could not understand why he felt a cold tide running between them every time he found himself in the presence of that face-powdered, arrogant, but strong and handsome young man of aristocratic origins. It was by no means because of those aristocratic origins, because Kostuna was aware that the Doukhobors needed followers from all social classes. Finally, since the young Verigin had submitted himself to life according to Doukhobor teaching and communal practice, what could he, Kostuna, have against the man? He was strong enough to persuade himself that Peter was not a disadvantage for the Doukhobors, but he did not like to be near him. And it had nothing to do with the fact that Lukeriya was an attractive woman of impressive mind and body. Kostuna had never felt any intimate feelings towards her. So in that regard he felt indifferent about whether Peter Verigin was going to travel with them or not. He even admitted as much to his little Misha when he was telling him what he had experienced while travelling with Lukeriya.

Misha was curious, and not satisfied with the report that his father gave to the *Sobraniye*, where, according to the custom, all villagers were present. As soon as they came home, he used the opportunity when Kostuna was alone at the table with food to tell him what had happened in the village while Kostuna had been away.

"Two times the mute Stevusha was first in the haymaking in the upper fields, and our Kuzmich defeated both Tartars who pulled the cart with hay to the big barns. And then, you know that Armenian merchant Ferhad? He brought goods from Turkey and the news that a drought had destroyed the harvest in Macedonia and that fires are burning on the Bulgarian shores of the Black Sea." Misha had been quick to disclose his news. Kostuna knew that meant Misha, in turn, was expecting his father to tell him about the adventures of his trip.

"Fine, fine, my son! As soon as it gets dark, make sure your mother and the other two are in bed, and then I will tell you about the Tartar Princess. Do you know what she is like? Her eyes are as black as coal and her hair as that of a Kirghiz and her cheeks and ears pink as wild rose blossoms in early spring. Not to mention her lips! If you could've seen your mother when she was a young girl..." The father intentionally flared the son's imagination.

"Did you go to Tbilisi?" Misha asked his father when, right at dusk, they crept out of the house and sat under the branchy Petrov apple tree.

He had built that city in his imagination from the stories and lies of people who had once visited it.

"We only passed through Tbilisi. We bought food supplies in the shop of some Georgian who owed us 50 kopeks change. He pretended not to have that many kopeks, but he didn't even have any more of the goods we needed. Lushechka jokingly wagged her finger at him and promised that we would come by his shop on the way back. It is a big town, Misha, as if you put ten of our Kars together. Their biggest church is in the centre of town, probably so that the priests can see from the bell tower what each believer is doing and persuade the believers that the Church is powerful, that without it the human community would be poorer both materially and spiritually. Not to mention the cross on top of the bell tower. I did not see one like that even in Kharkov. I have always asked myself why they build such big crosses on top of churches. There, when I found myself standing far down under that church symbol in Tbilisi, I understood that it is a weapon in the hands of the priests. They use it to threaten the disobedient and to warn good believers not to change their attitude or they will fall into disfavour. If while raising a huge cross on top of the bell tower of some new church one of them had thought about asking God for advice, I am sure that our Lord would have advised against it. Do you know why, Misha? Because crosses on bell towers are often hit by lightning, destroyed and burnt, and occasionally some believers are killed in the church."

"What are the people there like, Father?"

"Like us. Some have beards like me, some are beardless, like you. I saw one blind old woman who was sitting by a shop waiting for people to give her something. On her head she had a colourful shawl like that of our women, and she had only four fingers on each hand. It was hard to notice that one was missing. With our Alexey it is noticeable that the Tsar's soldiers cut his fingers off when they started their terror on us in the Azov. Lushechka gave her a piece of bread, and the old woman told her that she had come from the other side of the Caucasus, from the Dagestan. She was in a good mood and she told us that she had been born with four fingers on each hand because her mother had conceived her when running away from her husband high up to the glaciers of the Kazbek, where there were no birds, no beasts, not to mention a male human being. She said her mother was frightened by a flash coming from the sky and later felt a child in her womb. Lushechka has a good heart and wanted to give her something from her bag, but Peter warned her that a long journey was ahead of us."

"When did you see the mountaintops of the Kazbek?" Misha was impatient.

"The Kazbek is white both in the winter and in the summer. The snow left by the winter the summer cannot melt. We stopped by a stream, admiring the mountains shining in the distance, when horsemen wearing white turbans crossed our path. They make those hats using shawls. Do you remember when a few years ago young men came from the shores of the Caspian Sea to earn something by helping us sow the wheat? One of them had a hat like that and was playing with you children more than the others did when it was raining and we could not work in the fields."

"What did the horsemen want?" Misha asked quickly.

Kostuna told him the story:

They looked like Azerbaijanis, but they introduced themselves as Persian outlaws. They asked us to give them everything we had and then we would be free to go. Peter reached for his belt to pull out his long gun, but two bandits prodded their horses, the horses charged at Peter's horse, and both Peter and his horse fell down in the dust on the road. They pulled out their sabers to slay Peter. Kiril and I urged our horses closer to Lukeriya, but she shouted in a voice both commanding and dignified, a voice I had never before heard coming out of her mouth: "Wait! We are the Doukhobors!"

The bandits stopped, holding their sabers in the air above frightened Peter, who was lying in the dust, pressing on his horse's head so that it would not rise from the ground and the Tartars would not thrust the blades of their long sabers into the horse's bent neck. From the group of bandit horsemen one came forward with a yellow silk shawl over his face and calmly addressed Lukeriya:

"What are the Doukhobors doing in the mountains? The Doukhobors are in their villages."

Lukeriya was not easily confused. "That is where we live. We came here to meet with the Little Tartar woman in the Kuzbek."

Verigin's horse suddenly stood up on its legs and started shaking off the dust. Its eyes revealed that with its long teeth it wanted to bite the necks of the two horses that had pushed it to the ground. However, it decided against the revenge, realizing that it was not the right moment and that it would probably have bad consequences for all of us. In fact, it is hard for man to understand what was in the mind of that horse at that moment.

"With the Princess?" the bandit was surprised. The other two lowered their sabers. They were all for a few moments looking at Lukeriya with surprise and curiosity. Then the one who must have been their leader asked:

"What do you have to do with the Princess? And how do you know that the Little Tartar woman is in the Kazbek?"

"She is expecting us. Her merchants come to our villages. We agreed to meet in the mountains. When we saw you, we thought you were her soldiers. She promised to send a group of her soldiers to take us to her hiding place." Lukeriya was now trying to win the bandits over. In any case, she realized that mention of the Princess's name could help them a lot.

"If you are a Doukhobor, you must be their leader, Goobanova. I have heard about Goobanova. I do not know why you are making arrangements with the Little Princess. Tartars are warriors, and you…you are peaceful people. They say you do not go to war and you do not like weapons." The bandit was looking at us through the narrow openings of his eyelids.

Peter somehow understood that he was not in danger anymore and that the bandits had softened when they learned that the woman was Lukeriya, about whom many stories were spread as far as people from the Caucasus reached. Peter tried to get up, but the man with the yellow silk scarf pushed him with his foot back into the dust. "You lie down!

Feel what it means to lie in the dust. You do not look like a Doukhobor. You are aggressive and mighty. You must be the son of some kulak."

Peter, terrified, looked straight into the bandit's eyes, trying to foresee his next move from the way the shining of his eyes changed. He prayed to God to help him.

Lukeriya felt helpless and miserable. And with good reason. Since they had arrived in the Trans-Caucasian region, the Doukhobors had roused positive feelings toward themselves and their way of life among all the Caucasian peoples. Even wild tribes and bandits respected them. And now, unexpectedly...

"He is a good young man and an excellent Doukhobor. He lives the communal life with the others. He has even arranged business with the Tartar Princess," Lukeriya explained in a convincing voice.

The bandit went a few steps backward away from Peter and looked at him from the corner of his eye as if to see if the one lying down in the dust could fit the woman's description. Then, he gave a sign to the two standing above Verigin to help him rise from the dust.

"As for me, you made a good guess. I am Lukeriya Goobanova, the widow of the late Kalmikov."

"And we are the Princess's soldiers." The Tartar had suddenly changed his tone of voice. "We are returning from the Dnieper, from those parts that they expelled you from. Our Princess is not far. If you go with us, you will see her when the rays of sun redden above the highest mountaintops to the east. The night is ahead of us, Doukhobors." Then he stared at Peter's eyes, then at Peter's horse, whose gaze was still fixed on the two horses which had knocked him down to the dust. Peter understood that the Tartar was looking for words of apology to both of them, and he addressed the Tartar with dignity:

"I forgive you for this unreasonable attack on me. I have always admired your bravery and nobility."

The Tartar was surprised at Peter's words; he knitted his brows, passed his gaze over the faces of the other Tartars, patted his horse's neck and started off in front of the others.

§

The father was telling the story to his son, and the son was absorbing every word, admiring his father not only because Lukeriya had selected him among all others from the Kars Doukhobor region, and because he had had the opportunity to meet the famous Little Tartar Princess, but also mostly because in his father he recognized a man whom he wanted to emulate, a man who was both his father and his friend. With his Kostuna, Misha could talk about anything more easily than with his peers, and when Kostuna Chernov talked in the *Sobraniye* even the wisest and the oldest Doukhobors carefully listened and often sincerely approved his observations and suggestions. Misha was also proud that on several occasions Lukeriya had invited Kostuna to help her make a just decision when she had been asked to judge a community case of somebody's unseemly behaviour or cruelty. He only did not understand why his mother was unhappy when his father had to go for a couple of days to some faraway village where Lukeriya was needed as a judge. Then it occurred to him that his mother behaved that way, not because his father was away from the family and the community, but because, as Misha himself observed, the young woman was beautiful and smart, and her face and manner of speaking revealed her Russian aristocracy and goodness, and from her slanted green eyes a mightily provocative fire flashed out, inviting enjoyment.

Looking at his son's face, Kostuna saw that the boy was seriously thinking about something. Kostuna shifted his attention to the sound of cows mooing down there towards the big lake. Somebody is late with his cows, he thought. He did not find anything unusual in that, so he returned his gaze to his son.

"When did you meet her? The Little Princess," asked Misha.

"When? When it pleased her. And the way it pleased her. Although we were tired from the journey and from wobbling on the horses' backs, we could not easily fall asleep. The night was warm, so we did not need to pitch our tents. The Tartars settled themselves a little away from us among some rocks protruding from the ground as if a human being had planted them there. Our and their horses would occasionally neigh to conspire about something we did not understand. The Tartars were singing in low voices long into the night, and in the distance the sound of dogs and wolves howling was heard from time to time. The sky was covered with stars, and the moon was hiding somewhere behind the other side of the high mountaintops."

Just then, Mishka saw a meteor ripping along part of the sky above their heads. He thought how interesting it would be to explore those mystical realms, of which their planet was just an insignificant tiny particle.

"Weren't you afraid of night in those foreign places? And of those Tartars?" Misha asked his father.

"No. We were careful. The Tartars seemed sincere when they offered to take us to the Princess. I think that it never crossed their mind to cause us any evil because they were well aware that the Little Princess would never forgive them. She is their leader and is sacred to them."

Kostuna and Misha did not notice when Misha's mother, Pelagiya, approached them.

"What is with you two? Don't tell me you are talking about the hot-tempered Svrdlov. I don't believe that he once ate a whole basket of dry figs and hot sweet bread and that it hadn't been difficult for him to carry a donkey across the Efim's Marsh." Pelagiya was teasing them. Her broad hips gave her more charm than she would have had if that part of her body had been narrower.

"Don't be surprised, mother. Svrdlov said that he could jump and reach any star, if he only wanted to. But he wouldn't because there is nothing so beautiful as the sky adorned with stars." Misha was joking.

"I brought you some yoghurt so your throats do not dry up with so much talking," Pelagiya said as she put a wooden bowl of the delicious cultured milk between them. Then she went back into the house.

"Were you in the village when that happened to Svrdlov?" Kostuna asked his son.

"Yes," replied Misha.

"Why did he do it? I would have never thought that the old man was unhappy. It's been a long time since he stopped grieving for his son,

Ivan. I think it helped that people told him that those Cossacks who had taken his son later said they had put him with an honest and hard-working couple who had three more children. And see what he has done…"

"I was at home when I heard voices and screams that somebody had fallen into the abyss. I rushed there with many others, leaned over the abyss to see what was in its depth, and heard Svrdlov's shrill voice coming from down there:

"I won't go up! I won't grab the rope so that you could pull me out!"

"Grab that rope, Svrdi! Do not joke with us and do not act like a fool!" they shouted one after another.

"No! I tell you!" the old man was screeching from the depth.

His wife, daughter and brother Petrenko came from the field and begged him to grab the rope, but he kept screaming from down there that he would not and that they better go home.

"Only now do you care for me! If I grabbed this rope and you pulled me out, I would lose all that I have gained in this abyss. You would not care for me anymore. You would say that I played with you and then grabbed the rope tightly. I won't. You have never praised me for making the best scythes in Guberniya. You never said that my brandy stills are the best from here to Baku. Now when I decided to stay in this hole you started to care about me. I won't!"

The old man's daughter Nastyooshka was thrusting her head deeper and deeper into the cavern's opening in order to see her father better. She shouted that she was there too and begged him to tie the rope around himself so that they could pull him out. And the old man replied that he would fulfill any wish of hers except that one.

"Bear with me, Nastyooshka. Here it is different than up there. I feel that I am ever further away from people and from human wickedness and folly. Looking from here, life up there should be very different and simpler."

"What should be very different?" shouted Nikolko Popov to him.

"People put pressure on each other. See, if I have decided to stay in this hole, and if I feel better here than up there, why do you try to force me to return to you?"

116

The gathered people looked at each other, surprised at what old Svrdlov was saying. He was provoking them from the bottom of the abyss:

"Ask me something. Ask for advice and you will see that man thinks differently down here."

The people were quiet for some time; then Popov addressed Svrdlov.

"Tell us, Svrdloosha, why the sun gets born every morning."

"The sun was born one time and it does not get born every morning. We just do not see it at night because of these mountains and hills. If you were a bird to fly high up in the sky you would be able to see the sun all the time. It depends where you stand, my tovarish," Svrdlov shouted from down there.

"Why do cows have horns?" one woman shouted from the gathered crowd.

"To butt you in the bum to make you stop asking me such questions," Svrdlov shouted at her.

"Will the tsars and the church continue persecuting us?" asked the toothless Vasya and passed his gaze over the faces of those closest to him as if asking their permission to ask such a question.

"Everything has its beginning and end. They pushed us to the edge of the empire. We have nowhere else to go in Russia."

"Oh-ho-ho," laughed Kostuna. "Svrdlov was right. A man starts thinking differently in that hole. His words are full of wisdom, and wise men do not enjoy things other people enjoy. That is why we often think they are lunatics. Who knows where sanity ends and insanity begins, my dear Misha! It is almost impossible to be a good judge. If our tsars and vicars were in our shoes, they would not persecute us. And those who do not understand us should not be our judges.

"So tell me, how did the old man disappear?" Kostuna then asked Misha.

"The attempts to convince him were no use, the crying of his family, and the rain that started coming down harder and harder. They all knew that the waters would soon fill the bottom of the hole, and carry Svrdlov into some underground passage. And that is what soon happened. Svrdlov did not reply anymore to the cries and begging of his family. He wanted the people in our community to remember him for something big. If not for his scythes and stills, then for his disappearance in the abyss."

"The human brain is unpredictable. It sometimes creates things that other brains cannot even grasp. How can we grasp the fact that Svrdlov, in his right mind, decided to disappear from our lives in such a manner, wanting to do something ungraspable and big, so that we would remember him?"

"I later heard that some of the women were saying Svrdlov had been ill, and had even gone with Nastyooshka to see a doctor in Kars. He had not told anybody what the doctor had told him, but at Svrdlov's funeral, Nastyooshka found out that he would have died anyway within a couple of weeks."

They were quiet for some time; then Kostuna stretched himself, and Misha asked him to finish the story of the meeting with the Princess.

§

The horses woke us up. They were whinnying and snorting, squeezed together in a circle, their heads in the middle, their hind legs forming the edge of the circle, ready to kick. We jumped up and froze in fear. A group of about ten Tartars stood between us and the horses. They were not those whom we had come across the day before. In front of them was a woman with a young leopard. The animal looked at us, its front legs bent, its head stretched forward, following our every move.

"Don't be afraid!'" a clear woman's voice rang out. "This one only pretends to be brave and dangerous. He grew up in our tents, and eats what we do. When a cat raises its hackles at him, he hides behind my back."

The leopard seemed to understand what the woman was saying; he relaxed his tense muscles, sat in front of her and started licking his front paws. I hadn't seen a leopard before and had known about them only from stories. The woman approached Lukeriya, looked a her from head to toes and pulled down the heavy colourful shawl Lukeriya wore over her head. Her rich plait of black hair appeared, folded into a heavy bun.

"You are Lukeriya. I heard that the Tsar himself was surprised at your wisdom. You will have guessed that the Little Princess is in front of you. That is the name they gave me when I really was little. Time allowed me to grow up, but it did not erase that part of my name."

Between these two women a feeling of closeness spontaneously blossomed and they hugged as if they had known each other for years. Lukeriya introduced us to the Tartar woman, who just pointed with her hand at a strong young Tartar and said:

"Taras will be your host. He is a host to all who come to these Kazbek mountains."

She looked at Peter and apologized to him, smiling:

"They told me you had an unpleasant meeting with my Dniepers. They didn't know who you are. They say you looked like the Dagestan outlaw Suharov, and that one has caused us a lot of evil."

She led us through the forest, down a path that looked more suitable for wild animals than men.

§

"It seems that you, father, had the honour to be present at the meeting of two princesses," smiled Misha with satisfaction.

Long into the night Kostuna was telling Misha about the camp of the Little Princess and about the welcome the Tartars organized for them, about their games on horseback, about a hundred different dishes made from lamb meat, about children's races down the fast mountain river where they skipped from one stone to another.

§

At dawn, the Princess and Lukeriya went to a big tent covered with skins and decorated with colourful silk ribbons.

"I want to help you in case you need our aid," the Little Tartar woman started the conversation. Her face revealed strength and manly toughness. "Do not hesitate to ask for help if you find yourself in trouble. I personally feel some kind of obligation to help your people since your religion and your way of life do not allow you to raise arms against others. However, I did not propose our meeting only because of that. I am in possession of an object that belonged to your previous leaders. I do not know how it ended up in possession of a young Armenian merchant who wanted a handful of gold for it. I asked him to explain why he wanted so much, and he said that it is some kind of Christian holy object, that it is very old and worth much more than he had asked. He did not want to disclose how he had come into possession of it, but said he later found out that priests would have given an entire fortune to know where the object was. But this young fellow said he did not want to do that because he knew the object belonged to the Doukhobors." Having explained all this, the Tartar woman took the object from a concealed pocket. It was a tiny cube made of material that looked like amber, if amber can be clear light-green in colour. In the middle of that cube was a brain-like shape the colour of wild roses. Lukeriya took it and started turning it around in her hand in surprise.

"Have you ever heard about this holy object?" the Little Princess asked her.

With a feeling of respect and reverence, Lukeriya turned the cube in all directions, and penetrated its interior with her scarching gaze. After that, her smaragd green eyes looked into the deep black pupils of the Princess.

"I heard about it from my late husband. He had been looking for it for years and explained that bandits had stolen the precious relic from the Doukhobor leader Kapustin when they attacked him during his travels in Ossetia. He said that it is more important than the most powerful amulet, and that it is older than Christ himself. This cube is special. It is mystical and in this moment unexplainable to me. But I am grateful that you have returned this holy object to us."

Meanwhile the Tartars continued to entertain their other guests, offering them food and different drinks. They offered them their special vodka flavoured with the juice of rose petals, but the Doukhobors refused politely, explaining that their way of life does not permit alcoholic drinks. When the two women appeared at the door of the Princess's tent, Taras, their host, showed the guests the tents where they would spend the night. Lukeriya arranged that all four Doukhobors stay together

In the tent she told her companions about the Little Princess. Her impressions were fresh, full of admiration but also of surprise that the Tartars could live permanently as nomads, and that they managed to stand up against any authority trying to bring them under control, tame them and impose its laws upon them.

"We are different," Lukeriya explained to the Doukhobors. "We are similar to them in our rebellion against the state we live in, in our obstinacy toward their attempts to subdue us, but our mentality is completely different from theirs. They do not even think about settling in one area, building houses where they would live for a long time and where they would keep opening and closing the same doors. Weapons are sacred to them and they believe the only defence against the attacks of others is to be physically stronger than the attackers. To them survival means the ability to detect danger in time, so they can avoid or eliminate it. If your army is the weaker one, run away from the danger as fast as you can, so it doesn't reach you. But if you are stronger, fight to the death if necessary. They cannot understand our thinking that all men are equal and that all should have the same rights. The role of the individual is very important to them and one's position in the community depends on one's power and importance. The Princess cannot understand how we can live in fixed communities and wait for God to stop the evil doings of our enemies. However, she said that she likes us and she promised to help us in our travels and trades. Even if we need more workers in our fields during the harvest, their young people will come and help us."

Lukeriya did not mention to her companions the gift from the Little Princess, having remembered her husband's words that whoever had the object in his possession would be wise to keep it a secret.

Then, in the middle of the night, when even the occasional barking of dogs could not be heard anymore, that which Lukeriya and her company could not have expected happened.

All four of them were sleeping, tired from their journey and the events at the Princess's headquarters, so they did not notice when one Tartar entered through the door of their tent and started lifting the thick woollen cover from Lukeriya. At that moment from behind his back appeared the Little Princess carrying in one hand a big candleholder, with lit candles, and in the other hand her saber. She quietly warned the Tartar not to do anything stupid. Lukeriya and the others woke up and jumped to their feet. They quickly grasped what was happening, but the Princess calmed them down quickly. She said energetically, "Do not worry! Everything is fine. Not a hair of your head will be harmed when you are my guests. This greenhorn thinks he can have any woman in the world, especially when vodka gets the better of him."

With her saber the Tartar woman showed the young Tartar the exit from the tent; he bent the upper part of his body to the ground to apologize and he left.

"Forgive me!" the Princess said in a low voice. "He belongs to the group from the Amur. They are usually dignified, even when in contact with foreign women. You can now sleep calmly. I will be close."

She left without turning her back on them; then suddenly she thrust hear head through the tent's opening again and addressed Lukeriya: "Among your Doukhobors you formed a court of justice for the misdeeds of all members of your movement; I have heard that you dispense justice fairly and wisely. You managed to make an agreement with the Grand Duke Konstantin Romanov that the Doukhobors would help the army in the war with the Turks but not take part in the fighting. You introduced equality between men and women in your communities. But I am positive you haven't succeeded in changing the aggressive sexual nature of men. I know with certainty that you have had cases similar to this one that happened to you personally in this tent. It is not the leaders' fault. It is the Lord to blame, for he made men in such a way that they often lose their reason when they are close to an attractive woman and passion overtakes their reason. I could punish this one, establish a court of justice, but I cannot change the nature of male studs who would give us everything, even get killed for us, if we would open the door of our treasury to them."

The Little Princess did not wait to see Lukeshka's reaction. She had recited what troubled her, and faster than she had thrust her head through the opening, she pulled it out and disappeared into the dark. Lukeriya for some time looked thoughtfully in the direction where the Tartar woman had disappeared; then she heard the words of Peter Verigin, who proposed that they should not sleep until morning. He reminded his companions what had happened to him, but Lukeriya cut him short saying that in the Little Princess's camp everything seemed to be under her control, and that especially after that incident, nothing more could happen to them that night.

§

Later, after he parted with his father and went to his room in the attic to sleep, Misha lay dreaming about the Tartars and their Little Princess long into the night. Especially he kept thinking about the Tartar woman's words that men and women could be equal in everything, but not in love games, and that the Lord is to blame for male aggression. Since he had first noticed that the hairs on some parts of his body were getting thicker, he ever more wished to lie close to a naked female. Long after he heard his father's description of the Tartar Princess, every time he remembered her words he would feel his blood get hotter and start coursing wildly through his body.

10

The Caucasian peoples accepted the Doukhobors as a war gift from the Russian Tsars. Stories of imagination and admiration travelled before these unusual Russians, stories telling of their ability to refuse even the Tsar himself the right to force them to take up arms and to send them as his slaves to war. When local chieftains asked the Doukhobors how they could help them organize themselves and start a normal life on Caucasian territory, the Doukhobors replied that the best help would be to leave them alone in their villages and let them work freely on their land. That soil was barren, pregnant with rocks and sand deposits, and the summers were hot and without rain. The Caucasian peoples were surprised when the Doukhobors started digging canals to irrigate their fields, and when they saw how much bigger and better the harvest was in the parts the water had reached, they came to help the newcomers dig ever wider and longer artificial waterways. Tsar Alexander the Third himself was surprised when he met the Doukhobors for the first time in the village of Pokrovka in the Kars region, right next to the new border with Turkey, and he asked them how Mother Russia and the Crown could help them.

"Leave as alone, Your Highness, and we will survive. Or if you also do not like us, or if there is no place for us in our country, help us settle somewhere in the New World," replied Lukeriya Goobanova Kalmikova, the leader of the Doukhobors at that time. She appeared proud and defiant, and her face revealed the charm of a resolute middle-aged Russian woman.

"This soil is rough. It is different from the rich soil of Milky Waters. Summers here are dry and winters harsh. You are peasants. How are you going to water the cattle and crops?" the Tsar asked the crowd.

"We are digging canals to water our fields. We are bringing water from the mountain rivers," Lukeriya replied proudly.

When the Tsar asked one of the villagers in the crowd what he would ask for his children, that one replied: "To build them schools and help us educate them so that they do not become blind even though they have eyes, Your Highness. To make it possible for my son to get a higher education."

It was Kostuna Vasiliyevitch Chernov, father of the fifteen-year-old Misha. The Tsar was genuinely surprised at these words because he had heard different stories about the Doukhobors. The Tsar stared at Kostuna's light-blue eyes, full of incredulity and the sufferings of expulsion, but shining with wisdom. "What is your name? I thought that you Doukhobors did not like schools. In fact, that you tried to educate your children by yourselves. That you do not believe in public schools." Tsar Alexander was speaking to him in a friendly manner.

Kostuna was not shy. He, in fact, was happy to have a chance to talk to the Tsar, whom he considered an educated ruler, prepared to hear the opinion of the people.

"I am Kostuna Chernov. My great grandfather was a doctor in the Tsar's service. Why wouldn't my Misha be a doctor, too? You heard that we, the Douhobors, do not like schools. We do not like schools that teach against our beliefs and our way of life. Sir, we like learning, but not teachings that trample on learning, that teach how to kill and exploit people."

Both the gathered Doukhobors and the Tsar's entourage were surprised at and confused by Kostuna Chernov's declaration. Bishop Grigory, Mitropolit of the Trans-Caucasian Diocese, a man with a long grey beard and big shiny black eyes, dropped his gaze to the ground in front of the Tsar's feet, as if expecting from there an explanation for his unpleasant feeling of guilt before these people. Kostuna did not even look at him. In fact, he had avoided the bishop's gaze all along, firm in his belief that Grigory had played an important part in inflicting expulsion and suffering on the Doukhobor people. But the Tsar's reaction was different.

"O-ho-ho…" laughed Alexander III at Kostuna's sharp words. "Poor is a kingdom without wisdom. My Tsarina is in charge of education. I'll pass on your words to her and I'll insist that she talk with you about the education of your children. Where is your son? I want to take a good look at him. To see if in his face I can discover a thirst for learning."

"He is here somewhere, Your Highness. He is like our other children. On his face and in his bearing you can recognize that he is a Russian who expects much from Mother Russia." Kostuna looked behind the Tsar's armed entourage, and saw Misha. He signalled him to come and the boy was soon in front of the Tsar. His face was blushing, but his curious eyes were unobtrusively absorbed impressions of the Tsar's figure and clothing. The Tsar gazed probingly at him. His avuncular examination of Misha's face and body did not give the impression of a formal meeting between a tsar and one of his subjects.

"There is nothing about this boy's face that I would not want my grandson Pyotr to have," the Tsar thought. "If the Tsarina manages to see him, and if she gets a similar impression, we will find a way for him to come to our court. He must be smart and honest, this young Chernov." The ever-stronger gaiety enlivening his lips revealed he liked the boy.

"What is your name, young gentleman? And what happened to the top of your left ear?" asked the Tsar.

"I am Misha," the boy replied. "When I was little, we had a very nasty gander. He liked to pinch my ears."

"O-ho-ho…" the Tsar laughed again. "Your father says you like school."

Misha nodded his head to confirm.

"What do you want to study? Just don't tell me you want to be a sailor. I'm scared of the sea. Especially when I do not trust the captain."

Misha smiled and looked freely at the Tsar's dark irises.

"What do you think about your Tsar? Tell me so that I can improve if I am not good."

Not even in his dream could Misha have imagined that the Tsar himself would ask him what he thought about the Tsar. He did not like rulers, although he thought that somebody had to rule people.

"Do not be afraid, young gentleman. Tell me what you think about me."

"I heard that the French respect you a lot. That you like their philosophers and historians."

"Is it good for the Russian Tsar that the French respect him?"

"Yes, Your Highness. Russians love you, the French respect you.

"And the Doukhobors?"

Misha found himself trapped. He knew that the Doukhobors did not like rulers and that rulers had caused them a lot of evil.

"Depends on which Doukhobors. Some expect justice from you, and others are afraid of you. They do not wish anything evil for you."

The Tsar gave a big smile, and his bushy grey eyebrows met.

"You are a smart young Russian. You should go to school to become a politician."

The Tsar continued smiling spontaneously, and then he bent down towards one of his entourage, a tiny man with round glasses.

"Remind me of the conversation with this boy and his father, Sergey Davidovitch. We should not forget to help Misha go to higher schools."

That night during dinner at the Army Headquarters of the Kars Region, the Tsar inquired about the burning of the Turkish part of town and about the closure of the shops of some Jews who belonged to the Turkish Sephardic people. The commander, Anatoly Shukov, was not easy to confuse. He explained that the culprits were robbers who had come from all regions of the Caucasus, even from the parts bordering Persia; they had followed the army and plundered. There had been cases when even some Russian soldiers had participated in those doings, but their privileges had been taken away from them and they had been sent to the central provinces.

"But why were they allowed to burn the old Turkish town and the mosques?" Tsar Alexander asked reflectively.

The Mitropolit felt he should interfere in the conversation at that moment.

"The Turkish janissaries raided Tbilisi during the war and burned the old church by the river. Later some Georgians followed our Army and burned Turkish mosques in our region here. With resolute action, the Army's Colonel Vladimir Simonovitch Zdanov stopped that, and we proclaimed to the people that we would transform those mosques into churches so that they would not be burned again."

The Tsar was not satisfied. He frowned and looked somewhere behind the Mitropolit's head, as if scenting the smell of the burnings that had taken place.

"They even burned the town. Along these borders you never know how long one town will be in the hands of one side, and how long in those of the other. Because of these burnings and retaliations, all our border regions are empty. As a young prince, I travelled in Persia, Turkey and Europe. In Turkey I admired neat gardens, yellow tulips, and oriental hyacinths. I saw streets lined with chestnuts blossoming pink and white, and glorious mimosas. I saw fabric that I had never seen before, carpets, house decorations and an imaginative architecture of façades. Even warriors need to respect the achievements of the people whose army they fight, not to mention civil and church rulers. Do not forget that the Turkish sultan Ahmed the Third, after the battle at the River Prut when he was Grand Vizier and was fighting us, granted the plea of our Tsar Peter the Great and for the price of 230,000 rubles set him free. He did this out of respect for the Tsar and his person. Tsars go to war out of various interests, but there is no a priori reason for them to behave like barbarians toward each other. No more is there such a law for peoples and churches. New times are coming, gentlemen! Relations among people are changing. The moral values of people are changing, both in peace and in war."

Mitropolit Grigory looked askance at the Tsar and realized that his face had looked much happier when he was talking with the Doukhobors at the outskirts of their village close to Kars. And he had expected that the ruler would demand of those people that they return to the Mother Church and respect the Church authorities and laws.

"How did the Doukhobors behave after the war?" the Tsar asked Colonel Shukov. "Did they plunder and burn the town?"

'They did not, Your Highness. The Doukhobors are peaceful people. Though they won't join in fighting where human blood is spilt, they have helped our Army with logistics. Now in the time of peace, they work as hard as a colony of ants, and do not meddle in the affairs of others. Only, I hear that their leaders are ever more often asking to be allowed to emigrate from our country."

"And from their country too, Anatoly Osepovitch! Luckless is a country from which its people run away. If they do not bother anybody, if they do not get involved in any foul work, we should extend our hand and make it possible for them to have a normal life. They should not live crammed into their villages. School doors should be open for them and jobs available, just as they are for others in our country. The same should be true for those Turks, Jews, and Tartars…Do not you forget the son of that Doukhobor, Chernov!"

The Tsar cast his gaze at the Mitropolit, waiting to see how he would react to these words. The Mitropolit also felt that the Tsar was waiting for his pronouncement.

"There is a big problem in our relations with them, Your Highness. They do not want any contact with the Church authorities. They run away from the cross as from the devil, and when our priests show them the Bible, they take Tolstoy's books out of their coats and brandish them at the priests!"

"Wait a minute, Grigory! What would your priests do if someone brandished the Koran or Torah at them? Wouldn't they defend themselves with the Bible? I have a cross hanging on my chest, but not all people in the world do. Some use a cross as a symbol of their relationship with God, some use something else. Never will all people have the same belief nor will they belong to the same religion." With that, Tsar Alexander the Third concluded the conversation.

At the end of the dinner, The Tsar and his entourage were served the Doukhobors' borscht, then roast kid meat, the specialty of the Georgian mountain people…and in the end the Armenian sweet pie made of sour apples. All that was accompanied by red wine in long glasses from the winery of the Georgian kulak Shevarnadze. There was a rumour in those parts that Armenian merchants had secretly been selling that wine across the Ottoman Empire even to Budapest, where in the court of the Hungarian kings it was a match for the wines from French Provençe.

When parting with Colonel Shukov and the Bishop, the Tsar remembered to ask:

"What happened to the library of Vizier Selim in this town? Are those books safe?"

"They are, Your Highness. The library did not suffer much damage," the Colonel promptly replied, eager to give himself credit.

"I don't know what's in that library, but books ensure that the achievements of civilization in any era of history are recorded and saved from oblivion. In wars, women and books have been the greatest victims. The continuity of our development is in books, and women take care of the continuity of the human race. I know that rulers have different attitudes towards these two pearls of great price. But in hatred, we are often similar. When they asked Caliph Omar, after he conquered Egypt, what should be done with the Library in Alexandria, he said that all the books in the library that conflicted with the teachings and laws of Islam's Kur'an should be burned. If they had asked the same question of the Pope of that time in Rome, his answer would have been similar, and the library would have been burned. Ruling people should be different from that. In conflicts among empires and among peoples the achievements of civilizations should be protected. It is your task here, Colonel, to try to guard and protect our reputation before the human race."

Mitropolit Grigory knew that Tsar Alexander the Third, the last Romanov to bear this name, was a radical progressive and that it was better to hold his tongue. Maybe the Tsar would have asked another embarrassing question. But in front of the building—now housing the headquarters of the Russian units, and having only a decade before housed the headquarters of the Turkish janissary units—a fire was lit, its huge flame quickly reaching above the roof of the headquarters. Soon men in uniform gathered around the fire and started dancing. As

130

the fire became brighter and hotter, the dancing became more imaginative and faster. A couple of hundred Cossacks from the units that were part of the Tsar's entourage encircled the fire, their bodies performing a dance stolen from the tree branches of the forests along the River Don as they catch the southern winds from the Black Sea. Some linked themselves in line dancing, some danced in pairs, then singly. The soldiers competed for the Tsar's admiration; but they also competed in satisfying their souls' desire for dancing and happiness. From the crowd of other people in uniform, from the edge where the light of the fire and the powers of darkness met, a slow song started to rise, soft and drawn, then ever faster and louder, pouring forth feelings belonging to the centuries-old spirit of the Russian people.

During the Tsar's visit to that town at the western entrance to the Trans-Caucasus, dogs had their say too. They had come first from the neighbourhood, but the smell of food and the barking of these as they fought for better spots brought many dogs from the entire district. Now fed, and excited by brawls with each other, several dozen of the strongest and most daring seized the opportunity when a change in rhythm of the line dancing created a wide opening among the Cossacks. Running in an orderly file according to some rule of priority known only to them, the dogs rushed into the space between the fire and the dancers. It was as if they wanted to show the Tsar some of their skills. It is hard to uncover a dog's secret. Why they did that, no one knows, but it is certain that they, confused in that space between the people and the fire, started aimlessly running here and there; then they all started to follow one long-legged, brindle-furred dog. They ran in a circle almost equidistant from the fire and the dancers. The Cossacks did not stop their dancing, and the dogs understood that there was no danger to them in all this circular rushing. They continued to play their game. The Tsar whispered to those close to him that he had never seen anything like it; that nature had sent its runners to that play of human bodies. When the Cossacks started dancing in pairs, the long-legged brindled dog discovered the best place to dart between the dancers out into the dark night. The other dogs in a neat line did the same. Lagging behind was only one black-and-white fat shepherd dog, which had hurt his leg in the mad game and was hobbling. The choir of soldiers standing in the edge of firelight accompanied this dancing with their song:

Through the cold steppe the barefoot Tanyushka
Followed the man's footprints in the snow,
Oh, maiden Tanyushka, oh...

Cossacks did not spend their lives in the fields doing hard peasant work. They looked for relief in army service, the police and administration. Those who were in charge of the Tsar's security were full of energy and the ability to find ways to kill boredom in peacetime army service. From a distance, these Cossack soldiers all looked the same, whether on horseback or on foot, in uniforms or without them, always carrying a saber hanging from their wide belts. When you got closer to them, you saw that the Tsar's Cossack Guards were in fact men of various ages and body types. The first to come up with this idea was Tsar Nikolay I, who decided the Guard should always include soldiers of different ages and physiques in order to break their uniformity in coming up with stupid behaviour, which had often been dangerous even to those they were meant to protect. It was natural for the young ones to desire adventures of the body, while the older, feeling the transience of time, desired the reward of power and fame for their privileged position in the army. Strength and body instincts pushed the younger to adventure, while the older cooled them down with wisdom and calculation. Older soldiers were necessary because of the military experience that gave them skills to survive and see victory. And the younger? Without them fighting would not have been fighting. Lacking in wisdom, but strong and intent on triumph, they got killed or severely wounded, which made others fall upon the enemy to get revenge and to think less about their own lives and more about how to take life of somebody on the other side.

Tsar Nikolay I had demanded that his commanders not forget these rules, originating at least as early as the time of Egyptian pharaohs and Nubian princes. The famous Babylonian king Nebuchadnezzar, before battle with the Egyptians, ordered his commanders to put still-beardless boys and lunatics in the front lines, but to explain to them well what the helmets on the heads of the enemy looked like! And he won that battle in the south of his country. Then his wife, Meda, advised him to protect the northern borders of Babylon with a great wall. When he had secured the country from both sides, he ordered that, as a gesture of gratefulness to Meda for her idea of the great wall, his people build one of the wonders of civilization—the Babylonian Hanging Gardens.

To the younger troops you should offer war booty and the enemy's women and they will rush forward and die, which will in turn raise morale in the most important army ranks, which should lead to victory. "Victory is what matters in the battle," Tsar Nikolay I advised the soldiers and their officers in the Army Academy in St. Petersburg. "For if you do not achieve victory, you will be defeated. The same destiny awaits the defeated in all wars. It is always better to lose manpower in the battle than to lose the battle. The defeated inevitably face destruction, and the winners have a chance to build hanging gardens for their wives and to bring them satisfaction."

11

Tsarina Dagmar of Denmark, or, as Russians commonly called her, Maria Fyodorovna, visited the Trans-Caucasian regions of Russia about ten months after the visit of Tsar Alexander III. She was driven in one of the Tsar's well-wrought carriages, drawn by two pairs of charcoal black horses. Hers was followed by four almost identical carriages, in which travelled her servants, Minister of the New Provinces Yablonsky, and Minister for Education and Culture Semishev. Two elite units of the Guard provided security and travelled in front of and behind the carriages. In Kars, the Tsarina fulfilled the promise given to the Doukhobors. The former Turkish public school changed its symbols and brought in Russian teachers. Misha Chernov, along with about a hundred other students from the ranks of Kars' youth, found himself in that school. Overall, however, the response of the Doukhobors was sceptical and restrained. >From Spasovka, a Doukhobor village at the very outskirts of Kars, Paroniya Popov came to the school, along with two boys from the clan of the Popovs who enrolled in classes but left after two months. Only the Chernovs and the Popovs did not give in to the urging of the conservative Doukhobors to keep their children out of state schools.

Most of the students came from the families of army officers and public servants, but there was a noticeable presence of the children of Tartars, Turks, Jews and Armenians. Along with Misha, the school enrolled Boulisou, the daughter of Yakov Hasson, member of a prominent Jewish merchant family. Misha had known her since the Doukhobors had arrived here and started building their villages around Kars.

In the Trans-Caucasus, the Doukhobors very quickly developed agriculture, as well as the production of fabric, clothes and metal work.

Their merchant business was taken over by the Sephardic Jewish Hassons, who had stayed in their homes after the Turks had retreated from the Kars region. That family were not afraid of the Russian authorities. Knowing that Tsar Alexander was a righteous and enlightened leader, they did not expect that the Russian Orthodox Church could any longer demand that they accept Christianity, nor did they expect any discrimination, torture or expulsion. Just before the Tsar's visit to Kars, the Hassons had been in touch with part of their family who had remained in Turkey. The relatives had urged them to use the opportunity—the still valid postwar Russian-Turkish agreements—and move back to Turkey, where Jews had been living in peace for several centuries since the Turks had accepted them after their expulsion from Spain by the Spanish monarchy and the Pope.

"Why? We've had enough expulsions. I feel the Russians won't make any problems for us, and maybe we will remain welcome here," the oldest among them, Isidor Hasson argued. "This Tsar is prudent. All Europe is changing towards national and religious tolerance. New people from all parts of the Russian Empire are coming here and they will need us. We are lucky our next-door neighbours are the Russian Doukhobors, hardworking and honest people. No misfortune can destroy their optimism. They have been persecuted for two centuries by the rulers of their own country. They raise houses and cultivate land, and are then expelled to another place. And the Doukhobors build their houses again and cultivate the new land. And these here, these neighbours of ours, have already organized themselves, built their village, cultivated the wild land and are already producing enough not only for their own needs but also for exchange with others. They look like they are the descendants of that insubordinate and unrivaled demigod Prometheus, who, if the Greeks are to be believed, was punished by Zeus because of his capabilities and because he created man. So Zeus bound him onto the highest Caucasian rock and ordered an eagle to pick at his liver. What the eagle picked out during the day, Prometheus would, with his will and skill, make up during the night. I am not going anywhere. I have grown old, Yakov. I do not have time anymore to start all over again. You can, if you want, follow Uncle

Samuel to Anatolia, or you can go to America. But I am staying. Tsars and systems are replacing each other, I'll stay."

His son Yakov was not sure if his father's thoughts were the best choice for his family. He mentioned that for twenty-five centuries other nations and religions had mercilessly persecuted and killed Jews. "We have been destroyed in the waves of history. From the Egyptian pharaohs until today. And mostly by Christian rulers and the Christian Church. We are not Europeans by roots. We have been in somebody's cruel program: they realized that we are hardworking, that we know how to save and build, and by force they scattered us across the world. To work, to save, to create something, and then they take that away from us. They even mercilessly kill us, so they can take away from us what is ours and make us live in fear of being killed. They make it possible for us to create wealth, and then they take it away from us and kill us. Our golden age was in Spanish Andalusia during the eight-hundred-year rule of the Arabs. When the Pope and the Spanish King expelled the Arabs, they also expelled us. They demanded that we renounce what we are and convert to Christianity. Jesus was one of us, but our tradition and religion are older than Jesus. We refused, and they started to persecute us again and to destroy us in the whole of Europe. From November 27, 1095, when Pope Urban II gave his speech at Clermont-Ferrand in France, they have been committing genocides against us for more than one thousand years. I have a strange feeling that a new wave of history is not far ahead, and that somebody will again want to kill and persecute us."

"I am not afraid of the Russian Tsar and the Russian Church. Ever stronger movements of Russia's workers and peasants propagate equality for all people. These Doukhobors are greater pacifists than we are. If all others were after us, the Doukhobors would hide and defend us. I am not going anywhere. Also, there have been attacks on Turkey from all sides. They have been taking away her regions and cramming her all into Anatolia!" Old Isidor was firm.

The Hassons decided to stay. One of the youngest among the family members, the fifteen-year-old Boulisou, with other members of the family present, listened to that dispute between father and son. When she was later sent to the Civil School, along with Misha Chernov, she remembered her grandfather's words that the Doukhobors are great pacifists and that they do not judge people or nations on the basis of ethnicity or religion. Even though they are Christians, they do not carry crosses and refuse to follow those priests who wear terrible long black robes. Their obstinately individual Christianity removed a barrier between her and that handsome black-haired, blue-eyed boy, and made her cherish secret romantic feelings toward him. In fact, since she had seen him for the first time riding a white-spotted horse a few years after the Doukhobors had arrived and begun building their village close to her home, Boulisou prayed that parents not forbid her to see Misha occasionally and exchange some words with him. They had not had much opportunity to talk to each other, but when their eyes had occasion to meet, a strange sweet feeling flared up in each of them. One night, while her mother was telling her and her sister Rifka about the family of old Mordecai Wosk and in particular about his grandson Daniel, Boulisou guessed what her mother's purpose was and declared to her in an unusual voice:

"Mother, I want to continue school. You don't have sons to be merchants. Rifka and I have to go to school. If we can't do that here, there are many of them in Russia."

Mother was not happy about the way Boulisou interrupted her, but did not express her disapproval. She hugged them both and sent them to bed.

Misha and Boulisou were in the same class in Kars Civic School. Since the Hassons were busy doing trading, they agreed with the Chernovs that Boulisou travel to school—almost six kilometers away—with the Chernovs in their wagon. Misha's uncle Genadiy, who was very skilled in woodworking, had a family job to transport products from their village to the Hassans' shops in town, and from there to bring home the goods the Doukhobors needed. Thus Misha and the ever more beautiful and feminine Boulisou started to travel to school together. From the start, Misha felt his feelings stir whenever he found himself close to the girl, but he would quickly quench them, trying to convince himself that the two of them were too different, that there were too many barriers between them, from his youth to Doukhobor and Jewish traditions and customs. Boulisou had similar feelings, but she grew ever more hopeful that something would happen to make the barriers between them fall. She did not care whether or not barriers would remain between her family and his. She was not afraid when her mother mentioned Daniel Wosk because she knew her parents well. She believed that her father had asked her mother to mention Daniel to her, but she was confident that he would never impose on her his choice of her future husband.

While they were still little girls, her father, Yakov would often tell Boulisou and her sister Rifka that Jews should fasten each to other and how that was a very important way for them to feel safer and to survive. However, right after these words, he would advise his daughters against staying locked in their families and the Jewish diaspora, but instead that they should accept as theirs all the people whom they shared their lives with. And the mother? She was more conservative than the father, but she had a good heart, and her heart would not allow her to push her daughters into the arms of somebody whom they did not want. However, it would be commonly expected for a Jew to marry among Jews, among those of Spanish Sephardic heritage, who were of the same sort and had a soul full of the melancholy and passionate cultural identity they had brought from Spanish Andalusia. Before bedtime, in front of a big clay stove, with the flames finding cracks and escaping into the darkness of the room, the mother would tell them that marrying strangers is like pouring water into good olive oil. Boulisou would more often than not protest, saying that the worst thing is not to catch the train of changes that the new time brings. Her mother would reply without any trace of anger that Boulisou was speaking from her inexperience and youth, and that they should never forget they were Jewish, and that they needed to know the Hebrew language and at least the basics of the Spanish language.

Every day, in his two-wheeled cart pulled by a fat horse named Putaly, Old Hasson would travel to the town to take a look at his shops.

The war had caused him great damage, but the family managed to survive. For two to three years afterward, they had lived miserably, until the new state returned the shops to him and allowed him to continue his merchant business. Then everything came to life. The old man livened up too, feeling his desire to enlarge his business return. One afternoon he came from the town more thoughtful than ill-disposed. While eating lunch, he spoke to his wife Mary, twenty-five years younger, in a peculiar, speculative way. He asked her if she had had contacts with the Doukhobor women. She replied that they stuck more to their own, and were in any case rather timid and did not like to talk about other people.

Then the old man asked her:

"Have you noticed one Turkish woman, who is often there by the stream and in those woods down there? I have seen her five, six times, and she was always alone."

"Oh, everybody knows her," Mary was eager to answer. "I do not know if you remember the last days of the war. When the Cossacks were clearing this area of stragglers from the defeated Turkish army, they caught a group of Turkish young men who did not even wear uniforms or have weapons—and the Cossacks killed them by the stream. They say her son was among the dead. She did not know the young men had been killed; she believed they had been captured and taken away. They say she went to the town and asked one Russian soldier after another what could have happened to her son, and then one old Turkish man told her that her son had been killed by the stream.

"They say that during the day she would walk by the water—downstream, through the woods, and during the night she would be in town screaming. She could not find his body. Then in the fields down there she saw some herbs with red leaves growing in many circles, and she stared at them, smelled them and started to whisper as if afraid she would wake somebody up. There is a rumour that she said to that old Turkish man that her son had turned into those herbs and that he had told her to collect those red leaves and make tea, and in that way they would be together forever. Then last spring he whispered to her to sell those herbs as medicine and thus make a living for herself. She obeyed, and the word started to spread that that tea can cure women's diseases, and that even women who have always been childless will bear children. A few such cases have already been reported, and people now say that her son is coming back to life through the newborn of these women who could not bear children before."

"Anything is possible, Mary. If nothing else, that Turkish woman has found a way to affirm her faith that her son, in that way, is still alive, and has also found a way to make a living, to survive," Old Hasson pensively made his own affirmation.

12

On one night in May, a spring wind pregnant with freshness and discreet fragrances from recently awakened trees and grass disturbed Misha's sleep and he saw the moon casting its pale light between the branches of a big apple tree and through the window into his room. He thought about Boulisou and he felt that those pale rays of moonlight were whispering to him that he had the right to feel Boulisou's closeness, and to think and dream about her. Even to touch her while sitting next to her in the wagon behind Genadiy's back. Then his imagination freed itself from the earlier restraints and he pictured her lying next to him in his very bed and himself gently stroking her curly chestnut-coloured hair. She was more beautiful than any girl he knew. Her round head was adorned with a pure white face and dark eyebrows, arched like the new moon he would stare at through the window late at night. And her eyes were dark, with tiny round irises and long lashes…Her mouth was round and small, framed with lips the colour of the early wild rose blossoms when they cover the hills around his village right after the last snowfalls melt. He wanted his fingers to move from her hair down to her ever more prominent breasts, then to move up to her lips, and then to try to kiss her in the same way he had seen Ivoosha touching and kissing Lana behind a big walnut tree on her way back home from the barn with the fresh cow-milk. He did not mention it to anybody, afraid that Ivoosha would find a more secluded place for his and Lana's pleasures. It crossed his mind that nobody in the village would be happy about the love between him and the Jewess. He realized that even her family would not want him to dream about her, much less touch her. Then protest and anger awoke in him, as well as determination to disregard all that; he was firm that he had the right to feel that way about Boulisou. He felt his right to love her came from something older and more powerful than the restrictions promulgated by their ethnicities, religions and customs, and that their belonging to the human race was older. Across his mind the idea glittered that he would stand before the Doukhobor Council and criticize them all. He would tell them that it was nice they had stood against the barriers created for them by the rulers of Russia and the Church, but that they had fallen short of destroying their own barriers, and had failed in making all people equal. He decided he would do everything in his power to unite people and to try to become powerful enough to accomplish that.

Before his passionate feelings for Boulisou were stirred, he had felt the wind slipping through the ripe blades of barley, and had felt the moonlight's softness as it, on its way to reach the leaves of grass covered in dew, passed by the blue pregnant plums on the branches of the trees attacked by moss. He had also felt the longing gaze of the young boys recently having come of age as it starts to crawl over those parts of the female body that make women different from men. And now, when his feelings had come out of some previously unknown treasury in his chest and enveloped every part of the body of that proud beauty Boulisou, he suddenly realized he had the right to speak in the same manner as, hidden in the thick top of a cherry tree, he saw Lukeriya Kalmikova replying to the questions about love posed to her by a group of young Doukhobor boys and girls.

"You cannot look for gain in it. Love is not profitable in the way that deep ploughing can be, or in the way a hardworking man can earn money from his work. You cannot ask love to bring you material benefits. Love is a blessing. To our spirit it brings fragrant freshness and a pleasant tremble in the feeling that you gladly belong to somebody. And that belonging should give both parties another or more new lives that stay bound with us as long as we last. Love is a natural instrument of uniting people for the sake of reproduction, and it lasts at least as long as lasts the reproductive activity of those in love," Lukeriya said wisely.

At that time, Misha had not understood everything she had been saying, but he had remembered it well, believing that the time would

142

soon come when he would want to talk about it with the attractive Lukeriya. Now when in his thoughts he was embracing Boulisou, to all that he would add that love is a feeling above all feelings and that no less than Pushkin's ability in using words would be needed to describe it.

Before he fell asleep again, and it was not before the first roosters in the village started to crow, he decided to tell Boulisou that he was in love with her and to ask her about her feelings for him. He was not afraid of her answer, but he was afraid of not knowing how much she accepted the barriers between people.

Misha respected his father, Kostuna, but was not afraid of him. He had often heard his father telling the villagers that Jesus had not divided people according to their tribal affiliation and that all people are brothers and sisters. It meant, he thought, that his father would not object to his love for Boulisou. And his mother? She had always told the women in the neighbourhood that her Misha would be honest and smart and that he would be better in horseback riding than the Kalitvan Cossacks.

It took him a long time to reveal his feelings. One fresh morning, after the night rain that a wind coming from the mountains had blown away, Genadiy was driving the wagon, telling them how the night before some bandits had broken into the houses of the Turks on the other side of town, right on the border, and had killed one man and kidnapped three children. Genadiy feared retaliation from the Turkish border cavalry when the news reached them. Boulisou was sitting in front of Misha and listening to Genadiy's story. Misha admired the speed at which she had acquired the Russian language…He enjoyed looking at her long hair, the colour of ripe chestnuts, blown by the wind that had managed to squeeze past Genadiy's broad shoulders. He imagined how wonderful it would be to stroke her hair while Genadiy was talking. And she, as if aware of Misha's musing, reached out her hand behind her back towards Misha. Misha was at first surprised, then he quickly took her hand, afraid that the girl would change her mind. He felt a tremble from her chest reaching her hand and, quick as lightning, it spread over his body to overtake him. Later they avoided each other's eyes, embarrassed; then their love started transforming into a strong, life-long relationship, which was not blind and unscrupulous, but gave birth to feelings reaching much further than touching of hands and lightsome dreams.

One day when they were returning from school, Genadiy, tired by the daily work in town, was slumbering in his seat woven of brushwood and rye straw. The horse knew the way. Boulisou, having realized that a sleepy Genadiy would be no danger for them, slipped from her seat and leaned against Misha. He also slipped from his seat, and they embraced, pressing against each other on the wagon's floor, but quietly and carefully so that Genadiy would not notice.

"I love you, Misha, but I am scared…I think my mother would kill me if she knew," Boulisou whispered in his ear. Misha was holding and pressing her, wanting their bodies to become so closely joined that even their mothers would not be able to separate them.

Mesmerized by the play of their bodies, they became less careful and pushed against a hamper in which there were two chickens which started flapping their wings and cackling loudly. Genadiy gave a start and turned back, the reins loosened, and the bay horse Charouga, with a white patch on its forehead, got frightened by the chickens' cackling and ran as fast as his muscles allowed him. In that rush, both horse and wagon strayed off the dusty country road, and who knows how far they would have careered if it were not for a shallow muddy pond covered in reeds that stopped them. For a few moments Genadiy was sitting rolled up in his seat, and Boulisou and Misha returned to their places. The chickens calmed down, and Charouga waited for the water in the pond to clear and started drinking as if nothing had happened.

"What on earth made you push the hamper?" Genadiy asked them, turning his head back, his eyes bulging as if he was getting ready to punish them for what they had done. However, his expression quickly returned to normal again, and he smiled, scratching behind his ear: "I heard you whispering something, and that didn't bother me. Then the chickens started…Never mind, we are still lucky. If we had roosters in the hamper, our Charouga would have gotten more scared, so he would have carried us right into the lake. Now step down and let's help Charouga pull us out of this mud."

"We forgot to do the math homework, and our teacher Demidovitch is cruel. We were making plans how to defend ourselves," Misha lied.

Soon, at that very place, it happened that Boulisou and Misha started to feel even more strongly for each other than before. After the warm and rich summer, abundant and windy autumn, the cold winter with a lot of snow came from the Caucasus Mountains. The frost made nature still, covering it with its white coat and stopping its play with time. Like most hardworking harvesters of the forests, fields and waters, the Doukhobors spent their time at home, sharing news and telling yarns. During the holidays around Christmas, schools closed their doors. The villagers made well-trodden paths through the snow between their houses, and wrapped in warm shawls and fur hats visited each other, enjoyed eating winter delicacies, sang, and talked about what was happening in their villages, with their rulers, and in world affairs. That winter the talk was mostly about the meetings of their spiritual leader Peter Verigin with Leo Tolstoy. They believed both of them, but secretly reproached Verigin for claiming to be the spirit of Jesus Christ, and to a certain degree they felt that for Verigin's ambition it was not enough that he was just the leader of the Doukhobors. They found it strange that such a smart and handsome man could not learn from previous attempts by some of his predecessors to proclaim themselves descendants of Jesus and in that manner to put themselves above all other Doukhobors.

Only a group of Doukhobor children, accompanied by Yakov Hasson's daughters, defied the cold and played their games. The frozen lake attracted them most. In the middle of the lake otherwise covered in a thick layer of snow, ice could not form, as though heat rose from that deepest part of the waters. There the lake remained the same as it was in the middle of summer, and there would gather wild ducks and geese; they would catch fish and in the play of their colourful bodies would wash their wings. Among them, dignified in their defiance of the ice trying to overcome that oasis of warm water, and defying the onlookers from the ranks of ducks, geese, and children, two pairs of black swans would spend their days.

The previous summer Yakov had travelled all across the far Austro-Hungarian Empire to trade, and from there he had brought beautiful skates for his daughters. As soon as ice covered the surface of the shallower lakes in the proximity of the village, they would secretly, while the others in the village slept, sneak out of the house and practice ice skating. When she learned enough not to be ashamed before others, Boulisou told Misha that she would like them to go skating on the big lake. At first, he was surprised; then he said he would talk to Genadiy and ask him to make him a pair of skates from hard wood. The very next day Misha was ready for ice. He and Boulisou sneaked out of the their houses and went to the lake. Until that time, Mish had skated on his moccasins made of calf's skin, but skating on ashwood blades was something different.

Boulisou was helping Misha to stay upright on his skates. She herself would stumble if she tried to stop abruptly, or to turn before stopping, but she was much more skillful than Misha. He was rigid and insecure. But youth quickly found ways to make the body used to moving on ice. Soon Misha started skating by himself, refusing the girl's helping hand. And she, freed from her instructor's role, was skating more freely and beautifully. Misha was secretly admiring her skill, but even more the beauty of her body making moves on ice. Boulisou was much faster than Misha and she was boldly moving away from him, towards the unfrozen part of the lake. She wanted to fascinate him, to make him admire her openly. And she succeeded. A few times Misha fell down awkwardly while turning his head towards Boulisou, and she laughed. The ducks, geese and swans in the open water started moving faster and flapping their wings more frequently as if wanting to spray each other and compete with the girl.

Misha felt too hot in his thick grey sweater, which his mother had knitted for him the previous summer, and he went towards the bushes at the edge of the ice. He took off his sweater, and when he turned,

Boulisou was not there. A warm thought crossed his mind that she was lying down somewhere on the ice and that she had covered herself with snow so that he would not be able to find her easily. However, the girl was nowhere to be seen. He looked at the lakeshore, ran his gaze quickly back and forth over the bushes covered in snow, but she was not there. He heard the ducks and geese playing their game on the water and cackling, and he directed his gaze toward them trying to find any trace of Boulisou. But she was not there! Then he became very scared. It crossed his mind that the girl had skated towards the water and could not stop and had drowned. He did not know if she could swim, but he knew that wet heavy clothes could easily pull the body down into the deep water. And he rushed much faster than he would otherwise have done on his unfamiliar skates. He started calling, fearfully and quietly in the sudden silence he heard around him: "Boulisou...Bouly...Bouly..." Then panic made him scream, and he saw the edge of the ice in front of him, the unfrozen water and the ducks and geese running on it, and he threw himself onto the ice, digging in with knees and elbows and the toes of his skates, trying to stop moving forward. It is hard to imagine what was going through his head at that moment. It was more a chaos of fear, anger, love, expectation, hope, hopelessness, shame...than any structured thinking. And he stopped at the very edge of the ice, with his head over the water and his arms in it. In a flash he realized that Boulisou was not there and that now he was the one who needed help. He didn't dare move, sensing that the ice there was not thick enough and he felt he was swaying slowly up and down. Behind him he heard the terrible sound of ice cracking.

He suddenly heard the girl laughing and calling him from behind: "Misha! Misha!" He did not dare turn around. He tried gingerly to hold onto the edge of the ice and push back, but it was breaking in his hands. He felt helpless. He quickly followed his gaze down into the deep, trying to discover how far the bottom was, but it was dark down there. The girl stopped laughing; he heard her skating towards him. Boulisou had realized that Misha was just at the thin edge of the ice and that any moment he could be lost to the depths. She was afraid and prayed for her skates to go faster. When Misha could sense that Boulisou was there close to him, she shouted: "Do not move, Misha! Do not move! I'll pull your legs."

He felt her come down on the ice and stretch out on it and crawl towards him. The ice started to give away under their bodies and any moment it could break and give them to the water. In a split second Misha wondered what he would do if they fell in, and if he would be able to help the girl, and then he became afraid, for he remembered he did not know how to swim. But he would splash in the water with his arms and legs, like those ducks and geese, cry for help, grab Boulisou and push her onto the ice. He felt her hands getting hold of his pants and slowly starting to drag him backwards. At first, she pulled little by little, inch by inch, but she was pulling him. His arms were already back on the ice, but he did not dare to move at all. She was pulling him with her elbows propped against the ice, like the caterpillar of the cabbage butterfly when it becomes afraid of the abyss at the edge of the cabbage leaf, and slowly starts moving backwards. And Boulisou started pulling him to safety. The ducks and geese were not running on the water anymore, nor did they cackle. They were also watching the quiet struggle of the two young people, probably a struggle for life. The black swans made a passage through the crowd of small ducks. And when Boulisou and Misha were far enough from the edge of the ice and the water, and when they both started moving quickly on their knees farther away from the dangerous edge, the ducks and geese again started their playing and cackling, as if they were celebrating the happy ending of the two young people's drama.

Safely away from the place where Misha had been hovering above the water, the two sat on the ice, looking at each other and trying to say something, but they could not find words. Suddenly a strong feeling of joy overpowered them, their blood started to race and they fell into each other's arms while sitting on the ice. Tears ran down Boulisou's beautiful rosy face, and she pressed it against Misha's and whispered: "Forgive me. I did not want to…I wanted to tease you…" Misha did not feel even the smallest trace of anger or protest. On the contrary, he pressed his face harder against the girl's and he wanted to stay like that for an eternity. But the ice was cold, and the sleeves of Misha's thick shirt were already frozen. There on the water, surrounded by ice, snow and a heavy cold spell, the ducks and geese slackened their play and followed the swans. The swans would occasionally dip their beautiful heads and long necks into the water, giving a signal to the smaller birds that down there might be some food. And the ducks would dive into the water there, and the geese would also shove their heads into it as deep as they could.

Boulisou's mother was waiting for her at the house door, stared at her as if she had seen what had happened, but said only that her father had made a big mistake when he had bought the skates. In the house, Rifka's inquiring gaze asked Boulisou for an explanation of where she had been for the last few hours.

At his home, Misha could not lie very much. His frozen clothes, hands and face revealed that he had fallen into water somewhere.

"The water in the middle of the frozen lake attracted me, the ice started to break and I barely kept my head out of it," he briefly explained and moved toward the stove. His mother started screaming and embracing him, and then, when she realized that he was alive and needed help, she helped him change the frozen clothes, and later she was quietly talking with Kostuna and Genadiy.

13

"Paroniya, look down there at that miracle! Look at the river as it works its way through the glorious beauty around it." Misha thus interrupted the conversation of the passengers in the half-empty compartment of the train that was lazily crawling along a valley abounding in mesmerizing colours and sunlight. Two girls and two young men jumped to the window and looked at the river. The calm bluish-green water, as if making itself still to avoid disturbing that beauty with rushing and rumbling, carefully circled around a small island rich in glorious silver spruce trees bending towards the south, and in crests of rock covered with grey moss.

"The rocks look as if they had grown with the forest and chosen to gather close to the most delicate trees so they could grow taller. But while the trees bent under the prevailing wind the rocks continue to stand firm and tall." This first comment came out of the mouth of the dark-skinned and bony Grigory.

"To me that small island surrounded by the water looks like a nest protected by the wings of the mother bird," Svetlana added. "Look, doesn't the water of the river embrace and protect the island from anything that could hurt it!"

"It does not have to be the mother who protects. Among birds the father has the same role," chubby Seryoza quickly defended the male gender. His face, covered in reddish curly fur, looked more like the face of Pyotr, the youngest brother of Tsar Alexander the Second, than the faces of Seryoza's numerous family of the Nikolayovitch Luganovs.

"I am not talking about the river and the island," Misha interrupted them. "Don't you have eyes? Don't you see the women lying by the river and suntanning? I am not sure what's more attractive: they or the river."

Everybody laughed, and Paroniya, a plump girl with green eyes and fair hair, addressed Misha: "They are too far away to judge their beauty. It seems that to you all women are beautiful."

"Especially if they suntan by the river without clothes. You are too quick to judge how beautiful they are because your enthusiasm moves your tongue too fast," Grigory told him. "They haven't come to the river bank to suntan. Do you see those rakes and hay forks by their clothes? They have been working, Misha, most of this hot day, collecting dry hay, making haystacks, and bathing in their sweat. After that hard work they went to the river, had a bath and now they are drying themselves. Their clothes are drying because they had to wash them too in order to wash away the sweat and the smell of chaff. The water must be as cold as a snake when you touch it with your hand. I would rather see them when they were running into the water splashing each other to lessen the cold which was trying to get out of the boring river and creep into their hot bodies."

Everybody laughed at Grigory's musing.

"This train crawls so slowly that you could freely jump out, go to the riverbank, look at them carefully and try to figure out how many degrees their body temperature has gone down because of their wading in the icy water. You could return to this compartment before the train reaches those houses." Paroniya pointed at the village they could make out through the dark cloud of smoke coming from the huge sooty and noisy locomotive.

Those four moved away from the window. Only Misha was still looking towards the river and the women.

He took out a tiny flute, licked his lips with his tongue and started to play quietly. He was playing an old song about the beauty of nature in the eyes of man. He was playing and looking through the compartment window, and in his thoughts he was far away, in some God-forsaken place in the Caucasus. There, where for millennia the different streams of world civilization had been coming together and for an eternity living in fear that whoever was at the time more powerful and aggressive would start to kill and destroy. There, where, by the will of the powerful ones, the peaceful Doukhobors had been expelled, among them the peaceful members of the Chernov clan; there, where his Boulisou and their son Petro were, happy when they had an occasion to be happy, fearing that somebody would go berserk and fall upon them to take their lives and they would have no power to defend themselves.

It occurred to Misha that it would be really great if he could do what Paroniya had said, and, at least for a moment, leave the train, which, by that time, had for four days been rattling with deadly monotony along crudely fitted rails across the Siberian Steppes. He would not stop moving until he had reached all the way to that faraway place on the other side of the Urals where lived all those he loved. He hadn't seen them for more than five years, since the time when the agents of the Bureau for Protection from Internal Enemies had taken him from his father's house near Kars, in the faraway Caucasus, and brought him to the regional police station for questioning. They had interrogated him in a speeded-up procedure and condemned him to prison in Siberia. While they had been preparing him for the interrogation in the police station, a dark-complexioned officer had prodded Misha's ribs with his knuckles and in passing ground his teeth, making it clear to Misha what would happen if he were to be Misha's judge. They told him they had proof that Misha had been a member of the so called Kazan Bolshevik Movement for Liberation from Tyranny; that he had been an enemy of the Tsar's regime; and that he needed to sober up there, where cold northern winds blow all year round.

"To the Steppe, you smartass," a scrawny tall agent added his comment to the verdict, and showed Misha his long bony middle finger, whispering into his ear: "Long live the Tsar and Russia!"

After he completing his medical studies in Kazan, Misha had come home with his Boulisou because his great love was carrying their child; also, in the capital the antagonism between the Tsarist authorities and the united front of workers and the intelligentsia was growing ever stronger. Tsar Alexander III did not like war, but European political conditions forced him into conflict. He had to be cruel to neighbouring countries, and he often felt pain, knowing he made people suffer. He had to enter into the war with the Ottoman Empire because the interests of the European monarchies demanded confrontation with the far-flung and growing old Eternal State of the Ottomans, in order to corral it into the Anatolian Peninsula. As well, in the 1870s Russia's Romanov dynasty was showing less and less intellectual capability to confront the influences of the European revolutions, especially those of the French proletariat and their leading figures. Russia's intelligentsia and the workers and peasants, weakened by oppression, provided fertile ground for the ideas of these revolutionaries. The Romanovs realized they needed to modernize the empire, enable monarchial democracy, and face the European economic challenges.

Misha often dwelt on that memory, but never before had it occurred to him that the scrawny agent had maybe showed his middle finger to the Tsar and Russia, not to Misha himself. Considering that he was an agent, that hypothesis could be true because with such people one never knows whose God they worship. And for the first time it seemed to him that the scrawny agent had winked at him while he had been showing his finger, as if he wanted to say "We will soon be rid of such tsars and such Russia." Misha was trying to continue his train of thought by accompanying it with the sounds of his flute, gentle and drawn, escaping through the openings in the wooden instrument and then through the window, away from the shouting of the clumsy Siberian train, whose huge wheels screeched every time they followed a bend in the long journey through the Ural Mountains. Misha's own train of thoughts and the sounds of his flute, running down the slope towards the river they had left behind, were suddenly interrupted by the still immature bass of a bulky man with a beard.

Grigory warned that the passengers better prepare themselves as soon as possible for the afternoon entertainment of the gentlefolk from first class in the restaurant car. Otherwise, it could happen that their smiling escort for the journey from the penitentiary in Tomsk to Ufa, on the other side of the Urals, could be upset. Lieutenant Kozlov, instead of a smile on his pale face, might knit his eyebrows and raise his neatly trimmed moustaches and take them to one of the nearby centres for labour and correction of the too-smart brains.

The men put on their white shirts, and the women showed their naked shoulders, lifting their hair as high as their long black hairpins would hold.

"Gresha, I am sure you will charm that dishevelled lieutenant, who keeps telling everyone who wants to listen how it is a pity he obeyed his father and went into the army. If he'd had his way, he would have become a sculptor or a violin maker." Ever the romantic, Misha was encouraging his friend. Misha was obviously eager for anything to happen, even if it were the train derailing and rolling down the slope towards the river covered in lush grass and adorned with bushes in yellow blossom.

Gresha looked at him askance and continued to rummage through his suitcase. Apparently, he could not find what he was looking for.

"Take my belt if it fits you," Paroniya suggested, having realized what Grigory was looking for. "It is a bit wider, but it will work. I believe you lost many other things during that hassle when we were leaving the stage in the correction centre in Bratsk."

Misha observed the girl, her neck stretched and her head bent. The mischievous smile she flashed him confirmed his conviction that this solid, stable young woman was still ostentatiously making passes at him, just as she had been doing, with some inexplicable interruption, for years. He did not intend to give her any reason to hope for radical change in his attitude towards her. She had been trying to charm him since their school age. For a moment he remembered one of the many scenes, when Paroniya had bent over a wooden basin of cold water and scooped some up, pushing her wet hand inside the opening of her shirt above her breasts, glancing across the fence at the courtyard of the men's prison, where Misha had been washing his face. He believed that she had been choosing the time to have a bath and wash her breasts...that she had been waiting for him to come out before she ran to the basin. He smiled when he visualized his face at such moments, when he would every time pretend he hadn't understood Paroniya's intentions. He had never told her that he had always liked her, but that a woman stood between them, and nothing could separate Misha from that woman. Not the years spent in the Siberian prison, nor the inhospitable gorges of the Urals, nor the thousands of kilometers through the steppes on the both sides of the huge mountain chain—which, not only by its geography but also by the people's appearance, their customs, and even the way they danced at weddings, separated the European part of Russia from the Asian—none of this could separate Misha from his wife. Even if they hadn't had their little Petro, Misha could not imagine life without Boulisou.

Somebody energetically knocked on the curtained glass of the compartment door, and when he opened the door a crack, behind it appeared the lieutenant's angular head with its big bulging eyes and hairy eyebrows.

"I give you the amount of time it takes for the train to get to the first houses of Spasovka. It is not far. If, by then, you do not start *Prometheus,* you will be telling us that story without a break and without a sip of vodka."

The lieutenant held out his hand holding a canteen which, instead of water, contained vodka. Then he quickly pulled it back, with one hand pressed his saber to his leg in order not to trip on it when exiting, and disappeared into the corridor.

"He is not that cruel, this conceited artist, who is going to hiss at his father all his life for forcing him to become a professional soldier," the velvety voice of Svetlana Frolova was heard. She was one of the members of their artistic group. Her intense green eyes hidden by her fair hair reminded Misha of the small lake surrounded by willows with long slender leaves around which he had gamboled the best years of his early youth.

They were ready. The costumes, taking most of the space in their suitcases, were intended for the plays of Russian and European tradition, but there could be found some details that would pass as those from the civilization of ancient Greece. They failed to notice when Nikita Vladimirovitch Kozlov opened the compartment door again and pushed a half of his gawky head inside, but they heard his words:

"Grigory Rasputin, because of your insisting I allowed this tomfool comedy on the train. They have been waiting for you in the restaurant for half an hour already."

Instead of a reply, Grigory led the way through the door. The others hastily followed. On the other side of the windows of the rumbling train that crawled between tall trees of different kinds like a long black worm that had got lost in the blooming meadow, the Siberian summer day reigned. If man could return to the stage nature had designed him for, he would be its autochthonous part. Thus, on that rumbling train, which was trying to connect the disparate parts of Russia broken apart by distance and the uniqueness of its regions, man was a prisoner. In those train cars man travelled with a feeling that he was part of the machinery and that the most important thing on the journey across empty and inhospitable regions was to avoid being thrown off the fire monster which was dragging them along and moaning wildly while its metal wheels rattled and slid across the uneven joints of the rails.

From Bratsk to Ufa the train had a restaurant car. For this occasion, one section of its main compartment had been cleared and the tables and chairs moved to the larger section where the spectators were. According to their faces and clothing, one could assume that army officers and merchants dominated. Among them were a dozen women divided into two groups. Those in the group sitting in the middle of the audience were probably wives travelling with their husbands, and those cuddling close to younger officers were, by their clothes and flamboyant makeup, some of the "free women" who were almost a fixture on that train. One of them, Lana Kazimirova from Sasha, close to Ufa, wore a purple beret over the left side of her head of thick fair hair. She was pressing the underarm of a tall man with a light beard and, who knows how many times, whispering into his ear as if kissing him: "You'll keep your promise, will you! You saw I was a virgin. If I went back home, my father would skin me alive in front of the eyes of all the Bashkir folks."

"Naturally…naturally, Of course I will…I know you were…" Igor Yefremovitch Argunov comforted her, ever more unconvincingly. Argunov was a sturdy soldier from the border units of Russian troops in Kamchatka. As the train drew closer to the Urals and Ufa, he started blushing more and more because of the promise he had foolishly planted into Lana's heart so that she would agree to hide with him in the car where extra logs for the engine were kept and make passionate love. The more he thought about how his Maria, with their two giddy girls wrapped in her wide skirt, would be waiting for him at the train station in Ufa, the more his desire to be alone again with Lana in the car with the logs was turning into the idea that it would be better to jump out at some stop in the mountains and wait for a couple of days for another train.

Lieutenant Kozlov had chosen a chair in the first row for himself. He assumed that he was the most important person there and that all were full of respect for him, not because of his white uniform with red piping and the long saber in its white leather sheath, but because of his love for art. He also believed that he was there to watch over the cultural behaviour of the audience since the dramatic performance and the storytelling of Grigory's group was solely to his credit. He was thoroughly convinced the other officers in this audience were not mature enough even for army service not to mention some story about Prometheus. In those moments, when he did not have doubts about his importance among the people on the train, warm feelings spontaneously engulfed him, mixed with anticipation of revenge against the girl who had, without a moment of consideration, left him for a teacher who had come from somewhere in the Finnish flatlands. Some friends had advised him to pursue them and deliver punishment to the teacher for having dared to take the girl from him, but he had only smiled, believing that Larisa would suffer all her life for falling for the teacher's sweet talk. If he did anything evil to that man, Larisa would certainly hate him for the rest of her life; but this way…

Grigory explained to the spectators that the events to be described in the play had happened in nature and that he would try to make vivid the images of the environment. That controversial young man, who shared blood with some side roots of the Tsar's Romanov lineage, was a priest, adventurer, good friend; and for many who knew him and were persuading others to notice him, he was a mystic who knew the art of controlling the brains of those present and of imposing his illusions on them. Misha had met him in front of one of the prison buildings at the very beginning of his term of incarceration. There, in front of the other prisoners, Grigory had very successfully created the illusion that he was eating roast goat meat instead of the hard barley bread splashed with hot water. Later they had discovered a way to improve their living conditions in the Siberian prison by performing various plays and gags for the wardens and prisoners, which they enhanced with Grigory's rich illusionism. They had formed a theater troupe and in that manner they had made their prison days in Siberia more bearable. When Grigory had agreed with Lieutenant Kozlov, the commander of the prisoners' escort to the European part of Russia, to perform for the first-class passengers some story from the past of the human race, the lieutenant had enthusiastically expressed his wish that they perform the story of Prometheus. It seemed that the discontented Kozlov preferred stories in which outstanding figures face a tragic fate, just as, he thought, had happened to him.

Misha was standing at the centre of the stage, his hands pretending to shape clay statues, and then he withdrew the flute from his linen belt and started playing a slow tune which evoked the faraway past and noble feelings. Rasputin was creating vivid images of the environment:

"The sharp, rocky mountaintop reaches deep into the seeming transparent blueness of the sky, where the balmy sunlight creates an occluding membrane for the human eye to obscure the medley visible on bright nights which inspires thinking about the infinity of space around our planet and about our maliciousness in that space..."

Misha played the role of Prometheus. With one knee, he knelt on the food-stained rug of this Trans-Siberian dining car, while Grigory, through the power of his illusion, was creating the image that Misha was kneeling on the wide, soft leaf of a swamp water lily. Kneeling there, Misha mimed creation, tearing pieces of imagined clay from a liquidly grey mass and forming the hands of the statue, which resembled him in size and appearance. Special attention he paid to the fingers, which, with his every move, were more and more taking the shape of his own fingers. Grigory was speaking softly, but loudly enough for all to hear:

"If they had our fingers, many animals would show that they are much wiser than they seem. The major Greek God, Zeus, knew that enigma, and thus did not allow Prometheus to make any animals' fingers similar to those of the Gods. And although he gave Prometheus the task to create all the rich life on Planet Earth, he insisted that, unlike the Gods, every member in that chain would have a limited life span. When creating life on Earth, for the first time in his existence, Prometheus understood that nothing is immortal in the universe, that everything constantly moves and changes, since everything that comes to life at a certain moment is not eternal and thus cannot be immortal. Nothing in the universe is immortal, neither gods nor titans. All that is not eternal has limits, impossible to cross. And everything that has limits needs rules by which it manifests its life.

"Without rules also our Empire would be a basket of prunes and would be eaten by flea-ridden outlaws and good-for-nothings—scabby persons and bums," declared a man with a moustache and a chubby stomach, wearing a small hat on his head.

"It seems to me that not even the Siberian penitentiary could reform these men," a female voice expressing surprise was heard from the first rows.

Grigory waved a white handkerchief towards the audience in the manner of an experienced magician; then he turned it towards Prometheus and continued his monologue:

"Those people whom Prometheus forms out of clay and intends to fill with life and start a new species…they will, I am sure, only for a short time be the creatures Prometheus intended them to be; then they will break away from that idea and become inert, subject like everything else to cosmic rules, and that will drag them through time, regardless Prometheus and even their own ideas and desires. I know that such inertness exists, I know it is dependent on the laws of the universe, but I do not know where it originates and along what design it travels through time."

From his bosom he took out another, very large white handkerchief, hid his face behind it, and continued in a mysterious voice:

"Prometheus is now forming the creatures who would break away from the rules of the Gods and think they were masters of Earth, but only few among them would know that they could never understand where the path they were put on is leading them and that from that path they can go neither to the left, nor to the right, nor backwards, nor forward the way they want."

Somebody in the audience coughed, not hiding his disagreement. But he did not go beyond coughing. Grigory showed his face from behind the piece of fabric and continued:

"Thus far, Prometheus, according to Zeus's desire and request, had created a diverse chain-of-survival world on Planet Earth. He admired his creations, but their merciless struggle for survival, which Zeus instilled in them as soon as Prometheus rendered them alive, made him ever more discontent. In that chain the stronger had to eat the weaker to survive. When Prometheus asked the first among the Gods for an explanation, Zeus told him that the purpose of that decision was to make the cyclic flow of mortal life on this planet itself eternal, so that each species could survive only in the chain and that any breaking away from that cyclic life would lead to extinction. That cruelty in the relationships among the living forms on the glorious planet Earth was making Prometheus ever more uneasy and pushing him into impermissible disobedience of Zeus: the idea occurred to him to create creatures similar to the Gods, with a mind limitless in its potential for development; creatures who would not follow the Gods in their lecherousness and mutual hatred and who would, with their goodness and creativity, make life on earth less cruel; creatures who would be mortal and because of their mortality would try to render quality to every moment of their lives."

"The Bible says differently. God created everything, not some...Prometheus!" The one who had been coughing before had become braver now. When the spectators turned to look at him, they saw he was that same bald man with a parting beard who had been talking earlier about how Tsar Nikolay the Second would send troops to the border between Serbia and Bosnia to prevent the Austro-

Hungarian Empire from continuing to conquer European parts of the weakened Ottoman Empire.

"Prometheus is one half of God, Nikifor Yefimovitch," the lieutenant warned him. "This does not contradict the teaching of the Bible. I would like to listen to this story, gentlemen!"

The stares returned to Misha, playing the role of Prometheus. Grigory's baritone was heard again:

"First among Gods, Zeus, followed Prometheus's work closely. Since the war with his father, Kronos, in the Pleiades stellar system, when he defeated and supplanted that First among Gods and Titans, Zeus had considered the idea of leaving that part of the galaxy and starting all over again in some other suitable place. For that endeavour he needed Prometheus. He had given him the task of creating animate life on Earth. And Prometheus did. And now suddenly he was creating some Godlike clay figures, which looked suspicious to Zeus, and he decided to visit the greatest creator among Gods and Titans. He brought along Hephaestus, the great blacksmith-god, with the intention to ask him for advice after the conversation with Prometheus. Only Zeus and Poseidon, the God of the Sea, knew that Prometheus's real father was Hephaestus himself. Or so he claimed. They had always found it strange that Hephaestus had asked them not to reveal this everlasting secret. Zeus believed that Hephaestus maybe was not Prometheus's father, because, he, Zeus, at the time of the supposed love rendezvous between Hephaestus and Prometheus's mother, had secretly been enjoying her himself."

The section of the audience where the free women were sitting became louder, but the ear-splitting sound of the engine muffled the sounds. Like a heartless black monster, the engine slipped into a tunnel and pulled along the actors, the spectators, and all those other folks dispersed through patient, dreaming compartments. All their thoughts, feelings, intrigues, happiness and sadness—everything within their bodies was mercilessly pulled into the darkness mixed with the stench of the engine smoke, which stimulated in people illusions of quick transformation into something different from what they had been before entering the tunnel.

Grigory went to a window, and when their car left the roughly carved exit of the tunnel, he stared far across the river flowing from behind a round wooded hill, and he started to explain:

"A narrow stream coming from the higher parts of the mountain was noisily rushing towards the rippling turquoise-blue surface of the sea, wrinkled like the bottom of a shallow lake parched by summer heat. From the stream occasionally swarms of insects rose in a surge of uncontrollable instinct, as if they sensed some danger approaching; then, in the same unexpected manner, they would return to the stream."

Having eagerly waited for Grigory to make a pause between thoughts, louder than needed for others to hear him, a burly man with a patch on his right eye thundered:

"Lieutenant! What kind of story is this? I am bored. And something else. I do not like insects. Even here mosquitoes are bothering me. Before I managed to wake from my sleep by a swamp back near Irkutsk, they had eaten my eye. Why did this bearded lad have to mention them and add one more heavy load to my misery?!" The fellow made pause to hear comments, but the silence was broken only by Lieutenant Kozlov:

"That's how it is in the story, Ilya Goncharov. Everyone listened to this story with interest many times in the penitentiary. The prisoners listened to it and the wardens too. Why shouldn't we? I myself don't like it when somebody describes the murmur of a stream while we are listening to the rattling of this run-down train. But we should be patient. And what else would we do now?"

While Kozlov was speaking, two men approached him step by step, making their way through the crowd of spectators. One was wearing a light low-cut fur hat. When the lieutenant finished, the man with the fur hat whispered something to him. Kozlov jerked his head backwards to better observe the two men; then he slowly turned towards Grigory and Misha. Grigory followed that byplay and concluded that he did not like the two men at all, but continued to describe the scene from the story:

"Prometheus noticed the changes taking place in nature only when ever more persistent clouds of pale mist, coming with the wind down the mountain, started to creep in among the dozens of his sculptures.

He directed his gaze at the treetops and realized that they were uncontrollably and fearfully swaying in all directions. He did not need to guess. He very well knew that Zeus announced his arrival this way, by demonstrating his power and wanting to be recognized in that manner."

"Power often has a habit of brandishing symbols that make those who are oppressed and weak fall on their knees," declared a sturdy man in his thirties, with a big purple mark on his cheek.

"Hey, folks! What is this? This is turning into a political rally," thundered Goncharov, looking daringly at Kozlov.

Grigory did not let himself be distracted, and continued:

"That announcement of mighty Zeus's arrival aroused resentful anger in Prometheus, but wisdom warned him that patience is the best way to gain time. Zeus's chariot came floating down in the space between Prometheus and the stream, and, like the light autumn leaf of a steppe oak, landed on the soft carpet of mountain grass." All the spectators were taken by this illusion and, instead of Misha, they saw what Grigory was describing. "The First among Gods was now theatrically clothed, which only made him more ridiculous. He was followed by the unsurpassed but vain blacksmith Hephaestus. Unlike Zeus, who even in greeting was theatrically arrogant, Hephaestus bowed his body when Prometheus looked at him; in that manner he confirmed that he cherished special feelings towards the Titan and that they both belonged to the same level in the strongly hierarchical ranking of Gods."

The way the passengers followed Grigory's story revealed the degree to which they understood and the degree of their interest. Some rolled their eyes, asking themselves if anything interesting or relevant to their life experience would follow. Others were listening and watching in a disciplined manner, trying to get the most from what Grigory was telling them. Some had already started to analyze, and they discovered details that smacked of a satirical attack on their Russia's reality. And those crowded around the group of the free women were trying to mix with them inconspicuously and press against those body parts which most excited them.

Paroniya huddled close to Svetlana. She did not allow that blonde with long eyelashes, their tips knit with mascara, to think about Ruslan and his printery, in which, after completing the School of Journalism at Kazan University, they had printed many forbidden brochures directed against those who exploited peasants and workers and against the irascible Tsar's authority. She was a little jealous of Svetlana, for she knew Svetlana was in a hurry to meet her university classmate, who shared her political ideas and who would have become her husband, had it not been for the secret agents who had raided the printery just at the moment when Ruslan had suddenly decided to go to eat something by himself, even though they had always eaten together at the fat Galina Sokolova's beanery. She had not seen him since. In a hasty procedure they had condemned her to Siberian exile, not giving her a chance to see anybody before they included her in the latest contingent of those dangerous for the motherland and sent her on the long journey east.

Paroniya was indeed a little jealous of her friend from prison who had a reason to be in a hurry. Whenever she heard Svetlana talking about Ruslan and expressing her bitterness about the possibility that he had sold her out to save himself, or her fear that something could have happened to him that was more terrible than what had happened to her, Paroniya saw herself in a void, without a great desire to meet anybody and with no idea how to continue her life after prison. During her stay in the Siberian penitentiary they had managed to tear her away from all ties with the real world. Her inner life comprised two completely different states. Because of her, one scrawny prison warden had frozen stiff on a cold Siberian night watching the pale moonlight reaching through the window and lingering on her rosy face. When she was close to Misha, her hope would stir every time again that something would bring them closer, that they would make more of their relationship, full of uncertainty so far. Then, time again and again, she would realize that it had only been her self-deceiving, a waste of time. She would fall into a depression and try to pull herself out of it by escaping into her early youth and the games around the village houses and in the woods. However, her reminiscences of lost youth had brought melancholy, offering nothing fresh and tangible.

She would scorn herself when she occasionally found her thoughts turn to wishing some evil would befall Misha's Boulisou. She would often give herself a talking-to, saying that melancholy leads to endless dissatisfaction, that plunging into the past takes away from the precious time intended for enjoying every moment of life, and that it especially lessens the desire for optimistic plans. However, she did not venture further than the attempts to tear herself away from nostalgia. She was left with only the bitter feeling of reality and a desire to take part in any movement that would offer something new, some kind of escape from the stale and dreary life stuck between the Western-European rippling of the masses of the people and the Eastern cold detachment in the boundless far away.

In that state of mind, which was very close to a nightmare, she secretly cherished hope that one day a door to her and Misha's life together would open, even with Boulisou and her son Petro. Even in a situation where Misha would be a doctor in some hospital and she only his pharmacist.

Grigory was tireless. He started to ask himself if they had done the right thing by agreeing to perform a play from ancient times, but he could not back away now. And where could they go from that train, crawling as if through frozen eternity? He had a desire to mix with the audience and press his legs against somebody's buttocks. It did not matter whose; he only wanted something to change in that compartment and make time move faster. But now he had to play the first among the Greek Gods, Zeus.

ZEUS (to Prometheus): You made these clay figures bear likeness to me, to yourself...to us. When I entrusted you with the task of creating rich and diverse life on this planet, I did not tell you that the species should look like us! I thought you would stop at the most developed monkeys.

PROMETHEUS (his words and the lineaments of his face express pride and dignity): All we created before were simple forms of life without the possibility of a more serious development. I thought we needed somebody who would be able to perform more complex tasks, not just serve our hunting and leisure.

Hephaestus was circling around the statues and exploring them with his skilful eyes. The audience followed the conversation of the actors with interest.

ZEUS: What would be the role of these creatures similar to us?

PROMETHEUS (undeterred and ready for the conversation with Zeus): They would be able to create. It is a challenge. Why wouldn't we have creatures on Earth we could admire because of their minds?! And one day, when we decide to go to another planet in the universe, they would be able to rule life on this planet. Without them, we would leave this living world in a state of chaos.

ZEUS (unable to hide his surprise): You do not really think they should have our power?!

PROMETHEUS (unswerving): Their minds should have the capability for complex creations and be limitless.

ZEUS (indignant and offended): No way! No creature on this planet should have our power! If it happens, those creature would threaten us. The chain of life on Earth must be closed in a circle. Limited. It shouldn't contain even one tiniest link to divine power. What would happen when those creatures multiplied and gained a power of creation like that of Gods?

Zeus and Hephaestus remounted their chariot and disappeared into the stormy dark cloud above the mountain. Lying back in the comfortable seat of the chariot, Zeus asked Hephaestus what he thought about how they should punish Prometheus for his disobedience. Hephaestus replied, not revealing to the First among Gods that he agreed with Prometheus:

"If I remember well, your were thinking about Prometheus starting animate life on the Alpha-Centauri planet Dylan, after the completion of the program on Earth. Or starting it on Sirius's planet Jaime. After all, he deserves your devotion since he has created what the creators of your father, Kronos, could not have made anywhere in the Universe. If you are really asking advice from me, I'll sincerely tell you what I think even though I know very well that in expressing sincere thoughts one needs to be wise and that often one who is sincere gets in harm's way. Sometimes it is better to be quiet than be sincere. But, if you are eager to hear what I have to say, Prometheus is not a warrior but a creator. He is more like me than like you. He won't create warriors but creators. If I were you, I would send us far away from here, to some other galaxy, and I would leave those new Promethean creatures with only a faint recollection of the Gods. Let them talk about us and swear to us for eternity and beg us to forgive them for their sins."

Zeus became thoughtful and in his imagination projected the face of Prometheus against the very face of the God Hephaestus; then he smiled mysteriously when this time again he concluded that Prometheus was more similar to him than to Hephaestus. He wondered how Hephaestus had never come to that conclusion. Or maybe he had, but did not want to have an issue among the Gods about the origins of Prometheus.

In the group of men and women gathered as audience to this play, one middle-aged man with a moustache whispered to a woman with very blonde hair wearing tasty earrings, and pressed his body against her back ever more strongly:

"See, even in those old times there where some with brains. They will now take a break to rest. You promised we would go to that washroom at the end of the second car. Let's go."

"You have to be faster this time. Yegor has fever, but he might start looking for me. You know very well that even ill as he is, he would strangle both of us, if he finds out."

While the two of them were slowly sneaking out from the crowd of spectators, Grigory theatrically explained that Prometheus had blown a breath of life into his Godlike figurines and they had come to life.

"That's how the human race originated, according to the Greek myths. People came about because of Prometheus's creativity and his disobedience."

The spectators became animated. They realized the break had started and began commenting on what they had watched. Most of them encircled the lieutenant because it seemed to all that he was in some way the authority on the train. The most energetic one was Yelisaveta Andreyevna, a tall, thin, completely grey older woman.

"It is good, Lieutenant Kozlov, that you have fetched those actors to make this endless dreary journey more bearable for us. But why in the first place did they choose to perform for us this play about the creation of the world, so different from the teachings and the books of the Church? Maybe the late Tsar Alexander sent them here to rekindle the fire under the feet of the Church? My Vasily"—she pointed with her hand at an old man of enlightened looks and irrevocably thinning grey hair—"thinks this is connected to the forming of different parties in our country and could be revolutionary propaganda."

"What revolutionary propaganda, woman?! Haven't you ever heard about the ancient Greek plays and of Zeus and Prometheus? It is better that they tell us about this than that they talk about how our nobility is waging wars in Scandinavia, the Caucasus and the Balkans, and how our duchesses are having affairs with foreign diplomats and degraded officers," Seryoza Ivanovitch, a chubby teacher from Stoyanovka in Saratov region, drummed with his foamy baritone.

"It is best to get out of here until they calm down," Ivan Sergeyevitch Kalinin was thinking, and started to sneak out of the crowd. "Merchants shouldn't be in anybody's bad books."

Lieutenant Kozlov, with the instincts of an experienced officer, felt that comments should be postponed until after the meal. He spread his arms wide above his head and with authority suggested they should eat while the actors got ready for the continuation of the story.

"I wanted to say something more about…" Yelisaveta started to say from the crowd, but the lieutenant interrupted her in a brotherly manner:

"We know, we know, but you won't forget that. Let's drink some vodka to seal our bond of community on this train, my friends."

A bottle of the alcohol was immediately found in the hands of the chubby teacher, as if he had it ready to support the lieutenant's suggestion.

"Can I have one too?" Yegor Suvorov's voice, weakened and exhausted by sickness, came from the compartment door.

The teacher went to him in one leap with an eagerness probably induced by Yegor's obvious ill-health. He offered him a glass of vodka, but warned him:

"You should eat something. It's strong."

Yegor grabbed the glass from the teacher's hand as if somebody might snatch it away from him, drank it all, stretched himself from toes to top, shook his head from that whack of mightiness hidden in the vodka, and replied to the teacher:

"If this does not bring me back to life, food won't either. Where is my Daryushka?"

"Here I am, Yegorko! Here I am!" a female voice could be heard just when the heavy compartment doors slammed under the pressure of a sudden wind coming from the outside. She entered without the one with whom she had sneaked out in the middle of the story; she hastened to support her husband, putting her arm around his waist so that he would not fall. She looked at him in surprise, trying to discover anything unusual in his eyes. But those eyes were filled with images of the Azov's Voronyez, from which, still a boy, he had been expelled to Siberia because he had accepted the Doukhobor teaching and because he had been caught a few times with a group of people singing the psalms full of faith in divine justice. The teacher also stared at Yegor with extreme interest. He passed his gaze over Yegor's body, trying to figure out how much damage the illness had caused. Nobody could understand what illness the pimpled Yegor had. Daryushka had told them how he had fallen ill as early as Easter; more precisely, when he had returned from Bulgakov's lumber mill to celebrate the holidays with the family. Suddenly the pimples on his face had turned red, his ears become prominent and turned blue, and his voice become husky as if a bone of the brindled goose they had roasted for Easter dinner had stuck in his throat. Three times Doctor Tuzikov from the mill had visited him and every time he shook his head and left shrugging his shoulders. The first time he had told Daryushka to massage Yegor with diluted vodka and give him lukewarm chicken soup. He had repeated that order on the following two visits. For four days, Yegor had been raving in fever, and after eating the soup he would twist his body and breathe heavily. Only occasionally would he look more clearly and ask about the time of day. When doctor Tuzikov had visited him the last time, he had said that in Ufa, on the other side of the Urals, there was a doctor for such cases and that the mill would pay for the round trip for both of them. They were accompanied by Yegor's nephew Maxim, with whom Daryushka had disappeared during the play about Prometheus.

The train braked hard a couple of times before they entered the station at Chebarkul. Everybody crowded by the windows to see new faces. The people outside approached the train in a headlong mass; then they split up. Some rushed toward the train windows, offering cheese, bread, brandy, honey and who knows what else. Some crowded to the crude iron stairs leading into the cars. Some of these held suitcases with both hands as if afraid to lose them; some carried their loads concealed in swathes of cotton. On each side of the restaurant car was one first-class sleeper. The area in front of the entrance to those cars was empty. Only one passenger headed towards the closer of the two; he was short, bulky, and carried a leather bag in his hand. His legs were bent as if he had been on horseback all his life.

The Ural Mountains were bringing cold clouds to the sky, which had been clear before. Whenever the train curved through a switchback bend in the rails, songs accompanied by the sounds of an accordion or flute could be heard from the compartments other than those of first class. The melodies conjured the images of the wide spaces of the steppes and the collective autumn husking of the corn. As soon as the rails straightened up, the music was replaced by the monotonous rattling of the train wheels across the track joints.

Misha, Greshka, and other members of the group of actors received a hearty meal, ordered by the merchant Ivan Kalinyin. He told them they deserved a better meal, but in the restaurant there was nothing except dried ham, old hard bread, thin, plain borscht, hard sheep cheese, bad Caspian wine and Kazan vodka. Misha was becoming more thoughtful, as if trying to discern what he would face upon his return to the Caucasus. Grigory was provoking him, wondering what had made him change his mood so abruptly.

"Whisper to me, Mishka," he was telling him in a low voice. "Whisper to me what's happened, so I do not make stupid guesses. What happened? Are you fed up with this endless journey? Don't tell me you are becoming afraid of seeing Boulisou and your family. Don't worry. Your Petro will accept you. Even if he does not recognize your face, he will know the presence of his father."

Misha was staring at the members of the audience, who were finishing their meal, and one by one were going to the washroom and coming back from there adjusting the lower part of their clothing. He was listening to what this moustached and bearded, strong young ex-priest was saying, but Misha felt some strange chill engulfing him. He was in no mood to either think or talk. If he could at least get out of that train and sit by some big tree, and play his flute until he became exhausted...Through his playing, he would try to reach those he missed and to ease his pain and fear. He accepted Grigory Rasputin, and in some way had come to love him, and had not been offended when Greshka had refused Misha's plea to put the black metal cross he wore on a silver chain under his shirt. When Grigory mentioned Boulisou and Petro, a strange feeling crept through him along with the chill, like what happens when a hot potato is dropped in deep snow, where it sizzles and steams, irretrievably disappearing into the snowy depths. It was clear that the story of Prometheus had caused a change in his frame of mind.

"I don't know what it is. I am a little tired. I just want to find them even if my Petro does not recognize me. We'll get to know each other. It is easy for you, brother. There in Petersburg you will soon forget how they sent you to the Siberia to cool down, and your relatives of the Tsar's blood will undoubtedly push your way into the splendid salons or send you to Amsterdam or Paris to have fun. The worst thing that can happen to you is that the Tsar, accompanied by his consuls and ambassadors, looks at you askance, and when you get together at secret soirées with court ladies, laughs at your adventures and asks you which one of them has buttocks to your taste. It is easy for you, Greshka."

"You forgot something, Mishka. It could also happen that I pay dearly for that partying the Tsar would bless, and, in the best case, get a bullet from the gun of some red rebel. Or the Tsar himself could sacrifice me for the smallest part of his reputation or vanity. Or my friend and remote cousin, the Grand Duke Nikolay Nikolayovitch leaves me to fall into disfavour, as he did when they sent me to the Siberia for only one passionate touch with Anastasya, Princess of Montenegro, the sister of his brother's wife Militza. I have told you about their secret relationships and love soirées. By the way, I am still hoping you will help me when I try to conjure the arrival of Zeus and Hephaestus at Prometheus's workshop, as you used to help me in the Siberia."

Misha did not want to explain to Grigory that he was losing his concentration, and that every time he tried to conjure the images from his head for the audience, he felt some very painful process in his brain, as if in those moments that extraordinary brain matter was draining out of his skull.

"What is next?" asked Lieutenant Kozlov, approaching Grigory to consult about the continuation of the performance. "It would be good to continue without long nature descriptions and without big philosophy. Very few here understand that. Not everybody is as well read and educated as the two of us."

"Do not worry, Lieutenant. Fifty thousand years after Prometheus's act of creating humans, the great god Zeus decided to punish the creator of animated life on Earth, the God's own son Prometheus. Exactly because he had created humans and had generously been helping them to become creatures of an ever higher quality."

Lieutenant Nikita Kozlov saw himself in Prometheus's place. He remembered how he himself had started in that way, by doing good deeds in his village, Harashovka, close to Tambov. His father Vladimir was a merchant and had become rich by buying cheap vodka from the peasants in the entire region, then packing it in bottles coming from Rostov, affixing the invented label Vodka Tambovskaya, and selling it everywhere. He had mostly been selling it in the Don villages to Cossacks, who did not have time for peasants' work because of serving in the Tsar's armies. He could not sell anything to those Doukhobors who had stayed in their homesteads and accepted the demands of the Russian authorities to swear allegiance to them and pay taxes, because the Doukhobors had become more and more determined not to drink alcohol. His son Nikita, dreaming about becoming a big artist and about being greeted by people as God's miracle, started secretly to give his father's wealth to the poor: a hen to one, a sheep to another, flowers to yet another one, to some a piece of clothing or money. The father loved his son, but he'd had enough of Nikita's goodness. He asked the Cossacks for advice and they told him wisely:

"What art, what Petersburg Academy?! Send him to the Army for ten years on the other side of the Urals. That will drive the crazy ideas out of his head!" Thus, Nikita Vladimirovitch Kozlov, punished for his goodness, had eventually arrived at the Labour and Correction Centre in Bratsk. Even though in the army they had tried to bring him to reason and teach him discipline and unchanging rules, he firmly decided, while escorting the theatre troupe of prisoners to Ufa, never to return to army life. That is why he openly cheered for Prometheus even though it meant that he took the side of the one who would be punished. The free women, without any doubt, also took the side of Prometheus. Not only because he had dared to defy the great Zeus, but also because Misha was playing him and they were openly talking about Misha's handsome and manly stature.

Somebody protested in the central part of the audience. It was that short passenger with bent legs, who had boarded the train at the Chebarkul stop and now tried to bring attention upon himself.

"It seems that people had good models. It was enough for them to find out what the Gods were doing. Father Ignyati was right when he said: It doesn't matter what it is if it comes from God."

People around him stared with interest. Their gazes said, "And who are you?!"

"I do not meddle in God's affairs, but I say…I am from Zlatoust, Arhyp Izmailov."

It was obvious that those near him quickly understood that some lack of benevolence was emanating from the man. They withdrew from Arhyp, like the wave on a painter's canvas which becomes still above an inhospitable rock.

Misha was troubled by gloomy thoughts, as if he had had a bad dream. For days, actually since their train's departure from the Siberian wilderness into the civilization, he had tried to get rid of the objects of the chilling imagination of his own brain; he had tried to make jokes, tease some of the girls. However, a cold wave in his spirit had been for three years pulling him into the dark depths of feeling and premonition, ever since the bald Georgian Vaya Gelashvili had arrived at the Labour and Correction Centre and started talking about why he had been sent to Siberia. Misha's thoughts had become frozen when Gelashvili had explained how he, with a group of Georgian intellectuals sent to Rostov to school, had protested the harsh settling of accounts by the Tsar's authorities and the Church with the Doukhobors of Taganrogsk Bay, on the north side of the Azov Sea. Like Misha's own people, this community of Doukhobors had been expelled to the Caucasus. But conditions there were terrible. "They decided to completely destroy these people," Gelashvili had been saying, while gritting his teeth and clenching his fist. "They are taking away the children and sending them to fundamentalist Orthodox families, they are not giving Doukhobors work, are closing their schools, and letting outlawed Caucasian tribes attack them."

"Why did you try to defend the Doukhobors?" Misha had impulsively asked him at that time.

"They are good people with courage to oppose the Tsar's cruel and corrupted authority and the Church, which is deeply sunk in stinking mire. Allow me to confess to you something very private: the daughter of a carpenter of theirs, Popov from the Efremovka community, and I have been in love for a few years and I had the intention to marry her as soon as I finished mechanical engineering school. She is more beautiful than all Georgian beauties," he whispered to Misha confidentially, as if the Georgian beauties could hear him and spoil his plans with the exquisite Doukhobor girl. "Even her family had nothing against me, although I do not belong to their sect."

Misha had on a later occasion confessed to Vaya Gelashvili that he had been raised in a Doukhobor family himself, and that they had been settled in Kars; he had been trying to get more information from the Georgian about what had been happening to that group of the Doukhobors. "Maybe he has heard about my father, Kostuna. Or maybe," Misha had secretly hoped, "some word about my Boulisou and our Petro. Maybe…" Every time after such a conversation with the pleasant Georgian, Misha had been unhappy and his fear had become stronger. Once it had seemed to Misha that upon his mentioning Boulisou, Gelashvili's eyes had twinkled as if hiding a secret, and Misha had not dared prompt him to say what he knew because he feared bad news.

From one group of spectators came insistent requests for Zeus's story about Pandora and the box. Even as a character in a play, the First among the Gods knew that, being the most important, he had the right to be mightily uncooperative.

"Who is that Pandora and what was in that box?" the free women asked the question in unison.

ZEUS: "The decision to create Pandora was mine. However, Poseidon was consulted too. I wanted to create a human being who would become a relative of the Gods and bring more seriousness and responsibility to the human race. She had to be close to Prometheus to prove to him that Gods, too, have creative powers similar to his. Maybe even greater. And the box? When Prometheus started to openly help humans, when he started to steal wealth and power from the Gods, when he stole fire from us and gave it to humans, Poseidon and I decided to warn him seriously and to punish him in some way. But we could not directly either punish him or warn him. That is why we presented humans with temptation. We put evils in the box and gave it to Pandora with the order not to open it. But she confirmed our opinion about humans: that nothing is sacred to them. To them an order is an incentive for plotting how to disobey the order. To them a secret is an incentive for plotting how to reveal it. You know the rest. Humans got hold of the evils in Pandora's box and soon they started to serve them as great masters. How come Prometheus failed to instill in them protection against doing evil deeds?"

"Is there greater evil than the Gods' deceit of humans?!" the teacher Seryoza Ivanovic almost shouted. "To take revenge on each other, the Gods introduced evils to humans. And nobody had asked humans if they wanted to be created, nor what kind of creature they wanted to be."

The spectators started to stir and comment to each other. The short Arhyp was constantly moving around as if looking for something. Lieutenant Kozlov noticed him pushing through the audience, and when Arhypo got close enough, Kozlov grabbed him by the lapel of his coat and asked, smiling:

"Where are you going, Mister Izmailov? Wait for this performance to end, and you will have many opportunities to look each of as in the eye and to go behind our backs."

His voice did not show protest nor did his tone reveal what he thought about Arhyp. However, Arhyp's reply surprised both the lieutenant and those standing next to the two of them:

"I thought that the Tsar's Army would protect passengers on a train, and would not address them the way you have addressed me. Move that big hand of yours off my coat!"

While saying this, Arhyp rose onto the tips of his leather shoes to come closer to the lieutenant's eyes. His face was round, his small eyes a bit slanted, his eyebrows more grey than fair, his beard and ears both short and rounded, the skin of his face light with many tiny spots. However, his short arms were not moving, and Kozlov realized that it would be best to patch up the misunderstanding. He took his hand off Arhyp's shoulder and tried to apologize:

"I decided to tease you. Isn't it better that we tease one another than that we try to be smartasses and hiss at each other?"

"Your joke is rude, Lieutenant. I bet you are a Cossack from the Don. I also prefer jokes to gloomy faces. As for my pushing through the crowd of these good men, I have been trying to come closer to the one who is telling the story. I have heard he can tell fortunes, so I thought to ask him if we will get to Zlatoust on this train or I'll have to go on horseback across the Urals. I have heard that the Bashkirs have taken up the arms and that their groups have been attacking all who come their way."

"Don't worry, brother. The train has its escort. We can defend ourselves. The rebel Bashkirs know that."

At that point, Arhyp had already started moving away towards Rasputin, who was with the group of actors. Grigory was adjusting his wide collar of soft deer leather when Izmailov went behind his back, skillfully pressed the sharp tip of his knife through Grigory's fur cloak to his very skin, and ordered him in a low voice:

"Tell me quickly why you stole our cattle from the pasture? You better hurry to explain Zeus's verdict to the audience. Then follow me to the other car, but make sure you do not raise suspicion. If you do not obey, this knife is sharp and in my other hand there is a heavy gun. In the other car, you will tell our fortunes. Yours and mine."

Grigory was experienced with such situations. Similar things had happened to him while he travelled as an anchorite through the villages on the other side of the Urals. He knew that little bandit, in whom he recognized the village middleman and smuggler Urushka Golubov, from the village where the cattle had been stolen, was not joking and that it was easier for him to shove a knife between a man's ribs than to call the name of God.

"We were young and needed money for fun," Grigory told him in a low voice. "We had strength and youth, and a desire to have a good time, to travel as far as Moscow, but we did not have money. Your Prohor gave us the idea to steal the cattle, to sell them and to give him a quarter of the money."

The short man jerked as if somebody had driven a knife between his own ribs, was quiet for a while, then gave Grigory the order:

"Explain what happened to Prometheus and then go in front of me to the other car."

Grigory Rasputin stretched up on his long legs, stroked his long black beard and theatrically made a judgement:

"Zeus managed to get the approval of the Gods to punish Prometheus. The punishment was in keeping with the gravity of the offence in the eyes of the Olympian jury, and with the Titan's power of endurance: *You shall be bound to the rock on the mountaintop of Kazbek in the Caucasus. The black bald eagle shall devour your liver every day, and during the night the part devoured by the eagle shall be restored. And this shall continue for eternity!*

"Hephaestus looked at Zeus with anger in his eyes and cursed the day when he had finally confessed that Zeus was Prometheus's father and asked the First among Gods to keep that secret.

"'Your justice is very harsh! In your narcissism you destroyed your own father, and you now want to destroy your son! Poseidon asked me to pretend that Prometheus was mine to save your face!' Hephaestus uttered the last sentence in a whisper, turning his head towards Prometheus. The Great God Zeus pretended he had not heard the words."

Grigory made a bow, signalling to the audience that the performance was over. Just when he was stepping towards the compartment door, the voice of a woman was heard from the crowd:

"They bound him to the Caucasus, and our tsars have expelled the Doukhobors there. What symbolism! Prometheus was punished because he had created human beings and endeavoured to make them good. Our Doukhobors have been punished for their refusal to kill people and for their immunity to the evils in Pandora's box."

All those in the compartment became silent, but a squeaky voice, coming from the group who had followed the performance silently until now, abruptly interrupted the silence:

"The Doukhobors brought the punishment upon themselves. They have stirred people against authority and falsely interpreted the teachings of our Church. They respect neither the Cross nor the Holy Bible."

The group around the man with the squeaky voice moved a few steps away from him, so the others could see him better. He was tall, middle-aged, wearing a black priest's robe. Until then he had not been noticeable hanging around the free women. His face was fresh, with no trace of wrinkles, like the face of a girl, and his eyes small and sparkly, with big black pupils, like those of a bald eagle from the high mountaintops. Nobody had noticed when he had entered the compartment and joined the audience.

"Those like you, priest, have been condemning them," Teacher Ivanovitch declared. "From what I have heard about that movement, they must be good people. If they are against war and tyranny, they cannot be evil. They teach their children to be humble, generous, and to have purity of soul, to be patient, loyal, to regard all humans as brothers and sisters. And you, priest…I know you too well. You often travel on this train. I am worried that they have been sending you to probe our souls while we travel on the train. I see you here every time I travel by train to Siberia. Maybe you are also a merchant, reverend!"

"It's none of your business," the priest challenged him gruffly.

"Yes, it is. Your Church does not leave us in peace and freedom even in a train. Here also you want to have control over our souls."

"I did not say anything bad to any of you." The priest was defending himself, for no face expressed solidarity with him. "I am against all who do not respect our Church and authority. And those Doukhobors are against both of these."

"Against what are the Doukhobors, priest!? They regard all people as brothers and sisters and do not lay violent hands on anybody and they oppose all evil. We should adopt their life philosophy. I tell my students the rules that the Doukhobors follow in order to avoid evil: never be boastful or greedy; never become happy when somebody is humiliating other people; get rid of anger, envy, despair; and never perform any sort of sorcery. That's what the Doukhobors are, priest! All their lives they practice and develop the philosophy of the pure spirit, and avoid making barriers among people in order to hate those different from them."

"Do not praise them in front of me!" The priest's voice now expressed anger. "They are the ones who separate themselves from others. They deride the Church and the country. And these are sacred things for the human race. Without the church and state people would be beasts. Do you know where the Doukhobors got their ideas? They inherited them from that outlaw, Tsar Samuel, that Armenian who imposed himself on Bulgarians and Macedonians to be their tsar. And then he made them wage wars against Christians, against the Christian Byzantine Empire, which was the insurmountable bastion for all the conquerors from the East. Even worse, that Samuel supported the apostate Bogumil sect, which, because of him, spread from Bosnia and Dalmatia, over Macedonia and Bulgaria, and came to Armenia and Georgia, encircled the Black Sea and engulfed the Ukrainians and us Russians, all the way to Kharkov and beyond, almost up to Moscow. They fell out of God's grace, so they were destroyed. But their deep roots were not destroyed, so they reappeared in the form of these Doukhobors, just like any evil that lies low and waits for the right moment to sprout again."

"You are the evil, you human monster!" the teacher shouted, and started pushing aside those around him to get to the priest.

"Wait, you people," Kozlov cried out and put himself between the priest and the teacher. "Do not insult each other. I know the Doukhobors. I am from the region where they lived. I know they do not commit evil. But they also have flaws, as all men do. I hadn't heard the priest's story that their roots come from Samuel's Empire. But that's not important. I know of one writer from the Balkans who has written that humans are the creation of Satan, but have such a well-developed brain that they can choose to follow the divine philosophy of life. Come on, people, let's wash this away with vodka and song after the performance."

Most accepted his suggestion, and bottles of vodka started travelling from mouth to mouth, while Izmailov prodded Grigory with the tip of his knife, signalling him to head for the door. The train was moaning while climbing the slope in the bosom of the Urals, and from the chimney of the long heavy engine smoke was coming out similar to that coming from the tall chimney of the steel plant in Omsk.

Misha was pleased with the teacher's defence of the Doukhobors and felt blissful. Even the lieutenant's words sounded friendly to him. While the priest and the teacher were fighting against or for the Doukhobor way of life, Misha was having recollections of Doukhobor choirs singing happily, thrilled with the joyfulness of life. He remembered their unselfish communal work to produce enough for all; their goodhearted and wise old men, Kuzma, Nikolay, Vasily, Stepan; their mothers, who had worked in the fields, in the house, together prepared the winter preserves for everybody; their children who had joyfully anticipated each new day…Suddenly, in that very moment, he and Seryoza noticed that something strange was happening between Grigory and the short Izmailov, and they excused themselves to Paroniya and Svetlana, saying they were going to the washroom. Their absence among the girls, Kozlov readily filled.

Through the dirty glass of the dining-car door, Misha and Seryoza saw Grigory and Izmailov swaying on the unstable iron platform between cars. They were in heated conversation. No weapon was visible in Izmailov's hands. There was nothing suspicious in their gestures. Suddenly, a scream was heard from the engine and the train entered a tunnel. The darkness covered the scene between the two cars, and when the train came out of the tunnel, there was nobody on the platform. Misha and Seryoza hastened to the next car, but only dozing passengers were inside it. There was no trace of the two men. They asked people if they had seen them, but nobody had. Rasputin and Izmailov's disappearance from the train moving through the Urals towards Ufa remained a mystery. Lieutenant Kozlov sent a few soldiers to look for them from the locomotive to the last car, but they returned shrugging their shoulders. It was as if the two had disappeared from the face of the earth.

"It seems to me like some of Rasputin's magic," was the concluding comment of Lieutenant Kozlov.

The train stayed overnight in Zlatoust, and when at dusk after two more days they arrived in Ufa, it was raining outside. There were a lot of people wet from the rain waiting on the platform. Many of them were holding light bundles and leather bags over their heads. Misha and his company decided to spend the night at the Hotel Moscow by the train station. In the morning they parted. Seryoza took the train heading to Moscow, and Misha and the two girls waited for the train going in the direction of Kuibishev. Paroniya and Svetlana had also decided to travel in the direction of the Caucasus, to their families. The difficult journey by train, horse carriage and on horseback took a week. When he arrived at the entrance to the village of Pokrovka, Misha first met Genadiy, who had recognized him from a hundred-meter distance and rushed so eagerly to hug him that they both fell in the dusty lane.

"We knew you would come back," Genadiy said through his clenched teeth. "We have all believed in that. And your big Petro."

"How about my parents?"

"They are the same as when you left them."

"And Boulisou?" Misha asked in a faltering voice.

"She's great! Fit and strong and beautiful," cried out Genadiy. A group of people had already gathered around them, and somebody shouted:

"Here comes Kostuna as well!"

The father and the son stayed embraced until the mother Pelagiya separated them:

"Let your mother hug you."

Through tears she told him that Boulisou and Petro were having dinner at the Hassons. Soon Misha was riding his father's dapple-grey horse towards the two secluded houses just outside their village. Through the windows of the closer one, he could see a pair of oil lamps glow.

14

The end of the century was rapidly approaching the Doukhobors' villages and communities in the Trans-Caucasian region. Kostuna Chernov became increasingly afraid their movement was breaking down into several groups holding different positions about the vital issues of their way of life. He also did not like the families' rigid rules about schooling their children and the strong attacks from individuals and groups on those few who were sending their children to state schools. He knew that the Doukhobors would not have a future if they failed to school their younger generations and keep pace with society at large in educating the young. When his son, Misha, had gone to university in Kazan, the conservatives within the movement had strongly attacked him. And when the authorities had sent Misha to exile in Siberia, Kostuna had endured open mocking, even from some people of his own community. On a few occasions Kostuna was surprised by open disagreement from his brothers, Mikhail and Alexey, about the way he was raising Misha. They warned him these revisions of the traditional Doukhobor philosophy of life were unacceptable. However, when Misha, recently returned from exile, openly took the side of the progressive Doukhobors, Kostuna was pleased and felt he had an heir he could be proud of. Especially proud was he that Misha had completed the study of medicine and continued the tradition of their predecessor, Evstafy Chernov.

And Misha? As a greenhorn teenager, absorbing the stories and advice of his father and other wise people in the village, he'd had loads of plans. He did not want to stay in the fields of the barren Kars highland. Whenever he pondered on it, he realized that he did not feel this part of the world was his own. To him, mountains were mountains everywhere, fields were fields, rivers were rivers. Birds were birds everywhere, and mice were mice. And cats chased small rodents and birds, and dogs looked sorrowfully at the kitchen windows, and people told stories abounding in their own personal tastes and imagination. There was a clear division between the world of children and the real-life world of adults. And between the sensibility of females and the cockiness of men. A fool was a fool everywhere; an idler was an idler…But man is an animal and has legs. By trains and boats he can go around the world, as some did—the professor of geography from Petersburg or the members of the British Commission Agents Society. Man could live in any habitable part of the world. However, even if he succeeded in convincing himself that he belonged to the entire planet, somewhere deep in his soul he would cherish special feelings towards one of its parts. But not even in his dreams could Misha discover any feelings towards this Kars part of the world.

Now—after his schooling far away in Kazan along with the start of his married life with Boulisou, his journeys to Moscow, Petersburg and the Baltic harbours of Lithuania and Estonia; after his temporary exile to Siberia and the return to his small family in Pokrovka—he was not sure anymore that he was again at the right place where he could be happy and where he could do something for the happiness of other people. He was thinking not only of his family, about Boulisou and Petro, and about the community with whom he had blood ties and shared feelings, but also of the uncertainty whether the Lord would one day answer the silent prayers of all Doukhobors so that people of different opinions and instincts would leave them alone to live in peace in their homes. He extended this thinking to all the people living along the border with the Ottoman Empire, and along all other borders in the world, where the powerful divide people and protect their own interests. He was thinking about the family of the father of his Boulisou, her grandfather, uncles, aunts; about those Russian, and before that Turkish, and even before that Spanish Sephardic Jews, whose roots had for centuries been scattered across the various parts of the world because of human malice, in the same way as his roots and the roots of his predecessors had been scattered across Mother Russia. He was also thinking about the British journalist, Arthur Smith, from

Plymouth, who, with the great help and influence of Stephen Brown, Ambassador of Her Majesty Victoria, Queen of England, and that of the British friends of Leo Tolstoy, who managed to mollify the Russian Ministry of Foreign Affairs to allow two British journalists to visit the Doukhobors in the Trans-Caucasus, in order to study their way of life and to inform the public about those people.

Misha had met Arthur in Kars' hospital when the British journalist needed a physician's intervention in treating some strain of foot-and-mouth disease to which people from Western Europe had no immunity. Misha had been working there with the silent approval of Kars' Mayor Eliyas, since as a Doukhobor he was not allowed to practice medicine in public hospitals. When he saw Arthur, Misha could barely suppress his laughter because the nose of that man was so swollen and blue that he looked more like an Indonesian long-nosed monkey than like a distinguished Western European. His eyes expressed sadness and protest, as though dismayed by what a common foot-and-mouth disease could do to a human nose.

For weeks Arthur had been visiting Doukhobor communities and studying the life of these people. He soon realized that what he had seen was not only a specific belief in God and His ordering of life on Earth and in the Universe, but that it was a specific way of life, an attempt to organize people's lives on an equal basis so that all work for all and share equally; that there was no private property, unscrupulous fighting for profit, exploitation of man by man; and that there was no trace of any teaching or philosophy that would encourage hatred for any human being…There was no thinking about war and no acceptance of any authority or institution that would want to lead them into war. That man needs to vow obedience to God not to some human, even a tsar. Arthur had discovered the roots of the Doukhobor way of life in early Christian communities, except that there asceticism dominated, while Doukhobors had a developed sense of communal living and production. And then, he was almost convinced, the social relationships in Doukhobor communities were attracting ever more numerous followers of the leftist movements in Russia, which were becoming dangerous for the Tsar's regime and the teachings of the

Russian Orthodox Church. He did not like the Doukhobors' ideas about education and he liked the exceptions, like Misha. He did not like their refusal to accompany their songs with the sounds of the Russian instruments he loved, the Balalaika, the accordion and the violin, but he liked to listen to their choral singing of the psalms, hymns, and traditional Russian songs. He asked an explanation from Misha as to why the Doukhobors used lyrics drawn from Mikhail Lermontov's poems, and Misha briefly explained to him that the Doukhobors did not have prejudice when it came to art, and that they did not blame Lermontov for not living their way of life.

One afternoon after Arthur's nose had returned to elegant proportions, they were sitting on the benches in front of the orphanage in Pokrovka and listening to a Doukhobor choir singing Russian folk songs and psalms. On impulse, Misha joined the singers. From the inside pocket of his dark hemp suit he took out the flute and with the sounds of that small instrument started to accompany the singing of the Doukhobor choir. Arthur was very surprised. He had never before seen a musical instrument quite like it, and the sounds reaching him reminded him of the music of Pedro Sanchez, who played in the restaurant of the Hotel Belvedere in Portsmouth. That South American man had one day arrived at Southampton on the freighter *Bristol.* For some time he had made a living there by playing on the street, until one local newspaper published an article about his mysterious musical instrument. Very soon he ended up on the entertainment stage of the Belvedere's restaurant, where Arthur had encountered him. The flute of Sanchez didn't look at all like Misha's, but the haunting sound here in little Pokrovka transported Arthur back to the great city on the south coast of England.

When Misha joined him again, Arthur congratulated him and explained the reason for his surprise:

"I'd learned that the Doukhobors sing without the accompaniment of musical instruments, and now you disproved it. Furthermore, I am not familiar with that small flute of yours, and I have to admit, not even the instrument of Pedro Sanchez could produce such idyllic sounds."

"My uncle Genadiy made me the first flute when I was a boy. He showed me only the basics of how to play because he himself did not know very much. And I would play whenever I had a chance and I mastered its potentials and our choir accepted me. Some Doukhobors were angry, but as soon as they heard my flute, their anger would vanish. While in university I made my living by playing at student dances," Misha explained to Arthur.

While they were walking back to the house of Misha's father, Arthur asked Misha an unexpected question:

"Have you ever thought about whether it is good that people decided to be Doukhobors? I mean, to live in Russia, to be a Russian, but to live a life different from that of others and to believe in God in a different way than others, is not easy. Do not be offended, but I have also thought that it is not smart. You condemn yourself to isolation and to the animosity of the majority. "

"Oh, Arthur, Arthur! I have! I have often thought about it. But not in that way. In fact, the founders of this movement could have thought about it in the way you said. But I was born a Doukhobor. That way of life and belief is my tradition. Tradition is sometimes stronger than reason. However, there is a lot in that tradition that I love. Not only do I love it because it is ours, but I love it because I consider it good. It would be good if all people in the world accepted our love for all people. If every human being considered other people their brothers and sisters. If they excluded hatred, weapons, and war from their lives. If they were humane toward animals and if they were vegetarians. Do you find any of this bad?"

"No, Misha. I don't think it is bad. But what is bad about being an Orthodox Christian, as most Russians are? Why do churches and priests bother you? Why do you not like to carry their crosses? I know the Doukhobors' answer to these questions. But what do you yourself think about it?"

"Religion should be a personal matter for each man. I am sure that the Lord, if we had a chance to talk to Him, would say that all people are his creations and that no man has the right to kill people. If I have to belong to one religion, it cannot be any religion that fails to prohibit its followers from going to war. I personally, in my relationship with God, do not need any mediation by church or priests. It is very rational. First of all, churches and priests turn belief into institutions, and each institution has social and economic goals. In short, people have strong connections with God, so those institutions for their relationship with God are meaningless to them. Nor do they need any individuals who put themselves between people and God. We all know that religious institutions and their officials are the power that keeps people in submission. If I had a chance to avoid it, I would always gladly do that. As a Doukhobor, I can do that. And the cross. If there were no churches and priests, there would be no symbol of belonging to these institutions. The cross has nothing to do with God. All religions preaching belief in God have their symbols. They are all different and each signifies believing in God. It is absurd. Isn't it enough if man finds his own way of communicating with the creator of everything on Earth? Personally, God is a mystery to all of us, far beyond our reach. Nobody has ever seen God and nobody can describe his form. Would God require us to bow before him, to be afraid of him, to threaten each other with him as with a whip inflicting pain? It is absurd, Arthur. One who is a symbol of goodness would not ask people to be his slaves. He can only ask us to follow His goodness, to be the bearers of goodness and happiness to all living creatures. That's what we believe: God is in the soul of every human being."

"Oh, Misha, Misha! If all the Doukhobors believe the way you do, then I am not surprised that they are persecuting you. It is obvious that you threaten the interests of religious institutions. Tsars could secretly like you, but they would not dare to publicly express their admiration of you." Arthur was speaking in a low voice, and, what a coincidence, the Doukhobor choir there in front of the orphanage was singing a song by an anonymous poet:

They once asked a great Tsar
Why he persecutes those whom everyone loves
Why he takes their children away
and burns their cradles.

'To Love thy neighbour is fine,'
The great Tsar told them,
'But let others be loved by their neighbours.'

"Misha," the Englishman addressed him again, "have you ever asked yourself how it happened that the ancestors of the contemporary Doukhobors possessed the uncompromising courage to confront the state apparatus and the church oligarchy and create a new way of life—such a liberal and somewhat nihilistic philosophy of life—and a revised Christian religion?"

"I have occasionally thought about how brave and noble our ancestors were," Misha replied. "And what is your opinion of that?"

Arthur was silent for some time because in a flash he remembered his encounter with the London pianist Robert Girodo, a distant descendant of a radical faction of the French Huguenots. He remembered Robert's words that his Girodos had for two centuries been forced to look for their place under the sun only because they had dared to say they had an unbreakable human dignity.

"I am positive that those first Doukhobors were Russians with dignity and did not think that Mother Russia would persecute them so mercilessly because of their dignity. They were only a few hundred kilometers away from the centres of the Russian State and Church power; they were advanced food producers and exceptional housekeepers; yet they could not help but say they did not want to participate anymore in crimes against human beings and in playing with God."

"Oh, Arthur, Arthur! You must owe a big favour to the Doukhobors, you speak so highly of them!" Misha said in a tone of gratitude, and with unconcealed satisfaction he rushed ahead of the journalist to open the house door for him.

The next day Misha and Arthur went on horseback to a hill some distance away from the village; they sat on rocks covered in moss and talked till they became exhausted. They ended up telling jokes from Doukhobor communities. Before each of their meetings, Misha would collect precious anecdotes from his father and then recount them to the British man. He was just telling him about an episode that had happened in their Efremovka community. It was about a complaint by some villagers to their leader, Lukeriya, about a man named Stepka, who, secretly from his wife, was also living with two other women, who did not have husbands. Lukeriya told the villagers to be quiet about it until the secret was discovered by Stepka's wife.

"For these women it is better to have anybody than nobody," the wise Lukeriya told them. "If it suits them, its suits me too."

"How come you decided to come to this dangerous and rather wild part of the world to study Doukhobors and write about us?" Misha asked Arthur, after finishing his story from the Doukhobor community of Efremovka.

"I have written successfully about a group of Protestants in Ireland tortured because they had tried to rationalize many religious dogmas and change them to keep up with the times. As soon as I tackled this question, I gained enemies who tried all means to prevent me from informing the public about the truths kept in the police archives as special secrets. They physically attacked me, and once they even shot at me through the window of my apartment in Belfast, of which this scar is the best proof." He unbuttoned his shirt and showed a deep wide scar below his right shoulder. "They could not stop me. I exposed a group masterminded by the Police Secret Services and I sent some of them to jail."

While telling the last part of his story from the British Isles, Arthur jumped off the rock on which he'd been sitting and pointed with his hand towards the village of Bogdanovka, lying on the northern slopes of the neighbouring hill, and exclaimed:

"Look, Misha. There is a big fire in that village! Could it be that somebody's house or barn has caught fire?"

"No…" Misha stared into the distance and right away realized that it was not an edifice that was burning, but a big fire in front of the Orphans' Home. It was supposed to be a surprise for Arthur, but they had started the fire much earlier than planned. In fact, the present Doukhobor leader, Peter Verigin, had secretly arranged with the

Doukhobors in all the communities between the Black Sea and the Caspian Sea that, during the night between the 28th and the 29th of June of this year 1895, they burn all the weapons in Bogdanovka, the administrative centre of the Doukhobor communities in the Caucasus, to express their determination not to kill what God has created. Verigin decided in that way to make real the plans he had made with Leo Tolstoy to illustrate the application of Doukhobor philosophy, which condemns any participation in war and killing. Some members of the Doukhobor Movement went even as far in expressing their determination as to refuse to lay violent hands on animals and become orthodox vegetarians.

As soon as he realized that the fire had been started too early, Misha felt uneasy and begged his eyes to help him see better what was going on down there. There were a lot of people around the fire, but the crowd was suddenly becoming bigger as groups from all sides joined it. He hadn't noticed the small clouds of dust in the fields around the village, raised by horse-drawn carriages and Doukhobors on horseback. Yes, they were Doukhobors. Their horses were heavier and slower than the horses of the other groups and tribes in that region, for the Doukhobors used them only for work in the fields and for the transport of goods. The horses of the Tartars, Armenians, Dagestanians, Azeris and others were mostly used for riding.

Arthur, surprised not only by the fire but by all the activity around it, asked Misha what was going on. He explained that those were Doukhobors coming for a gathering in Bogdanovka to burn their weapons. Then both of their eyes were caught by a large cloud of dust approaching the village from the direction of the Wet Mountains. Misha right away realized they were not Doukhobors because the cloud was moving much faster than the villagers' carriages and a lot of people must be in that cloud.

"It is the cavalry! The Cossacks!" Misha exclaimed all of a sudden and rushed towards the spot where their two horses were grazing on low branches. Arthur did the same, and soon the two riders were approaching the village from the hill. Their fear that something bad would happen intensified when they heard gunshots and when the entire village became covered in a grey cloud of dust, in which only from time to time could be seen the flames of the fire in which the Doukhobors' weapons were burning.

While they were dashing downhill as fast as it was safe for their horses, behind a copse of beech trees they saw a group of unfamiliar riders, led by a huge man with a black beard wearing black robes. Misha did not want to lose one single moment to find out who these people were, and especially who the priest was. While rushing down the hill, he tried to think of some acceptable explanation. But the chaos in Bogdanovka was too immediate and terrifying for theories. Thoughts about what was happening in the village crowded his mind, none of them optimistic. As soon as he'd learned about the preparations for the public burning of the weapons, he started to worry about retaliation from the Tsar's authorities and the functionaries of the Church. Now his imagination, spurred by fear, created images of what was transpiring within the clouds of dust and smoke obscuring the village, of what might be happening to familiar people, his father, uncles, and even his Boulisou and the young Petro.

This entire event, and the atmosphere of hellish chaos in which Cossacks armed to the teeth were pitted against defenceless Doukhobors, Arthur Smith described in a newspaper article which disturbed the European public and finally placed the case of the Russian Doukhobors, whom Mother Russia had terribly tortured for the last two centuries, on the European political and humanitarian scene.

15

"You see what is happening in our country! You see what they are doing to innocent people who do not ask anybody for anything except for the right to their own way of life and belief. Now is the moment for the world to put pressure on our Tsar to allow the Doukhobors to find somewhere else in the world a country better than our Mother Russia. Hear what is written in the *Daily Chronicle*!" Lev Nikolayevitch Tolstoy was addressing his friends Pavel Biryukov, Ivan Tregubov, and Vladimir Tchertkov, in his house in Yasna Polyana. Then he read aloud a copy of the letter that Arthur had sent to his newspaper in Plymouth.

...Right at the foot of the hill Misha and I fell into a cloud of dust raised by the men on horseback and by the people chaotically running in all directions. We hadn't reached the fire yet, but the shouting, the terrible screams of the people and the gunshots were a clear warning of what was happening. The cavalry had attacked the Doukhobors with guns, and sabres, and whips. The soldiers on horseback, wearing white uniforms, fell upon the men, women, and children; they were whooping to express their joy at the brutal settling of accounts with these innocent and unarmed folk. I am surprised that they didn't stop the two of us right at the entrance to the village. We soon reached the huge fire, which made that terror look mystical and surreal. In spite of the hell instigated by the cavalry, the Doukhobors were still sitting around the fire, women and men together, dressed in their traditional clothes embellished by the men's low fur hats and women's shawls. They were sitting, but even at a quick glance the surprise and fear were clear in their faces. They were sitting and singing the Psalms as loudly as their

throats allowed them, to muffle the terrible noise of the other folk and the cavalry.

The fire was spectacular but at the same time frightful. It took up a third of the area of Manchester Stadium, and the flames were reaching the height of Big Ben in London. They must have brought there hundreds of horse carts full of dry logs. Through that hellish muddle of flame and smoke, I saw in the fire hundreds of old hunting guns, soldiers' rifles with bayonets, sabres with silver hilts, ammunition cases...On cremated uniforms twinkled colourful medals for war service, having been attained in who knows which wars and in what times. I know that various antiwar movements in the world have organized unforgettable protests against wars and their murder of innocents, but nobody in the world has ever made something so magnificent as this bonfire. It was the most wonderful symbol of humanism in the course of civilization on our planet. There, in that fire, which was devouring weapons kept hidden for decades to defend homes and families, human dignity was flaring up. In those short moments, while I was trying to memorize the most illustrative images of this Doukhobor protest against war, weapons, and attacks on human life, I saw the people before me as the greatest pacifists on our planet and I was proud that, at least in that moment, I belonged to them.

When I took my gaze from the fire and focused my senses on the chaos developing around it, I again became astonished, seeing the horror that people were doing to other people. The cavalry was massacring everybody without interruption, one by one, unvaried retaliation against young and old, women and children. Some soldiers were slashing the bodies of all of those in front of them and around their horses. One soldier raised his sabre as high as if facing a huge dragon from the fantastic stories of Russian mythology, not terrified helpless people under the foaming head of his black-spotted grey horse, people who shared the same roots as he. It was the sabre of the Russian rulers and their Church elite in the hands of the common man, who no later than tomorrow could find himself in the same situation as did his victims on that warm early summer night of the year 1895.

A little bit further away a few manly Doukhobors were defending a group of women and children with lengths of wood, while the solders were using sabres. The cavalry horses, accustomed to attacking human beings, were nonetheless afraid of wooden bats in men's hands; they raised their heads towards the sky, rearing on their hind legs. The soldiers got the idea to wheel their horses about ten meters away from the group of people, lift their guns, and without aiming start firing at the crowd. First the wooden bats started falling from the men's hands; then the defenders started falling to the ground, followed by the women and children. The soldiers quickly dismounted their horses, approached the group to see the effect of the firing of their guns and started screaming wildly at those who were trying to lift the bodies covered in blood:

"Sing the oath to Tsar Nikolay; fuck your Psalms!"

No more humane scenes of Golgotha were occurring behind my back. A group of soldiers were whooping while singing Cossack war refrains and using their horses' chests to push Doukhobors into the fire. The Doukhobors were reaching out their arms and heads towards the horses' chests, but the horses kept pushing them, heads averted from the people and the ever-closer heat of the fire. When the first flames started scorching them, some people jumped into the fire, and with their bare hands picked up glowing-hot pieces of wood and started throwing them at the horses and the soldiers. The horses backed away in fear of the smouldering logs; some dashed to the other side of the pyre, carrying their angry riders with them; suddenly there appeared a strong white stallion carrying on his back a man in an officer's uniform decorated with yellow ribbons. He started shouting:

"Slash them in the name of the Tsar and God! Slash them and throw them into the fire!"

Waving his unsheathed sabre, he lunged at the people trying to smother the flames on the clothes of those who had jumped into the fire and thrown the firebrands at the cavalry. The commander of the blood-crazed Cossacks clearly had the intention of taking somebody's life himself, but suddenly, from the smoke and dust on the other side where the civilians were slowly retreating, Misha, on his foam-covered bay horse, darted in front of the commander and spread his arms.

"Slash me, the Tsar's servant!" he exclaimed to avert the attention of the squadron commander.

The Cossack paused with his sabre above his head, stared at the rider, trying to recognize him, and then, without thinking, savagely spurred the ribs of the frightened stallion. The animal reared, preparing to jump at Misha and his mount, but froze in that position when all the noise was suddenly silenced by the peal of trumpets coming from the dense cloud of smoke and dust on the other side of the fire. Captain Praga, the enraged officer, whom everybody in that part of the world knew by his evil deeds, abruptly settled his horse and listened carefully as the clarion notes of the trumpets drew nearer. The rest of the cavalry emulated its captain. Praga's hat had been lost in the dust under the horseshoes, and his dishevelled hair fell over his forehead and covered his eyes. At that moment he had forgotten his intention to vent fury on the unarmed Misha. The people had stopped moving, except those still trying to combat the insect-like flames devouring the clothes of those who writhed in pain and attempted to extinguish themselves in the dust.

When the pandemonium around the fire ceased, and the dust and the smoke settled, the scene of mayhem in front of the orphans' home in the Doukhobor village of Bogdanovka was revealed. The bodies of the dead and the wounded, covered in blood and dust, were scattered everywhere. The Doukhobors who needed help received it from those who had had more luck. From the direction where the trumpets had sounded came a group of soldiers riding in file; they wore white uniforms with black buttons, and garrison caps on their heads. Riding at their head was the Tsar's famous Colonel Seratov, a bulky man with thick black moustaches and swollen lips. Next to him rode Prince Ospinski, and on the other side, the Governor of Elysavetpol, Nakashidze. They stopped in front of Captain Praga; the Prince spurred his horse and approached him, holding an unsheathed sabre high above the captain's head:

"No! There is no law that gives you the right to kill these people! If you do not revoke your order for the cavalry to kill them, I will split your head!"

It was the end of the bloody massacre of the Doukhobors at their fire of protest, in which they had burned weapons designed to kill those created by God. When I moved away from the fire trying to find Misha Chernov, I saw groups of riders approaching across the field. Later I learned that they were Georgians, Tartars, Armenians, and Turks from the neighbouring regions of the Caucasus. They had heard what was in store for the Doukhobors, so they had set off to help them in their trouble. Above the village, on the slopes of the Wet Mountains, stood a group of riders carrying the orange-triangle flag of the influential Tartar Princess, who, having learned of the authorities' preparations to renew their pogrom against the Doukhobors, persuaded Prince Ospinski to hasten with his entourage and stop the massacre in Bogdanovka. That Prince, a Romanov like Tsar Nikolay II, had earlier shown signs of devotion to the Doukhobors and had met several times with Leo Tolstoy.

Afterwards, I found Misha in a group of the Doukhobors from his village who were, with great, piety putting the bodies of their dead into carts and tending to the wounded. There I saw the corpses of two children, of women with terrible bloodstains on their clothes, and one man half roasted. It was, as Misha told me, Igor Kalmikov, from the village of Pokrovka.

Russian authorities and the Church have been persecuting the Douhobors for almost two centuries. They have been horribly terrorizing those people, whose way of life and religion is free of any aggression, and who consider all people their brothers and sisters, and who do not want or need to display any symbols for the God they carry deep in their souls. Church and State attempt to eradicate them. They confiscate the Doukhobors' homesteads, and take away their children, expel them to Siberia, kill and burn them. Their official leader, Peter Verigin, has been expelled to Siberia. Is there any power on our planet capable of stopping the extermination and forced exodus of these innocent Russian people?! Their leaders told me that the majority of the Doukhobors would gladly accept emigration to somewhere in the world free of persecution. These are very diligent and honest people. Their religion does not permit committing evil deeds. I plead to all individuals and organizations of the free world to join their forces to help the Doukhobors. Please, send your suggestions and opinions to the editorial office of our newspaper.—Arthur Smith.

Tolstoy and his friends were speechless. With silence they expressed their compassion for the sufferings of the Doukhobors. They were looking through the window at the abundance of the sunny day in the trees which were piously expressing their gratitude towards the warm summer.

"And Verigin...In face of all this, he has recently sent a new message to his followers with the request to eliminate smoking, alcohol and meat-eating from their way of life! 'We need to follow our principles in our relationship with animals and to completely cease the violence against these innocent creatures,' he declares. Gentlemen, we must ourselves make a declaration."

On that day Tolstoy and his friends, Biryukov, Tregubov, and Tchertkov, wrote an appeal to the world to help the Doukhobors, or, as the Doukhobors at the time referred to themselves, the Christians of the Universal Brotherhood. Because of that appeal, the Russian authorities expelled Biryukov and Tregubov to a small village on the coast of the Baltic. Tcherkov was permitted to emigrate abroad on account of his noble origins and his mother's friendship with the Tsarina. The great Tolstoy, friend of the Tsar himself, they could not touch.

16

Misha, with the convoy carrying the dead and the wounded, returned to the village of Pokrovka. Many needed his skill as a doctor. There were no medical supplies in the village, so Misha tried to send two men to Kars' hospital to bring what was needed. However, the authorities were doing all they could to isolate the Doukhobors from the rest of the world, and the cavalry sentries prohibited exit from Pokrovka. The villagers took the wounded into their homes and decided to bury the dead on the following day. While Misha was sterilizing Evgeny Popov's wounds with strong vodka, Kostuna, pale and breathing heavily, rushed into the room, stopped in front of Misha, and said that during the events in Bogdanovka some unfamiliar horsemen had arrived in the village and taken away a number women. Among them was Boulisou.

Misha tried to react without panic, but could not keep his face and body calm as he faced his father.

"Where have they taken them?" he asked after a few moments.

"Nobody knows. They headed towards the lake, but then they went somewhere toward the Wet Mountains."

At that moment the father and grandfather of Misha's Boulisou, along with Genadiy, rushed into the room. They announced that they had organized a group of people to go in search of the women who had been taken, but again the cavalry sentries would not allow anybody to leave the village.

Only now did Misha realize the full horror of what had happened, and in bewilderment he asked his father:

"Where is Petro? Have they taken him too?"

"They haven't!" Kostuna quickly assured. "He is at home and cannot stop crying. A few times he tried to break away in order to look for his mother. We had to physically restrain him. He saw them take her."

"We can sneak out of the village towards our houses," Boulisou's father, Yakov, declared. "I'll find a few Armenians to go searching with us."

"Of course, I'll go too," Misha exclaimed. "We'll find a way out of the village."

"Me too!" shouted Kostuna.

"You won't go without me. I'll find them in the mountains," exclaimed Genadiy and jumped for the door to show there was no time to waste.

"I first have to go to the Kalmikovs," Misha said more calmly. "Two of theirs are among the wounded. Then we will set forth. Bring anything you have for defence. And food...Do not use any tired horse."

Just as Genadiy was crossing the doorstep in order to go and get ready, the others about to follow him, Misha stopped them:

"Wait. The night is coming. Soon it will get dark. It will be easier to sneak by the guards in the dark. Let's meet at Kostuna's place in an hour."

"Papa Isidor and I will go home," Boulisou's father declared resolutely. "When you are ready to go, come and collect us."

The night was dark, with a lot of wind and occasional lightning coming from beyond the Wet Mountains, from the giant peaks of the Caucasus. It was not difficult for the group led by Misha Chernov to sneak out of the village on the side where the river sometime in its mischievous past had made steep, tortured banks. There, towards the new border with the Ottoman Empire, which was still Ottoman but less of an empire, they made their escape. In the course of time, natural changes had turned the mad river into a stream that would dry up in summer, in the same way as the former Turkish power had been turned by the end of the nineteen century into a mere memory of the terrifying monolith it had been. As that memory faded, it took with it into history the fear European kingdoms and dukedoms had of the danger from the East. The Hassons, father and son, who had made it home and waited outside the doors of their neighbouring houses, mounted their horses and silently joined the group from the village.

The riders tried to move eastward quietly to avoid detection, but as quickly as possible because they assumed the mysterious brigand abductors would naturally be hastening towards the Caucasus, where any search party would have a hard time finding them. Misha was riding parallel with Genadiy, and images from various grim scenarios were going through his mind. In each of them was Boulisou, usually powerless to resist the bandits in any way. He would also see images of Boulisou running in the night through ravines, bumping into bushes and trees, leaving a trail of blood on the rocks. He was trying to see her face and those burning dark eyes of hers, her hair blown by the speed of her body and the wind. On a few occasions, he almost spurred his horse and rushed to greet her, and then reason reminded him it was only his fear and desire transformed into images from his imagination. It seemed to him that he heard his Petro in the distance calling his mother in the wind, and something from the mountain replying indistinctly, unintelligibly.

The younger Hasson, Yakov, was clenching his fists tightly, begging his ears to bring him any sound that would confirm his daughter was somewhere close by, and his eyes to suddenly discover her in the darkness of the night. Deep in his soul, something was whispering to him that Boulisou had made a mistake by having dared to find a husband among the expelled, especially when young Jewish men on both sides of the border had expressed their interest in her.

The old Hasson and Kostuna knew that looking for the bandits and their Boulisou in that stormy night in that part of the world was the same as looking for a kernel of wheat in the stream of a rising river.

Far into the sleepless night, when on the tops of the Wet Mountains thin beams of light started to appear announcing the arrival of the day from the east, Misha was painfully startled from his stupor by the vivid mental image of a group of unfamiliar people with a priest in black robes on the hill from which he and Arthur had rushed down towards the chaos of Bogdanovka. It suddenly seemed possible to him that the Doukhobor women had been kidnapped under the orders of some of the enraged clerics. That thought overturned all his previous calculations and he felt a little relieved, for if they had been kidnapped on the orders of the Church, the worst would not happen to her, and there was a possibility he could find her. Yes, Misha thought; it was better if the kidnappers were connected to the Church organization than if they were white slave traders, who would take their prey somewhere far to the east and south, and sell them to owners of harems, to the wealthy, to owners of brothels and to innkeepers. Yet he felt a lump in his throat and bosom because even in this case he might never see his Boulisou again.

Morning found them among the gorges of the Wet Mountains as they and their horses rested in a valley surrounded by tall trees. The storm had passed with the night. They continued moving and searching, but on that day they did not discover anything that would assure them they were on the right track. Nor did they on the next day. They visited the Georgian villages and inquired among the Georgians and Tartars, but nobody knew anything. Then they met a group of Dagestan people who told them they had been in the mountains since the snow had melted but had noticed nothing unusual lately.

Misha's mood was changeable. When the attacks of new thoughts alternately gave him hope or brought anguish from hopelessness, he would behave accordingly. At one moment he entertained the strange thought that maybe as a group they were less lucky and that he would be more successful if he separated from his companions. He caught the opportunity when they made a stop by a lake in a hollow high in the mountains, and, while the others were busy looking for a spot to lie down and have a rest, Misha disappeared in the bushes under which he discovered an animal track leading downhill, parallel to a stream running down from the lake. He was moving slowly, stopping frequently and listening attentively in order not to miss possible sounds of voices. When he had gone far enough that his fellow searchers could not hear him, he felt as if something whispered to him to start calling:

"Boulisou, Bouuli-i!..." Misha was shouting, and then he would become quiet to hear if somebody called back. He was moving and calling. He came to the foot of the mountain, and with a great faith that he would hear the voice he was hoping for, he called Boulisou. Misha was shouting through mountain meadows, down the trails lined with bushes of hawthorn and sloe berry, through the woods thick with underbrush, down the clear waters of streams, across pools and small lakes. He was calling and listening, but the only reply was the flutter of the wings of forest birds and the song of the mountain wind touching the branches of bushes and trees. When he came to a gorge through the bottom of which a fast stream was running, again he started to call. He suddenly heard somebody's voice reaching him from the depth, and he happily called again: "Boulisou-u-u." Somebody's unintelligible words again came back to him and he became thrilled. Blood rushed to his head, the pace of his heartbeat quickened, and his eyes and ears strained to help him as much as they could to discover who was calling him. He called again several times, and the same murmur returned to him. He suddenly realized it was only an echo of his voice, distorted and subdued because of the unevenness of the gorge. He sat on the thick, branching roots of a tall branchy beech tree. He stared at the distance where the gorge disappeared. He put his head in his hands and looked down at the depth.

"Help me find her," Misha whispered to the stream far below; then he carried his whisper with his gaze down the long mountain gorge until it was stopped by the white bosom of one of the Caucasian mountains in the east, behind which must be another world. A thought reached his consciousness from the nightmare of his mind: Maybe it is better than the one here. Maybe people are better there, not doing evil to each other as here. Then he felt powerless facing that distance, and again, as who knows how many times in his life, he realized that he was only a tiny human creature. And people are people. When feeling happiness and goodness, they do good deeds. When their mind submerges into the cold and dark depth that creates hatred and aggression, they do evil deeds. While staring into the distance of the gorge, he took his flute out of the pocket under his right arm and started playing. All that had been making sound in that part of the mountain became silent and only the unusual melody of the flute was heard. He played a song about a black swan who, swimming among ordinary ducks and geese, would stretch its neck high and spread its wings to show its beauty and pride, and glide on the lake like a queen using her elegant bearing and splendid clothes to give flavour to the ball in the Tsar's court on the River Neva. Boulisou loved the times when Misha played that song, and he was completely sure that if she were anywhere the melody could reach her, she would find a way to contact him. He made short pauses between the parts of the song and pricked up his ears to catch any response to the sounds of his flute. Except the weak echo of the last tones before each pause, only heavy silence reached him from the gorge. He realized that his Boulisou could not hear him and that it was long since he had left his party, so he hastened to return to the mountain. He soon heard his people calling him.

When they had almost lost hope, they met a group of armed Tartars who told them that the Princess had heard about the abductions and would certainly take action if she learned anything about the kidnapped Doukhobor women. Realizing that the entire region knew about their search and that they would be contacted if anything was discovered, the search party decided to return to their homes.

During the night they sneaked into the village, avoiding the cavalry sentries. The people in the village did not know any more than they did about the vanished women. Time was passing. It was not only the Doukhobors who were searching for the lost. Many in the entire Trans-Caucasus were doing that. However, it was in vain.

Misha dedicated all his days and nights to the search for Boulisou. He left Petro in the care of his father, mother and Genadiy. His face expressed sadness, and wrinkles were attacking him. He was taking on the appearance of an old, eroded landscape. Even before, his understanding of life had lacked solid systems and strong priorities, and now the unexamined principles upon which his life was structured started shaking more and more. A good part of his ancestral nature recoiled from the social ties, science and religion that had evolved around him. Now for the first time in his life he faced a dilemma about what was most important to him, and more and more he favoured his own status in the natural world with the partner he had chosen himself—Boulisou. Everything else was in one way or another given to him by the environment he had been born into, by the time in which he lived, by his first and last name, by his father, mother, by his stature, intelligence and religion. Even the practice of medicine had come to him by chance...Boulisou was the only choice he had made himself in these complexities of life. Maybe this was the reason he cherished a very different feeling towards her, compared to everything else—a feeling that included love, belonging, desire, insecurity, hope, and a vision of the future...And now she was not by his side anymore. That emptiness was heavier than any pain he could have imagined. When he was searching for Boulisou, hope governed him at first, later the feeling of fear and lack of strength, and then again faith in the impossible, even a presentiment of something mystical which would bring them back to each other.

Misha's relationships with the family of his Boulisou had been reflected through the prism of his relationship with his wife. When the two of them had sung in union early in the morning like nightingales, he had wanted to hold all the Hassons in his embrace. When, on account of some triviality or simply because of a natural desire to stay away from Boulisou for some time, his feelings had become harder and more confused. He had felt a colder wave of emotion toward her parents, her grandfather and grandmother. Only his feelings towards Boulisou's sister had always been stable, very close to his understanding of the relationship he would have with his own sister if he had one. Since Boulisou had disappeared, he had often reexamined his feelings towards her family. He would become suspicious that the Hassons had abducted Boulisou and sent her to some of the numerous members of the larger family out there in the world. Then, what had happened to the other kidnapped women? He would get angry at his brain for being capable of producing such thoughts. But time took its toll; the initial sparks of distrust transformed into a serious suspicion. He recalled then her father Yakov's argumentative disagreement with his daughter's choice of a life-partner who was not Jewish. He connected that recollection with the almost inexplicable fact that the Hassons had stopped asking Misha for medical assistance when one of them fell ill. Now they wanted access to Petro.

One night, after a long visit with his friends in the orphanage, Misha felt a need to visit Boulisou's family. It was a clear but cold September night, and Misha decided to put on an autumn coat which the old Hasson grandmother, Maribel, had knitted and given to him after he returned from the prison in Siberia. When Isidor Hasson's house appeared from the darkness, he noticed that the only light was coming from the wide, shingle-roofed terrace. On the outer sides of the terrace thick vine grew. It had small black grapes, which the Hassons had brought from Ankara because of their sour taste and sweet smell, before the Doukhobors arrived in the Caucasus. The vine was so thick that it was hard to see if anyone was sitting on the terrace. Misha heard conversation coming from the other side of the grape curtain, and he had the thought that this could be an occasion to find out something about Boulisou. He recognized the voices of the old Hasson, Isidor, and his wife, Maribel. They were having a heated debate even though he knew they were quiet people capable of controlling their emotions. After he heard the first sentences, he realized that they were talking about him and Boulisou, and that they were of different opinions. In acrimonious tones Isidor was repeatedly saying to his wife that he had made a mistake by not having listened to Yakov, for having failed to prevent his granddaughter's feelings towards Misha from ending in love and marriage.

"What are you trying to say? That the tragedy of our Boulisou happened because she married Misha? It does not matter who he is and what roots he comes from; at the time when they decided to get married, Misha was the best choice for a young woman in our entire region. And they married far from all of us, there in university, because they were afraid of us. They did not trust us, fearing that we would not respect their love and wisdom. And they lived to be a credit to us all. You want to deny that? You want to prove them right for fearing us so long in the past?"

"You are not listening to me, Mary! All that you are telling me I know. But you saw what happened. I am sure our Boulisou would be with us or somewhere with one of ours, in a safe place in these evil times, if she had chosen otherwise. If she had gone to the Woskov family, she would be in America now. Even then Mordekhay was telling me that his Daniel and the one who would be his wife would right away go to America where his brother Benjamin lives. And you see; now we have neither our Boulisou nor her son Petro, whom they do not want to give to us so we could teach him about our tradition and religion. I pray God not hear me, but each day I am more afraid that we won't see either of the two…"

"Don't talk like that, Iso. They are both alive, and you are talking like that!"

Misha's heart was racing and his voice started to rise from his lungs to his mouth. Just when he was feeling the muscles in his legs tightening to jump over the fence of the terrace, so he could demand an explanation of where Boulisou was, Isidor almost burst with anger and reprimanded his wife:

"If Boulisou were alive, we would have already heard something about her. I am also lying to myself and expecting to hear something about her, but there is nothing." The choking of tears thickened Isidor's words. "Do not praise any more her Misha or the Doukhobors! If she had not gone for one of them, she would not have been kidnapped. The whole of Russia has set on doing away with them. And he!? I believed in him like you did. He could have taken her wherever he wanted. They could have gone to work wherever they wanted. If only he hadn't held to their teachings so strongly! If he had listened to my brother's urging, they would have gone to Turkey a long time ago, and who knows where else in the world…"

"Wait, Iso! Misha is one of us. Why are you talking like that? He is having a hard time, the same as we."

"I know he is," Isidor was crying freely now, his words a blubbering wail. "I know…I don't have any more hope that we will ever see our Boulisou again. If at least Petro were with us…He and his mother are alike. He is like our Boulisou."

The old grandmother Hasson was also crying. Tears were running down Misha's face as well, and through the tears he saw the image of Petro's face, resembling that of his mother. While he was quietly walking away from Isidor's house, Misha felt ashamed of his suspicion that these grieving old people were the ones who had kept Boulisou hidden. The tears were dripping on grass already covered in dew and making wet the socks in Misha's summer sandals.

Old Isidor was right. From his first days Petro had resembled his mother. As he grew and matured, the only distinction between the two of them came to be the manliness of his form; the rest was a copy of his mother, Boulisou: the round head with fine facial features, the thick black hair and the arched eyebrows, the charcoal black eyes and teeth like a string of pearls. When he saw his mother being taken away, he was eight years and three months. He had started to get to know his father better after Misha returned from Siberia, and until his mother's disappearance their relationship had evolved to the stage where Petro accepted Misha as a friend, calling him "Otyec" Misha, while the other children in the village, having grown up with their fathers, called them "Batya". That word carried a lot of respect, the love of a child towards a father, and the feeling of belonging. The two of them had not reached the stage when Petro would call him "Batya". Now when the mother was not there any more, little Petro was sleeping by his "Babushka" Pelagiya, and sometimes by the "Dyedushka" Kostuna. At bedtime, the dyedushka and babushka would tell him stories in which good people fought evil spirits and monsters, and the good people would win in the end. When the story ended, Petro would always ask if that good being would find his mother and bring her home. He accepted the other relatives of his father with the tenderness of a child, but they could never compare with Kostuna and Pelagiya. With Genadiy, though, he had not only blood ties but ties of friendship because Genadiy did not have children and he showed great affection for Petro. In return, little Petro's affection for him was even greater.

17

Tsarina Alexandra woke up when a sunbeam, reaching from behind the ridges of the hills rippling away into the interior of Mother Russia, built a spectrum of twinkling colours on the waves of the just-waking River Neva, and blended with the white and green marble from the Urals which covered the walls of the Tsar's Winter Palace in Petersburg. Only through the places where the curtains were not carefully drawn did the beam reach into the interior of the Palace. There, like a magician, it opened the Tsarina's eyes and made her stretch contentedly. She looked to the other side of the bed where the last Russian Tsar, Nikolay Alexandrovitch Romanov, would customarily fall asleep before her when their usual midnight infatuation was consummated. After a bad dream about finding his wife, his great love the Tsarina Alexandra, the former Alix of Hesse, in bed with the court writer and harp player Yegor Tihonov, he had not been able to sleep again for a long while. Morpheus at last overcame him once more, so thoroughly that now he could not wake up. The Tsar had been frightened by the mysterious dream, for which there was absolutely no foundation in their real life. Later he recorded it in his secret diary as one of his life's great oddities, and in that text he emphasized the oddity: how he had dreamed he suddenly entered the Tsarina's chambers, ran towards the bed in which she and her lover where enjoying their embraces, raised his hand to slap one of them, but stopped it halfway to their heads. Instead, he had puffed up his trembling chest hidden under the pink silken bathrobe, opened wide his turquoise blue eyes, and with fake surprise and his mouth strained in pain, had hissed in the Tsarina's face:

"I wanted to kill the one who revealed your secret to me! Maybe you are not a match for a Tsar. Maybe your rank is that of the one you have in your bed, Alix!"

That morning, almost three years after the massacre of the Doukhobors in Bogdanovka, Tsar Nikolay II had his midnight's bad dream, ending with him rushing out of the palace to get as far as possible from their marital bed. In his dream he was running away barefoot over the waves of the murky Neva from some horrible people whose faces he did not want to even see. They were closing on him, and he could not run fast enough to escape.

The sun was trying to ruffle the Tsar's light hair, the colour of unripe apricots, but it could not reach his face dipped into the soft white silk pillows stuffed with fine down from the chests of polar owls.

The Tsarina quietly got out from under the thin cotton bedcover, put on a long, lightweight white morning dress, and walking barefoot on the floor of hard Siberian oak, reached the window. She picked up a pair of binoculars from a small table there, and, as she had always done when the sunlight enticed her to leave her bed, she looked through the binoculars at the wide spaces above the river and at its broad cultivated banks. The sun had just peeked from behind the ridged top of the hill at the eastern entrance to Petersburg. Her gaze rested on the bell tower of the huge Saint Peter and Paul Cathedral, then passed over the sporadic buildings among the vegetation growing on Vasily's Island, and slowly, like a feather floating from the eagle's nest when the eagle accidentally nudges it towards the ground deep under the tall crown of an ancient cypress, her gaze came to rest on the lightly rippled waters of the wide river. There, flowing through the city in which Peter the Great had experienced his first love with the daughter of the renowned Dutch diplomat Peter Van Dajk, St. Petersburg's famous river lazily flowed towards the Gulf of Finland, as if it regretted leaving the beauty of this proud Russian city. Right away the Tsarina discovered a flock of white swans in the ripples, and a lot of white bottles floating on the water's surface. The swans were a permanent decoration on the Neva, but the Tsarina was puzzled by the mysterious appearance of white bottles. She quickly made a connection between them and the bad dreams that had recently been haunting her as well. The mystic Grigory Rasputin, wearing his black cape and carrying in his right hand a long rosary made of yellow amber, had constantly occupied these dreams. Every time he appeared, he would be holding a sick boy in his lap. The boy, whom she would name Alexey Nikolayevitch Romanov, was to be born a few years later to live his short mystical life. If the Tsar had not listened to the Tsarina and had instead given his son the name Alexander, maybe the royal lineage of the Romanovs would have continued. In the generations of Romanovs since Paul the First's two sons Alexander and Nikolay had both succeeded to the throne, all the first-born sons had been named either Alexander or Nikolay. The exception was Alexey, first and only son of Tsar Nikolay the Second and that was the end of their royal lineage.

The Tsarina rubbed her eyes to make sure she was not dreaming and then looked at the river again. The bottles were floating slowly downstream and the swans were swimming toward the riverbank to avoid touching them, since for the regal birds as well the floating objects represented a mystery. Without any hesitation, the Tsarina rushed to the heavy doors of her chamber and noisily flung them wide. In the antechamber there sat a sturdy young man with yellow trimmed moustaches who wore the uniform of the Palace Guard. He jumped up from his chair when the doors slammed against the wall and he saw the Tsarina before him.

"There are some bottles floating on the Neva. Call all the guards and courtiers and bring me every bottle you can reach!"

The guardsman understood and rushed out of the chamber. The Tsarina returned to the window and tried to count the odd objects floating on the river. Awoken by the noise, the Tsar reluctantly got out of bed and called out: "What's going on, Leksi! What bottles were you talking about?"

"Come to see, my Lord! Bottles are travelling down the Neva. The lost and the innocent have always sent messages in this manner. There is something mystical this morning. Let us hurry to the riverbank!"

The Tsar was not willing to hasten since his recent dream seemed more than enough for that day. The Tsarina quickly changed her clothes and ran down the stairs towards the nearest exit from the palace. The same guardsman was running towards her from the direction of the river carrying two white bottles in his hands. She took one and saw that it had no sticker or any sign on it; the white colour of the bottle's surface concealed its contents. She thrust it back into the guardsman's hands, and in a trembling voice, ordered him to pull the stopper from its mouth. Through the bottle's narrow neck, the Tsarina saw there was a paper inside. Again she ordered the young man to pull the paper out. The guardsman removed a clip from the insignia of his hat and the paper was soon in the Tsarina's hands. She was trembling while reading it because she was afraid of its content. It was a letter from faraway Siberia, from Doukhobor leader Peter Verigin to Tsarina Alexandra, herself.

I apologize for sending one more letter after the one I sent two years ago. Since then, the life of us, the Doukhobors in the Caucasus, has become more difficult. We pledge and hope, since you are both Tsarina and a mother, to ask the Tsar again to grant us our plea. The best way to govern us would be if we were placed somewhere, in one place, where we could live and work in peace. We would be willing to pay all our state obligations in the form of taxes; we only refuse to be soldiers and to pay for the Army. If the government cannot accept this, grant us the right to emigrate to some country outside Russia. We would gladly depart for England or even better for America, where we have many brothers among the followers of Jesus Christ.
Peter V. Verigin

The Tsarina raised her eyebrows and became thoughtful while looking at the paper in her hands. "Why have they written to me?" She whispered. "I am only a foreigner in this country." Footsteps behind her back interrupted her thoughts. The Tsar was quickly approaching her. At the same time, a group of courtiers and guards coming from the direction of the Neva was also approaching her. They were carrying dozens of white bottles in baskets.

The Tsar was not surprised by the letter, but was surprised by the coincidence between the event and the dream he'd had. From abroad and from inside the country, he had recently received many messages and suggestions that he should quickly and efficiently make decisions about the Doukhobors. He was aware of the effect that Lev Tolstoy and his friends' efforts had in the world. Even Nikon, the top man in the Russian Orthodox Church, had suggested that it would be best to throw those hot coals into somebody's lap far from the borders of Mother Russia.

"We will order the Okhrana to examine the case. We are going to find the perpetrators, Your Highness!" the chief of security at the Winter Palace quickly reported. He wanted to add more words in order to assure the Tsar of the effectiveness and safety of his security service, but Nikolay II, known among the people as "Bloody Nikolay," simply tapped him on the shoulder, took the Tsarina by her upper arm and led her back into the palace.

"Do you want to hear my opinion and suggestion?" the Tsarina asked him.

"The letter is addressed to you, Leksi."

"What you have been doing to those people will cast a historic blot upon Russian rulers. If I were you, I would go to the lavatory and try as hard as I could to wash my face. It is never too late for a good deed. And God will find a way to reward us for the good we do."

Instead of a comment, the Tsar pressed the Tsarina's underarm a few times with his short, well-groomed fingers. This time he was not wearing the white gloves embroidered with the golden symbol of the Russian Empire. As they approached the huge gates of the Winter Palace now open to receive them, the rays of the sun glimmered strangely in their hair.

Not long after the event on the River Neva, a breath of spring enticed Tsarina Alexandra to sit on a wooden bench in the glorious Tsar's Park while her ladies-in-waiting were playing some childish hiding game. The Tsarina heard a soft song coming from behind the tall trees. The voices were rich baritones led by a sweet soprano. The Tsarina pricked her ears like a deer listening to the sounds around her, and forever recorded in her memory the lyrics sung by an unknown choir:

The early morning awoke the seagulls by the River Neva.

Tufts of mist in the heart of Petersburg
A cold breeze from the north around the Tsar's Palace,
And above from the bosom of the wide hill
Arrived flocks of snowflakes from the waking winter.

Over the Neva the shrilling song of the Doukhobors,
Pleading for kindness from the Tsar and Tsarism.
Give us back the worm bosom, the old songs, the fairytales,
And the embrace of our Mother Russia.

We are also her children, only of a different heart,
captivated by a strong desire, love and hope.

While the Palace rests silent, mired in anger,
The cold wind brings tears to the crying Neva River.

18

Paroniya returned into Misha's life the same year that Boulisou disappeared. They ran into one another in front of the glassware shop of a young Turkish merchant. Without seeing the face of the woman struggling to carry some heavy window panels to her carriage, Misha hastened to help. He held onto the panels from underneath, helped Paroniya straighten them up, and was startled when he saw her face.

"Is that you, Parushka?!" he asked in surprise.

Paroniya was also taken aback, but happy to see him.

"What are you doing here? You were in Tbilisi for a long time. Have you returned to Kars for good?"

"Yes, I have, Mishka." She looked him straight in the eyes. "There I only had a job. Here are all the people I love. My family, friends…"

Misha sensed that she wanted to say that he was here too, but all that had passed between them made them careful when choosing their words. For her part, Paroniya knew that Boulisou had been kidnapped and that Misha had been looking for her all over the Caucasus. She said to him, as if confessing:

"I have also been asking after Boulisou. All sorts of people come to my pharmacy, including those who live and work outside the law. Nobody could tell me anything helpful I could report to you as good news. One man from some Azerbaijan mountain tribe told me that Uzun-Bey has new Russian women in his harem, but later I found out that Boulisou is not among them."

She was looking at Misha's face to see his reaction, but Misha's gaze was closely examining the distance above her head. Her hair shone handsomely wavy and light, as it had when the Siberian breezes had tossed it while they worked as prison labourers building the road from Bratsk toward Zeleznogorsk. When she had left Kars a few months after their return from prison, Misha had felt both a cold emptiness in his chest and relief at her disappearance from his life. Now when he saw her again, he felt the same chill vacancy, and he was not sure whether he was happy to see her or wanted her to go away permanently.

"I am happy to see you, Mishka," Paroniya said quietly, as if afraid of her words. "I am sorry about Boulisou…I can't forget you. I love all of you. Boulisou and your son too…"

Misha felt her words like the splash of a warm wave washing over him. He felt content. He saw her as a woman who had been offering her hand to him for years, and whose presence close to him he had in some way long desired; but he had never accepted her offer. Unexpectedly, a sigh escaped from his chest. He bent his head towards the ground, and felt a need to tell her what he had been afraid of since the time he had fallen in love with Boulisou:

"I am happy to see you again too, Parushka. But we both know we cannot let our feelings loose and allow them to develop into something more between us. We do not have that choice. I cannot, Paroniya…"

"I know, Mishka…I know! You do not need to explain. It's best if I go," that beautiful woman almost whispered. "I have a lot of free time. I'll keep trying to discover something more about Boulisou. I have a feeling we'll find her. How is your son? He must be a big boy now. Does he still take after his mother?"

Misha, overwhelmed with all these questions and with the offer of help in looking for Boulisou, did not know how to answer. What he was certain of was that this woman was again close to him, a little older, more reserved, but she was there. It crossed his mind that, since their first encounters when they had been children, Paroniya had expressed feelings for him and shown special interest, but had never been aggressive in offering a more intimate relationship. Boulisou had come a little bit later in his life and had kept Paroniya at a distance. Now it seemed to him that time had not brought a change in the feelings of Paroniya's heart toward him, although he could not have guessed it from her words. He was feeling what she was feeling. And he became nervous.

"What are you doing here?" he distractedly asked.

"Isaac has offered me the manager's job at the pharmacy. The same work as in Tbilisi."

"Is there anything new in your life, Parushka?" He let the question slip without any calculated intention.

"There is, Mishka. I am older, a little heavier...I do not care as much anymore what I wear. I am more sentimental towards my parents."

Misha was quiet, and then she realized that he was not satisfied with her answers.

"There is nothing new in my personal life," she said quietly and looked at the empty space between their feet. "Svetlana is with me. We haven't parted since we became friends in prison. Nothing has changed in her life either."

Misha knew for certain then that the old bond between the two women remained. And her words confirmed that their relationship still expressed more affection than most friendships. An old, tormenting thought came back to him, the idea that Paroniya, waiting for some mystical door to open between herself and him, had tied her life to Svetlana's to compensate for what she had hoped so long to get from Misha. Misha was troubled; he felt guilty about Parushka's unfulfilled love. But he could not help it. He sometimes thought that it would be great if both Paroniya and Boulisou were his, but traditional moral and social beliefs made this impossible for Boulisou, at least. It was far from the understanding of love and life which the Sephardic tradition had instilled in her. As for the Chernovs, his father Kostuna had often secretly visited the widow of Stepan Kalmikov. Even his mother knew of this, but pretended not to. He had never blamed his father, nor thought that Kostuna had sinned against his mother, Pelagiya.

Paroniya interrupted these thoughts:

"I'll be away frequently because I'll be travelling and purchasing medicines for the pharmacy. I'll keep trying to find out more about Boulisou."

"Thank you, Parushka," he said, looking at her face thoughtfully.

"Will I be able to see Petro?" the woman he had cared for from her girlhood asked as she climbed into her carriage.

"Of course," Misha hastened to say, feeling that it would be better if Paroniya immediately urged her horses to pull the carriage away. When she looked back from a distance of about twenty meters, Misha was still standing at the same spot, gazing after her.

19

"Look! Here comes Grandpa Vasily! He's coming through the willow grove as if he's hiding from something. He's holding a snake in his hand!" exclaimed a stout, light-complexioned young man with a big dark scar stretching from his left elbow to his shoulder. He'd seen somebody coming down from the direction of Hedgehog Hill, and he recognized Grandpa Vasily by his skipping gait. When he came close, even one who did not know him would have assumed he was a wise man always ready for a talk and a sip of goat yoghurt.

"How come you recognized him from that far, Ivan?" Uncle Andrey Baulin wondered. "He is my dad, but in that person skipping through the willow grove I would not have been so fast to recognize my own father. I thought it was some mischievous young man from the other side of the hill, trying to draw the attention of our girls with that skipping from leg to leg. It's nothing of the sort, but our old-timer—with a snake in his hand! "

The group of ten men hoeing up potato hills stopped hilling and leaned on the handles of their tools, watching Vasily approach. The party of women bending to put potato seeds into the hills also stopped working; they somewhat straightened their backs, stared at the snake and impatiently waited for the old man's first words. They knew he was bringing some news or a piece of wisecrackery.

Vasily stopped skipping and his gait became lazy, as if he wanted to try their patience yet further. There was a mysterious smile on his face and his gaze was locked on the immobile yellow eyes of the rather fat snake. He held the snake's neck in the firm grip of his knobby hand, his thumb pressed between the two bones of the snake's lower jaw so it could not pull its head free.

"Look, folks!" exclaimed ruddy and plump Pavel Savenkov. "This is that greyish snake that bit Varvara's cow down there in the swamp. Yes, it is that one! I recognize it by its tail. It pulls in its tail like a pig when sensing somebody's dog nearby. I have hit it on the tail with a stick a few times while it was slithering into the ooze and I broke it in two places."

"That's why I caught it," declared Vasily, caressing the reptile with his gaze as if proud both of himself and of the snake. "I knew it was the one that had bitten the cow, so I brought it here so we can put it on trial."

The women laughed, and some of the men got hold of their hoes to continue hilling.

"Wait! Wait, you frogs! I have two pieces of news for you," the old man disrupted their intention.

"Let us hoe, Grandpa! Look how much more work we have and the day is getting on," exclaimed Ivan.

"Have a little rest, Vanyooshka. It's a long time till the evening. Kostuna's Mishka has returned from Bogdanovka. He says that on the other side of the lake he met that Turkish woman who sells herbs; she told him that sailors had told her about some bandits from beyond the Caucasus selling women to traders on British ships docked at Batum, who were transporting these women to America. She swore by Allah that in one of the groups she had recognized Misha's Boulisou. Misha is now raving in the village. It is not clear whether he is happy to have heard that Boulisou is probably alive or howling because by this time they have probably taken her to America."

"Ohhh…" the female party sighed in surprise.

The farmworkers started talking in their groups; the men came out from the shallow furrows and the women put down their baskets of seed potatoes there. They all came closer to Vasily as if trying to read on his face whether he was joking or telling the truth.

"Wait!" said the old man. "You are going to hear it from Misha himself when you return to the village. Pavloosha has gone to the Lower Meadows to tell Kostuna the news."

"Has the Turkish herb lady seen some of our women? Has she seen Fyodor's Agafina?" Alexey wanted to know.

"I don't know. Misha did not mention any other woman," the old man replied.

"Come on, and throw that snake on a rockpile. It's not the one whose tail I broke. It was darker than this one," Pavel said, then added very seriously, "We can't try it...It is not guilty."

The snake started to wriggle and flap its shrivelled tail as if it had understood Pavel's words and was approving of his suggestion.

"Let it be, Pavel. Let it be a bit more. If you knew how it is cooling my hand in this hot weather, you would not suggest that I turn it loose."

"What's the second piece of news, Vasya? Tell us quickly. Time is passing," suggested Andrey.

"Are you ready to hear?" the old man asked them mischievously.

"Tell us, Grandpa. Tell us what else happened," pleaded Ivan.

"I'll tell you if you continue working till the evening."

"Tell us, Vasya!" The air filled with the voices of a dozen people.

Vasily lifted the snake above his head and backed away from the circle of people around him. When he'd gone six or seven arshins he turned to looked behind him. He saw a stretch of rocky ground away over on the other side of the stream, and exclaimed:

"Wait till I let the snake go, and then I'll tell you. I'll be right back."

While looking at his grandfather walking away, a strange thought occurred to Ivan. He knew that Grandpa Vasily could never be a judge because he was incapable of being impartial. He always chose his own side—family, neighbours, friends. Ivan also knew that the old man lacked the wisdom to stay calm when others confronted him. But he loved Grandpa's way of avoiding disputes with women. He would never forget his old Vasily's advice that it is better to sit on a coiled snake on a hot spring day, when it has just slithered hungry and angry out of its winter nest, than to do wrong to a woman. He was engulfed by the unpleasant memory of a story about Grandpa's sister Fedoseya. The story had it that some shepherds raped her while she was watching cows graze in the field. None of the shepherds returned home after that. Their youth had not been capable of cooling the ardent blood that tempted them into wrongdoing. Folks assumed the shepherds were afraid of the revenge of Fedoseya's brothers and had left, never to come back. Ivan then remembered his grandfather's advice when he caught Ivan staring at the curves of the female bodies walking by. Using sweet words, Grandpa lectured Ivan, saying that women are made to ease men's anger, to sew troubles into a cloak of fragrant colourful flowers, and to always offer a man the comfort of a cozy home and a pleasing touch.

"Here I come! Listen!" the old man's call interrupted Ivan's thoughts.

"News came from as far as Petersburg! The Tsar has decided to organize a celebration of Pushkin's birthday. He proclaimed him a Russian idol. He asks people to perform line-dancing all over the country in Pushkin's name."

"I did not know that Tsar Nikolay loves art!" Gresha Savenkov declared. "His advisors must have influenced him to show the people something he is not. It must be the Tsarina who convinced him. She knows what art is."

"He knows everybody loves Pushkin and he wants to use the celebration to unite this destabilized Mother Russia of ours," Vasily explained. "The celebration is going to be around Christmas."

"That's fine, Grandpa, but why is this announcement important to us?" asked Melaniya Baulina.

"It is important. Wait and you will see it is important," Vasily suggested. "The Tsar has made one more decision to unite the country."

They all raised their heads and pricked their ears to hear better.

"He agreed to let Doukhobors emigrate."

They all froze as if they had not understood the old man's words.

"Whoever from our communities wants to leave Russia, he can do it at his own expense. And without the right of returning."

They were quiet for some moments. Pavel interrupted the odd silence. He jumped into the air as high as he could, followed by Ivan, then by some women; then they all started to jump in the field by the freshly turned potato hills. They started screaming and dancing. The scene was similar to that of the valley of geysers by Aralsk, when the warm waters become quiet in the bosom of the earth, collecting more heat, and then suddenly burst towards the sky from holes big and small, geysers of all sizes that in their fall towards the earth mix and start bouncing against one another. Some of the men threw their hoes into the dug-up mounds, and the women started singing their favourite psalm:

Haste and help me,
I desire a free space in my life...
Not even the night is forever.

The joy ended as strangely as it started. Out of the group came forward Maria Kooznetsova, a middle-aged, large woman who took off the kerchief from her head, undid her long black hair, raised her face towards the sky, and bent it down again to kneel and start kissing the soil like a madwoman. Most of the folk lowered their heads towards the ground as if overpowered by Maria's feelings.

"How are we going to leave our Mother Russia? How are we going to go to the foreign world?" Maria was saying through tears. Then she raised her head towards the sun as if afraid of being heard by those who could not understand how she felt:

"I wanted the day to come for us to depart somewhere. That the terror over us would finally stop. But now, something is choking me. It has choked my..."

The woman wept helplessly. The others felt compassion. Vasily was first to recover, and he went to Maria, put his hand on her head and told everybody like a sage:

"Politics is to blame for everything. The greed for power. I don't blame them. They do not see things the way we do. Politics is not about the rational. It manipulates with the irrational."

"And the Church, too!" added Dmitry.

"Now, get back to work!" the old man exclaimed. "You promised you would continue working till the evening."

They all obeyed, grabbed their scattered tools and started hoeing the rows of potato hills. Some women started singing the psalm about the happiness that visits those who believe in it, and all the hoers joined in song yearning for that elusive happiness. Vasily moved further away so as not to be in the way of the women who were walking to fill up their baskets from the wooden tubs of seed potatoes. His gaze wandered away over the diggers, rushed across the plain to the west, and climbed the barren top of a hill bathed in sunlight. There, on top of that hill, Vasily saw a group of soldiers on horseback, lazily moving somewhere towards the north. High up above the soldiers, a flock of eagles hovered, seemingly disinterested, as if relaxing after a tiring day. Vasily knew well that eagles never fly up into the sky from treetops to have a rest. His thought was interrupted by a bright object that, like a bolt of lightning, lanced across the blueness of that portion of the sky where the eagles were masters. It left behind a tail of light.

"I see them often at night. I don't know what this one is doing here in the midst of the day," whispered Vasily without visible agitation. "That toothless Pelagiya would claim this is God's sign that he is with us and that every single evil time will end. I do not meddle in God's affairs, so I won't babble about how to interpret his signs."

20

Kostuna did not oppose the decision of his community's Council of Elders, the *Starosta,* that he be the one to make the lists of the families and individuals who wanted to emigrate to some other part of the world. They still did not know what the British authorities would offer as a destination since the plan that the Doukhobors emigrate to California or Hawaii had recently been abandoned as too expensive. There had been a serious suggestion that they move to the part of Manchuria under Chinese control, but the Tsar's authorities did not approve it. It seemed they wanted to move this "difficult" fraction of their population far from Russia's borders to prevent any possibility of their return to the motherland.

Age had already started gnawing at Kostuna's body, but his mind was still clear and unwavering. He was happy for days when he heard the news that the pressure from Lev Tolstoy's group in Russia and his admirers throughout the world had convinced the Tsar to permit the Doukhobors to emigrate to a part of the world where they would not be persecuted because of their religion and way of life.

"If it were not for Tolstoy, they would not have allowed us to leave," claimed Simeon Perepolkin, a middle-aged, strong man with flamboyant moustaches, who came with a group of people to their orphanage to check how many people had decided to emigrate.

"I have occasionally doubted their genuine devotion to us and our movement. You see, I thought that Tolstoy was only practising his philosophy on us. You see…I am aware that great people use masses of ordinary folk to magnify their glory, as some of our own leaders have done. Look…They have proclaimed themselves the descendants of Jesus…"

"Wait! Stop, brother!" everybody exclaimed in one voice, and Kostuna tried to undermine the negative effect of Simeon's words.

"It was not easy to prevail under all the attacks on us. We, too, had to use cunning and tricks. And now, thank God, the door to the world is opening for us. There everything will depend on us."

Simeon blushed, realizing it was not the time for criticism.

"It was not only Lev who helped. Many of his friends in the country and in the world have helped too. Peter Verigin himself has written a letter to the Tsarina pleading to let us live freely outside Russia. And also, great help came from British, American, and French journalists who revealed to the whole world the truth about the crimes committed against us. What's more, the European Alliance, headed by the government of the British Queen Victoria, strongly demanded that the Tsar approve our emigration," Kostuna explained, feeling obliged to provide official information to everybody about the remaking of their destiny.

"How is the collection of money for the ships and passports going?" Mikhail Nagornov wanted to know. He was Simeon's nearest neighbour, a man whom most outsiders would identify as a Turkman rather than a Russian. His unusual slanted eyes and thin black beard and moustache made him appear different not only from the others in his community but also from the members of his family. He often made jokes at his own expense, saying that the Lord was bored always seeing the same faces in Pokrovka, so he brought him to this world to be different.

"It's going well in our community. Our people are selling their properties with Armenian merchants and Jewish shop owners as agents. The Turks from Kars are buying a lot, as if they are expecting this region to be returned to Turkey."

"It seems strange to me too, Kostuna. Maybe in that manner they want to help us to raise enough money for the journey." Mikhailo was musing aloud.

The doors cracked open and into the room came two women and several men, all from the family of Fyodor Ivanovitch Fedosov. When they realized what Kostuna and the others were talking about, Matrona

Fedosova, a large woman with a broad forehead and a prominent bosom, asked:

"Is there any news about the aid that was promised from everywhere? Maybe we in our village will be able to collect enough money for ourselves, but many others won't. They say that families from Bashkitchet and Karaklis want to leave but do not have money. Nobody wants to buy their properties. It is similar with our people in Azerbaijan."

"We are just talking about that," Simeon hastened to reply, quickly softening his conversational style. "There will be help from people in Russia and the whole world, but the greatest responsibility is on us. There are rumours that some folks are asking too much for their properties, houses and cattle, as if they did not care enough about leaving. Tolstoy is going to help. And Tchertkov. And many others. In Britain, they are collecting money for us, but it is only symbolical."

The Fedosovs sat on long benches, and Matrona addressed Kostuna:

"Kostya, write this down. We are all going. Baba Ulyana was a little iffy. She said she is old and ill, and would not survive the journey. But when she realized that we all want to leave, she agreed too. If she hadn't, maybe Grandpa, Ana, and her sons wouldn't have accepted either. Thus, we are all going into the world. She has one condition though: that we bring the seeds of our Petrovka apple, of the early red plums, and of the black mulberry. The Hassons have found buyers for our houses and the cattle. Our land we will give to those from our community who do not want to leave."

All those present jumped up and started hugging the Fedosovs. Those who had first decided to leave were afraid that many would decide to stay. Family and friendship ties had brought them close to each other through the years of their battle for survival, so it was hard for them to imagine such rich relationships damaged or even completely lost.

21

Misha could not find out anything for certain about Boulisou. What the Turkish woman who collected herbs in the red fields had told him almost destroyed any hope that he would ever learn how his wife had disappeared. Most difficult for him was the absence of any reasonable idea about where to look for her. In the beginning, people had helped him, looking for and inquiring about her, but as the time passed their help became more and more just verbal support. He would occasionally even get angry. Those whose continued help he expected with most confidence started to talk to him in such a tone, and with such a lack of ideas, that he grew certain that they wanted to tick off this case from the list of their obligations. Even his father had once whispered to him that he should normalize his life and that it seemed to him that his daughter-in-law had disappeared forever. Misha would have expected to hear such words from anybody but Kostuna. He became so angry— and told him to his face and his grey moustaches never to repeat what he'd said in front of Petro—that for the first time in his life he left his father without saying a word.

Neither did Misha have any more patience with the Hasson family. In the beginning they had cooperated in his search for Boulisou. As time passed, his patience toward old Isidor and the father of his Boulisou—and theirs toward him—changed into mere tolerance, and then they started to avoid each other. It seemed to Misha that the Hassons had accepted Boulisou's disappearance and with that began to reject Misha as their son-in-law. He persuaded himself that for them, without Boulisou, there was no Misha. They and Kostuna agreed that Petro would stay with the Hassons from time to time; the Hassons took care of his clothes and toys, which Grandpa Yakov bought on his travels. Aunt Rifka got more and more attached to Petro as if in some way trying to compensate for the loss of his mother. Misha finally understood that they had reverted to the conviction that Boulisou's disappearance was linked to her stupid decision to marry him. Rifka had once confessed to him that they were now trying to force her to marry the Woskovs' Daniel, and she had promised Misha, as if that was important to him, that she would refuse and would rather run far away from the family. She also told Misha how somebody had informed the old Hasson that Misha had been seeing Paroniya Strelayeva and that they would like it most if Petro permanently moved to their house.

Life in Doukhobor villages completely changed when the news came that the Tsar would allow the Doukhobors to leave Russia. All the relationships among people and especially within families focused on the decision about moving. Not in one single family were the members unanimous in their decision. There was always somebody who was of a different opinion and who measured the decision against or for in a different way. Suddenly, the hierarchy of core values became destabilized. It was not the most important thing anymore to follow long-term life strategies and to make long-term plans and to put on an air of safety and happiness. Everything suddenly revolved around the decision to stay or to leave. Some families, now that they had a chance to choose, suffered great turbulence in their emotions as well as their thoughts, unlike anything previously experienced. Anxiety increased. Many experienced disintegration; links between some people were severed and it took a long time to spin new ones. A polarization occurred similar to a rope-pulling contest when people divide into two groups and start pulling in opposite directions to see which group is stronger. And then somebody from group one decides to join group two, and vice versa. Essential for everyone was to provide all the money they could. Those who decided to leave needed as much as possible for the journey. Those who decided to stay needed to help those who were leaving by making financial contributions and also by buying possessions the emigrants could not take with them so that these things would not fall into the hands of people outside the community.

Misha's anger at his father abated after the family's decision that they would all leave into the world, but he confronted him again when Kostuna complained about leaving behind some cows and horses that he was specially fond of.

"You complain about leaving behind the spotted and the dapple-grey cow, and the black and the bay horse...I love them too. I even love that hobbling she-dog. But you are not saying anything about our leaving even though Petro's mother and my wife is not going with us and we are maybe leaving her in the hands of criminals, in a terrible misfortune."

Kostuna became thoughtful looking at his son's longish black hair. He shook his head as if he did not understand anything and went into the house without saying a word. While looking disinterestedly at a straight streak of smoke rising towards the sky from the neighbour's house, Misha for the first time caught himself wondering if Petro would accept another woman to replace his mother. For a moment he saw Paroniya's face in his mind, her beautiful round head, long hair and dark eyes. Then his mind pulled out an image of Petro and Boulisou embracing each other and laughing till they dropped. Misha knitted his brows. He reprimanded himself and went towards a group of men and women in front of Genadiy's house. While he was slowly walking towards them, the terrible thought crossed his mind that maybe that ferocious commander of the Tsar's Cossacks, Praga, could reveal some clues leading to Boulisou. He stopped, thrust his fingers into his hair and begged his brain to come up with an idea of how to reach Praga. Genadiy noticed that something strange was happening with Misha and ran towards him.

"What is it Mishka? What is with you?"

"Wait." Misha was thinking. "Maybe you would be able to find out better than others. Do you know where that bloodthirsty Praga could be?"

"Praga," Genadiy was surprised. "Why do you need Praga?"

He waited for some time and when he concluded that Misha was expecting his answer in a flash, he stuttered:

"I don't know! Wait…I know they were saying how he was out of favour for some time when newspapers started writing about what he had done to us in Bogdanovka. Yes…Wait…Oh yes! There was a rumour later that he had gotten killed. I think somewhere there…Oh my God, yes near Saratovo…Somewhere there…"

Startled by this news, Misha shook himself as if finally realizing that he was facing Genadiy and he muttered:

"You say he has been killed…Oh, why did I think of him?!"

22

The winter hadn't started yet but in the Canadian capital city, Ottawa, snow fell. The Russian Prince Hilkov, together with Aylmer Maude, Minister's First Counsellor, and James A. Smart, Deputy Minister, entered the office of Canada's Minister of Interior Affairs, Clifford Sifton. Without waiting for them to finish the formal greetings and enquiries about each other's health, the Minister informed them:

"Gentlemen, everything has been agreed upon! Our Government is accepting the Doukhobors! Only try to avoid half of Russia knocking on our doors…" He smiled and offered his hand to Prince Hilkov.

"Prince! Your mission has succeeded. I congratulate all three of you, and, please, send my appreciation to the great Tolstoy. I have decided to personally purchase a hundred copies of his book *Resurrection*. Under normal circumstances, I would buy only one, for my library, but since the money goes to the Doukhobors, I am buying a hundred. I am positive that my country will soon be receiving new citizens of the finest quality, and that they will be pleased and happy with us."

After that, Minister Sifton went to his office doors, opened them and gave a sign for drinks to be brought in for a toast. When all four of them raised their glasses filled with dark Canadian whiskey, Prince Hilkov noticed the powerful drink trembling in his glass. "I have never before thought that our Doukhobors would finally have to go on a long journey across the ocean, into the unknown," he whispered into the dark liquid, brought the glass to his mouth and drained it.

SECOND
PART

23

About one hundred riders of the Russian Border Army on the Caucasian border with Turkey were slowly moving up the hill along the road covered in deep snow. They rode strong Ukrainian heavy horses, with long manes and prominent chests, whose broad hooves, like snowshovels, left behind a wide, compacted path. They were moving in a formation of five horses to each rank, obviously wanting to groom the snow-covered mountain road for somebody's carriage. It would not seem serious enough, nor proper, to conclude that the very learned, but egoistic, Tsar Nikolay II had decided to travel in his carriage in such snowy weather from the border town of Kars to the Black Sea. Steam from the hot and sweating horses billowed into the cold sky, while the riders were well wrapped in their long grey army overcoats and wore high fur hats on their heads. In front of them, the commander of the unit was riding a tall black horse, making sure the unit did not stray off the road.

When they arrived at the final hillcrest, the commander gave the order to dismount and let the horses have a rest. >From the top of the hill they could see far away, both in front and behind them. Before them appeared the dark-blue Black Sea and a several kilometer wide stretch of the coast not covered in snow. Along this entire zone of the coast, as far as their eyes could reach, there was but one human dwelling. Deep beneath them, about ten kilometers distant, they could discern the Georgian Black Sea harbour of Batum. Off shore, beyond some smaller ships, there were two huge steamers standing in from the open sea. Out of their chimneys, dark smoke rushed in a straight line as far as possible away from the inhospitable sea depths. Even the surface of that vast water looked alien, mysterious—a heartless, aloof immensity. To the brave, it appeared a call to daring, especially when the lowering sun made a twinkling furrow of light on its surface, looking like a path to eternity.

When the cavalrymen turned to the other side of the hill to see what was happening on the road that their horses had trod, they saw the wide groomed path through the wintry expanse covered in snow, disrupted by occasional groups of dark trees; the path first went down behind them, then up the hill that was longer and higher than the others; it then disappeared in the depths behind the top of the hill towards the giants of the Caucasus Mountains covered in snow. While the soldiers were looking at the wide groomed path, somehow looking like the Great Wall of China if seen from the peak of picturesque Guancen Shan, the path became alive up there far away, close to the top of the tall hill. A dark moving mass started flowing down the path towards the depth between the two hills. As it drew closer, people and horse-drawn wagons could be discerned in that living mass, the way when you approach a moving file of ants you start noticing what each of them carries in its jaws to some new dwelling. The mass of people and wagons moving in a ragged column from the wide Caucasian spaces covered in snow towards the sea had no end.

"About five thousand of them have set out on this journey. If the train succeeds in passing from Tbilisi to Batum, it will mean that these Doukhobors from Kars and Elysavetpol have chosen a much more difficult way than their brothers to leave the fatherland. Even at the very moment when they are leaving their country, they do not trust the Tsar's authorities. They feared their train might be toppled down into the abyss, so they decided instead to go on a difficult journey on horses and in horse wagons. So the Tsar sent us to groom the road for them in the deep snow. I am sure many of them will give up their journey across the ocean once they see the wide Black Sea and start getting loaded into those ships." This pronouncement was made in a gurgly voice by a tall moustached soldier from the group next to the commander. The soldier unwrapped his thick green shawl and revealed a long muscular neck with prominent Adam's apple.

"I don't know what I would do if I were in their shoes," a neatly shaved young man added while pulling pieces of ice from his horse's mane.

"If they did not cut the umbilical cord that connects the newborn baby with its mother, a new life would not be able to start. These Doukhobors have chosen a new life, and each new life starts with great unpredictability and pain," was the commander's verdict. He mounted his horse and the others followed. The long column of soldiers on horseback started going downhill towards the harbour of Batum.

The other column, the snowy caravan of the Doukhobors, was moving along the groomed snowy road, following its winding path. From a distance, the caravan looked like a snake moving slowly down a dune of sand in relentless Sahara's heat, wriggling to avoid rolling over and drowning in the sand. But that seemingly uniform mass consisted in fact of a multitude of horse wagons and individual riders. The wagons kept distance from each other to avoid the possible misfortune of one becoming the disaster of many. The wagon horses, whose main task now while they were going downhill was to brake the force of inertia, were hot and tired, and above their bodies a long winding cloud of steam was rising. In the wagons sat people wrapped in warm cloaks; they were quiet and thoughtful. Their faces, red from the cold, clearly revealed the state between their uncertain past and an unpredictable future. Only one among them in each wagon, the one holding the reins, was exasperatedly active, making sure the wagon kept going in the right direction—slowly. The men on horseback made the caravan more alive because they were moving between the wagons, criss-crossing the voids among them. In the immediate vicinity along the sides of the caravan, the silence of the snowy day was being broken by the sounds of the shouts of those in command of the animals and by the deafening noise of the brakes.

The Chernovs were in the front part of the line. Kostuna had command of the first horse wagon, while Genadiy, Stepan, and Nikolay were on horseback. Misha and Paroniya rode their horses along the line to offer emergency assistance if needed. In their backpacks and the bags safely fastened to their saddles, both of them carried medical supplies in case of an emergency. Misha was a very skillful rider, bent low in the saddle over the horse's neck in the manner of the Cossacks from the Don River. During the planning for division of duties in the caravan, Paroniya had offered to help Misha because she would be able to bring a lot of supplies from Isaac's pharmacy. Misha liked to be close to that woman, even though every time he thought about Boulisou, it would put cold water on any involuntary thoughts about physical contact with Paroniya. In fact, he would ever more often find himself daydreaming of carnal pleasures with his pharmacist, and after that would become thoughtful for a long time and avoid conversation with other people.

When they went closer to the wagon driven by Phillip Shishkin, a fifty-year-old carpenter who had been one of the first to have decided to go to Canada, his sister Anastasya addressed Misha from inside the wagon:

"Mishka, is that pack of wolves that attacked Morozov's horses last night still following us?"

"I haven't seen them since we crossed to this side of the hill. Maybe they gave up when they felt the warmer air from the sea," replied Misha and went forward to the front of the line.

"Are there wolves in Canada?" the fourteen-year-old Ivan asked his mother, Anastasya, and pushed his fur hat to the top of his forehead.

"Why wouldn't there be!" Instead of his mother, the reply came from his younger brother, Yegor. "In those papers about Canada, it says there are more wolves there than in Russia."

"I'm afraid of them," said the one. "I hope we won't live in a place where there are many of them," said the other, as they confessed brother to brother.

The caravan did not stop on the crest of the last hill above the sea. As their wagons reached the top, nobody among the Doukhobors could hide their relief—gentle triumph in their eyes and a reserved smile on their faces. Even the animals, probably feeling the warmer air and the nearness of night, became more lively and did not ask for a rest. When the head of the caravan reached the lowlands, instead of the snowy path they faced a muddy gravel road and the cavalry unit which had been grooming the path for them all the way. The cavalry's task now was to escort the Doukhobors to the dock in the harbour where they would board the ships. The caravan was now loosely extended because as soon as wagons reached the coastal zone, which was not covered in snow, they could move much more quickly. Both people and animals knew it was the end of their exhausting journey from villages engulfed in the bitter cold winter to the harbour, where they would say farewell to Mother Russia and go to a new life.

In the coastal area of the Black Sea, the evening sun awaited them. The men took their cloaks off and stretched as if just getting up from their beds after a long, tiring bad dream. As soon as the wagons stopped for any reason, the animals also stretched their limbs and necks, trying to drive out the weariness accumulated during the long journey through the snow. However, the horses, of which there were hundreds, did not make any sound. And the people were quiet too. They experienced such turbulent feelings that they were robbed of the instinct for a big conversation. The only words to be heard came from women warning their children not to go far, while the youngest were either sleeping, or crying to express their frustration.

In front of the harbour of Batum many representatives of the authorities and the organizers of the journey by sea bade them welcome and informed them that getting aboard the ships would start the next day, strictly according to the lists. The Doukhobors faced spending one more long night in their wagons under the open sky, but now removed from mountains, freezing weather and deep snow. The city of Batum had never in its history seen so many people, animals and wagons, all camped in the valley behind the harbour waiting to embark the huge ships anchored in the bay beyond the docks. The authorities and the citizens of Batum for hours brought food and water to the Doukhobors and their animals, and near the previously prepared piles of wood, fires were lit. Potential buyers for the Doukhobors' horses, ordinary folk and horse-dealers alike, observed the animals from a distance, making their own calculations about prices to offer.

The train with the other Doukhobors had not yet reached Batum even though it should have arrived hours earlier in the afternoon. Nobody knew when it might appear.

24

Misha was immobilizing the broken arm of a young man of the Obetkov family, who had jumped out of the wagon just when they were going down the slope of the last foothill into the valley where Batum lay. Young Obetkov jumped down to help the horses keep the wagon from sliding over the edge of the road, under which the slope stretched down into rocky depths. A few other men had come to his aid, but the wagon nevertheless turned over and broke the young man's arm above the elbow. Misha decided now to take his time and set the man's broken bone and immobilize it using splints. While he was tightening the bandage around the splints with the help of Paroniya, and explaining to Obetkov what to do to ease his pain, Genadiy approached with long strides over the uneven snow.

"Mishka, Batum's doctor has arrived and says he wants to see you. I had a hard time finding you," the old man gasped, his face revealing the fatigue of the long journey they had all undergone.

"I'll be there right away. Just wait until I finish bandaging the wing of this brave falcon. He behaved like a hero while I was setting the bones. He didn't let out a sound!" Misha praised the young man. "Parushka, where will I find you when I come back? We might need to visit a few more patients."

"I'll be near Uncle Nikolay and his family," she replied.

From the moment the caravan left Kars, Paroniya had been overcome with happiness and triumph, feelings she neither could nor wanted to hide. For a long time she had been thinking how nice it would be if she and Misha could go somewhere far together. Now, when they were leaving, if she had the power to make them move faster, she would do anything to have them on the ship as soon as possible. And to always have somebody needing her and Misha's help. It seemed to her that Misha desired the same, not only to be close to her but also to move away from the cursed Caucasus. To start building a distance from the past. She believed that Misha too, in that cruel Caucasian land, had felt like a bird in a huge cage, into which so many other creatures were crammed that it made the birds' feathers stand on end.

Misha was soon hastily following Genadiy and making his way through the crowd of people, wagons, and horses in order to meet Batum's doctor. He had been in that harbour several times before, but had never thought about seeking out the doctor.

"What does he look like?" he called out to Genadiy. It occurred to him that it might be somebody who had attended the Medical School in Kazan. Maybe they would even recognize each other.

"How does he look?" Genadiy repeated Misha's question. "I am sure he is not so exhausted and deprived of sleep as you. The man is just like any man. I'd never guess he is a doctor." Genadiy was vague. It seemed strange to him that Misha inquired about the looks of that doctor.

In fact, the man, the doctor of Batum, looked more like an innkeeper tending his bar than a physician. When he and Misha met, they first examined each other before they held out their hands in greeting. They seemed the same age, except that Misha's figure evoked respect and confidence in his skill as doctor. The other one could have been the most qualified specialist in the world, but no one who saw him would believe that he could cure people. They might entrust him with the duties of some municipal office, or with an inn full of food and drinks, even with the uniform of the captain of some transoceanic freighter, all that—but neither his face nor his figure matched his profession.

"I was told that your Doukhobors had arrived in Batum in this wretched winter thanks to your commitment in the caravan during the journey. They say you managed to help everybody who needed you." This improbable doctor's bass voice drummed in a subdued manner. He was examining Misha with his big black eyes. "I am Mikhail Jugashvili," he added, not taking his gaze from Misha.

Genadiy felt he should leave them, so he found an excuse by saying that his family might need him.

"I have heard about you, Doctor Chernov. I have also heard about your tragedy. I mean about what had happened to your wife. I haven't married yet, but I can feel for you. In some way, it is perhaps better to go through one's life without a family. The heart aches less and you sleep more peacefully. Do not reproach me for my comparison. I know how we bachelors feel, but at the same time I feel compassion for you and allow myself to speak about married people such as yourself."

Misha was quiet and only with the nodding of his head did he show he was following Jugashvili's strange manner of introducing himself.

"If you think nobody needs your help, we could go to the fat Bolso Kapanadze's and have some refreshments."

In the inn they saw people who looked very different from Misha's Doukhobors. One group were loud and spoke fast in some strange dialect of the Russian language and did not notice when the new guests entered. The others were sitting in a dimly lit corner of the big room and it was difficult to discern what they looked like or where they might be from. The only things that caught Misha's eyes were the glass jugs of wine on their table and the black fur hats on their heads.

"I know that many Doukhobors do not drink alcohol. What can I treat you to in this Batum paradise?" asked Jugashvili. His heavy voice drummed between the walls of the inn.

"Something with no alcohol in it, if there is such a thing here," replied Misha.

"We have good cider made from Georgian apples," they heard the rough voice of a middle-aged woman who was lazily approaching them. "It has little alcohol."

"Cider for Doctor Chernov, if there is nothing better, and for me a jug of Bolso's black beer so that I leave as little as possible for him. He has gained so much weight because of that drink that he's larger than any barrel in the cellar. Where is he today? I wanted to introduce him to my colleague," Jugashvili added chattily. His strong voice beat out in such a hearty manner that one could easily conclude he enjoyed interrupting, at least for a moment, the conversation of the others around him.

The waitress—probably the innkeeper's wife, Misha thought—did not reply to the loud doctor of Batum, as if not finding herself obliged to respond. The group close to them continued their rancorous conversation, dominated by words about a strike, the exploitation of the dockworkers and threats that the owners would soon have a reason to be very worried.

Jugashvili was curious to know if Misha felt that the new life for the Doukhobors in Canada would mean the end of their troubles, and if he was still hoping to find Boulisou. He was sceptical about the course of the development of the political situation in Russia and complained about the life of a doctor in such a rough harbour town as Batum.

"Ever more frequently there are ships coming from the West with merchandise but also with people who do shady jobs. They secretly trade in liquor, cigarettes, and women who go directly to the brothels in Western metropolises. It is hard to watch all this and lack strength to stop the evil. Some might say, why worry about things you cannot change, but…I feel like packing my stuff and moving to somewhere in Russia away from the sea. But I was born on this shore and know it would be difficult for me to adjust to a completely new life in the interior."

Misha refrained from pointing out that for Doukhobors life in the interior had more than its share of evil. He had no desire to explain to Jugashvili that it was better for his people to risk being persecuted and maltreated in Canada than to put up with that in their own country. For it is easier to endure suffering brought about by foreigners than to experience it from your own people. And Boulisou? A thought crossed his mind that maybe somebody had crammed her too into a foreign ship and that she might be suffering in some western harbour. Maybe the Turkish woman near Kars had been talking true.

Misha would rather discuss any other topic than talk at length about the Doukhobors and their departure into the world. And especially not about his Boulisou. While for a moment he stopped paying attention to

Jugashvili's stream of thoughts, fragments of the conversation from the table next to theirs reached him. One of the men, now speaking in a lower voice, was explaining why he did not want to carry a load of amber on his ship to the Bay of Varna, on the Bulgarian coast of the Black sea. He mentioned the name of a Turkish solicitor named Murat and his unfortunate encounter with a Russian naval vessel.

Before Misha felt pressed to reply to his colleague's questions, the waitress brought glass mugs with thick handles and two wooden jugs containing the ordered drinks. As they were pouring their cider and dark beer into the mugs, Misha and Jugashvili noticed two burly men from the table in the deep, dark corner of the inn move away from that group and slowly approach the ones discussing dubious aspects of sea-trading. The way they moved and their attitude clearly indicated they did not have good intentions. Jugashvili was looking at them in surprise and his face revealed increasing anxiety. The two men wearing black fur hats went to the table and one of them spoke with an obvious effort to make his voice sound calm.

"We said until eight," he said. "It's past eight."

One of the people closest to the men with fur hats took out his pocket watch, opened the lid, and replied, also calmly, without turning his head toward the two men:

"This watch is not showing eight yet. Seven is an unlucky number for me, so I won't do anything before eight."

As he spoke the last words his face flushed red. The others sitting at the table with him turned towards the men in the fur hats, keeping their hands in the pockets of their short warm coats. The three others from the table of men with fur hats slowly started walking towards the table around which tensions were rising. From the corner of his eye Misha noticed the innkeeper's wife poking her head around the service door and swiftly pulling it back. Then, everything happened very quickly. Some of the men sitting at the table pulled guns out of their pockets and aimed at the men wearing the fur hats. The two closest fur-hat men grabbed the man in front of them and threw him like a toy at his friends holding guns. A few shots were heard, muffled among the throng of struggling bodies, and some men, obviously hit by the bullets, started screaming. The others jumped on each other, and, instead of guns, they held knives in their hands. It was difficult to discern who was fighting with whom, but it was clear that screams were coming from more and more throats.

Misha and Jugashvili also reacted very quickly. They jumped up from their chairs and pranced a few steps backward, trying to stay afloat in the situation. Some of the fighters were already on the floor. One was crawling on his knees trying to escape toward the door when it burst open and into the inn rushed policemen with guns and sabers ready for the battle. A few shots thundered over the agitated group of fighters and broke bottles of liquor on the shelves behind the bar. The crowd, having been busy fighting until now, suddenly stood still, surprised at the vigorous police intervention. The opposed parties started moving away from each other.

"You two, lie down on the floor and put your hands on your back," one of the policemen ordered, pointing with his fingers at the man who had looked at his watch and the man who had said it was after eight o'clock. Policemen rushed at them and tied their hands, lifted them in front of the commander and served each of them with a barrage of blows to their ribs. Both of them slumped as though to fall, but the policemen grabbed them and half-dragged them towards the door. "The rest of you, follow us in two files!" shouted the one in charge and they all exited the inn.

"Do you know what is going to happen now?" a biting voice abruptly called from the dark quarter of the room. "The police are going to confiscate their money, with which they were supposed to pay me; in a few minutes they will remember that the doctor is here and somebody will come to fetch him, so he can attend to the wounded. They are obviously not seriously hurt since they managed to walk away. And who is the losing party? Me. I am always the one who gets screwed, Doctor!" The owner of the inn, Bolso. "It would be better if I hadn't gone to fetch the police. If they had killed each other, I'd be able to collect money from their corpses!"

And in fact, in just a few minutes, two policemen came through the door and addressed Jugashvili:

"We need you, Doctor! One took a bullet in his shoulder, and two managed to get stabbed in the stomach despite their thick coats."

When Misha returned to his people, they told him nobody had looked for him. Both men and animals were in deep sleep, and the full moon was high above the harbour and the anchored Canadian ships. Paroniya did not come to look for Misha, nor did he think it was a good idea to look for her. Only sporadic barking of the harbour dogs could be heard; they did not come close to the parts of Batum where the Doukhobors were, but they signalled that they were aware of that mass of strangers and their horses.

The train with the Doukhobors from the region of Tbilisi arrived sometime before dawn. It was decided that the people wait for daybreak in the railcars. On that train came the son of Lev Tolstoy, Sergey, whose task was to do everything in his power to enable these people to have a safe and easy journey across the ocean, and to have the least painful start possible in the new country. The great old Tolstoy could not come with them. But nobody among the great in the world was as close to them as he, and nobody had helped them as much to prepare themselves both psychologically and materially for this definite breaking of bonds with their roots in Mother Russia. Peter Verigin, whom the great part of the Doukhobors respected as their leader, was—at this time of such huge historical importance for them—spending his years in exile in Siberia.

25

Boarding the ships went very slowly. The Chernovs were in a group of several clans, while six other groups were scheduled to get aboard before them. However, in the early morning, before the feeble light announced sunrise behind the mountaintops in the distance towards the Caucasian summits, the Doukhobors had to complete a deal with the merchants who took most of the horses and wagons. Some were given as gifts to the families who had decided to stay, and soon a much smaller caravan of empty wagons set off for the journey to Kars. The emigrants spent the rest of the morning organizing the groups and loading food and clothes onto the ships. Small boats were used for that purpose. They were being loaded at the docks, and then ferried their cargo to the two ships quite distant from shore. Doukhobor volunteers did most of the work with the organizational help of the Tolstoys' friend, opponent of the Tsar's regime and tyranny, the persecuted and convicted Leopold Sulerzhitsky, who was now out of prison. He rushed from one group to another, from one team of workers to another, his face red from the cold wind rather than from running around. With his swollen cheeks, the short and pointed chin and the narrow slits of his eyelids, he looked like a worker from the Turkish contingent who had volunteered to help load the cargo onto the boats, rather than one of the Russian volunteers who were bringing the goods on horse-drawn wagons. That group of Turkish workers was employed by the German entrepreneur Sepp Richter, who owned a wide net of oil storage tanks on the shores of the Black Sea. When Sulerzhitsky had met him in Batum a couple of weeks before the arrival of the Doukhobors, the German oilman, always lost in his thoughts, told him that he had been born in Hessen, like Tsarina Alexandra, and that he would financially help the emigration of the Doukhobors to Canada only because the Tsarina was devoted to them.

More and more grey clouds were gathering in the sky and the winter wind was blowing from the north. The groups pressed together to protect themselves from the cold. In the middle of the groups were the children and the elderly, around them the younger women, and the strongest men formed the outer rank against the ever-colder wind. They were slowly moving in a circle, keeping their feet and bodies warm, and transmitting the warmth to the others. Those outside the circle were, as if by some rule, taking turns to shift their places with those not directly exposed to the cold. Their struggle against the icy wind looked like the struggle of golden penguins for the survival of their newborn young on the terrible Antarctic ice.

The Chernovs were in the group who were boarding the colossal transoceanic steamer *Lake Superior,* owned by the Canadian company Beaver Line. Misha, Kostuna, and Genadiy were among the first to join the team tasked with organizing a big kitchen and dining room in the ship because the existing ones were far too small for the needs of the Doukhobors, who liked to eat in large groups. Leopold Sulerzhitsky introduced Misha to the ship's captain, Taylor, who was surprised that he had not been informed there would be a doctor among the emigrants.

"We have a doctor and his three assistants on our companion vessel *Lake Huron*, and here on *Superior* we have two nurses experienced in treating illnesses among those unaccustomed to long journeys across the ocean. I'll introduce you to Vera and Emily right away. They will be pleased if you decide to help us and offer your medical knowledge," the captain addressed Misha, in an almost fatherly manner.

Taylor was of medium build, muscular and solid, steadfast of mien. A man to respect. On his long journeys on the sea, in the endless battle with sun, rain and wind on the enormous expanse of water, during the uncertainty of storms and epidemics of diseases, he had earned deep wrinkles on his forehead and around his eyes which gave him an air of experience, wisdom and self-confidence. Captain Taylor embodied all the qualities that travellers about to spend a month crossing the ocean on a ship would like to see in the commanding officer—finding assurance there of a safe passage, and thus ameliorating their ever-present fear of the hazardous unknown. A passenger would want to see the image of such a captain when saying words of prayer to God in times of trouble, asking the help of the one whom he deems more powerful than a human being.

"I'd be happy, sir, if I could help even though I would be happier if nobody needed my help. I am one of those medical practitioners who are the most pleased when the folks around them are healthy. On this ship there will also be my colleague, Paroniya Strelayeva, who is a pharmacist, and who has brought a large supply of medications in her luggage to meet our needs," Misha said to Captain Taylor, while with his gaze he was spontaneously searching the growing mass of people on the upper deck of the ship. However, it seemed that Parushka's family had not yet arrived.

Vera and Emily were pleasant young women, each attractive in her own way. If the Captain had not told him they were highly experienced medical nurses, Misha, in his first contact with them, would have thought they were missionaries because their faces emanated the desire to be accepted as representatives of something full of love and saintliness important to all. Especially Vera. Her eyes revealed motherly care and comfort, something of the innocent gaze of a holy woman, and a spark of warmth inviting love without carnal debauchery. Briefly introduced to Misha, the two of them stood back and, without a trace of open curiosity, let the youthful Russian doctor's face permeate their memories vividly and permanently, feeling something close to the dreaming eroticism young people often experience when they encounter a person who resembles the one from their nightly imaginings. After Misha went away to help the group building dining tables and benches, Emily spontaneously admitted to her friend:

"I have always imagined Russians differently. In my imagination they were either slightly built, yellow-haired and bow-legged, or giants with long beards and greasy hair, short-tempered when working, cruel in war, and truculent and insatiable in love. This doctor seems like a cross between what is best in Russia and what is most elegant and sophisticated in our West." Vera looked approving of these words, but remained silent, so Emily continued:

"He is tall, so you need to lift your head to admire him; nicely muscular, so he instills respect; his gait is swift and elegant as if he practised ballet in Jean Dion's Montreal group; and he is arrogantly sensual as if the colour and the shape of his lips were patterned on the nudes of the Québecois painter Horatio Walker. It won't be easy for us to be close to him on the journey across the Atlantic." Emily was talking as if to herself, while the chilly wind tossed the streaks of her black hair in the direction where Misha had gone. She smiled when her gaze met Vera's, whose wide open eyes with big greenish irises reminded Emily of John Paul from Office No. 172 of the Canadian Ministry of Health. In Emily's smile it would be hard to discover a spark of disbelief that her reply to John's love offer would be positive when she returned from Russia.

The Strelayevs embarked the ship just before the loading platform was closed. There, three officials of the Harbour Master's Office along with army security guards were checking passports and immigration documents. In front of them, set out on a long wooden table in dishes painted red, there were bread, salt, and water, which symbolized the Doukhobor way of life. When they reached the table, each emigrant standing in line touched all three dishes with the fingers of one hand and put the fingers to their lips as a symbolic farewell to their fatherland. Some of them cried while performing that act; their tears dripped on the table, and in those tears were images and stories about them and those dear to them, images which belonged to the time they were leaving behind. Some wiped their tears carefully with the other hand, gathering determination to sail into a life more worthy of man by boarding one of these foreign ships. Some were looking back at the mountains behind their backs and whispering. The whispering of each was very personal and each whispering was unique, just as every man has something that makes him different from other people.

The emigrants building the dining room on the *Lake Superior* were surrounded by a group of children, whose parents had told them to stay away from the railings of the ship, beyond which threatened the turbulent sea. When walking between two groups of children, Misha noticed his son, Petro, his back turned to Misha. Petro was involved in earnest conversation with a few of his friends. Misha managed to catch a few phrases from one of them who, seriously as a grown up man, was explaining that in Canada he would continue telling his little sister and brother bedtime stories about the legendary giant Bash-Chelik and the Siberian white tiger.

"Maybe those people over there have some good stories, but nobody will be able to forbid me to tell my brother and sister our stories," the boy with curly hair covering half of his forehead and both ears declared in a raised voice.

"Their stories will become ours too, Koozka. My mother used to tell me bedtime stories. And grandfather too. Since my mother is no more…" Petro stopped talking as if not knowing how to continue; then he started wiping his tears with his hands.

In his bosom Misha felt Petro's sadness because of his mother and hurried to join the workers.

As soon as he saw him, Kostuna left the group that was making long dining tables and called to Misha while approaching him:

"Have you seen that woman from Voronyez?"

"What woman?" asked Misha as they met.

"The one who was brought in by her brothers. Four of them. They came by train with some other families from the Azovsk district. I think their last name is Antonov," Kostuna gave the news to his son.

"What about that woman?" Misha interrupted him. "You started talking about her and now you are telling me about her family instead of explaining why you mentioned her."

"If they haven't called you, they will. I think she hasn't healed yet. They said she had visited Batum's doctor before they got her aboard the ship. He gave her some liquid to drink…" Kostuna was speaking confusedly.

"What happened to her, father? What hurt is she suffering?" Misha interrupted him again.

"She drank very strong pickling vinegar on the train when they were already close to Batum. The kind you have to dilute. She wanted to kill herself. Maybe because her face had been so badly burnt nobody would be able to recognize her. I heard one of her brothers saying how she had been burnt last year when their sheep wool caught fire in a storeroom. They hardly managed to save her. I haven't managed to see her face; they say it is disfigured. She covers her head with a thick black kerchief. The same brother told us that she had lost her voice because of the vinegar, but Batum's doctor hopes that her ability to speak will return."

Misha was listening to his father, unsure whether he should seek out the woman right away or wait for someone to call him to examine her. "Maybe she is not seriously hurt since they haven't asked for my help yet," he was thinking, turning his head around trying to see the woman with a black kerchief over her head, or somebody else, the captain, the nurses, or Parushka…At that moment he saw Paroniya approaching him, accompanied by her father, Pyotr Anastasiyevitch Strelayev.

"Mishka! It is terrible. That poor woman must be suffering a lot. Have they told you? We were transported in the same boat. Her brothers are some strange people. They are short-tempered and unpleasant. She is hiding under the kerchief, and they are mostly quiet and stick to their group. They do not allow anybody to get close to her, especially not to ask questions. Then one of them explained what had happened to her," Paroniya quickly informed Misha. To help her, Misha interrupted:

"I know, Parushka. My father has told me everything." He turned to Paroniya's father. "How do you feel on this huge ship, Pyotr Anastasiyevitch?"

"I have no feelings yet, Mishka. When we get further away from our shores, both of us will know better how we feel," Paroniya's father replied in an unusual way, looking Misha in the eyes as if searching for the answer to Misha's question there.

"I think so, too. We need time to realize how we feel."

While speaking, Misha had been searching all the visible parts of the ship. Suddenly, his eyes opened wide and he exclaimed:

"Look, Parushka! There are the Canadian nurses. They are going to help us during the voyage. Let me introduce you to them, and then we'll go together to see that woman."

Accompanied by First Officer Griffin, they all went to the cabin where the Antonovs were accommodated; at the door they met two of the brothers. Paroniya explained to them that they were the ship's medical team and that Doctor Chernov wanted to see their sister. The other two Antonov men appeared at the door. The brothers were quiet for a moment; then three looked at the fourth, who must have been the eldest. Without saying a word, he went back into the compartment and soon returned with their sister, whispering something to her. She turned her head towards the newcomers, trying to see them through the black knitted kerchief. The oldest brother spoke in her name, rudely, showing no desire for cooperation:

"She can't speak. You must've heard what happened to her. The details are not important. Last year her head got burnt when our sheep wool caught fire. We barely managed to save her. And on the train, she drank strong vinegar that she had hidden in her luggage, maybe because she did not want to settle in Canada looking like that. She lost the ability to speak. Her hearing is impaired too. The doctor in Batum helped her and gave her the drink she needs to take."

"May I check your sister?" Misha asked in a raised voice. "The captain of the ship has asked me to help those who need medical assistance."

The oldest brother looked at his sister, then at Misha, and then nodded his head and signalled to Misha with his hand that he could approach her.

After meeting the Antonovs, Misha could not dispel the feeling of uneasiness he experienced when the woman took off her kerchief. She had turned her head away as if she did not want to look at Misha. He held her shoulders, ever so gently turned her head towards him and for a few moments held her there, looking at her face. What he saw would be difficult even to imagine. There were many scars and dark recesses on her face. Even though she had no eyebrows and her lashes were very thin, the narrow strip around her eyes was undamaged. Her lips were very badly swollen, so she could not close her mouth. He noticed that her eyes brimmed with tears almost dripping from her eyelashes. Misha, as soon as he spotted the undamaged band around her eyes, felt an unarticulated suspicion creep upon him. If this woman had been burnt, then it must have lasted for some time to cause the damage to her face. The strip around the eyes couldn't have escaped such a fire. That portion of her face would have burnt as well, along with her eyelids and eyes. It must have been something other than a fire. It must have been some strong acid, thrown at her face. She'd had time to close her eyelids tightly and instinctively retract her eyes deep into their sockets. "No, no! Something is wrong here," Misha thought, his suspicion growing. And her brothers seemed very odd. They kept distance from others and only one of them communicated with the outside world. And only as much as necessary. And also, not very politely. However, Misha tried to hide any trace of his suspicion, not only from the brothers, but also from everyone else, including even Paroniya, Vera and Emily. Thoughts were running through his head like a storm. For a moment he felt he could not control these thoughts that started to mix with images. As if by a command, his mind focused on the image of the injured woman's eyes in her disfigured face. Those gentle eyes, the colour of chestnuts, reminded him of somebody, and Misha frantically examined his own memories. He became scared of the thought that those eyes were familiar to him, close to him, and that they wanted to take him to the time when that person's face was not disfigured.

"What did the doctor in Batum give her to drink?" Misha asked the brothers, who were standing in their group a few steps away.

"Some liquid. Here, you see," again it was the eldest who spoke, and handed Misha a bottle.

Misha opened the bottle and smelled its contents. He gave it back to Antonov without comment. He took the kerchief from the woman's shoulders and wrapped it around her head. Then he went to Paroniya, Vera and Emily and asked them if they had permanganate.

"Yes, we do," Emily replied right away.

"Help her bathe her mouth, and throat as deeply as possible, with permanganate. The Doukhobors have sheep yoghurt. Let her drink a lot of it. We have to take good care of her for a few days," Misha said pensively, feeling growing pressure in his chest, and ever stronger determination in his thoughts.

"No, no, no..." Misha was whispering to himself while walking towards the central compartment of the ship where Captain Taylor was monitoring the placement of the last group of the emigrants. "I should not hide my suspicion from the captain. He seems to be a very reasonable and sympathetic man."

The captain first listened to Misha's report with a cheerful face, then with surprise, and then with surprise growing into worry. He was quiet for a while, looking at Misha's face, then at the shore where there were no more Doukhobor emigrants. There by the side of the ship, the last boat was unloading its live cargo.

"I saw those people when they were boarding the ship. One of my officers introduced them to me and explained that the woman was hiding her face because it got burnt in a fire. I did not insist on checking what had happened to her. I did not think it necessary. After your report, Doctor Chernov, I can only tell you that we will try to investigate the Antonovs and find out the truth. Here on this ship, I can disclose it to you, I have two security officers. Of course they are undercover and only the crew and myself know about them. I'll put you in touch with them as soon as it is convenient for them. Please, do not do anything on your own. I do not want any unrest on the ship. I have experience with Russians."

The captain let these words slip from his mouth, then realized that maybe he should not have ventured into a characterization of these people. Misha used that pause to insert his opinion about the captain's assessment of Russians and asked him resolutely:

"Sir, I have great respect for your countrymen. As for Russians, I probably know us better than you do. These people here are Russian, but they are Doukhobors. There is no aggression in our philosophy of life."

"Doctor Chernov!" Captain Taylor's voice revealed no desire to further inflame the discussion. "I was not talking about you, the Doukhobors. I know a lot about your philosophy of life. However, among these people there could be a handful of those who do not think the same way you do, or who have infiltrated themselves amongst your people. I do not want to prejudge anything, but there is a possibility of infiltration. Many non-Doukhobors from your part of the world want to go to America, to Canada. As for aggression, I am leery of those whose aggression arises naturally out of a need for defence. I fear those who attack out of pleasure, or because they do not know of another way of achieving a goal. I fear aggression that is part of one's philosophy of life, present even in harmless play, even in a game without competition. With such people you never know when their aggressive instincts will flare up in their brains. A few of them in the mass of people we have on board could be disastrous for the peace, security and harmony of the ship. I believe, even without that problem, we are going to have some undesired accidents. There are more than two thousand people who are travelling for the first time so far away…Do not be surprised if some lose their nerve, if they become seasick, if we get cases of dysentery, and if some become afraid at night on the ocean. Not to mention storms. Prepare yourself, Doctor, to struggle, along with me and my crew, so we can transport these folks to the Canadian shore with a happy outcome for all."

Then they both became silent, looking at the people around them, who were more and more retreating to the accommodations designated for them and their families. The captain put his hand on Misha's shoulder, looked at him in a friendly manner, and asked:

"Do you think, Doctor, that injured woman can safely go on the journey with us?"

"I think it is better that she goes with us than that we send her back to the shore, sir. I believe, here on this ship, we are going to either confirm or dismiss my suspicion about the Antonovs," Misha told the Captain before taking his leave.

When the boarding was over, all the Doukhobors went out onto the top deck to wait for the departure into a new life. Neither nature nor the people could hide that something extraordinary was happening on this day. Fog was advancing from the Caucasian mountains, hiding an ever bigger chunk of land from the people, as if trying to make it less painful for them to say goodbye to that part of Planet Earth, where their origins and those of all the generations of their people before them lay. Orange and yellow bands across the cloudy sky to the west signalled that the sun was trying to touch the sea. There where the clouds were less thick, colours were transparent. There were even spots in the sky where the sun penetrated through the clouds and its broad rays fell on the rough seas. The thickening banks of fog were approaching from the east.

And the people? On both ships they did the same: they gathered on the open deck waiting to say goodbye. Misha was with his family. He looked up at his son, Petro, whom Kostuna had put on his shoulders so the boy could see better. Misha struggled with the thoughts that overwhelmed him. He was not happy. His reason was telling him that he should rejoice. But his feelings…Oh, is there anything as hard for a man as to think he should be happy, but instead to feel sadness engulfing him, keeping him away from happiness! Misha had never felt like this before. He knew he had much to be happy about, like all his countrymen on the Canadian ships in the Georgian harbour of Batum on the eastern shore of the Black Sea. It occurred to him that even the name of the sea symbolized these moments that mercilessly separated the time before this day from the time that was coming. The Black Sea…Misha wondered, looking at his son's hair tossed by the wind, if they would enter a new life when they crossed the Black Sea, went through the Bosporus Strait and exited into another world. Was that strait the same as the narrow neck between the two parts of an hourglass, through which sand flows from one bulb to another? Then it crossed his mind that they used to send the most notorious convicts to this part of the world from the other one, so they could never return. It is how the God Zeus punished his favourite Titan, Prometheus, of whom he knew with certainty that he was his own son rather than the son of the God Hephaestus. The Tsar's family, the Romanovs, one Tsar after another, more the Tsars Nikolay than the Tsars Alexander, had been persecuting the Doukhobors because of their noble way of life and their rational way of believing in God; they had expelled the Doukhobors to that same Caucasus, where Prometheus had been expelled and bound. It took thousands of years for Zeus's wrath to lessen enough for him to free Prometheus from the bonds and from the eagle who had been devouring his liver every day, while it took the Doukhobors several centuries to obtain the right to look for some other part of the earth where they could be free and where others would not kill them because they were Doukhobors. Misha hoped that moving to Canada, to the new world, would mean freedom for all of them. Yes, it would if they were accepted for what they were. He knew for certain that the Doukhobors were not bad people. They liked to work, they did not want to be a burden to anybody and they did not wish unhappiness to anybody.

At last the ships' sirens signalled departure from the harbour of Batum, the clanking of the chains used for weighing the anchors was heard and thick smoke gushed forth from the black tops of the tall funnels. Decks shuddered, and the transoceanic giants started crawling out over the rough seas. The people started measuring the movement by the widening foamy trail left on the water behind the ships. It seemed the waves became bigger then, as if to arrest the motion of these human inventions, and broke with increasing force against the prows of the steamers, raising curtains of glassy foam.

The Chernovs stayed together in the huge mass of the Doukhobors; they were part of that life which was mercilessly separating from the land, where generations of their ancestors had been born and lived, where their roots were and where they had been persecuted, ruthlessly terrorized. There were about thirty of them in the broader family of the clan who had decided to emigrate to the new world. However, this big mass of people on the ship *Lake Superior*, as well as those on the other ship, knew that the land was not to be blamed and that it mourned their departure in its own way. Man's blind desire for power was to blame, for it demands absolute obedience and wants people to think and breathe the way rulers order them to.

Misha wanted to spend these moments with the other Chernovs, but not for a single moment was he away from his Boulisou. His thoughts were bitter because the peons of that power, evil men, had brought misfortune upon him, his Boulisou and their son Petro, even though they did not deserve it at all. "The powerful keep the world obedient and change it as they like it," Misha thought while gazing at the contours of the hills not yet completely covered with the shrouds of fog. "It is the desire for power, not human spirituality. The desire for power forces the human spirit to look for solutions. It is in human nature to go wild when some power is obtained and the desire for more takes control. It becomes insatiable. The inertia of power pushes man, without regard for boundaries, into infinity and makes him forget he is only a human being. It pushes him blindly to go straight forward and to measure everything around him and in him according to the arshin of power, and it makes him sooner or later face a wall against which he crashes.

Misha, at this moment, also thought about their leaders, who, to say the truth, had given impetus to their movement, but some among them had failed to prevent their desire for power from getting the better of them, and allowed themselves to become greedy, to desire part of God's power. None were among them now. "Yes," Misha whispered ever more loudly, "the power of the Doukhobors is in their determination to endure even in the biggest tempests of their times and to not let anything break their spirit. My Kostuna, and my mother, my Petro, and my Genadiy, my uncles…" He did not say Boulisou's name, but he had a feeling the she too was coming with them. Tears were running down his cheeks. He looked at his little son and saw Petro in tears too. And Kostuna's wrinkled face was running with teardrops. Not only were the Chernovs in tears; all the faces he could see were weeping silently. Thousands of eyes were trying to stay as long as possible on the land they were leaving behind.

As the ship gained speed, its distance from that familiar land grew more and more quickly. Crossing the waves behind them was *Lake Huron*, similar in size and shape. Misha heard a song coming from the crowd of people gathered at the rounded stern of the ship, first quiet, then stronger and stronger. Soon all the passengers on the ship were singing. It was a choir of people accustomed to singing even in the greatest storms. Now their song was sad. It came from the depths of their feelings for the land they were leaving behind.

Down Molohnie Waters near the Azov Sea,
Not even storms did extinguish the sun.
Through our memories streams murmur.
Hey, hey, Mother Russia!

The crowd was singing and tears were continuously running down their faces. Their eyes were struggling to see through that liquid coming from the special compartments in their bodies where feelings reigned. They were wiping their eyes to make them clear so they could impress upon their memories every detail of the scenes they were leaving behind. But those images had become distant and small, blending with the fog, which was trying to help these people lose sight of their land and the land of their ancestors as quickly as possible. The water over which they were sailing was becoming wider and more merciless. Kostuna felt his grandson Petro pressing against his head and felt the boy's tears on his brow.

"Nature is also crying with us," Kostuna interrupted the singing. "Do you see how the wind is snatching water from the tops of the waves and splashing it on us like tears?"

Nobody heard him because the song suppressed all other sounds. Not even the noise of the mighty ship's engines was heard anymore. Between two songs they heard another coming from *Lake Huron*. Kostuna and Pelagiya were holding hands, and little Petro was holding onto his grandpa's hair.

"I feel sorry, Kostuna!" Pelagiya almost shouted so that her husband could hear her. So that everything in that maddening world could hear her.

"I feel sorry too, Pelagiya!" Kostuna shouted to overpower the volume of the singing.

Misha could no longer see the land because the fog had taken over the stretch of ocean behind them. His gaze roamed over the people and he saw some embracing each other tearfully, and recognized more sadness than joy in their embracing. A flock of seagulls drew his attention. They rose into the air from the ship's funnels and from the upper deck, swirled around, then hastened towards the land. Soon he noticed another flock of these white and grey objects flying east. They were all going back.

"They always return to their shore." Captain Taylor's voice startled Misha. He had approached from behind while the folks started to disperse and go below to the accommodations designated for them. "They know exactly how far from land they can stay with the ship, and when they realize it is time to return, they rise above our decks, make a couple of circles to find the most suitable air current, and then return to the land. It seems as though they sail with us to keep us company, and when they know they've gone almost too far, they make those farewell circles and fly back. The most daring ones wait until we reach the spot from which a human eye cannot see land anymore. Then they also rise in the air, and communicating in shrieks known only amongst their own, they return to their home shore. Some who are sick or unsure if they will have enough strength to return stay behind on the ship. Those ones stay feeling sad and fearful as if they knew that over there they will encounter different seagulls who will not have warm feelings for them. When we approach the other shore, before we catch a sight of it, we hear the shrieks of its seagulls coming to meet us. It is always like this, Doctor. More than thirty-five years I have sailed the seas and observed seagulls."

The night was approaching from the east. A big group of the Doukhobors had remained on deck, and were singing the lyrics of a Lermontov song:

From the life I'm not expecting anything,
And I don't regret whatever past;
I'm looking for a freedom and a peace.)

26

When the Canadian transoceanic ships passed Beykoz at the eastern entrance to the Bosporus Strait—which, according to many cartographers, separates Europe from Asia, and which, according to many historians, has inexplicably for thousands of years of the history of our civilization tempted many conquerors to traverse it to reach the other continent with their armadas—only then did it occur to the many Doukhobors aboard that they had left their moorings and gone on a journey of no return. Not even when the belligerent sultans of the Ottoman Empire conquered it did that long narrow passage from the Black Sea toward the Aegean and Mediterranean Seas become peaceful. Now, facing the powerful European alliance led by the Austro-Hungarian Monarchy, which was openly screaming in anger to announce its fateful advance deeper into the Balkans at the end of the nineteenth century, the Turkish Sultan Abdul Hamid II could get no sleep. He was suffering from an insidious pain in his liver and from annoying hiccups, which gave him such a headache that he became terribly angry at one of his most respected physicians, the learned Ibrahim Malkotch, because he was unable to stop the freakish spasmodic heaving of his guts. When he almost lost hope that that nuisance would ever stop, he remembered his Aunt Shefika's cure: to administer an enema to his rectum and to spend a couple of hours on the toilet. That suffering was upon him just when the ships carrying the Doukhobors passed through the portion of the Strait overlooked by his palace on the outskirts of Istanbul, where the Sultan spent Anatolian winters. When the learned Ibrahim explained to his padishah, the Sultan, that the song of a thousand throats was reaching the exalted sultanic ears from the Russian Doukhobors on Canadian ships, Sultan

Author, Rifet Bahtijaragic with Charlie and Michael Chernoff in front of Peter Verigin's house in Veregin, Saskatchewan

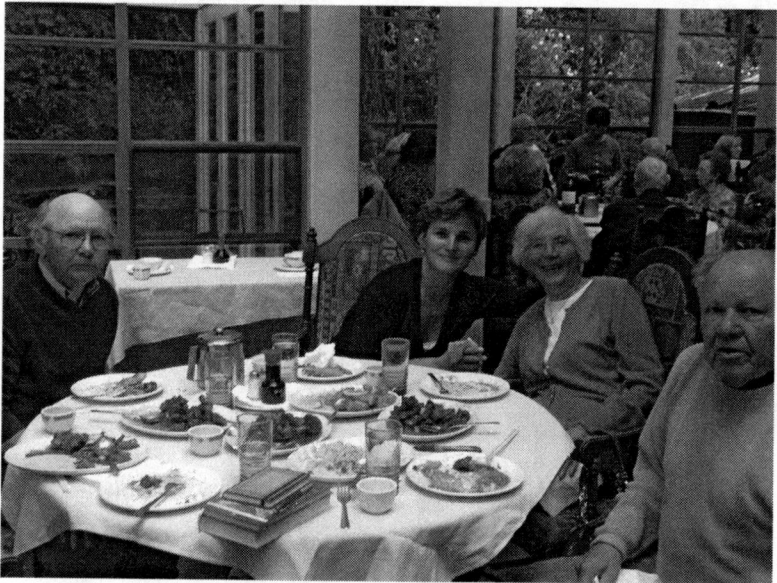

After meeting in Vancouver 2009; from left:
Michael N. Chernoff, Norma Bahtijaragic,
Michael's wife Dorine and Charlie N. Chernoff

Charlie (Koozka) Chernoff supports his younger brother Michael (Mishka) in front of their boyhood log home where both were born. They both attended a rural one room school (Whitesand Valley) that taught grades 1 to 9. Circa: summer 1937

Michael (Mishka) and Charlie (Koozka) Chernoff with their tame owls at their boyhood home. Circa: 1943

Nikolay (Nick) Mihailavich Chernoff and tame owls. Circa: 1943

Misha Chernoff and family. Circa: 1925 Standing, left to right: Peter (Petro) Chernoff, Peter's wife Leesoona and Nikolay (Nick) Mihailovich Chernoff.

Seated, left to right: Peter Chernoff (Petro's son), Paroniya Chernoff (Misha's wife), Misha Kostunavich Chernoff and George Chernoff (Petro's son).

Mavroona's descendants on her 100th Birthday Celebration in Kamsack, Saskatchewan, October 27, 2008

Standing, left to right: Cheryl Chernoff, Carlotta Chernoff, Reid Foose, Catherine Chernoff, Brooke Foose, Michael "Bruce" Chernoff and Dina Chernoff.

Seated, left to right: Michael "Lucas" Chernoff, Charlie (Kuzma Nikolayevich) Chernoff, Maud (Mavroona Kuzmayevich) Chernoff, Michael (Misha Nikolayevich) Chernoff, Stella Chernoff, Nyah Chernoff and Dorine Chernoff.

*Chernoff, third from left, marches into the Winnipeg Arena with his
team representing Canada,
during the World Curling Championship in April 1978.*

Doukhobors' celebration in Castlegar,
British Columbia, Canada – 2009

Doukhobor Prayer Service in Castlgar,
British Columbia, Canada – 2009

Abdul perked up, forgetting his hiccups, and he summoned his advisor for relations with Russia and Persia.

"While I was on the toilet, I heard the song of those emigrants from Russia, who do not want to carry the cross, and I remembered that Russian tsars had settled them in the Caucasus in order to take forever that part of the world from us. Note, my loyal Avdaga, that in not many years from now Russians will root out their tsars and we will gain back what is ours in that region."

The advisor wondered silently at why the Sultan had so urgently summoned him to communicate the prediction that had occurred to him while sitting on the toilet and listening to the Doukhobors' song from the Canadian ships. Nobody knew at that moment what was going to happen to the last descendants of the Romanov tsars, but one thing was certain: The Sultan had forgotten his horrible hiccups. At that moment Sultan Abdul didn't remember that he had recently dreamed about a strange beardless young man, a cadet of the elite Army Academy in Thessaloniki.

In his dream the Sultan asked his official historian, Harkun, who and from where that cadet was, with his charcoal-coloured moustache and eagle-like eyebrows. Harkun said he was afraid to answer this question.

"I've had enough of being afraid all my life!" shouted Sultan Abdul. "Tell me what is in your fear? I was scared of my brother Murat, worrying that our father might pronounce him heir instead of me; then I was scared if they would deliver the captured Russian Tsar to me even though I did not know what to do with him; then I was scared if the reforms of the state and the army would work, and if my eye would dry up when the eye plague attacked me; then if the rebellious Greeks would break into Smirna...I am no longer afraid of any fear. Speak, Harkun!"

"The young man will be condemned to death and they will hasten to pardon him and offer him a promotion several times. He will close the door behind our last sultan, he will commit great atrocities against our own people, and after all that he will be called the Father of Turks— Ataturk!"

"That very lad?!" The Sultan pointed with his long bony index finger at the young man of the honour-guard platoon standing in front of the fountain in the Academy courtyard. "He seems to me like all the rest of them: young, scrawny, with burning eyes…How do you know he will turn into all that?"

"I can read it in his eyes, my Padishah," replied the Sultan's historian, with no sign of fear anymore.

"Could it be that you will prove to be mistaken, Harkun?"

"It could, my Padishah. It could; just as I could be proven wrong when I record events in history books differently from what really happened so that I do not make my Padishah angry," Harkun smiled, knowing the Sultan would forgive him the joke he made.

"You know what I mean, Harkun? You are a historian and you record past events. I do not think Allah has created you so that you can foretell the future." The Sultan said this without any anger because of the prediction Harkun had made; simply because Abdul believed that people are not capable of knowing what Allah has in store for them.

At that time the horn of the *Lake Superior* was blown a few times while the ship was exiting the Strait, passing the last edifices of Istanbul. It signalled a warning to the crews of some larger sailboats to clear the way for the huge steamship. In the corner of the dining room, a crewmember, Second Officer James Cannigan, was talking with a group of young Doukhobors. James had already joined the Doukhobor choir and his gaze was merrily moving over the faces of younger women, by now free of the fear of the ship and the sea. They were talking about everything that the officer wanted to know, while feasting on the still fresh Doukhobor bread, the salt and water still on the table. The Canadian man wanted to add fish and dry meat to the feast, but the Doukhobors refused.

At the moment when the ship was passing by some big mosques, James asked the young Doukhobors something he hadn't dared mention before. "They told me you are Christians, but that you do not respect the Bible. What's wrong with that book, which, according to many, has come to us from God?

The Doukhobors were surprised at such a question, but the cheerful Gresha Kalmakov replied without much hesitation:

"It is the same with the Kur'an, which the Muslims in those mosques follow. They also say that their book is holy and that it has come from God. We do not believe in that. People wrote these books so that they could impose laws on the followers of their religions."

"But what is wrong with them?" insisted the officer.

"It is wrong to claim that these books are given by God and people cannot change and supplement them. These books should be subject to changes because they reflect the level of achievement of human society at the time when the texts were written. They contain the history, philosophy and ethics of those times and of those societies. Nowadays, all that has changed. Those books need to be changed and refreshed by the truths of the times people have gone through since, and are going through now. Then they could represent the laws and the norms of human behaviour. Otherwise, who nowadays can reasonably follow codes of behaviour imposed by people who lived and wrote hundreds, thousands of years ago?"

The officer was surprised at Gresha's explanation. It seemed to him it was better to change the subject, but his gaze returned several times to Gresha and he shook his head. Only now did he understand why the organizer who had sent the ships for the Russian Doukhobors had demanded that there be no priests among the ships' crews, as well as no Bibles or crosses in the dining rooms and sleeping compartments.

Both old and young passengers returned to the upper deck, sang psalms and were looking at Istanbul, which was disappearing astern. If one could judge based on the choice of songs and the pitch of their voices, the Doukhobors sounded the more cheerful the further away from Mother Russia they went. It was especially true for the children. Petro was most frequently in the group which included the children of the Popovs and the Tarasovs, for they shared the same compartment. Kostuna was in charge of monitoring that group. Paroniya often warned him to keep an eye on them all the time because among the children was a dwarfish girl named Anushka. She was already eighteen but of the size of the six-year-old Ivan Tarasov. When some child inadvertently started to stare at Anushka, Ivan would approach and bravely explain how she was so small because she was a twin sister of the giant Gavril, and while they were in their mother's stomach, Gargo, as his friends called him, was voracious and ate more than she did so that his sister was born tiny like a white ferret when it comes out from behind a rock. Gargo had the same thoughts as Ivan and he felt it was his duty to look after Anushka and protect her all his life. Even now while the children were running across the deck and the dining room playing hide and seek, Gargo was sitting on a pile of ropes following their game. He did not intervene when Anushka hid in places close to the ship's railing or when she ran as fast as she could to find a place to hide, but he always knew where his sister was.

While one group of older Doukhobors were discussing whether the snow-covered mountaintop far away to the west was the Greek Mount Olympus, Gargo noticed that the oldest brother of the Antonov family was looking at the children and that his gaze often stayed fixed on the mischievous Petro Chernov. Gargo had developed a sense of protectiveness while looking after his sister Anushka, so he immediately became suspicious of that brawny, bearded man. He decided to find out why the man was so interested in his group, especially in Petro, whom everybody loved because of his wise words and honest reasoning in conflict situations. At one moment the young giant noticed how that annoying Antonov knitted his brows and smiled maliciously while looking at Anushka as she was running on her bent little legs toward a pile of bags behind the kitchen to hide there. It was too much for Gargo, who lost his patience, got up and walked towards Antonov. That one, realizing that the young giant did not have friendly intentions, turned away and went to a group in which two of Captain Taylor's sailors dominated. Gargo went back to his spot and sat down. Having observed the Antonov a little bit better, Gargo brooded on his suspicions about that man and doubted he had good intentions. He definitely did not seem like somebody who liked children.

"I am of the same opinion, Gavrilo," Misha's voice surprised him. "Something must be wrong with an adult who does not like children.

We have to carefully monitor that bearded man." Misha, too, had been watching, and had approached Gargo from behind. He put his hand on Gargo's shoulder.

The young man was surprised at how Misha was able to read his thoughts, but was not in the mood to ask the doctor about it. What he heard was enough for him. He respected Misha and felt close to him since the doctor had put so much effort into curing the carbuncles on Anushka's neck and shoulders. And for the doctor's son, Petro, that little rascal who could make Gargo laugh until his stomach began to hurt, the giant would do anything if the boy needed his help.

"I feel sick in my stomach," Gargo complained to Misha.

"If you have been eating too many prunes, I know what that's about. The pain will go away."

"I haven't. I had sheep cheese and grandma's dried rye bread, suharei, for lunch. I also drank a lot of water. Maybe it's from the water," Gargo suggested to the doctor.

"It is much better than what some suffer travelling on a ship for a long time."

"I think, Doctor, it is not the seasickness. I used to spend a lot of time on the lake in a boat. I especially liked to fall asleep in the boat while the wind was blowing and making the boat sway," Gargo said in his melodic rough baritone, which had already started to sound like a man's voice.

Suddenly they heard noise coming from the other side of the ship and folks rushed in that direction. Misha also hastened to see what was happening. Gargo hurried to gather the children and Anushka so that they could follow Misha. There, on the other side of the ship, a school of dolphins was pretending to race the *Lake Superior* across the waves coming from the west. The onlookers enjoyed the synchronized performance of the dolphins, admiring their elegant bodies as they arced to the surface and the swift movement of their fins when they went under the water again.

While Misha was walking slowly through the crowd toward the ship's railing and monitoring Gargo, Petro, Anushka and some other friends of theirs, he felt himself in a strange state of mind, similar to the one that Grigory Rasputin had described to him in Siberia, a state between reality and imagination. Misha thought it was because of tiredness, or because of the monotonous rising and plunging of the ship, a symptom of seasickness; but none of this could explain the state of consciousness that overcame him. He looked more carefully at the faces around him and saw that their cheeks were swaying, their eyes plunging into their eye sockets, their foreheads knitting. Then he made a wish that the man in front of him turn his head and smile at him, and he did so. In a flash he remembered that the mystic Grigory had talked exactly about this, trying to teach Misha, and that he had attempted it in front of Grigory, but it hadn't often worked. However, now this psychic state suddenly came over him, giving him a special power and self-confidence, something he had never felt before.

To test his ability, he looked at Alexey Shishkin and made a wish that he adjust his fur hat on his head. And Alexey did it. Misha saw a group of dolphins still swimming parallel with the ship and playing their leaping game. He made a wish that they start spinning in the air as they jumped out of the water, and they started spinning before diving back into the sea. He repeated his wish a few times and it worked. He looked at the faces of the people around him and noticed their astonishment at what they were witnessing. It works after all, Misha said to himself a couple of times, and a strange happiness engulfed him. He looked at the dolphins again and made the same wish, and as they jumped out of the water, they spun in the air. He quickly glanced at Gargo and saw astonishment and incredulity on his face. His Petro was rubbing his eyes and staring at the dolphins. Many other people were doing the same. Misha realized that he had mastered the same skill Rasputin practised in their camp in Siberia and on the train across the Urals.

"Incredible," Misha whispered and turned his head away from the dolphins and the sea. "Based on the expression on the faces of these people now, the dolphins are behaving normally again and the minds of the people are back to normal. This is me. What I am capable of doing could be far beyond what most people can do. What my mind can do participates in schizophrenia as well as in the illusionist's ability to transfer the creations of his mind into the minds of others. It is phenomenal. I have always thought of the people who could do things like this as mystics, but now…Well…" Suddenly it occurred to him that it was just a moment, an unusual activity of his brain, and he became afraid that he would not be able to repeat it, so he decided to try it again. He turned towards the sea and saw the dolphins coming out of the water and jumping in an ordinary manner. He saw people pointing at the dolphins and complaining because the dolphins had stopped spinning in the air. Misha saw Gargo in front of him, holding onto the railing of the ship, and he made a wish that the young man climb the rails as though to jump into the water. Gargo did that, stepped onto the broad top railing, and straightened up, looking at the rippling sea. People started to scream, the young man's giant body started to sway, and Misha made a wish that he jump back onto the deck. Gargo did that. Misha saw people swarming around him, asking why he wanted to jump into the sea. Gargo was looking at them in surprise, trying to convince them that he had no desire to jump into the water.

Misha saw Captain Taylor with a few of his people as they were talking to a group of Doukhobors and he approached them. Taylor asked him for his explanation of the odd events that had happened within the last ten minutes, and Misha shrugged his shoulders.

"I saw you out by the railing," Taylor said. "Is it possible that the volcano Etna exploded and that it affected some people and even some animals in those strange ways?" the Captain asked, not seeming to expect an answer.

"I don't think so, sir," Misha answered nevertheless. "Etna is too far to have an effect on the minds of the people on the ship. Maybe it was just a manifestation of the seasickness, sir. Some kind of illusion, a mirage that affected some of us."

As soon as Vera, Paroniya, and Emily joined them, Vera started to comment eagerly:

"The three of us were behind the laundry place watching the play of the dolphins. We couldn't see you, but we were there all the time, and did not see the dolphins spinning in the air, and all these folks are saying they were spinning. We also did not see the boy wanting to jump into the sea. If he had climbed the railing, we would have seen it."

"It is more than strange," the Captain commented concisely, obviously worried. "I and all my crew on deck saw everything the people are talking about."

When night fell, the people on the ship could see the distant pink light from Mount Etna in Sicily. In the clan of the Popovs, down in the lower compartment of the ship, old Ivana was trying to convince the others that volcanoes in the sea warm up the water around them, and that in that water animals change very fast and some become huge. Many ships sink because of that and sailors often see mermaids as they sit on rocks and sing. Others were adding their comments and their versions of the events. Other families on the ship were spending the night in a similar way.

27

Captain Taylor had a habit of getting up when the dawn started to overpower the darkness of the night. He preferred being in the open sea, where no land was visible. He enjoyed following the slow early tide of daylight, long before the first rays of the sun appeared, as it slowly conquered an ever bigger portion of the sky. The more the daylight spread where the sea and the sky touched far to the east, the more twinkling stars started to disappear. Sometimes that first light of the approaching day would create a semi-circle there above the sea, as if a rainbow had permeated the entire spectrum of its arch with the light of a full moon. Some time later, much brighter and dressed in lively hues of yellow and pink, the rays of the sun would pour out from the surface of the sea and start their magic colouring of the east. These images brought about sublime feelings in the Captain and created some mystical connection in him not only with nature on earth but also with the universe, so he cherished these feelings as part of the deepest and the most intimate history of his life. He loved it the most when through the bright semi-circle of the approaching day he spotted long-stretching flocks of cranes, storks, geese, and wild ducks on their journey from the frigid north to the spaces of the warm south, and then in the opposite direction. In the fall towards the south, in the spring towards the north. Along all the meridians of the northern part of our planet…In the southern hemisphere those temporary migrations went in the reverse order. He saw these flocks wherever big ships sailed. Even before he was hired by the Canadian company Beaver Line, while serving as first officer on the British steamer *Boston,* W.H. Taylor enjoyed observing the laws of nature in the parts he was sailing through, and he was extremely happy when he discovered even a small detail that great world naturalists had failed to notice. He was especially proud of being one of the first seafarers of the end of the nineteenth century to come up with the theory that the Gulf Stream was showing a tendency to move closer to the shores of Greenland each year, and that each year in midsummer the border of green encircling that huge island, covered in snow and ice-bound, was becoming wider. As corollary to his theory, the Captain warned his crews of ever more frequent icebergs to be spotted along the east and south shores of Greenland, even in the middle of winter. Through all this he admired the birds, which infinitely keep improving their flying skills and their ability to follow wind patterns and air currents. He had never detected any confusion among birds when they were in the zone of confrontation between the currents coming from the north and those from the south. He disagreed with those who claimed that avian navigational skills are only natural instinct; he believed that birds' small brains have faculties which men's big brains often cannot understand. Thoughts like these made him feel that he was creating the world he observed. When the sun appeared on the horizon though, it would mercilessly take over the main role in the scenery, and the Captain would feel the fading of his own importance in that earlier mystical moment when day and night met, so he would retreat to the ship's bridge, where the first officer was waiting to report the events that had happened during the night.

On that morning, when Captain Taylor went out on deck to watch the victory of day over the darkness of night, he was surprised to see Misha Chernov standing by the railing, looking towards the east. For all other passengers on that huge transoceanic steamship it was still too early to come out onto the cold upper deck. Approaching, the Captain was surprised one more time when he heard that Misha was playing a small flute. The Captain stopped about twenty steps behind Misha and listened to his music. It seemed to the Captain that the music which was coming out of the tiny tube had its origin in the depths of the sea; it had something of the sound of a music shell when placed to the lips of a Polynesian fisherman, or of a tiny harp in the hands of an Isfahan girl who was in love; it also had something of the spring Mediterranean breeze when it touches the branches of a Bosnian birch tree standing on the hills facing the south; it had something of the gentle voice of a blue-eyed Russian girl from the valley of the Don River on the very shores of the Azov Sea. The melody, counterpointed by occasional loud surges from the waves, sounded like whispering about our human desire to reach happiness, like a call of the spirit to all people to make a chain of happiness and hope and to spread it from faraway places in the east to faraway places of the deep west. To feel happier and safer. Misha was playing and looking towards the east, where the sea was being permeated by misty light coming from under the surface, announcing the inevitable advent of day. Then he stopped playing, sensing that somebody was approaching from behind; he turned and saw Captain Taylor, who hastened to greet him.

"Doctor Chernov!" the Captain declared, a note of pleasure in his voice. "I am very lucky to have come on deck so early. To what do I owe this opportunity to hear your enchanting music?"

"I woke up very early, sir. It is obvious that something in my brain, which I cannot control, did not want to miss the opportunity to meet you here at the sunrise," Misha replied. "And the music? This is my flute, which my Uncle Genadiy made for me when I was still a teenager. I often play it when I am by myself."

"But you Doukhobors sing without musical instruments."

"We take pleasure in choral singing, but occasionally we play some instruments," Misha explained, smiling. "This tiny instrument is my great friend when my spirit desires to communicate with something I cannot reach, or with nature."

"Are all of our passengers in good health, this morning, Doctor?"

"I believe they all slept well except the old Andrasov. Since yesterday he has been suffering from heart arrhythmia and increasing chest pain. He is close to a heart attack. I'm worried that he hasn't responded to any of the medications I gave him," Misha explained. "He is old and weak. However, I am certain that his problem is of a psychological nature. I believe he set off on this journey because all his family did. Otherwise, I am positive, he would gladly have stayed in Mother Russia."

"Hm…" The Captain's answer was unintelligible. Then he turned in the direction of the movement of the ship, and stared at the darkness still thick to the west. "When the day pushes the night into the ocean, if it is not foggy there at the exit from the Mediterranean Sea, we will be able to see the Rock of Gibraltar. If you have never seen it, you will realize as soon as you lay your eyes on it that on the other side of the Rock life is different. There, beyond the mythical Pillars of Hercules, the old Mediterranean world ceases to exist. No more will you have a feeling of being embraced by ancient Mediterranean civilizations. You won't be obsessed anymore by entire encyclopedias of stories from times long gone. You won't suffer from some strange morality or history. You won't live by the rule of emotions; instead most of these functions will be conducted by the brain. On that other side lies a huge ocean, and beyond it the new world. Everything is different there: the present life and tradition. Life is action there. In this world that we are leaving behind, inheritance is inside the human spirit. Over there, beyond that darkness in front of us, inheritance is material possessions that your ancestors leave to you. In this eastern world they leave you history as inheritance. And that is often the history of power, a product of aggression. Over there…There they do not study history. Only one type of philosophy is real there. All philosophies have been reduced to one: It is essential to reach the state of consciousness where anything abstract is wrong, and where all life calculations are reduced to simple mathematics. The truth is in the concrete, the visible, the attainable. Over there the meaning of life is something tangible, determined by itself, and has a measurable produced value—wealth."

"Sir, I expect tolerance there. Freedom…I doubt that people are not aggressive there too. We have been forced into the new world by intolerance and aggression. If I understood you correctly, aggression is creative there. I do not think that aggression is inherent, natural in man. Given by birth. Truly, aggression has its roots in egoism, is inbuilt in any human being, but, in my opinion, aggression is a product of the environment in which man lives. Our Doukhobors have built opposition to war and war conditions into their philosophy; they have chosen communal life and the dominance of collective ownership over private, and have reduced egoism to something useful in society. We have personally proved that in that manner aggression among us has mostly been subdued and hatred reduced to the minimum. Instinctive resistance to attacks on individual and collective ways of living is not hatred. Struggle for survival is not hatred. I am not in favour of Tolstoy's teaching that one should love one's enemy and one who hates him; however, I am not advocating that one should hate. Real Doukhobors among us do not hate. They are surprised when they feel somebody's hatred."

Captain Taylor was thoughtful. His gaze wandered over the water expanse ahead of the ship. He was thinking about the young doctor's words. His wife had been abducted, he had been expelled to the far corners of his homeland, he had not been allowed to work and his people had been killed. And he talked about how man should not hate. He had been subjected to the worst kind of aggression, and he condemned aggression in man.

"To be honest with you, Doctor Chernov: if you expect to find a society free of aggression and hatred in North America, you are mistaken. For sure, there is more tolerance there than where you come from, but people are just people even in the new world. Your sect, if I may use that term, is a Christian one, but it is different from the Christianity in Canada. I do not think you will be persecuted and killed in Canada, but you will be different. You would be less likely to face difficulties in Canada as well if you were the same as everyone else..."

"Sir, I am glad that I can talk to you freely and that this deck is still deserted. And that the Rock of Gibraltar is not visible yet. However, I believe in a higher level of democracy in Canada. What I know about that society gives me a reason for hope. It is enough for us if you are not going to persecute us because we pray to God differently and have a different way of life than other people; we do not commit evil deeds, we love work and honesty, hate no one, and attack no one. Our religion is not aggressive. But it will certainly be competitive. That is a good thing, sir. It is good for other religions as well. Without competition there is no progress. If there were only one direction in religion, if there were no small streams of new ideas and new currents coming into the rivers of religion, all religions would turn into swamps with lots of silt and pond-scum on the surface."

"Are you really an optimist, Doctor?"

"I am, under one condition…It will mostly depend on whether the Doukhobors will be able to weave into their way of life the sense of need to adjust to the time in which they live and to the uniqueness of other groups of people. It depends on whether they will have the ability to adapt. If they show the ability to adapt, they will avoid the danger of assimilation or persecution. It is going to be a great challenge for these people, sir. If they isolate themselves from others, it will be harmful."

"It is difficult to be a prophet, Doctor. In your case prophecy is in Doukhobor hands. In fact, it is in the quality and wisdom of your philosophy of life. I can tell you that for the people amongst whom you are going to live the most important thing is that you earn your own bread and that you work hard for the one who employs you. I have heard that your people are stubborn and unruly. That is not good if you expect to be accepted in your new surroundings," the Captain challenged Misha.

"We are stubborn when it comes to unconditionally refusing to go to war, not taking oaths to rulers, not wanting churches and church hierarchy. There are differences among us too, as in any other group of people. If we are unruly and stubborn, others made us that way. The centuries of persecutions, torture, isolation, abduction of our children, rape of our women…The powerful ones have made us the way others see us. However, they see us in a biased and inaccurate manner because we are different."

Misha was pleased to have had an opportunity to talk with this Canadian whose face revealed that he was a good man even though it was the face of a captain and required respect and subordination. Captain Taylor was also pleased with the new information about the Doukhobors and about this young man whose face revealed suffering and uncertainty but also enormous willpower.

"I have been informed that the Antonovs are strange people," the Captain said, changing the direction of the conversation. "They constantly keep an eye on their sister and they are always together. But their papers are fine and their names are on the list of the immigrants. Do you still have the concerns about them that you voiced when we sailed?"

"To be honest with you, I still have some doubts that I cannot clearly define; it is not logical that they have kept themselves isolated and are refusing any initiative from the outside. They say that it is best for their sister to be left alone. I worry because of that mystical veil around the Antonovs, but I still do not have answers to my own intimate questions," Misha confided in the Captain.

"Here is Gibraltar, Doctor!" Captain Taylor cried unexpectedly. "I hope that the British Navy won't stop us and waste our time ransacking the ship. They know about our mission."

The Captained hurried to the ship's bridge. Through the small windows, inside the wheelhouse could be seen the back of First Officer Griffin, who had charge of the vessel in Taylor's absence. Far in the distance, several miles in front of the ship, under the tall rock, which in fact was a high hill that dropped into the sea almost vertically, there were the lights of the harbour.

On the wall of the office of the Governor of Gibraltar there was a picture of Queen Victoria, and on the marvellous golden crown resting upon her charming head sparkled diamonds from the mines of Central Africa. In the inn of the bald James in Cardiff, some Irish sailors once claimed that the chief of the treasury of the famous diamond mine at the provincial centre, Bangui, had swallowed the diamonds. Two Welsh missionary priests disembowelled him and took the gems. The story does not say how the diamonds, which went to the jewellery shop of a Jewish man in Plymouth, ended up on the Queen's head. Nor does it say what happened with the two missionaries.

28

The ocean's water was different from that of the Mediterranean. As soon as they passed the Portuguese Horn of Cabo de Sao Vicente, the waves doubled in size, and the Mediterranean deep blue colour started losing its nuances of the blue and became greyish green. Those aboard the *Lake Superior* experienced alternate spells of cloudy skies and sunny periods with sudden rain and cold northwest wind. However, there were signs indicating they were still in Europe; they passed by groups of green islands surrounded by coastal rocks of light colours; the few houses on the island hills had red roofs made of baked clay; the houses' white walls made of crushed stone dominated the scenery. *Lake Superior*'s pitching and rolling on the ocean's rough surface became steadily more violent. There were more and more passengers on the ship suffering from seasickness. There were rumours that some passengers demanded to be put ashore in the first British harbour or they would jump into the ocean. They were relieved when the word was passed that Captain Taylor promised they would stay two days in the Scottish harbour of Aberdeen because the steamers needed to be loaded with coal for their journey across the Atlantic. As the ships were emerging from the Strait of Dover, passing the French city of Calais, the news spread that a girl was born to the Kurbatov family; she was immediately named Atlanta.

On the same day passengers woke Misha to tell him that old Fedosov was in great pain and that his eyes would open frequently, twinkling as if some strange flame lived in them, they shut suddenly as if they could not stand the light and the smoke from the tallow candles. Misha rushed one deck down, where the old man's family was housed, and saw Parushka and Vera by the bed made of reeds. They told Misha the old man had grown ill after a long period of calmness; white froth mixed with blood was coming out of his mouth in irregular intervals. Fedosov's eyes moistened sporadically with each stab of pain in his chest and left shoulder-blade, but Misha did not notice any sign of fear of death, which was imminent, and the old man seemed to be aware his end was near. When Misha put his hand on Fedosov's forehead, trying to find out whether the man's mental absence was the result of high fever or simply a sign that his life-functions were ceasing, the old man's wife, Matrona, came closer to Misha and whispered so that Fedosov could not hear:

"Misha, last night he told me that in his dream images from his life were mixing with those he had never experienced, and he said that he believed his final departure had already started. Maybe that is the reason he is not groaning and complaining about great pain. Only, he cannot hide the spasms that run from one side of his forehead to the other when the pain comes."

As soon as they left the Fedosovs, Paroniya told Misha that the oldest Antonov had taken to going onto the upper deck frequently; he would stare at the sky and whisper something as if praying to God.

"Or to Satan, Paroniya..." Vera interrupted her. "Or rather I would say that he does not pray to anybody. There are anger and insubordination in his eyes."

And his sister? According to what Paroniya could read in her always teary eyes, she did not want the hope of prayer. Some strange inner pain would often make her eyes glow and she would turn her head away to hide that tiny expression of her psychological state. She breathed ever more heavily and, oddly enough, she would frequently stare at the face of the oldest brother as if trying to read something there, but Paroniya could not figure out what. She more often refused food, even yoghurt, which was by now anyway very scarce among the supplies of the ship.

"She averts her eyes as if she were scared of me or ashamed before me. Then occasionally I notice a heave in her chest and twinkling in her eyes as if she wants to tell me something; then she looks at her brothers and turns away," Paroniya said to Misha. The tone of her voice revealed an aura of the mysticism that surrounded her encounters with that woman.

Misha's thoughts about the Antonovs' sister went further. He became surprised at his own conviction that the woman was suffering from psychological pain, that what had happened to her physical body was much less painful than what was happening in her soul. This growing conviction was driving him closer to taking desperate measures to discover whether his unspoken suspicion that the Antonovs were not her brothers was justified; he felt he was very close to a terrible discovery. Whenever those thoughts came over him, he became afraid of the unconvincing but compelling intuition that these people, the Antonovs, held a secret that could lead him to Boulisou. On that morning, while he was listening to Paroniya, that thought struck him like lightning appearing in a cloudless sky and disappearing into the distance faster than the eye could follow. Without any sound. Without thunder. However, Misha did not yet want to disclose to anybody how he felt about the Antonovs and their "sister".

While *Lake Superior* was approaching the shoulder of the British Island that juts in the direction of Scandinavia, they entered a zone of colder wind thick with drifts of tiny snowflakes. The upper deck was becoming slippery and less safe for walking. The people retreated into their accommodations and tried to organize social life to make time pass more easily. Often songs were heard from below decks, and they sounded like the howling of the wind which was blasting over the foamy ocean waves, hitting the colossal body of the ship, rearing above its decks and plunging again into the waves on the ship's other side. Mixed with the deep low tones of choral singing, the odour of food often crept onto the deck, especially the odour of cooked sour cabbage and boiled prunes. Snow was trying to cover the upper deck but it was prevented by the strong waves crashing over it.

Grandpa Fedosov passed away silently, without saying farewell to anybody, two days before they reached Aberdeen. His tearful Matrona claimed that at the end he had smiled with his eyes closed, as if in that manner he wanted to end his journey through a life full of uncertainties and defiance. Whenever she recounted her last moments with her husband, she used a crumpled grey handkerchief to wipe her eyes in which there were no tears. It seemed the springs of that liquid had dried out long ago, so she could not express her feelings in that way anymore. However, the somber cast of the wrinkles on her forehead was a sign of her mourning and her protest against the definitive departure of the man with whom she had had five children and with whom she had spent more than fifty years. While whispering her farewells to her dead husband she sincerely forgave him for his youthful fooling around with some girls who had failed in finding a suitable match for marriage; she even forgave him for his affairs with some women whose husbands had either been expelled to Siberia or perished in the authorities' bloody clashes with the Doukhobors. She even insisted, without a desire to explain why, that Ana Ivanovitch, a vivacious old woman from the family Vasilenkov, attend the funeral. When people approached Ana informing her about the wish of the Matrona Fedosova, she quickly found an excuse, saying that she was too infirm to attend such a funeral even if for a cat, not to mention for a human being. After the funeral there were rumours along the ship's decks that Ana Vasilenkova was an old flame of Fedosov's, and that she took a place in his heart right next to his Matrona.

The death of Fedosov was the cause of the first big wave of excitement on the ship. The crew, as soon as the news of the death of the old man reached them, started preparations for the burial, which was to take place in the ocean waves. The family was horrified at the news and became firm in their decision that the old man should be buried in soil. For them even the thought that his body could be thrown in the water was horrible. Many passengers took the side of the Fedosovs and asked for the funeral to be in Aberdeen. Even though Doukhobor custom called for little formality in funeral rites, it seemed below any human dignity to simply throw one of their own into the depths of the sea. Captain Taylor resolutely refused that they wait for two days for the funeral because his company rules required urgent removal of the body from aboard ship. He explained that there was a danger of disease, even an epidemic, should the body stay on the ship longer than one day. To convince the most determined objectors that these were the company's rules, he showed them the by-law document with its clear regulations.

Misha found himself in a difficult position, between the demands of the Doukhobors and the ship's regulations. The Doukhobors expected his explanation that there was no danger if a dead body waited so short a time for burial on land, but the ship's crew stood clearly and uncompromisingly on their position. Captain Taylor again disappeared behind the door of his cabin and searched the ship's documents to find the British regulation that did not allow foreigners who died on international ships to be buried in British harbours. The family members and the Doukhobors who had supported them in their demands for a funeral on land had to give in, so with a common family procession, without any speeches and stories about the deceased, Grandpa Fedosov was put in a coffin wrapped in a Canadian flag, and placed on a platform which was tilted until the coffin rushed down from the ship and disappeared in the depths of the ocean.

"I believe if he knew, he would not mind being buried in this way. He always avoided our village cemeteries and said that we should not assign too much meaning to something that does not have a value," Matrona said to those who were trying to express their dissatisfaction with how the old man was thrown into the ocean. That old woman, experienced in life's sufferings, had quickly accepted the new situation and defended it with dignity.

In Aberdeen's harbour it took two days and nights to load the coal for the journey across the Atlantic. During that time, mostly because of the harsh winter, the passengers' activities took place below decks. Both old and young people told their traditional stories, sang and made jokes at the expense of those present. They all laughed and nobody was offended at the joke directed his way. Women took care of food and hygiene, and when they had free time they knitted warm woollen vests, gloves, and socks. The further away from Mother Russia they went, the more they removed the veils of secrecy from the stories of their previous life. It seemed they wanted to get rid of that secret burden in their memories. As time passed the ship's crew more and more often joined the Doukhobors during meals. They especially liked rye bread, borscht, sour cabbage with sheep cheese, thick bean soup and coffee made of roasted wheat. They also liked the drink the Doukhobors made by fermenting rye and oats. Two sailors drank the liquid from the barrels containing the sour cabbage, and not being used to that refreshing drink, they spent two days in the toilet.

Right before dusk on the second day of their stay in the Scottish harbour, for no reason known to the Doukhobors, the first officer on the ship was replaced. The Captain's former second-in-command, Griffin, left the ship, and not long after his departure Captain Taylor and a few of his colleagues on the upper deck greeted the new first officer, Robert Ballard, who was, as later disclosed, descended from the French Ballards expelled from their homeland during the persecution of the Huguenots in France. Scots near Aberdeen had offered them a home, and two generations afterwards most of the Ballards moved to Canada and the United States. Robert was proud that he had managed to persuade his son William to complete veterinary studies and in that manner avoid his father's destiny of constant travelling on the wide sea.

After leaving the Scottish harbour, *Lake Superior* no longer sailed close to the *Lake Huron*. That ship was not visible when they passed the Faroe Islands and continued sailing towards Iceland; they saw nothing on the horizon except the wide ocean. The weather was changeable; spells of snow and icy rain alternated with sunny periods. However, the winter would not let go. As they were moving further towards the north, the temperature continued to fall. As the weather grew harsher, the folks in their accommodations were wrapping more and more woollen covers about themselves. They were sleeping longer, as if the chilly weather stirred their biological sensors to signal the brain that longer sleeps would make the journey feel shorter and the approach of land seem sooner. They did not mind if that land was colder, but they wanted the feeling of helplessness to stop as well as the state in which any initiative was impossible.

One day before they sighted the first fjords of Iceland, suddenly two children fell very ill. First, they started coughing quietly; the cough came from the depths of their lungs and it was followed by a slow but permanent rise of body temperature and by redness in their cheeks. Misha assumed it was a light pneumonia and suggested that the parents give their children more nutritious food and one tablespoon of fish oil in the morning and at bedtime, as well as cooked dry fruit. However, the following morning both children had such a high fever that they refused any food, even water. They even tried to give them frozen yoghurt from their meager supplies as the Canadian nurses suggested, but the children started vomiting and fainting. Panic was born on the ship. Captain Taylor even consulted his crew about what would be the best thing to do, but nobody could suggest anything better than what the medical team had already done. The only hope was if the children could hold on for two more days until they reached Iceland and the nearest hospital, at Reykjavik. However, both children died within hours, right after midnight.

Misha, Paroniya, Vera, and Emily felt the death of the two children as their own failure. They suffered the next blow when, close to dawn, the news reached Misha, almost simultaneously from both families, that the children might not be dead because their eyes occasionally opened on their own and strange red spots appeared on their necks. Right away the entire medical team rushed to the nearer of the families in grief. Misha did not have an explanation for the red spots on the boy's neck. Then he saw with his own eyes that the left eye of the boy opened slowly. The boy's mother started screaming and mentioning church, priests, the cross, and the Bible.

"I don't want Satan to escort my son to the other world!" she screamed, hitting her head with her hands. "If there was a priest with the cross and the Bible here, everything would be different. Tell them, Dmitry Stepanovitch, what I told you before this journey! I knew something bad would happen if there were no emissaries of God on this ship. See my child, Dmitry!..." She was pulling her husband's sleeve and pointing at the uncovered head and chest of her dead son. "Didn't I tell you we shouldn't go! I knew...I knew..." the woman screamed, hitting her bosom with her hands. "There is Satan here. As soon as I saw that woman with the burnt face, I wanted to jump into the water with my only son. The people who are with her are not human. I saw how the big one was staring at my Oleg, devouring him with his eyes..."

"Wait, Spasenka...Doctor Misha is here. He knows what happened to our Oleg," Dmitry tried to console her. It was very difficult to separate her from the child's body.

Misha was confused. He knew that within a few hours a dead body could change the position of the head or limbs, and that eyes could open after being shut by caregivers. But he did not know that eyes that are open could shut again and that red spots could appear on the body after death. When he discovered the same thing on the body of the other boy, whose parents, brothers and sisters were silently saying their farewells to him, Misha went to Taylor's cabin. He described the odd events to the Captain and asked him if he had ever experienced anything similar while travelling on the sea. Taylor was quiet for some time; then he patted Misha on the shoulder and told him almost confidentially:

"Doctor, I have seen many different cases of death on the sea. Something like this, I have never seen. It has happened that during long winter journeys, some have frozen to death and have been found behind some deck structure and dragged into a cabin. A few hours afterwards, occasionally red spots appeared on the skin of these dead bodies, especially where the frostbites were. And their eyelids would occasionally move. However, I believe it was because of the thawing. We cannot do much here, Doctor."

Misha did not say anything after the Captain's explanations. He was still obsessed by the case of the mysterious death of the two children. He was bewildered with the combinations his brain was making. When the Captain added that those cases he had experienced happened on ships where, as a rule, there were priests with all that they use in their services, Misha informed Taylor about the screams and words of the deceased boy's mother and about her mentioning the Antonovs and their sister.

"Doctor Chernov, I have been receiving information that the case is being investigated ashore. Some of my people suggest that family be handed over to the police in Iceland. I am close to making that decision so that we can relieve the people on this ship of the strange burden of mystery which surrounds this family."

Hearing the Captain's words, Misha became afraid. He knew the mystery centred on the misfortune of the Antonovs' supposed sister and that the cause of her misfortune was not what the oldest brother had told them. He felt deep inside that here lay a connection with his Boulisou, or at least news leading to her. However, he hoped time would bring him some opportunity to reach a conclusion, or eventually to act.

While on the ship, and it would be for two more weeks, the Antonovs were in a kind of prison. They associated with no one. They were under surveillance. Finally, Misha thought, the pressure of their isolation from others on the ship would force them to make a move that would shed more light on their case. And now, the Captain was telling him that he might put the Antonovs ashore in Iceland!

"No," shouted Misha, and the Captain looked at his face, surprised.

"What 'no,' Doctor Chernov?" the Captain asked, not sharing Misha's agitation.

Misha did not have an adequate answer nor time to think.

"I am trying to find out the medical truth about what happened to the face of that woman. I am close, sir. Iceland's authorities won't consider that family important, and they will give them a chance to continue the journey on the next ship. It will be helping those people to avoid justice if they are guilty. I beg you to leave them on the ship, and I will inform you about everything I find out."

The Captain moved his gaze from Misha to the snowstorm outside the cabin's window.

"You were the first who brought my attention to the problems with the Antonovs, but you haven't yet explained your suspicion of them. Tell me honestly, are you hiding something from me?"

Misha knew that the conversation had turned to something of the most immense importance in his life. Under no circumstances did he want to be separated from the Antonovs and their sister.

"Sir, Captain Taylor! Allow the people to say their farewells to the dead children. Tomorrow, after the funeral ceremony, I will visit you and tell you in detail what I have found out about the case of the Antonovs."

The Captain looked at Misha's face for a long time, especially at his troubled eyes; then spoke quietly, bringing his lips close to Misha's ear:

"I think you probably have some idea about the Antonovs and the disappearance of your wife, Doctor. Is this true? You have my deepest sympathies, only I don't want any incident to happen on this ship before we arrive at Saint John's Harbour. I know that you Doukhobors do not like use of any force in human relations and I hope that in the case of the Antonovs there won't be any breaking of that rule. My crew controls the situation, but a surprise could always happen."

Misha left the Captain's cabin very disturbed. He blamed himself for not being active enough in dealing with the four brothers who kept their sister in total isolation from other people. That fact alone would make even a child do something. But it seemed to Misha that he had hesitated to confirm or dispel his doubts because he was afraid of something, something he was still unsure about. He probably did not rush to take action of his own initiative because they were on this ship in the middle of the ocean as though in a cage and because the constant motion of the ship made people apathetic and reluctant to act when it was hard to predict the outcome.

During the preparations for lunch, Kostuna sat next to Misha. It hadn't happened for a long time and Misha curiously turned his head towards his father, trying to read in his eyes what his intention was. Within the last two years both of them had felt a distance grow between them and they attributed it to nature, to their aging. At the same time, Misha had been happy to see Kostuna and Petro building an ever stronger friendship. They were becoming closer than was common between a grandfather and a grandson, especially since the disappearance of Boulisou. However, Misha's happiness had been spoiled when he found out that Kostuna was often drinking alcohol with the old Hasson, even though it was against Doukhobors rules. On one occasion when the two of them were alone, Misha told Kostuna that he knew about his addiction to alcohol, and Kostuna replied briefly that he had the need for it and that he was able to control his addiction so it did not become excessive and that he wanted to keep it a secret that he did not follow the rules of their teaching. Even though the old man did not ask, Misha told him that he would not tell anybody, not even his mother, Pelagiya.

"Would you like a vodka?" Misha suddenly whispered to his father, winking discreetly.

Kostuna looked at him, not believing his ears.

"I am joking, Father. It's been a long time since we made jokes with one another. Time pressed on us, so we forgot what is the most important in life: to laugh, to make jokes…"

"You are lucky you did not inherit the addiction to alcohol from me. That vice will end with me," Kostuna said, quietly defending himself.

"What do you mean, Father? Even though I did not inherit it from you, the same vice might appear in some of your grandchildren, great grandchildren…"

Neither the father nor the son wanted to continue the discussion about Kostuna's secret.

"We have to talk about those Antonovs," Kostuna said, deciding to change the subject. "They are some dangerous people, Mishka."

"Why do you think so, Father? Everybody on this ship knows they are strange. I find them strange too. But you think they are dangerous?" Misha wanted his father's perspective.

"That polar bear, the oldest brother, I do not like him at all. His eyes are full of aggression and hatred. I do not know if you noticed, but recently he has started walking around the ship, but he does not join any group. His eyes glare like those of a hungry wolf."

"Tell me what it is, Father. What's troubling you?" Misha looked him straight in the eyes, smiling gently.

"Maybe it is because you are a doctor and you force open the door of their self-imposed isolation…That bear is more frequently coming close to us and staring at us as if we were in a cage. Especially at our Petro. He neither smiles nor says anything, but his eyes are active. He watches Petro like a beast its prey and waits for a chance to jump on it. Even Petro has noticed that and asked me why that giant is circling around us. I have started observing him more seriously and discovered something that needs to be checked." Kostuna was talking more openly now.

"What should be checked?" Misha asked and took a plate with food that Pelagiya handed him.

"I have noticed that the brothers are more frequently using rude language when talking among themselves, and they quarrel. Especially the one among them who always wears a grey shawl around his neck is becoming more nervous and often talks heatedly to the giant."

Misha was quiet, not wanting to interrupt his father's explanations. However, the tension in him was growing, prodded by the feeling that he should openly confront the Antonovs in order to find out the truth; especially the truth about their sister.

"That poor woman..." Kostuna continued as if he guessed what Misha was thinking. "She more often comes out of the door of their compartment and sits on the floor holding her head between her hands. I would say she is crying but I cannot see her tears. That bear says she has lost the ability to speak! I could swear by everything dear to me that she occasionally exchanges a few words with her brothers. There is something fishy about the Antonovs."

Misha picked up a spoon and started eating the potato soup with dumplings. Kostuna picked up a spoon too. Both of them realized that much had been said. Misha suddenly remembered that he had recently dreamed about the Antonovs' sister and that she had told him she was afraid of the waves on the sea. He remembered the dream and concluded that he was obsessed by the case and that his brain, oppressed by suspicion, was trying to find a way to relieve the pressure. He looked at his father and noticed that he too was struggling with unspoken combinations of thoughts. He directed his gaze at Petro and saw that the boy was staring at both of them. His face was red from the hot soup and the steam rising from the plate. Misha saw how Petro was holding his face above the steam, enjoying its pleasant warmth. As if somebody outside his mind had concocted a plan for him, Misha decided to visit the Antonovs' sister right after lunch. He decided to take Petro with him, obscurely sensing that the boy's presence at the meeting with the Antonovs might help provoke the strange brothers to loosen the shield they had built around themselves and their sister.

Misha was surprised when Petro accepted this plan to visit the Antonovs with unconcealed interest.

"Are you afraid of seeing that woman's face?" Misha asked him while they were going down the stairs to the lower deck.

"No!" the son replied firmly. "I want to see her better. Children are telling all sorts of stories about her. The other day Greshka told me he had seen that big man embrace her and pull her through the door into their room."

Misha flinched but did not comment. Maybe if she is their sister they keep everyone away simply so that she doesn't feel embarrassed among outsiders, he thought. However, his feelings did not confirm that thought. He almost wished that the woman were not their sister. He could not dispel his suspicion about their whole story and secretly expected his suspicion to be confirmed.

The Antonovs' door was shut. Misha knocked a few times and suddenly the door opened and the figure of the giant appeared, bent as before because he was much taller than the opening. Obviously, he was surprised to see Misha and Petro.

"What brings you here, Doctor?" he asked unwelcomingly.

"Paroniya told me that your sister's condition has improved these days. I want to see her."

The giant stood looking at Misha and Petro with his eyes wide open, thinking.

"I am close to deciding to forbid you to come here. I won't say you are either a good or bad doctor, but the other day two children died on this ship. I would not blame you for the death of the old man, but for that of the children…"

Misha did not take his gaze off the giant's eyes. His irises were of a colour between green and yellow, and were not round like a human's.

Their shape was elliptical, like a cat's. From the time he arrived on the ship, it had been obvious that he did not like children, and now he was blaming Misha for the death two of them. That giant, Misha concluded in a split second, had decided to play more openly.

"Why did you bring this boy? What does he have to do with my sister and her treatment?" the giant asked, not changing his posture in the door frame.

"This is my son, Petro," Misha replied louder than necessary for the host to hear him. "His mother disappeared more than two years ago, so he is most frequently with me."

Misha did not notice any unusual sign in the giant's eyes, but he retreated farther into the room and with his hand signalled them to get in. The other three brothers and the woman got up from a long wooden bench covered with a thick woollen blanket. In her hands the woman was holding a ball of yarn from white sheep's wool and wooden knitting needles. Misha noticed that the woman was staring at Petro's face and that her eyes opened wider and then narrowed as if she was trying to see better. Then she turned her head away. Misha looked at Petro and saw surprise in his eyes. The giant also noticed that something was amiss. He looked at his sister while frowning and hastened to report:

"She has been feeling better since she started to drink a lot of yoghurt. There is a change in her voice, the sounds she makes. If she could speak, we would understand her."

The woman turned her head toward Petro, then she looked at Misha. Then she fixed her gaze on the giant's face, as if she wanted to ask him something. Misha noticed her eyes become watery; tears could any moment run down the blue scars under her sparse eyelashes. She put a black kerchief over her face and her hand reached toward Petro. At that moment Petro grabbed Misha's hand, started squeezing it, plunging his nails into it, and screamed. Under the kerchief, the woman, too, screamed, and ran into the farthest corner of the room. Petro continued to scream. The woman also, making sounds that could have come from the caves of the sea; then with her hands she started hitting the wooden wall of the room.

The giant opened the door and ordered Misha to leave their compartment. Misha held his son in his arms. Petro was still screaming. At the door Antonov thundered at Misha:

"As soon as I saw the child, I became upset. For her it is the worst when children see her face. She is ashamed and starts to cry! Go away, Doctor! My sister is fine! Go away!"

When they had climbed onto the upper deck, Petro calmed down. He looked at his father. Misha could tell that his boy's heart was beating madly, and tears filled the spaces between his nose and cheeks.

"What is it, my son?" Misha asked.

Petro tried to speak, but a new burst of tears choked him. Some people were approaching them, and among them was Parushka and Uncle Stephen.

"Mama..." Petro managed to say. "It is Mama..."

The boy shoved his head into his father's bosom and cried. Misha also felt tears in his eyes, his chest started to heave, and he clenched his fists as if holding onto something that somebody was trying to take from them. Recently it had often crossed Misha's mind that it could be Boulisou. She was of the same height, but somewhat chubbier, of the same hair colour, the scarred nose small and slightly turned up. However, he was afraid to admit to himself that it could be Boulisou. He was terrified of the truth. One morning while he was playing his flute, standing alone by the ship's railing and looking at the waves that were rushing in front of his eyes, he had asked himself if Boulisou, if that was really she, had a reason to hide her identity and not ask for help from him and other people on the ship. Then he remembered that she could not speak, and that Antonovs were always near her.

"What happened, Misha?" asked Paroniya, and her worried eyes rushed over his face. "What happened to Petro?"

The others also expected Misha's reply. He only shook his head as if saying it's not that important, and carried Petro toward Kostuna, Pelagiya, and Genadiy, who were rushing towards them.

"Petro, do not say to anybody why you are crying. Listen to me, my son. Maybe it is not Mom."

"Yes, it is, Father! It is..." Petro whispered in his father's ear, realizing there was a reason to be quiet. "I recognized Mom's ear, Father. And..."

"It's fine, my son! You will tell me later. Only me..."

As soon as they came, Kostuna took Petro from Misha's arms, and Pelagiya and Genadiy asked at the same time:

"What happened? Did Petro fell down?"

"Everything is fine. It's nothing. You, Father, and you, Mom have spoiled him, so he cries easily," Misha pretended to scold them.

That same night, while they were passing among Iceland's small islands, all the passengers went out on deck and looked in wonder at what they had only heard about in the stories of sailors serving on Russian ships. A strange light made various shapes in the sky partly covered with small clouds. It rushed like an arrow and then suddenly flipped to the other side of heaven's vault and changed colour. It was greenish, then turned into nuances of orange, then purple. It arrived in waves as if the sea mirrored itself in the sky, then its lines competed with one another to see which one of them would disappear fastest into the uncertain distance where the cold sky and the wide sea met. The ship's crew explained that it was the Aurora Borealis, which occasionally wanders much more to the south than people would expect.

29

Ballard, the new first officer, was a short strong man in his forties. Unlike his predecessor, he formally greeted all whom he met without many words and with a forced smile in the corners of his mouth; in this way he made it clear what his role was and asked for cooperation so that they all could cross the wide ocean more easily and reach the Canadian shores. However, when he was not on duty his face emanated unassuming goodness, which meant offering without asking for something in return. When Misha saw him for the first time, in his blue officer's uniform, Ballard reminded him of jolly sailors walking along the Neva Prospect in Petersburg. He had seen them for the first time when as students at Kazan's university he and Boulisou visited the capital of his youthful dreams.

On that sunny morning while the ship was approaching Greenland, trapped in whiteness, Robert Ballard appeared on the upper deck instead of Captain Taylor. He came a little later than it was the Captain's habit to greet the new day. Misha noticed Ballard as soon as he appeared at top of the companionway from the lower deck. Not wanting to interrupt the song, Misha played more quietly as he began the last aria of a composition that sounded like music of the Canadian Squamish Aboriginals from the Pacific Coast, alone in their long wooden canoes in the narrow waters of Howe Sound, deep beneath the jagged summits of the Coastal Mountains in the backdrop of Vancouver.

"Doctor, when I saw you and heard the sounds coming from your tiny musical instrument, I thought it was the opening tune of *In the Steppes of Central Asia,* the symphonic poem by your Alexander Borodin, but I didn't see anybody except you out here. Your music is perfect. If I were a painter, I would right away throw myself at canvas in order to capture this rippling ocean the colour of the light blue sky this holy morning. Today is the day of the birth of Jesus, according to the Orthodox calendar, and nature has given us a gift of this beautiful light and colours in the open sea. I see nothing around us except this water of an unusual colour adorned with rippling waves and up there the cold vastness of the sky, whose numerous bustling oases of fluff play hide and seek with the rays of sunlight. Here on this deck there are only the two of us, and far away on the surface of the water there is an occasional iceberg of brilliant whiteness. All this is unusual, Doctor. The two of us here on the deck, and the strange colour of the sea and the sky, and those icebergs tiny in the distance. Nothing like this did I expect this morning." Misha was surprised at Ballard's lyrical talkativeness. This morning the first officer seemed different from the way Misha had perceived him in their earlier encounters.

"Sir, we are moving in the direction of those icebergs. Don't you think we might collide with them?" Misha asked the officer as if he had thought of the question in advance.

Officer Ballard, surprised, looked Misha directly in the eyes as if he were looking there for something more than Misha's question.

"Don't worry. We are the sailors of the northern seas. Those hills of ice could be dangerous at night, in a storm, when we do not expect to encounter them and when we cannot see them. But in daylight they are just part of the beautiful scenery. However, it is unusual at this time of the year. This is the time when ice forms, not when it breaks into huge icebergs." Then the officer suddenly asked, "What is the situation with your Doukhobors? I mean what is the health situation?"

"Under control, sir. It is better than I had expected. These people are very strong. They are used to both good and evil. And they are surprisingly adaptable, they quickly adjust to new conditions. Their desire to reach the goal makes them strong. Hope is the builder of their immunity," Misha said.

"I understand your people very well. My roots too are soaked in suffering and hope like yours. I originate from the numerous lineage of the Ballards from French Provençe. When my ancestors joined the humane Huguenots, the state and Catholic Church rulers threw them in the ocean. On the other side of the English Channel people who owed them nothing welcomed them and housed them. Long after that, they followed the tide that brought them to the eastern coast of Canada; they walked to the interior, to Quebec, Manitoba, and Saskatchewan, and there they started a new life. As a youth, I returned to Great Britain. I became a sailor in Scotland and I travel on the sea. I do not want to become attached to any corner of the earth because the destiny of my ancestors haunts me."

"How strange," Misha replied. "I carry a big part of your story in me. However, it is just happening to me, while you already have it in your genes. Doukhobors or Huguenots, it does not mater...If you think with your own head and live your life accordingly, the powerful ones will plot against your life. Thank God there are seas and ships, so we can move from one corner of the world to another...In search for our land...For a land that will accept us as her own."

The beautiful morning lured some other people out from below decks. Groups of people formed by the railings of the ship. People turned their faces towards the rays of the sun that bounced from the tops of the waves back into the sky as if coming from the depth of the sea. Through the openings of the companionways a quiet women's song was heard; it sounded more like the buzzing of bees in the hollow of an old oak tree than like sounds made by human beings.

"They must be making breakfast for us," Misha observed, turning his head towards the nearest companionway, from which the song was reaching their ears.

"Ah yes. I am impressed by your unity and reliance on each other. I come from a world where private property is sacred and where people even in the most social of communities try to hold onto their privacy. You look to me like a huge compact family. In the Western world families are splitting up, the relationships among close ones get spoiled because they get the smell of money and material interests. And you...I am aware that you have developed a new way of life where material interests are collective, and where relationships among people are based on the feeling of belonging to the human race. To be honest with you, I do not share enough of your understanding to be able to live like the Doukhobors."

"It is not easy, sir," Misha said shortly. He had suddenly lost inspiration and ceased his modest contribution to Ballard's attempt to become close to him. Unexpectedly, the ship had entered a strange weather zone, mystical, more like dream than reality. It was different from anything these people had in their memory, so nobody, not even Misha, fully realized that they were entering something unusual. Above them the light fluffy clouds had closed ranks to hover in a screen through which the sky could still be seen. Because of the clouds and the filtered spectrum of the hues of sunlight, the colour of the sky became a pale, otherworldly green, and the clouds to the east acquired an orange lining. Light, sparse snowflakes were spiralling gracefully from above; it seemed as if they were attempting to defy the force of gravity, to avoid falling in the water and disappearing without a trace. If these people had senses to register the feelings and whispers of that in nature which isn't alive, they would probably have been able to hear screams from the crystal snowflakes when they finally realized that their hope and effort to avoid falling in the water were in vain.

"Look, sir," a now delighted Misha addressed First Officer Ballard. "These snowflakes also fight for their collective life."

"What do you mean, Doctor?" Ballard asked quickly.

"Don't you see that with some strange energy they are trying to weaken the force of gravity and stay away from the waves of the sea as long as possible? If there were a solid surface below them, where they could continue living although assimilated in the mass of snow, maybe it would be easier for them. Maybe in that case they would not so much resist falling on the surface. In this situation, I feel they see the water as imminent death. I would not be surprised if I could hear their whisper, calling a strong wind to lift them into the vastness of the sky and to prolong their life. Sir, doesn't this remind you of us Doukhobors? Of our struggle for life…"

Ballard's wide smile stretched his charming cheeks. He looked at Misha's face then he looked at the greenish sky through the tiny snowflakes.

"If I follow your impression, that would mean freedom is up there above those clouds. There where there are no restrictions to free movement and freedom in general. But, Doctor, I am afraid of that freedom and that limitless space. I like it most when after a journey on the sea, I see a rock behind which there is land. I am too heavy to dream about freedom or about the life of these light snowflakes."

They were both surprised to see so many people on the upper deck admiring the beauty that surrounded them. Ballard, as if he had suddenly remembered something, asked Misha to excuse him and, avoiding collisions with people around him, he hurried towards the bridge. Misha joined the nearest group, who were using all their senses to enjoy the extraordinary display of nature around them. Frail snowflakes were settling on people's hair and wool-clad shoulders as if even now fighting to avoid breaking the branches in the crystal structure of their bodies, fighting to preserve their beauty. The children moved away from groups and reached with their arms towards the sky, happy when a snowflake decided to accept their offer. They would look at that snowflake with curiosity as if it was something alive that landed on their small mittened fingers from somewhere in the universe.

"The ship is slowing down," noticed Hristo Bure, a blond young man whose eyes were of a strange green colour similar to that of the sky above the fluffy clouds.

"We are approaching the icebergs!" shouted one woman, pointing with her hand in the direction where the ship was sailing. All the groups of people started moving forward to better see the floating icebergs. Everyone started crowding into the bows of the ship as if being pushed there. In that mass of people Misha spotted Kostuna, Pelagiya, Petro and some others from his family. They were only about ten steps in front of him. Beyond them he saw some of the Strelayevs, but Paroniya was not among them. Then he was astonished to see the Antonovs' "sister" with a black kerchief on her head pushing her way towards his family. The oldest Antonov was hurrying after her, followed by the other three brothers. The people did not understand what was going on, and they were getting out of the Antonovs' way. Misha tried to move faster through the crowd to get closer to them, but people were so crowded together that it was not easy. *Something is wrong.* This thought frightened Misha as he continued pressing through the crowd towards the Antonovs. He realized they were trying to get closer to his father and the other Chernovs. He forgot about his consideration for others and started pushing people out of his way, feeling ever more strongly that the Antonovs were not rushing forward in order to see the icebergs.

From the moment when somebody's hands suddenly clamping his shoulders from behind made Misha stop, events started unfolding unpredictably, with furious speed. Misha understood that the strength of somebody's hands was deliberately holding him back. He turned his head and saw Captain Taylor, without his captain's cap on his head. He was at the front of a group of his crewmen, who were almost pressed against his back. That position made him appear even more important and powerful. There was a flame of ferocity and determination in the Taylor's eyes. His wide, fair eyebrows were drawn so close they nearly joined, and as punctuation of that determination and ferocity a tuft of his reddish hair touched the spot where the eyebrows met.

Misha was extremely surprised. His brain couldn't immediately grasp the situation, but in a split second he decided not to react before hearing the Captain's explanation.

"Doctor, the Antonovs have made a move! Now it is my turn! They are dangerous people! Their status is suspicious! And their intentions! Keep away from our encounter with them!"

"But, sir, they are right behind my family. He was looking at my son…" Misha tried to find words.

"Get behind me, Doctor Chernov! I am the captain of this ship! I give the orders!…"

"That woman is my wife!" Misha cried, trying to free himself from the Captain's grasp. Two crewmembers grabbed him, and the Captain and the others continued forcing their way through the throng in order to get to the Antonovs as quickly as possible. By the time Misha managed to free himself from the hands of the Captain's sailors, the woman with the kerchief had reached the Chernovs. Over there Kostuna had been holding Petro close to him, surprised at the commotion of people who rushing towards them. He had not been afraid because he had no idea what was going on. His eyes revealed fear only when a few steps from him he saw the woman with the kerchief, followed by the giant in full swing. Instinctively he pushed Petro into Genadiy's hands and stepped in front of the woman. She pushed him away violently and with the force of a beast snatched Petro away from Genadiy's arms. Carrying Petro, the woman rushed towards the railings right at the bow of the ship, shouldering aside the startled people. At the same time Kostuna and Genadiy blocked Antonov's way and threw themselves at him, realizing that somebody needed to stop him. He trampled over them like feather pillows. The throng of passengers now understood that Antonov did not have good intentions so they moved as a mass to block his way. It was not easy. He was flinging aside the folks around him and getting closer to the ship's prow. When the woman with the black kerchief, holding Petro in her arms, jumped like a cat onto the broad triangular platform where the ship's railings met, the wind blew the kerchief off her head and completely revealed her burnt face. Antonov got to her, jumped onto that platform at the top of the railings and snatched the child from her arms. She lost her balance and almost toppled into the sea. Only at that moment did Petro start to scream, reaching with his arms towards his mother. The other Antonovs were standing by the railing in order to confront those who tried to attack the giant.

Along with the Captain and his officers, Misha got to the space in front of the Antonovs, the woman, and Petro. The Captain understood that the seriousness of the situation and stopped some five steps away from the Antonovs. Petro was still screaming, trying to wriggle out of the giant's hands, and in his screams the words "Mama...Mamushka...Mama..." became more recognizable. The woman remained still, clearly realizing that the boy was in danger and that any reckless action could bring the risk of death upon her son. The giant did not wait for the Captain to start speaking. He thundered so that they could hear him well.

"Captain, drop the big boat into the water and give us clothes and food! We will take this boy with us to be safe!"

"You do not stand a chance of surviving in the ocean on that boat!" the Captain shouted.

"You don't worry about us! We are close to the shore of Greenland!" the giant shouted again, as if to encourage himself. His frequent glances at the other three Antonovs revealed that he was trying to keep control of the situation.

Misha's heart was beating wildly, and frantic thoughts about how to save Petro and Boulisou were running through his head. He spontaneously looked at the water of the ocean and saw mercilessness and threat. That Antonov, who was holding his son high on the ship's railing, belonged more to the monstrosity of the water than to the people on the ship. The functions of Misha's brain, stunned by his nightmare vision, began recovering. One by one he saw the images of that giant on the ship's bow and those of the giant priest on the hill above Bogdanovka on the day when the Tsar's cavalry had massacred the Doukhobors. He was the same man. In a flash Misha realized that Antonov was the priest and part of the gang that had been kidnapping Doukhobor women and probably selling them. He could not understand why that priest, with three others who were probably priests as well, had used the disfigured Boulisou as a shield and set out on the journey to Canada with them. Antonov's scheme clearly included Petro, but at that moment Misha could not imagine what infernal plan the priest had concocted. He remembered Rasputin's words that he could help himself and others in greatest danger if some vile human being caused calamity. Through the power of his mind. Through the magic of illusion! Misha tried to concentrate, to switch roles with the men in front of him, but it did not work. He felt pressure in his brain, the mysterious energy he had never understood. He was trying to control it, but the power remained inchoate, far from use. There in front of him the Captain was trying to gain time to think of an efficacious way of overcoming the giant. He was slowly getting closer to Antonov and the other three men. Looking at the expressions on their faces he concluded that the other three were not a problem. The people made a living wall enclosing the confrontation in the ship's prow, and the three men displayed no intention to attack this barrier of massed bodies. The

Captain realized that the three lesser Antonovs were under the control of the giant, and if he were neutralized they would be forced to their knees.

The beginning of the resolution to the sudden trouble on the *Lake Superior*, ten miles south of the shore of Greenland, came from the group in which were Kostuna and Pelagiya. As if in agreement, they simultaneously stepped from the crowd into the empty space between the Antonovs and the ship's crew and shouted:

"Take us instead of Petro and his mother! We will go with you into the boat!"

The Captain and the crew stepped towards Kostuna and Pelagiya in order to pull them back into the crowd, and Misha charged at the giant like a beast instinctively rushing to fight a predator. The Antonovs pushed aside the people who encircled them and rushed at Misha, but the Captain and his people in a split second fell upon the backs of the giant's "brothers". The huge Antonov started to sway on the ship's railing, as though undecided, and Boulisou with the sudden strength of a tigress plucked Petro from giant's arms and threw him towards Misha. The giant hovered over Boulisou like an eagle, and paused for a moment, trying to read her intention in her eyes. The buttons on his shirt had fallen open on account of the powerful movements of his body and Misha saw a big black cross on his chest. Misha was now certain it was that priest from the mountain. Boulisou looked at the water behind Antonov, jumped at the giant's neck and before he could regain his balance she pulled him backward into the waves of the ocean.

Misha caught Petro before he hit the deck and immediately they both looked back at Boulisou and the giant. Instantly Misha realized it was the end of his and Petro's Boulisou. She had decided to resolve the crisis with the Antonovs and save her son by sacrificing herself. He realized she had abandoned hope of returning to him and Petro because she had persuaded herself that she was not anymore their Boulisou, for whom they had been searching and longing for years. She saw herself only as ugly, disfigured, and destroyed in the terrible misfortune after the kidnapping. Who knows what she had experienced in that nightmare of a few years! In his Boulisou's final act, Misha deciphered her message asking for forgiveness and understanding. Asking to be remembered the way she used to be and the way they loved her and not to blame her for leaving them forever of her own will. In those nightmarish moments Misha felt that mysterious power of his brain engulf him and he transmitted it as a suggestion first to Petro, then to the others who were looking at them. He saw Boulisou firmly gripping the giant's neck as they fell towards the waves, and saw them plunging into the water just as the ship was passing by a huge iceberg. In the minds of those present Misha's mind created the illusion that the criminal fell into the water, but that Boulisou started to glow with the beauty of the girl he had fallen in love with even as a child when Genadiy used to drive them to school, and that she was with her outstretched arms reaching towards the snowflakes falling from the thinly clouded sky, lingering briefly above the railing of the ship slowly sinking and rising with the waves, and then herself simply rising into the sky.

"I succeeded!" Misha thought, and the weight of the misfortune that had hit him and Boulisou suddenly became lighter. He looked at Petro, who was looking at the sky breathlessly. Misha turned to the people around him, and they were all looking at the sky with their eyes wide open in surprise.

"Mama..." whispered Petro looking at the sky. "My Mamushka..."

"Boulisou..." whispered Misha, looking to see if the head of the woman he loved would appear around the iceberg that the ship was passing. He believed that through the transparent surface of the ice he saw Boulisou pull the giant ever deeper into the water, and the huge iceberg hid them from his eyes. He winced when he realized that her face was not disfigured anymore. He looked at his son's eyes and in them he saw Boulisou rising through the snowflakes, her round face and black hair, red lips smiling as if she wanted to leave them this image of her forever.

"Father, I saw Mom," Petro whispered in Misha's ear. "I saw how she went into the sky. That ugly woman is not my mother. My mother is beautiful," Petro whispered and through tears looked up, stretching his arms towards the sky. From there quiet light snowflakes were slowly falling on his face and eyes. "Did my mother go up?" Petro asked through tears but with a smile on his face.

"She didn't, son! Only her image. Your mother is always with us. She can't go anywhere away from us," Misha whispered and cried. Petro was surprised at Misha's words, and he looked him seriously in the eyes, put his head against his father's and embraced him with his slender arms.

The Captain gave the order to stop the ship, but the force of inertia had dragged them pretty far away from that iceberg. They slowly turned back, returned to the iceberg, searched to see if they could find the bodies, but could see nothing except ice and the furious ocean waves. When all of them realized that the search was in vain, the Captain ordered the ship to resume its course. Kostuna, Pelagiya, and Genadiy embraced Misha and Petro, and so they all returned to their compartment under the deck of the steamer.

After that event, when Boulisou definitively settled in the souls of her Misha and Petro, the people started talking, trying to resolve the mystery that had happened on the ship *Lake Superior*, close to the southern shore of Greenland. They knew Misha Chernov had played a big part in what they had seen, but they did not ask him about it. Misha went into seclusion and until they reached the Canadian shore at Saint John's he did not socialize with anybody except Paroniya, Vera, and Emily, and his close relatives. Weakness came over him, followed by some strange lethargy and lack of interest. Then for a few days he suffered from an inexplicable sickness in his stomach and chest, which occasionally paralyzed his thoughts and his ability to concentrate. And his brain?! If he were not immersed in medical science, he would in his feebleness have constructed the belief that some strange power had entered his brain, much stronger and more creative than himself, a power beyond his ability to control. He felt that the grey matter in his skull was rapidly expanding as if it was going to explode, then shrinking to a point of helplessness where all the rational activity stopped. He applied beyond-human power to try to control his mind and became afraid of its disobedience. Then he felt a desire to play his flute.

He tiptoed into the huge bunkers of the ship intended for storing coal and wood, much depleted now, and started playing. He played a melody spontaneously improvised by his fingers, and felt the strange process in his brain easing away into music and becoming weaker. The sounds of his small instrument brought to him images of Boulisou as she was sinking on the back of the giant into the depths of the rough sea, and those of Boulisou triumphantly suspended in the air, slowly disappearing among the snowflakes. Soon Misha felt only a slight headache and he realized he had managed to take control of his brain. His knowledge of medicine was inadequate to explain the processes that had threatened to overwhelm him, or the miraculous cure that the sounds of his flute had performed.

Petro cried for a few days, looking at the sky; he often came close to his father and embraced him as never before, and for the first time since Misha returned from Siberia he started putting his ruffled head against his father's bosom.

Before entering the harbour of Saint John's, Captain Taylor and Misha embraced each other, happy that the journey was over. Taylor placed his hands on Misha's shoulders, looked him in the eyes, and said in a friendly manner:

"Doctor Chernov, I am happy that you have arrived in my country with your people. Not only are you a good doctor and a good man, but you also possess skills that in the most difficult circumstances offer solace to people's eyes and hearts. It took me several days of deep contemplation about all that had happened to realize that you had directed our perceptions in the final departure of Petro's mother, the woman you loved. A good man searches for the good in the most extreme situation, when most people kneel down, powerless."

THIRD PART

30

In January of that last year of the 19th century the East Coast of Canada was trapped in ice. The cold wind from the north froze the rain that came from the Atlantic; there was such a thick layer of ice on the surface of the land and on rivers and lakes that people feared it would not start to melt until the next spring and summer, and would linger until the first heavy rains of the fall. The ice made people shut themselves in their homes, and made cattle stay in their shelters; it broke everything that was breakable in the forests and parks, broke telephone cables, and sent children from schools and office workers from their jobs on an unpredictably long vacation. Aboriginal shamans observed the results of nature's anger with suspicion and explained that people had offended the Great Spirit and that he had sent a warning to them not to be involved in desecration of what he had created.

When, approaching the harbour of Saint John's, the ship *Lake Superior*, tired from her long journey and the struggle with the ocean waves, made a signal requesting from the harbour authorities a place to dock, long and heavy icicles started to fall from the eaves of the harbour buildings, making a sporadic cacophony as they smashed on the thick layer of ice already covering the ground. More than two thousand three hundred Doukhobors crowded onto the upper deck and greeted the town trapped in ice with their choral singing, the biggest choir ever heard until then on the west shores of the Atlantic. The singing notes of that great choir went sliding inland across the icy surface all way to the line where layers of deep snow replaced ice. The sounds drowned in that soft cover of snow, sinking down to the hard Canadian soil which each member of that gigantic choir imagined in his own way, different from all others. It is certain that none of them had imagined that their first encounter with their land of dreams and hopes would be when it was trapped in such extreme winter. However, as soon as the steamer neared the harbour's buildings, out of them came people of all ages welcoming the passengers on the ship by waving small flags. The Doukhobors also lifted their thousands of hands into the air to greet them; then on an impulse they started jumping up and down on the upper deck in groups and individually, shouting and stepping hard on the wooden planks in the rhythms of old Russian folk dancing. Their euphoria at this first glimpse of Canadian hospitality stopped at the ship's railing, beneath which there was still a broad stretch of rough water between host and guest. Some of the folks on the harbour's docks tried to respond with a similar play on land but at their first attempts to dance they started falling down on the ice and getting up again, continuing to wave their flags in the direction of the ship. The other big surprise for the Doukhobors was the clothes of these Canadians. They did not wear heavy coats and thick hats nor warm boots and gloves out there on the ice, its surface rough from the wind which should make people's feelings freeze even behind the windows in their warm rooms.

At the most prominent spot on the foredeck of the ship stood Captain Taylor and some of his officers, together with Misha Chernov and the other medical workers. They embraced each other, then waved their arms towards the shore, then embraced each other again and squeezed each other's hands in happiness. The mission to transport the Doukhobors from the Caucasus to Canada had completely succeeded. Captain Taylor had successfully brought from Europe to the American continent the biggest group of humans in his career on the sea.

Suddenly, signal flags appeared on the Harbour Master's building. Taylor frowned at them and turned to Misha. "They ask if we have had any serious communicable diseases on board."

Misha thought of the two children who had mysteriously died. Reluctantly, he mentioned this to the Captain. "I'm not sure what that means. Probably they will want us to go into quarantine."

Taylor gave orders to one of his officers, who hurried to the *Superior*'s signal platform. A message was sent, and more flags appeared on the official building. "I fear you are right, Misha. They say quarantine will be required. And they don't have the facilities here. We will have to go on to Halifax. But don't spread the word just yet. Let them all enjoy their celebration. They have excellent cause for it."

On the shore, two men as yet unaware of the quarantine news also had a special reason to celebrate. These were Russian Prince Hilkov and the representative of the Canadian Ministry of Immigration and Internal Affairs, James A. Smart. They squeezed each other's hands, smiled and patted each other's shoulders. James Smart was Deputy Minister and greatest support to Clifford Sifton, Minister of Immigration and Internal Affairs for Canada, who widely opened the door of immigration to that country because there was a danger of great influx from the populace of the United States of America to the uninhabited parts of Canada. It would, without doubt, pose a danger to Canadian unity and independence. There had already been frequent pushes from the south to annex some parts of Canada to the United States.

And Prince Hilkov? That jolly and always charmingly dressed prince, great friend and admirer of Lev Tolstoy, a man with a broad chestnut-coloured beard and an even broader forehead, was probably the happiest among all since by helping the Doukhobors from Russia he had managed to erase at least part of the blemish from the faces of Russia's ruling dynasty. If he were not Prince Hilkov, Tsar Nikolay II and the Russian Orthodox Church would have sent him to Siberia for at least a few years on account of his open sympathy for the Doukhobors.

Misha and Petro Chernov did not participate further in the jolliness and singing of the others. Unobserved, they left the group of their Chernovs on the foredeck and retreated toward the stern. Since their Boulisou's final departure they had felt detached from ordinary reality and from others who waited impatiently to reach the Canadian shore. Misha embraced Petro more frequently and Petro ever more openly redirected his feelings for his mother to his father. Never before had he gazed at Misha so questioningly and for such a long time while Misha was talking to other people. When the ship approached the shore of their new country and they saw it covered in ice and snow, its colour seemed to Petro like that of the sky on the day when through the snowflakes he saw his mamushka smiling and, with her eyes wide open, rising into the heights.

"Batya." Petro slipped the word out unintentionally. He had never before addressed his father in that manner. He looked at Misha with surprise, as if Misha had said something Petro had not expected; then he gazed at his father's sad eyes and said:

"Batya, did Mamushka arrive in this country as well? That snow over there coming out of the big water is of the colour of the sky on the day when Mamushka went up."

"Oh, Petro...my son...She did arrive for sure. I told you she would never leave us. She is now in our hearts. In yours and mine, my son. Only her body went up and she entered your and my heart and nothing can chase her out from there."

Petro was looking at his father's face as if not sure whether Batya was serious or only wanted to console him.

"Where are we going now?" asked Petro when he noticed that the ship had stopped before reaching the dock. "Are we going right away there where we will build our house?"

"Not right away, my son. First, we will spend some time isolated from other people because they are afraid that we have brought them some diseases from our country. Also, it is winter in Canada. When you see big flocks of birds returning from the south and flying towards the north and when you start feeling it is hot in that big coat of yours, then we will go there where we will build our house."

Petro, his face serious, followed his father's hand as it moved from the direction of the south to the north. He started imagining how the birds from these flocks that Batya had mentioned would follow Misha's guiding hand so that they did not get off route. He wanted to tell his father that he was now feeling better knowing that his mother was with them, but out of the crowd of the people facing the shore and singing appeared Dyedushka Kostuna and Babushka Pelagiya and while approaching Misha and Petro they started talking in unison:

"Where have you two been? They say we will be put in smaller boats and sent to a quarantine. Do you know, Mishka, where the quarantine will be?"

"Wait! Why all this noise?" Misha replied smiling. "Where they take others, we will go too. And on this ship, not in small boats. We are going now again on the ocean toward the Canadian harbour of Halifax. The Captain said there is an island there, with fishermen's huts and other buildings. They emptied the island so that we could settle on it for some time while any danger of the illness which took the two children passes."

"Mishka, maybe it is not fair for me to say, but I have a feeling that the rulers of our new country want to isolate us from Canadian people for a long time, so that as much as possible of what we have brought with us comes out. I do not mean diseases, Mishka. I mean what we have in our heads. I suppose they know very well who we are and where we come from, that we have been expelled and that we are their guests now…Authorities are the same everywhere…" Kostuna hastened to share his fears with Misha.

"Wait, Kostya," Pelagiya intervened. "Who knows what they think we have in our heads? But they have accepted us as their own. See these people on the shore waving at us as if their closest relatives had arrived." She was trying to protect her son from the attacks of Kostuna's unusual inspiration.

"It would be hard to empty our heads of what we have brought in them. From what I know about us, the more they try to make us similar to them, the more we will look for additional strength to resist that," Misha tried to follow his father's thoughts. "That will be especially true among those of us who are older. Younger people have a chance to choose—and follow what they perceive as better and wiser regardless of whether it comes from our tradition or from what these folks on the shore have acquired in their struggle for life."

"We'll see…For now it is better to be quiet and wait for time to show what is better and wiser," Kostuna added in a low voice, reaching with his arms towards Petro, who listened with only half his attention to the conversation of the adults. The other half focused on the sounds coming from the shore.

Misha was not scared of closed space, nor a space surrounded by water, but already in the first days of their quarantine on Lawlor Island he felt such depression that he started thinking about the effect of isolation on human feelings and the mind. On those days he contemplated his desires and plans and concluded they went in a circle, actually a cursed circle within which ideas about the outside world did not dwell. It seemed as if that world did not exist or did not have anything to do with these people inside the circle. Isolation makes man entertain irrational ideas about life and forces him to build unreal relationships both with people and nature. On this island, in the quarantine, people were enslaved both in space and time. The truth was they were all equal, with an equal destiny. However, Misha thought, there was no benefit from that equality. That equal destiny did not mean happiness for an individual. Neither happiness, nor consolation. Even when they knew the isolation would last only for a short time and for sure it would become just an unpleasant memory. Misha felt how his brain had already started to harbour negative feelings about the outside world of freedom.

These days Misha felt a warm air coming from the southern Atlantic. He saw how the ice started to retreat further away from the shore and on the mainland he saw people walking quickly and children running from tree to tree. He caught himself thinking that it was not just, that those people over there did not have more rights to freedom and happiness than he and his people confined to this island. He started feeling tiny prongs of jealousy even though he could not see their faces. Then he realized he was foolish and had lost touch with reality. He laughed at himself and saw Petro freeing himself from Grandpa's embrace and running towards a group of children who were heading for a small wood of tall leafless Canadian maple trees.

"Petro…" Misha thought. "Does my Peter deserve to spend his life in isolation?!" These thoughts overcame his consciousness. In the past he had questioned certain regulations of the Doukhobor way of life, and now in quarantine his thoughts became rebellious. With pronounced dissatisfaction, as if reading someone else's written text, he started telling himself: "Who will benefit if the Doukhobors here isolate themselves from other people? If they crowd themselves in their communities and organize their traditional way of life independent of the established rules of the Canadian way? We could keep our values, but we should not ignore the values that our hosts have created—the Canadian people. I think Verigin made a big mistake when he sent instructions from Siberia that we organize life here on the principle of communal living. No, no. This by no means could be happiness that would lead us into the future. No, no," Misha whispered, searching with his gaze for Petro's group of children among the Canadian maples. It suddenly occurred to him that he did not want his Petro to live in isolation in this land of hope. He was certain that Petro, when he grew up, could be at the same time a good Canadian and a good Doukhobor. Without living in isolation. He would be able to communicate with God in the manner of the Doukhobors, be against war and tyranny, against churches and priests, but without being isolated. Isolation brings most damage to the one who isolates oneself. Could the philosophy of isolation entail freedom? "No," Misha concluded. "Isolation is self-imposed slavery. Also, if the defenders of isolation believe that in that way they would be able to preserve the purity of their way of life and of their beliefs, they are terribly mistaken. They will conserve only one stage of civilization and stay on that level. In the same way as the people who accept the Bible and other holy books as the eternal rule of how to live and think. But man is not created in such a way that he stops his development. His brain knows of no boundaries, just as Prometheus created him to be."

In later days, Misha mostly remembered the quarantine that had awaited them at the entrance into their new life in Canada by his firm decision to allow neither himself nor his child to be imprisoned by anybody's intention to force them into the receptacle of their ideas, like cabbage into a jar.

While he had been a child listening to his father's stories in which Verigin, their current leader, had often been mentioned, Misha had cast around Verigin an aura of holiness. However, while he had been growing up and thinking more deeply about himself and the teaching he followed, he had turned more and more against leaders who impose their recipes on other people. Especially against those who had been pushing the Doukhobors into isolation from other people. When he came to understand what isolation meant, having spent time on the ship trapped in the unending wideness of the ocean and now on the island, still surrounded by the waters of that ocean, realizing how human possibilities stultify in such circumstances, he decided to tell others that the choice of freedom is wiser than the choice of isolation. "When you come to somebody's house, if you would like the host to accept you, you have to accept him too," Misha concluded before the cooks started calling out that lunch was ready. Walking towards a long wooden cottage where there was a huge dining room for the Doukhobors, he met Captain Taylor and First Officer Ballard, who had to endure the quarantine just like the Doukhobors.

"Gentlemen, how are you feeling surrounded by the Doukhobors on this isolated island?" Misha asked them with a smile on his lips.

"I think very similar to how the Douhobors feel being surrounded by other people," Ballard replied.

"It is hard for me to be isolated on something that does not move. Isolation on a ship is not the same as isolation on an island. A ship eventually arrives in some place, and I can get rid of isolation on its decks, see the waves breaking against the bow and the wake spreading astern. When the ship arrives in my harbour, I rush home to hug my wife and children; then I go to the inns to hug some friends. On an island?…" Ballard spoke as if reading Misha's previous thoughts. "An island will never take anybody anywhere. Anyone who wants to be rid of it must jump into the sea and swim to the shore."

Captain Taylor remained silent. He had almost one more month to look at and listen to these people he had transported on his ship. He was never quick to reach conclusions about others. Although at sea he was master, he would not even allow himself to act as judge except when certain that he was not wrong. In many ways, the Doukhobors were like other people in the world. The way they treated each other, how parents treated children and children treated parents, the way they emotionally responded to their surroundings, clearly visible in the way the lines on their foreheads moved—a lot of that was agreeable to a stranger and instilled confidence and sympathy. Their songs, brought from Russia's vast regions and from ancient psalms, stirred emotions. But they were different. Taylor scolded himself at the thought that in spite of everything he would not like to live close to them because every contact with them required a lot of delicacy and consideration to avoid offending them…

His thinking about himself in contact with these people was again interrupted by the voice of Robert Ballard, who addressed Misha:

"Doctor, have you decided where in Canada you would like to live? I would prefer to see you somewhere in Montreal or Toronto. There are many more possibilities for doctors in bigger cities."

"Good question, sir! I have to go where my people are sent. I am no prophet. It is hard to guess what will happen later," was Misha's ambiguous reply.

"I'll give you my address in Montreal. I am mostly on the sea but my family is at home. Even my son, William. He is studying veterinary sciences in Montreal. Next year he will finish his studies. Your people are farmers and cattle breeders; they will probably be allocated farmland where pioneers are needed. Maybe my son would like to work somewhere deep in the interior of Canada. In any case, if a parent can be objective about his child, I believe he is a good man and hates the idea of war and instigating pain on any living being on earth. I am also at your service if you feel a need to contact me."

Misha did not have time to thank Ballard for his warm offer because there on the shore, near the facilities the fishermen used for unloading and processing their catch, they heard children's shouts:

"Whales! Whales!…"

Soon a big group of people gathered on the foreshore admiring the huge tail fins of these sea giants. They were moving very fast close to the shore and every time they appeared on the surface of the sea they created a cloud of steamy exhalation and tiny drops of water. A few children started throwing stones at the school of five or six whales, imagining how their stones hit the hunched backs of the whales and ricocheted into the slow waves rolling toward the shore. However, these images were only the children's imagination because the whales were far from their reach.

"I bet your Petro is there with the children," the Captain's voice was heard. "Children are the same everywhere. If people did not grow old, they would be mischievous, unpredictable and much less dull. In harbours children often throw stones at ships. Once, in Boston Harbour, they threw a stone in the eye of my stores officer, so he had to spend the rest of his life with a grey patch over his ruptured eye. Was he a strange man! In harbours, while the rest of us would go out to restaurants and promenades, he would sit on a chair by the ship's railing and draw what he found interesting in the harbour. In each of his drawings there was one beauty with black eyes and black hair, always in a different posture but always charming and inviting. Sometimes in his drawings she would be sitting on a bench by the sea, sometimes on some old wooden fence right by the water, sometimes she would be swaying down the promenade in front of white stone houses, sometimes with the toes of one of her feet she would be touching the water as if checking its temperature…He confessed that only once had he taken her out for dinner, in Veracruz in Mexico, and three jealous Mexicans had threatened the next time they saw him with her to plug out his other eye so he would no longer be able to see any woman in the world. Somebody must have cursed him so misfortunes targeted his eyes." The Captain was talking while the children ran along the shore following the school of whales swimming away towards the south.

Since their arrival in the quarantine on Lawlor Island, every morning before breakfast and in the afternoon before dinner the Doukhobors had collectively spoken their prayers and sung songs. Their prayers and songs were pervaded by words of gratitude and hope directed at the Creator for having given them a chance to find a hospitable corner on earth for themselves. Nobody among them, not even in songs, did even think about asking the Creator why he had given them such a destiny and why in the first place he had given them a reason to pray asking for help. Why had he punished them and not those who had persecuted them and destroyed their property? These people did not ask for anybody's apology for their misfortune nor did they doubt the goodness of the Almighty. It seemed that in their philosophy of life it was more important for them to direct themselves and their future generations to live in accordance with what they perceived as God's will. And now when they found themselves on Canadian soil, they believed it was God's will that they had been brought to the best place on earth and that it was the reward for their goodness and love toward all people.

Misha joined the group of his closest relatives in singing with the others, feeling how these songs gave him additional energy and some inexplicable bliss. Even Petro would sing, though he secretly believed that these ceremonies should be shorter so that he could have more time to run around the island and to sneak a hand into the pocket of his Grandma's apron where she was hiding cookies for her grandson.

While the Doukhobors were singing, Captain Taylor and First Officer Ballard often joined a group of their crew members playing cards in a wooden hut which fishermen had also used for playing cards and other types of leisure activities to fill the time between fishing expeditions when mending of nets and boats was done. >From the huge clay furnace for heating and for smoking fish, occasional small sparks followed by gentle crackling reached the card players. When among the card players Ballard saw the second officer, James Cannigan, whom he had known even as a mischievous teenager on the streets of Laval, a town growing ever more into the bosom of Montreal, Ballard asked him completely seriously:

"James, is it really true that you are planning to ask Marusha's parents for permission to marry that beauty?"

James did not react to Ballard's question. He was looking at the cards in his hands as if Ballard had not said anything. The other three men at the heavy wooden table raised their gazes at the First Officer and their faces revealed they were expecting that James's reply might make them laugh. When he realized that James did not intend to answer, Ballard asked him again and neither his words nor his tone reveled that there was anything not serious in what he said:

"Are you in love, old son? You probably are because you devour her with your eyes any chance you get. She is a beautiful and healthy woman. But I think they do not want to mix with others, the Doukhobors. Aren't you afraid that her parents might refuse your offer?"

"I am not afraid," James replied briefly.

"Really? I do not think it doesn't matter to you," the First Officer was curious.

James raised his look from the cards to Ballard. His eyes revealed he welcomed Robert's questions. As if he himself had provoked Ballard to ask.

"Bob, I am in love with her. She charmed me immediately. Since what happened with Natalie, I thought that no woman would ever interest me. That I would rather go to brothels and pay streetwalking beauties in Caribbean harbours than have a serious relationship with a woman. Since I saw Marushka I have felt my face burn and blush. I became ashamed of thinking all women were like Natalie. This one is different. >From her downcast gaze I can read her feelings. She at the same time loves and respects men. Yes, I'll beg her parents to let us marry, even if they reject me."

"They will reject you, James," the bearded Owen told him. "They believe they will survive as a particular group of people if they stick tightly to each other. If they do not mix. They believe mixing would destroy their movement. I am not inventing things, James! The fat Greshka told me that. The one who made fun of himself because of his fatness, saying he would have an advantage if the ship started to sink. He has enough lard around him and a stomach as huge as a bellows, so he is not afraid of sinking."

"What did Greshka tell you?" asked Captain Taylor, who until now had been only a passive observer.

"He told me that neither Russian tsars, nor Church ministers, nor brutal Cossack soldiers, nor harsh winters, nor hunger, nor many other misfortunes had been able to turn them from their religion and their way of life, just because they had all been together, and all shared happiness and misfortune together. He told me exactly what we are talking about. That others would quickly swallow them, make them blend with others, if they started marrying those who are not followers of their movement. He said they could decide to sing different songs, to again take up the habit of smoking and drinking vodka, to pay taxes to the government, to send children to public schools, but they should not marry others," the bluff-mannered Owen patiently explained.

"Oh, ho!" said James and everybody took their gazes from Owen and looked at him. "Both you and the fat Greshka have forgotten about love. Nothing could stop love growing in the hearts of two people. My dear bearded Owen, as Navigator you should know that love has two powers in itself: the creative one and the destructive one. It will create all the conditions for those who love each other to start living together, and it will destroy all barriers, those of state, religion or property, or any other, against those two living together. You think I would have so simply accepted when Natalie told me she was leaving me? I would not if she hadn't sat next to me and started to cry as if asking God to forgive her for her sins and told me she was in love with that cute female teacher I was telling you about. With a woman! I could not stop her because I understood exactly that: love creates and destroys. If you try to block its way, it will take you over a precipice just as the great power of the water of Niagara would take you if you tried to stand at the edge of the waterfall. That's why I swore there was no longer a woman for me. But love conquered me, Captain."

"If they do not give her to you, James…" Taylor continued.

"We will run away as far as we could. She loves me too. She says the Doukhobors won't lose anything because she will die believing in their teaching, for she knows it is the most humane and the purest. She asked me if I had anything against her belief. I said, and I tell you, that I don't and that I love her just as she is."

Owen scratched his chestnut beard, stepped towards James, hugged him and squeezed his hand. Others winced, not expecting such a gesture from Owen, and started hugging James as if he had already married Marushka.

From the big cottage for dining, the song of a thousand Doukhobor throats reverberated on the island. Marusha was there singing with the others and often glancing at the wooden hut where James was defending their love and playing cards with his colleagues.

31

In the second year after his arrival in Canada, Kostuna fell seriously ill. When they had reached the endless flatland of the Canadian Prairies after leaving quarantine on the Atlantic Coast, the Chernovs found long wooden shacks specially built for the Doukhobors, where they were to spend the rest of the winter and continue to live until they could build their own houses. Kostuna did not expect their accommodation to be like the houses they had left behind in their former country: the not very comfortable shacks they were housed in did not cause him depression or dissatisfaction. He did not visibly react when he noticed Pelagiya's worried look as she complained about her fears that Petro lacked variety in what they could give him to eat, and had started to lose weight and grow pale. Kostuna also did not react when he realized that many in their colony had almost lost patience. Some complained very seriously about the troubles caused by the harsh winter and long distance from a bigger settlement. Nor when he discovered that some distributors of state-aid supplies took care of their own interests and cheated Doukhobors of their food. He neither opposed nor supported the expressions of dissatisfaction by those who showed low-spiritedness and impatience and were saying ever more loudly that the Canadian authorities had accepted them to demonstrate their humanitarianism to the rest of the world, but in fact only wanted to use the Doukhobors to populate some of the vast regions of uninhabited Canadian territory stretching from the east toward the Pacific Ocean. They had settled them on reserves like the Aboriginals. And that had been done in cooperation with the Doukhobors' leaders. But on a few occasions at the meetings in his community Kostuna did indirectly accuse Doukhobor leaders and the organizers of the immigration of having asked the authorities to settle them in uninhabited territories where the Doukhobors were to build their villages away from other Canadians. And he was very surprised when his son Misha decided to ask the authorities to change the location where they were supposed to build their own village and insisted that the new location be on the higher land embraced by the great curve of the Assiniboia River, some five kilometers away from the location the state had designated for them.

"Why do you prefer that location to the other?" Kostuna asked Misha and the tone of his voice revealed not only surprise but also displeasure. "Why into the jaws of that river so that we always fear floods? Or give an opportunity to those who lose their spirit to meet their death in that water before they realize how foolish they are. Finally, Misha, the winters here are harsher than ours, and by water winters are always harder than away from it. And if we faced trouble that meant we needed to flee across the water, I would not know where to run nor how."

"We are farmers, Father. Summers here are often hot and dry. What would happen to our crops without water? There on the high ground we could build our houses, and there by the river we could plough, dig, plant, let our cattle graze," Misha explained to him. "We could swim, Kostuna! Ride in boats, catch fish, if somebody wants to eat it. If our people want to focus on crop-farming, we could easily dig canals for water and irrigate our fields. We dug them in the Caucasus, in that rocky soil, why not here? Finally, Father, maybe the authorities will not let us build on that hill, so why worry so much about it?"

Dissatisfaction and anxiety did not abate in Kostuna when they started cutting trees and making houses up on the high ground above the river. Every day he became more and more thoughtful, spoke fewer words, and became impetuous when he did decide to talk. He less frequently teased and played with Petro, and did so less spontaneously. Then, during the second summer of hard work in his colony to prepare that beautiful soil for planting, and build the houses of their new village, he started getting spasms more frequently; with his hands he would press the right side of his stomach under the ribs, breathe heavily and wander away from everyone, especially when he was certain that no one was watching. Pelagiya secretly followed his every move, afraid he would discover her, for she knew that he would be embarrassed and that he would scold her for spying on him. Then once, when they were refreshing themselves with water from a small lake near the area where they were helping to clear the bushes and a thick layer of grassroots, she complained to Misha. Misha went to his father without hesitation. He was on the other side of the lake, stretched on the prairie looking at the empty hot sky. Misha sat next to him and looked him in the eyes.

"Father, what's wrong?" he started in a gentle voice, as if afraid that Kostuna would get up and leave refusing to talk. "It seems to me you are not feeling well, but you are not saying anything. I go around to cure people in our communities and you do not want me to help you."

"Mishka, I am fine. Who told you I was ill? It must be your mother. She is capable of inventing my illness so that it suits her soul to look after me. It's nothing, Misha!" Kostuna also spoke in a low voice, not wanting to change the position of his body.

"I have observed you many times, and noticed that you have been pressing your stomach in pain, that you have become thoughtful, that you whisper to yourself and breathe heavily. What's going on, Father?"

Kostuna could not find an escape and he confided in his son.

"I am having problems with my stomach. But it is not stomach sickness. It is the sickness of the soul. My soul hurts, Misha. Since we made the decision to immigrate to Canada, I have been feeling bad. I have never felt worse than now. It is not because we lack normal living conditions, but because some fear has come over me. It is worse than my horror at what happened to our Boulisou on the ship. The pain under my ribs does not worry me so much, but the great changes that I feel do worry me. I am not ready for them. Only now do I realize that we have come to a country that we do not know. We do not know their language, our customs are different and God has not appeared to give us advice. This aid from the state and good people will soon stop and for hundreds of kilometers around us there is nothing. I am afraid they have pushed us into the worst part of this huge country and that for us it will be worse than for Aboriginals because this is their land in which they have their roots. They have gotten used to each other and it will take a long time for them to get used to us. Who knows how all that will turn out?"

Misha knew that Kostuna would eventually accept his counter-arguments, but that his soul would stay unchanged, and not because he could not accept reality. He realized it was only the beginning of a nightmare in Kostuna's consciousness and that any new day might bring a higher tide of the irrational and the paranoid to his feelings. It was an illness Misha did not have a cure for. He thought if his father could be able to suppress the paranoia by regaining his faith in Misha and in the other people around him, the pace of the illness conquering him would be slower.

"Father," Misha addressed him, like a friend, not like a counsellor, "we are Doukhobors! We know that life is according to God's will and that we have chosen to live serving the good. Now the most important thing is that we build for all of us, especially for our young people, our Petro, the conditions for a normal life in this wilderness. And we can do that. Our powerful tsars persecuted us, as did the powerful Russian Church, and we prevailed."

During a pause while Misha waited for his father's reaction to his latest words, from all parts of the village which the people were building together, various sounds and human voices reached them. Somewhere from beyond the house they had built for the family of Vasily Grigoriyevitch Popov, came the even sounds of a long saw used for cutting roof corner boards. Somebody called out a few times for Sashenika to bring a cord for the plumb bob and instead of a human voice the reply was the gruff bellowing of a cow somewhere in the fields towards the river. From the other side was heard the dull banging of a heavy hammer on some thick post, which they were probably hammering into the ground to use as an anchor for the foundation planks of the new house. A group of girls pulled a heavy wooden cart carrying two barrels of water on its platform, laughing at two boys stooped to the ground trying to move a pile of heavy boards. They didn't realize that anyone was behind them, so they were straining at the boards with their cute young bums turned towards the girls. A few yellow-brown dogs chased a group of children trying to tear a length of cloth from their hands.

The Doukhobors had agreed that each village should have two rows of houses and between them a broad road where their social life would take place. Between the houses, as a rule, there should be no fences and the recommendation was that the houses should look alike and be almost of the same size to avoid jealousy. In the middle of the village would be built an Orphans' House. Misha had had a plan to create a square in the middle of the high plateau above the river and to make streets along the four sides of the square. However, the Village Council of the Elders, the *Starosta*, had decided to follow the instructions of Peter Verigin, Lev Tolstoy, and his son Sergey, whom the Doukhobors, in the absence of their leader Verigin, respected and accepted as their counsellor. Because Misha had a medical practice, the village had decided that his house, in which Kostuna, Pelagiya, and Petro were also to live, should have one more room than other houses, for use in treating the ill.

From the construction work in the village Misha's gaze slowly travelled to the field a few hundred meters away across the lake. On that day a dozen women were ploughing that part of their field. They were leaning into wooden bars attached to a thick rope at the end of which was a heavy metal plough. They were followed by an older man who steered the plough, which they were using to prepare the wild surface of the fertile soil for the spring planting of seeds. As if following Misha's gaze, Kostuna addressed his son again:

"Do you see, Mishka, our women over there in the field? They are ploughing glacial soil that has never been ploughed. The problem is not in the soil but in the roots that have become interwoven during thousands of years and it will take years for the fields to become like those we had in our country. At least they could have given us more oxen and horses so that our women would not need to pull the ploughs! Your mother is old, but the other day with a group of women she pulled the plough..."

Misha struggled to find the right way to take part in his father's thinking and to comment on his words. He knew they had to use whatever was available to till as much land as possible for planting with seeds of wheat, beans, cabbage…The oxen and horses they had received as help were far from what they needed, so that women had to take the place of men who were needed for cutting trees, bringing them from the woods, and building the houses. Many opponents of Doukhobor settlement in that region were secretly taking photographs of these women who, instead of using oxen and horses, pulled the ploughs and tilled the soil themselves. They published these photographs in Canadian newspapers which attacked the authorities, claiming that those Russians to whom they had opened the doors of their prairies were people of low culture and that they should not have been settled in areas where cultured Anglos-Saxons should live. Misha Chernov was aware that they were launching these attacks not out of a desire to help the Doukhobors and prevent such toiling by women, but to use this propaganda in their pre-election struggles for political power.

"Father, we are going to make this soil the best bread-basket in the world and our future generations will be proud of what we are doing today," the son gently scolded the father, not taking his gaze off those women who were pulling the plough through the uncultivated soil of the Canadian Prairies. "And those women down in the field, you know very well, Father, are from the family of the old Arhyp Samsonov. You know the Samsonovs do not let animals work for them. Do you think that's wise?" Misha's voice became a hiss. "Is he a better Doukhobor who lets his women toil on the land instead of animals, instead of oxen and horses? Such people demonstrate their humanity to animals by letting women plough in this hot weather!"

Kostuna was surprised. He did not expect from his Misha such a violent attack on what Kostuna also found immoral and inhuman.

"You don't think that I support such tendencies in our movement? I also think it is stupid and immoral. I wish I could meet Verigin and his counsellors somewhere so I could quickly get such theories out of their heads. Your mother went yesterday with the women to plough so that she would not be a black sheep. The other women came for her and she went with them."

"I know why Mother went with them. She went so that tomorrow, in the time of the harvest, some people would not be able to say that we received the same portion as others even though we did not toil as much as they. However, not everybody is like our Pelagiya. There are some who dodge hard work and receive their equal portion. It is like that now. But I think that such collectivism and solidarity won't last long. A hard worker will not tolerate a lazy one, Father. Now, it has to be like this!"

"It is true, Mishka. We will...I am of the same opinion...We will..." stammered Kostuna, obviously wanting to stop the conversation and go away from his son. The older he got the more awkward he felt when near Misha. It seemed that he was losing his previous importance in the family and being prepared for some corner in the house where, as he imagined, he would spend the rest of his life. But Kostuna did not want that. He preferred to depart this world before they put him in a corner. Fear of losing his importance in the family weakened his will to live and brought on depression, which Pelagiya had been noticing since their arrival in Canada. She realized that in Russia her husband had stood firmly on his ground and that here on this Canadian ground he no longer felt himself to be the useful pivot of the family. Kostuna realized he was getting older and that he had jumped out of the time and space that belonged to him into some alien space and time. Kostuna's fear that he could lose his place amongst the people closest to him grew into a kind of paranoia, which Misha thought could turn into aggression. He knew his father was a calm and reasonable man, but illness is illness.

When Kostuna got to his feet and started to walk towards Pelagiya and the group of women on the other side of the lake, without waiting for Misha to follow, he turned back and said in a serious voice, his gaze fixed on something beyond Misha's back:

"Recently that Aboriginal who brings us chicks and ducklings to raise in our village has told me that established farmers in this

Assiniboia are unscrupulous and would sell the whole world for a dollar. He confessed there are some Aboriginals who do not like us, but the farmers only like their profit. He said they had even secretly incited some radical groups in their tribe against us to make our life miserable so that we leave this territory. I heard they are instigating some Métis from Manitoba against us as well. It is the same movement against us which managed to persuade the leaders in Fort Edmonton not to let us settle in Alberta. Here they could not harm us because at present their parties do not hold power in the country. People are afraid that the Liberals might lose in the next election and then anything could happen."

Misha lacked arguments against Kostuna's words. He knew much more than what his father had told him but he considered such events a normal beginning in a foreign country, which many claimed as theirs even though so much of it was wild and inhospitable. However, he also saw that their Doukhobor village was acquiring the shape of an organized settlement, that new strong houses were being built for many families, that the teams of their lumberjacks and carpenters were also turning out more and more of the necessary house furniture, that the area of cultivated land was every day becoming bigger, and that the soil was very similar to the fertile *chernozem* black soil of their native land, there beyond the Azov Sea, about which he mostly knew from the stories of the old people. Also the mosquitoes in their new land in Assiniboia, about which there were rumours that it would soon became part of the new Canadian Province of Saskatchewan, were similar to those of the flatlands between the Rivers Dnieper and Don. He trusted the Government Counsellor for New Immigrants in Canada, Mavor Maud, who had on a few occasions told Misha that Canadian Government expected the Doukhobors to be a great help in turning that fertile uncultivated land of the Prairies into the biggest bread-basket in the world. He had also advised them to build a few grain silos by their village before merchants and profiteers came up with that idea.

And Paroniya? Paroniya's family had been settled in a group of Doukhobor families about ten kilometers east of Misha's village of

Spasovka. As a rule, Doukhobor immigrants in Canada gave their Canadian villages the names of their villages in Russia, believing that in that manner they would lessen their nostalgia for Russia. After Boulisou's death, Paroniya had first seen it as a chance for her and Misha, but some strange feeling of participation in Misha's tragedy made her patient in order not to sully his love for the lost wife and the mother of his son. She left it to Misha to signal his feelings to her after Boulisou's tragic departure from their lives. But now, when Misha's wife was no more, the feeling of belonging to Misha was growing in her more than ever and she was ever more impatient when they met or when they went together to help somebody who fell seriously ill.

Once when they were riding towards the village of Prokuratovo in a carriage drawn by Misha's horse, they were silent, as if afraid to talk. Fierce wind was blowing from the east and making waves in the tall grass of the flatland. The mane of Misha's grey horse, different from other horses because of a big black spot on his forehead, was blown so violently that it seemed the wind would start tearing it off his neck and make it disappear in the grass behind their backs. The sky was heavy with thick dark clouds so pregnant with moisture that they were almost touching the surface of the prairie. When the narrow country road turned around the lake, shallow along the shore and adorned with tall marsh grass from where occasionally came the tiny shrieks of small ducks, they felt a smell of smoke coming from the east. They soon saw a black screen of smoke over towards Kirilovka, so that the smoke and the dark cloud blended into a curtain between them and the nearby village.

"Mishka, the prairie is burning over there!" the worried voice of Paroniya interrupted the silence. "There is no flame, but there is a dark curtain of smoke…"

"It seems to me too that the dry prairie grass is burning. The wind is coming from that direction. If it does not start to rain, it could bring trouble to our village."

Paroniya looked at him with her big wide open eyes and, not hiding surprise, she said in protest:

"The fire is far away from your village, Mishka. It looks like my Prokuratovo is burning! We have to hurry there to help them should they need us."

"Don't worry, Parusha. Prokuratovo is on the right from the smoke, and the wind is blowing from the village in the direction of the fire."

How can he be so calm? Paroniya was thinking. There are a lot of elderly people in the village, and we only have four horses and three pairs of oxen for about two hundred souls. Should they try to run away from the fire, many will be roasted! But when behind the huge smoke screen she saw the rocky hill above Prokuratovo, she lifted her head towards the sky and clenched her teeth, scolding herself for not having noticed that the village was not in the path of the prairie fire before Misha mentioned it.

Misha raised his eyebrows, looked at Paroniya, sucked his upper lip, as if assessing her thoughts and intentions. Who knows what that innocent brief scene moved in her brain, but she bent her head and leaned on Misha's shoulder. Misha was surprised. He did not expect it in such circumstances, but all his body shuddered in satisfaction and he found his eyes fixed on her breasts. In a flash he realized that the touching of their bodies floated on currents of wind mixed with the smell of smoke and opened their windows to each other. Behind them nothing mattered anymore, neither Misha's love for Boulisou nor the limits prescribed by their understanding of morality. Without giving the horse any signal to stop, Misha grabbed Paroniya's head, pressed it against his and started kissing her without any feelings of guilt. Hands fondling each other behind the blowing mane and the horse's fluffy tail, they searched for the place into which their passionate feelings were pushing them, and they were drinking from each other's lips, so they for a moment forgot about the fire, about Prokuratovo, and about the danger that the wind could spread the fire to Misha's Spasovka. Only when the horse realized that something strange was happening behind his back and that Misha was no longer holding the reins in his hands did he stop, and Misha and Paroniya realize that they needed to signal the horse whether to continue forward or to retreat before the danger that was approaching them.

Misha had received the horse as a gift from the Aboriginal man Manidu, of the Chippewa tribe, after Misha saved his son from the venom of some yellow-green snake which Misha had never seen before. Later he found out that those unusual poisonous snakes from the Prairies' swamps are common and that their only predator is the long-legged eagle, which sometimes dives into the water rushing after the prey it discovers from great heights. The grey horse, like other Aboriginal horses, had a strong bond with nature, and with wide open eyes was looking in the direction of the smoke and snorting more and more, probably trying to tell Misha that they should make the decision immediately to avoid the fire.

Misha and Paroniya realized that by letting their bodies continue their love folly they would lose precious time, but, wanting to quench their desire, they looked even more carefully at the dark screen of smoke and were relieved to discover that the wind had started changing direction and that the fire was now moving to the north, towards the river. Prokuratovo was far from the river, the grey horse needed a rest, and the two of them time for fulfillment of their passion. Misha signalled the horse to turn around in the direction they had come from, and when the horse had done that, Misha made him stop and he returned to Paroniya's embrace. Their equally intense instincts led them into the old intricate play of love, from which they would forge a marriage, and give birth to their son, whom they would name Nikolay, Nick Chernov. Whenever the two of them later pondered over their memories from that time, both tried to find a justification for their folly in the vicinity of the burning prairie. On one occasion, when they were sitting on the trunk of a maple tree which had fallen in a storm, its branches immersed in the lake, Misha placed his hand on Parushka's already big stomach, trying to sense the beats of Nick's tiny body, and a thought crossed his mind, so he said:

"Love is stronger than anything," he said in a confessing voice. "The instincts that prod feelings of love are not under human control. They originate in the creative intentions of nature and are stronger than any norms and morality established by humans. Love is the healthiest human feeling. It is not only an elixir for the soul but also the most efficient nourishment for the human body. It appears suddenly when two people meet and an inexplicable instinct draws them towards each other. It is some kind of natural biological magnetism, not within the power of the human intellect. When two people create a union based on a desire of their intellects, it is often not the true natural love. There is calculation in that, serious life plans…But it is not real natural love. That one originates in the most naïve sphere of human personality and all calculations are alien to it except looking for the fastest way to reach the loved one," Misha expanded his original thought.

"Ah, Mishka…Wait! I know you are a doctor and you know a lot about the human body, but I did not know that you are deeply interested in this type of psychology. Babushka Tarasova once told me there is nothing stronger than a woman's feeling towards a man when she chooses with her heart to spend her life with him and to have him father her children, but they married her to a man from whom she would run away even in her dreams so that he could not catch her."

"Why do you mention Babushka Tarasova?" Misha was surprised.

"I don't know why she assumed that I was interested in that long-legged son of her brother Stepan. Having assumed that I would marry him, she persuaded him and both his and my family that it would be best for both of us to marry each other. They cooled down when somebody told them that I was living with Svetlana, and that in fact I am in love with you. When the long-legged bulbous Ulyan heard that, he started turning his head away from me. I am not sure what he detested more: me with Svetlana or me with Misha Chernov.

"One should not be ashamed of love, Misha. I have been waiting for you for more than fifteen years and I'm proud of us. Even if Boulisou could see us, I would not bend my head before her," said Paroniya, and Misha was thinking the same, but Parusha's words were reverberating in him like some kind of defence against his own lingering echo of guilt. Waiting so long for Boulisou to disappear so she could enter his life. He was certain that very few people would wait as patiently as Paroniya had to enter the life of their loved one.

"I have no right to ask you about Svetlana…" Misha replied, but he had decided to clarify with Parushka the relationship between the two of them. And he did it now when her allusion to Svetlana prodded him. It seemed to him that Parushka had mentioned her friend on purpose to eliminate once and for ever that secret from their life. "…But I would like you to," he finished.

Paroniya became serious and thoughtful. A few times she looked Misha directly in the eyes, then returned her gaze to her stomach, inside which was their child.

"Svetlana is my sadness, Misha. We started to sleep together in the Siberian prison—because we suddenly found ourselves separated from everything we knew, among unfamiliar people, out of fear of that schizophrenic state of mind in the Siberian penitentiary. Then we realized it was the best way to save ourselves from the lecherous wardens. So they would not rape us. When they became convinced that we were lesbians, and that we detested men, they left us alone. Maybe they wouldn't have, and maybe they would have taken revenge on us if there hadn't happened to be the beardless Onyegin, a nurse, whose job was to take care of our hygiene. He was huge like a bear, and his whole heart was filled with bereaved love for his partner, whom those macho wardens had drowned in a water trough for pigs. Only because he loved Onyegin! He was as gentle as the most gentle girl, so it was not difficult to drown him. Onyegin was protecting the two of us and no warden dared to approach us."

"Why is Svetlana your sadness, Parusha?" Misha asked, moving his hand from her stomach, where Nick was developing, to her shoulder.

"Svetlana was convenient for me because I had persuaded myself that there was no other man for me but you. And you were not there. You were not mine. Being close to her body made it easier for me to wait for you. But she…She loved me. She thought the two of us would spend the rest of our lives together. When I confided in her after seeing you for the first time in Kars after our return from Siberia, and explained that I was waiting for you, she became sad. That's why she did not come with us to Canada. She stayed behind, disappointed and hurt, and made a decision to live alone."

"To be honest with you, Parusha, do you know what I was thinking there in the penitentiary when I stretched myself on the bed and put my hands under my head? Every time I imagined you two together, I would see images of those children who where created in rape and would disappear, whom their mothers drowned in that large cesspool underneath the women's toilet. Then the mothers would cry for days and refuse food. And those warden beasts would pull those drowned children out of the excrement with long hooks and cross themselves while they buried the tiny bodies in that long ditch behind the corn field. They would gnarl like rabid dogs at your huts, pick flowers in the fields and put them on the grave-mounds where they buried the newborns. Then again at night they would drag you out of the bedrooms and rape you."

Paroniya remained silent for a moment. Then she said, "It is better not to go back to those images, Mishka. Those memories are not making us happy."

Not long after that fire on the prairie Misha received a message that three Aboriginal men were waiting for him by the river on their dappled horses. It did not surprise anybody because Misha would often go to the nearby Aboriginal reserves to help the sick, when Aboriginal shamans were not successful. Aboriginals were coming closer to the Doukhobors villages but were not entering, probably aware that the new settlers had not yet got used to their race of people.

One of the three men was Manidu, a strong man with pleasant facial features, longish black hair and unusually big blue eyes. The other two were young men with a cheerful gaze and thin moustaches. They dismounted their horses and lifted their arms in salute to Misha.

"I can see you are very different from us Chippewa, Doctor. I have heard that some white scientists claim that the American continent is not our land and that we came here from Asia. In fact, thousands of years before the white man, but they say, nevertheless, we also originate from somewhere else. You explained to me that you too have come far, from the region on the border between Europe and Asia. But we are not like you. You make villages very differently from the way we do. We do not like to put houses in rows, and you make them all the same as two eggs are. We scatter houses in all directions, one under a

346

huge tree, the other by water, the third on top of the hill…One is round like our tents, the one next to it is narrow and tall, the other with its roof reaching the ground…And yet you, Doctor, treat us as you treat your own people…"

"We are different, Manidu," Misha agreed. "If our tastes are different, it does not mean there are more differences between us than similarities. We are humans. Both you and we. We speak, have feelings, know what is right, remember the past, plan life, try to pass our best experiences on to our children…If somebody undressed us and mixed us together, and observed us from a distance so as not to notice the colour of our skin, he would say that we are the same. Nobody would know who is who." The two men regarded each other like brothers who had been estranged. "But what brings you to our village, Manidu?"

"To warn you, Doctor. When I was a boy, I heard stories from our people who live there by the Great Lakes, about what had happened to the ones who had come from your country before. Many settlers did not like them and tried to do them harm. Something similar could happen to you too. We have talked about it, Doctor. A few weeks ago, some farmers from the area under the line where the state plans to build the railroad visited our chiefs. They secretly offered to us a lot of money, guns, ammunition, whiskey, flour, salt, and sugar if we would try to scare you into leaving this territory. Our people refused that but some might accept. Recently too a group of foreigners has appeared; they look like you—white men—and they have asked us if we wanted to trade with them. One of them has asked about your son a lot."

"My son?!" Misha looked at him in surprise. "Why my son?"

They were silent for a few moments; then Misha asked, "How did he look, the one who wanted to know about my Petro?"

"He is older than you, but to us you all appear similar. He was wearing a neat coat like those that Americans wear, tight pants, and high leather shoes. His nose was bumpy, more like mine than yours."

Misha felt thunder and pounding in his brain. His memory jumped from one face to another and questions amassed without any order or sense. Who could that be and why? Why his Petro? That's what those

347

who abducted and killed Boulisou had tried. It suddenly occurred to him that he had lost any trace of the three Antonov brothers. When they had arrived at Saint John's, at Captain Taylor's request the police had taken them away and he had not seen them since. Rumours about them had stopped after that. Misha tried to recall their faces but he was certain that none of them had such a bumpy nose as Manidu described.

Manidu advised that Misha keep his son in the house for some time. Then he offered to take Petro with him because nobody would be looking for him in the Chippewa village. He could attend school with their children if Misha did not mind that the school was under the jurisdiction of the Anglican Church. Misha thanked him in a brotherly manner but decided that Petro should stay at home with his family. He asked Manidu to try to find out some more about that man who had inquired after his son.

'How is your son Ayawamat? Has the fever come back since my visit to your village?" Misha wanted to know.

"He is as healthy as a bison. All day long he stands in the swamp and preys on fish. When he catches one, he throws in into the bag on his back so that a fox, coyote, or bald eagle won't be able to steal it from him."

"I also caught fish in a lake when I was your son's age. Nobody in the village could catch a fish with bare hands as easily as I could," Misha said, not so much to brag about the skills of his youth but more to find some similarity between Manidu's son and himself.

"But you do not eat fish, Doctor!" suddenly said the young Chippewa who had a dozen long black hairs on the tip of his chin.

"When it comes to food, not all Doukhobors are the same. My clan eats fish, and when I was a young fisherman we also ate chicken meat," Misha explained.

Manidu was looking towards the river as if imagining Misha wading into the water and waiting for a fish to come close. And Misha? He did not know why he now recalled the stories he had heard from the seafarer Ignyatiev, who had lived near the Doukhobor village of Bogdanovka in the foothills of the Wet Mountains in the Caucasus.

While the adults attended the council meeting in the Orphanage, in front of the Orphanage Ignyatiev would tell stories to the children. When he mentioned the warriors from Aboriginal tribes, he described them as merciless while fighting their enemies, and very merciful in peace. With these thoughts running through his head, he thought of a question he wanted to ask Manidu:

"Can I ask you something very different?" Misha addressed the Aboriginal man.

The man looked surprised, and his eyebrows touched while he tried to guess Misha's question. When he realized he was just wasting his time, he nodded:

"Ask me, Doctor. I will answer if I can."

"Recently you have been helping us more than those who should be helping us, so I would really like to know why. Your kindness is very welcome, but it is unusual."

The Aboriginal man smiled, then put his fingers between his lips, pushed the right cheek out with his tongue, gazed towards the east beyond the river, and started speaking in a voice full of pride and dignity:

"Doctor, we still do not trust white doctors. And yet we asked you to come to our village and help cure my son, and that old woman who had broken her hip when she fell in a hole between rocks, and then the stubborn leader Bodaway...There is something agreeable about you Doukhobors.

"First, we also migrated to these prairie regions from the east. I think I haven't told you what our legends say about why we came here. You came here because tempests created by your leaders pushed you into the sea. And we left from the Atlantic coast when in the sky above our tribe appeared a big sailing shell that was moving slowly towards the west during each day and during the night it stood still, high above our wigwams, waiting for the daybreak. Our shamans understood that God had sent us a ship to invite us to follow it into a better future where white people coming in big ships from the east wouldn't attack us. That shell dragged us every day more and more to the west until we reached this prairie, home of bison, deer, fish and healing herbs.

"Second, you came to these wild prairies and you are not warriors. You do not carry weapons. A people can survive here only if others are scared of them. Weapons are the law here, Doctor. It would be the best if we didn't need them, but..."

"Manidu, we came to the land that by natural law belongs to you. You were the masters here before the arrival of the white man. Isn't that reason enough to hate us?" Misha asked, sensing it was a convenient moment to find out more about the people who surrounded them in those wild prairies.

"That's how our ancestors felt when white people started coming here. Nowadays it is different. We know that we cannot resist the pouring in of the foreigners, not only white men. We accept Canada as a country of all the people who live in it. I do not want to talk about justice when it comes to the division of land nor about corralling our people on reserves. We have also come to this land from the east. There is space here for all of us. And for many more people. We probably need more land than you because you are farmers, and we live off hunting. But we are also slowly taking up farming, and taking other jobs. Some among us are already working in the railway construction. We also need money to survive. That's how it is nowadays."

When they mounted the bare backs of their horses to follow a route around the Doukhobor village of Spasovka, Manidu told Misha:

"Your Petro is a sturdy boy. It won't be easy to steal him. But people would do anything for money. I'll try to find out more about the man who was asking about your son."

The Aboriginal men left by circling to the east of the village, where the grass was taller and the stands of Canadian maple more frequent. Misha was not too much worried about Petro, but he wanted to find out more about that man who had inquired after the boy. It must be somebody who had some connection with them. That man, obviously, did not want to do harm to Petro because he could have found a way to do that already. And...But anything was possible. Misha's thoughts focused on the Antonovs, but he realized it could also be traffickers of children who sold them to wealthy, childless Americans. However, Petro was already fifteen and Misha dropped that possibility.

Dusk gathered about Misha as he returned home. He heard a song coming from the direction of the lake, which one arm of the river supplied with water. With the song the Doukhobors were celebrating another successful day. It was a hymn to the sun and rain. The builders were making more and more houses, and those who were preparing the soil for planting tilled more and more of the fields; the women so successfully organized the production of fabric and woollen clothes that they had enough for the merchants who had started visiting them not only to offer their products for sale but to buy from them. Woodcrafters were able to make furniture and wooden dishes that the merchants desired, so that now they had enough orders to keep production going for the entire winter. From humanitarian organizations in Canada and America, like the Quakers, they were receiving the seeds of wheat and vegetables so that there was no doubt they would be able to plant every single part of the soil they tilled.

Although they didn't avoid farming, the Chernovs focused more on handicrafts. They were especially skilled in working with wood. Misha's uncle Genadiy was famous far away for his joinery skills. Everybody in the village wanted to have at least one piece of his furniture, and the merchants offered to buy all the wooden birds, bears, and wolves that he could make. Realizing that it could be a profitable activity on a larger scale, Genadiy set about training many young people in the village to shape the wooden sculptures. Petro had already learned a lot from Genadiy, so that his contribution to the family budget was considerable. Whenever he received money for his sculptures, and he preferred to make fish and birds, he started teasing his father, showing him the money and saying he would be able to earn more money from his sculptures than Misha from curing people. In fact, the Provincial Ministry of Health was giving Misha only a symbolic salary for his medical practice, limiting it to the Doukhobor villages. However, a government official for immigrants had recently suggested that Misha have his medical diploma recognized, for it could happen that his salary be determined by his Canadian licence. Also, there might be a need for Misha to practise in a wider region, beyond the region of the Doukhobor communities. The level of Misha's fluency in English was now high enough for him to communicate in the official language of his province.

When the cold breath of winter from the north was again felt in the region of the Doukhobor villages, the news arrived in Spasovka that Marusha Nikolayevna from Tambovka had eloped with James Cannigan, that curious and smiling second officer of the *Lake Superior*. Her brothers and cousins went in search of them, but Marusha's father, Nikolay, was faster than they. He reached his daughter and future son-in-law when they were crossing the Whitesand River and hid them in the swamp watered by the river during the fall and spring rains.

That year winter came earlier than the migrant birds announced it. Canada geese had not yet begun to fly over the Doukhobor settlements in Saskatchewan, nor foxes to get closer to villages, when one night in early October it suddenly became cold. The following morning the smaller streams and lakes were skimmed with ice and by evening there had been so much snow that the boys and girls in Spasovka formed teams to shovel it from in front of the houses and along the central village road. The cousins Vasya, Stavro, and Vasilisa picked up Genadiy and Petro to go together to visit the Bondarevs, who had organized a party where they would sing old Russian songs and psalms. They invited Misha, but he preferred to remain with Pelagiya, Kostuna and Paroniya, who had already put many halves of white potatoes into the oven of the big metal stove, and were preparing crumbled cow cheese with onion. They had the left-over borscht from lunch. Kostuna was feeling nausea and Misha stayed near his father in case his condition worsened.

In order not to miss the roasted potatoes with cheese, Genadiy and Petro left early from the party at the Bondarevs, whose house was at the other end of the village. Petro was still singing in a low voice the lyrics of the song they had just sung at the party:

The Hindu and the African,
All races on earth,
And the Mongol and the Caucasian
All are going to be one family.

Genadiy suddenly placed his hand on Petro's shoulder and whispered to him to stop. From one of the houses in front of them, they heard quarrelling. The female voice was loud. From the Bondarovs' house the singing of the choir could be heard.

"That sounds like the voice of Praskoviya," Genadiy pointed with his hand in the direction of the house from which the sounds of the quarrel were coming. They stood for some time in the middle of the broad road and the wind from the north was throwing the dry snowflakes into their faces. Through the narrow windows of some houses the light of oil lamps was reaching the street. The voice of the quarrelling woman mingled with the loud bellowing of a cow from some distant barn. Genadiy and Petro started moving slowly and soon reached the house from which the quarrel could be heard. Now they were certain that the female voice was that of Filat's wife Praskoviya, and occasionally Filat's calm tenor could be heard as well. Genadiy and Petro instinctively stopped to hear what was going on.

"You have destroyed my life!" Praskoviya was hissing, and Petro squeezed Genadiy's thick coat sleeve. "You shut me in the house to clean and wash and give birth to children, and you got yourself a job at that blind merchant's and are away all day! Who knows what you are doing there!"

"We are working, Prashenka. Do you think that Peter would give me a salary if I did not work? I work like a donkey and do everything Peter tells me to. And more, so he does not fire me. My salary comes in handy for us and the others in our community," Filat was trying to calm his wife.

"Do not make up excuses! I have no use for your salary. I do not even see it. I cannot even go to that store to buy something because I don't have a cent."

Praskoviya became quiet for a moment, and Filat was probably thinking that her attack had stopped. However, only then did the woman really give him hell:

"I won't have it any more! I can also find a job. You do not deserve me! You are the biggest mistake that could have happened to me," Praskoviya was now shouting. Filat was quiet. Genadiy reached for Petro's hand, intending to proceed home, turned his head to see if anybody else was walking through the village, and Praskoviya continued with the same intensity:

"What have you done for me? I am no different than a cow. Other people earn money and buy their wives a piece of clothing from Boston or New York. And you...Have you seen what Anton bought for Jasenka? And their children...I wear what our great-grandmothers used to wear. Always the same! I would like to have some of the things that come from America."

Then Filat protested much more loudly.

"Prashenka, stop! See how you are talking! You praise me in front of other people! You make me look big. And when we are alone, at least once a week the anger comes over you and you start hissing. You say I have ruined your life. But I share everything with you and our children. I do not have more than you do. And I did not forbid you to do whatever you want. If you want to work in the store, to collect healing herbs and sell them, to...Do whatever you want, just leave me alone once and forever! Why are you praising me in front of others?"

Filat's voice was still fairly calm. But Prashenka continued screaming:

"If I told them the truth about you, they would feel sorry for me! They would say how worthless a girl I was because I couldn't find a better husband than you! Plus a widower with two children!..."

"Why did you marry me, Praskoviya? I did not force you to marry me. You sometimes say you would have died if you hadn't married me. And what's wrong with my sons? They are grown up, they work as others do. Both want to go to work in the railway construction. You used to respect me. How come your respect is gone now? I am sure it has nothing to do with me. It seems that even before you became dissatisfied I was just a statue in your brain. Now you are kicking that statue with your legs to break it. I haven't been able to make your secret plans come true. Be careful, Praskoviya, when that statue starts falling down, it might hit you in the head."

"Are you threatening me? Should I not have expected anything better from you? To whom have I given the best years of my life?!" the woman was squeezing out the words through tears.

"I am not. You are doing that to yourself. I am supporting you in the path you once chose. Our brain constantly offers us different paths to walk along in our lives. Swerve off the path we have been walking together and find yourself. It seems to me that some wind has suddenly made your wings spread, Praskoviya. It is not the doing of a normal brain. Close your wings until you see where that wind comes from and where your wings might take you."

For both Genadiy and Petro the conversation was becoming more and more interesting. They had never known the Filat and Praskoviya who were now revealing themselves in the cold night. Genadiy started questioning whether the husband and wife had been different people before or just that hopes and expectations had made them hide their real feelings. In fact, Genadiy concluded, man is a very complicated creature and it is difficult to measure him by using the same yardstick every day. Probably, men are formed by the circumstances they live in, and when the circumstances change, people reveal what before was hidden in their character, maybe even deep in their genes. A plant cannot grow without a seed. Once in front of the school, the biology teacher Howard had told farmers that seeds of some types of grass could be conserved in the soil or rocks for decades, even longer, and when the conditions for their germination are created, they start to sprout. It must be similar with people.

Filat became quiet. Praskoviya was silent too. Petro started stamping his feet with the cold. They both started to move, but Praskoviya, as if she knew that somebody had been listening and wanted to make him stay, continued in the same tone of voice, full of anger and tears, and Genadiy pulled Petro under the porch of Filat's house so that they could continue listening but also hide from the freezing wind.

"People see things! Women tell me they are surprised that I live with you. Nowhere in our Doukhobors laws does it say that a woman must put up with her husband. They say I am beautiful, smart. I could be a tsarina! Rich widowers are proposing to me. Women tell me how that tall Scotchman who is buying Genadiy's wooden sculptures is interested in me. He said, when he saw me, that he would marry me right away if I were not married already. The women told me that. Melaniya told me that too…She said you treat me as if I were in prison…and that I deserve a better life."

Filat apparently lost his patience. He raised his voice and probably jumped to his feet:

"So you are telling others nice things about me to make yourself look better! It is rotten, Praskoviya! I would have never thought that you are such a rotten person. Do whatever you want! I am not going to stand in your way! If you want, I'll tomorrow gather our elders to give you permission to leave me. If necessary, I will say only bad things about myself so they give you your freedom!"

"Now you tell me that! Why didn't you say that before. Now when I have three children with you…"

"Do not worry about them, Praskoviya! I'll stay with them. You follow your path and I will stay with the children. That Scotchman hasn't remarried yet. Go to him! He is a great man who will offer you real life, not me…Leave tomorrow, if you want! I am not a doctor to offer an expert's opinion about your psychological condition. But I know that you have put a blindfold over the eyes of your heart and that you are dragging yourself to a precipice. You won't be able to come out unless you take off that cover. Even if you take it off, it might happen that you remain on the precipice your blindness has taken you to. It was not without a reason that old people used to say that dazzle can damage the eyesight and that attractive things are, as a rule, not good. Often a glaring light hides the abyss in front of one's feet, Praskoviya."

Somewhere from the back of the house a child's voice was heard; it started calling its mother and crying. Probably the children had patiently tolerated their parents' quarrelling until they started talking about divorce and family separation.

Genadiy and Petro could no longer listen to it. They were surprised at what they had heard because they had both believed Filat and Praskoviya to be an exceptional couple and that they had lived happily. They became embarrassed for having stopped to eavesdrop on that strange quarrel between husband and wife. They quarrelled now when in the new country, in which they were born again and had a long difficult life path in front of them; instead they should hold each other's hands because it is safer and easier to live like that. The night became colder. On the way home Genadiy confessed to Petro that strange things had started happening among the Doukhobors. Since people had started to go to work outside their communes, especially since that group of workers had gone to California, things had gone bad with some families.

"I have heard about it too, Uncle Genadiy. It seems that our villages have become too small for some people. Many have started to think differently than before. Especially women. I have heard open talk that our way of life should become more liberal," Petro said.

"That there should be more self-initiative," Genadiy continued young Petro's thought. "I also believe that people should not follow the same rules all the time. Especially those imposed by others. It seems to me that the human mind and feelings are not stable. People desire changes and novelties.

"Who knows, my Petrusha, what is going to happen. And what the future will bring. When a bird sees that the cage door is open, it rushes out believing it rushes into freedom. If you told the bird it was wrong, it would peck your forehead with its beak. But, in fact, it itself does not know what awaits it on the other side of the cage's door. Maybe a hawk. Maybe a mate. I also do not know what will come out of a block of wood when I start working it to make an animal. It happens to me that after deciding to make an eagle with spread wings, the piece of wood

I plan to use to make a wing gets chipped, so I change my plan and make a beaver. Who knows how your life will go on and the lives of those younger than you. What awaits us is full of challenges and uncertainties. They influence our decisions about how to live."

When they reached the doorstep of Petro's house, Genadiy signalled Petro with his hand to stop so that he could tell the youth some more of his fear.

"It would be best for Filat and Praskoviya to take a while to think. These times here are foreign to us, especially to us older people. We are now going through a storm of time we were not born for. In a storm it is best to find good shelter and lie low until the bad weather passes, just as birds, hares, and beasts do. If you do not, you risk much more. Storms can destroy things built in previous times. Petro, maybe it is easier for me than for those who have a wife and children. Maybe it is better for me to have a chance to hug you once in a while than to wait for a wife to attack me in the way Praskoviya just now attacked poor Filat."

The warm room full of the smell of borscht, cheese, and potatoes awaited them inside the house. Pelagiya first offered them a glass of yoghurt to refresh their throats after singing at the Bondarovs.

32

Kostuna and Nikolay never met. Kostuna died while he was dipping pieces of rye bread in the warm fennel tea. In his last moments he was aware he was leaving and offered one hand to Pelagiya and the other to Petro. He blinked a few times as if trying to tell them something, then closed his eyes, his hands dropping onto the woollen blanket. On that day in the afternoon, Paroniya gave birth to Nikolay. As soon as he felt oxygen and opened his mouth to breathe it in, he started screaming and kicking with his arms and legs as if he wanted to go back to his mother's womb. The women washed him with warm water and wrapped him in a soft blanket they had been keeping since Petro's birth. His grandpa Yakov had brought it from Istanbul. Then they put the tiny red-faced Nikolay on Parushka's breasts. The mother was looking at her son trying to figure out if she would recognize him if they had brought him in a group of a few other newborn babies. As soon as he felt he was close to his mother, Nikolay stopped screaming and with his tiny fingers grabbed his mother's thumb, which she had offered him. The little Nikolay grabbed his mother's digit not to let it go until the end of her life as all newborn babies had done before him and would do into the future.

Misha was not around when his father was dying nor when his son Nikolay was being born. Early that morning men had come from the Doukhobor village of Terpeniye to fetch him because the oldest sister of Ivan Vasiliyevitch Potapov, Efrosinia, had had a high fever and cramps in her stomach for the whole night. As soon as Kostuna died, the family sent the young Mikhailo's son Seryoza Chernov on his fast bay horse to Terpeniye. It took him about five hours to get there. Misha and Seryoza returned to Spasovka at dusk and found the house and the street outside full of people. The whole village had poured into Misha's house. They wanted to mourn Kostuna and at the same time offer little Nikolay a finger so that he would go easier through his life.

While he was going through the crowd to reach the house, within which Kostuna's body was laid out on the new bed that Genadiy had made for Kostuna and Pelagiya, many family members and villagers hugged Misha. Through the sounds of song performed by a big group of men and women, the words of condolence as well as a few nice words for his Nikolay reached Misha's ears. When he reached the doorstep, the singing of the Doukhobor choir attenuated to a solemn diminuendo, so he managed to hear condolences from Alexander Popov, who, having heard the news of Kostuna's death, had come from the nearby village of Nadezhda to be with the Chernovs.

"Kostya was a respected member of our community. He lived his life honestly and did not hurt a fly. He departed in the same manner. Pelagiya said he died holding her hand and Petro's. Mishka, there was a miracle in your house today—your son was also born," Alexander expressed his feelings to Misha.

Embracing his mother, Misha entered the room where his father's body was lying. Only the body of his Kostuna was in the room. The other parts of the house and the yard were full of people, and Kostuna's body lay alone in the room on the bed Genadiy had made. If it were not for the red roses Pelagiya and Boulisou had embroidered together onto the white counterpane while Misha was in Siberia, the remains of Kostuna Chernov would have looked miserable, so lonely and isolated from the crowd of people gathered because of his death. That revelation made Misha melancholy and uncomfortable, and made him feel sympathy for all human beings born to travel through life in this and that way just to leave, in the end, as alone as they came. With the one difference that one enters life from mother's warm womb, and one leaves life cold and stiff, facing an uncertainty that forever stops one's breath. The times before birth and after death are the same, unknown to people. Both are spaces of human imagination in which men unconvincingly create magical worlds through which the human spirit travels along the paths to eternity. Only in these imaginary worlds is man the master of his life, Misha was thinking as he looked at his father's body, because in real life he is only a pirueta moved according to somebody's design. If my father Kostuna had been able to choose his life he probably would not have chosen to depart from us in this country, so far from ours. Maybe he wouldn't—the thought occurred to him while he was looking at his father's blue eyelids and his yellow pale face—so blindly have followed some leaders who caused him more harm than good.

Then it occurred to him that he was like his father. Maybe even worse because he had had a chance to choose a different path in his life, but he was like a chip from that old block. And he asked himself, "What will happen with Nikolay? Is he going to follow the same path..."

Petro entered the room where Misha was saying goodbye to his father. Genadiy followed him, his face revealing—especially within the past few years—the relentless and ever more visible passing of time. He gave Misha and Petro time to hug each other tightly and their eyes to become misty. Then he hugged Misha, muttered something about Kostuna's departure, with his sleeve brushed the tears running down his cheeks, and slowly left the room. Petro was staring at Grandpa's body and then looked through the window into the distance.

"Why did Dyedushka die? Why did he leave us?" Petro suddenly asked his father. He looked into Misha's eyes as if to prevent him from avoiding the answer.

"Because Dyedushka was old," Misha replied, his voice faltering.

"He was not that old, Batya!" Petro whispered.

"And because it was God's will, son," Misha added.

"Why God's will, Batya?!"

Petro was looking at his father with his eyes wide open.

"God decided that it was time for Dyedushka to leave us," Misha said, still hesitant.

Petro again looked through the window as though expecting help from there.

"I do not understand, Batya. How can God decide that our Dyedushka should die?! What kind of God is that to take our Dyedushka from us? We haven't done anything bad to God."

"We haven't my son. I do not understand either. Certainly God thinks differently from us. We, in fact, do not know how God thinks."

Misha was speaking in a low voice and staring at Kostuna's body on the bed.

"But it is not fair, Batya. Dyedushka always said God is just. How then could he have taken Dyedushka from us?!"

Misha felt pressure in his chest. He did not want to answer Petro's questions as a doctor, who knows very well why people die. His answers came from his feelings, from the deep spirit of his people, among whom his Petro had grown up and whom he understood. While he was looking at his son's face, Petro's broad dark brows and eyes the colour of a burning coal reminded him of Boulisou. He himself did not know why that thought crossed his mind at that moment, and he realized that the wrinkles on Petro's forehead contained one more spirit in them, the spirit of Boulisou's roots reaching him from the enormous distance of time and space. He felt guilty and embarrassed. He took his gaze off Petro and cast it on the floor made of wide oak boards whose grooves bore witness to the age of the tree they had been made from. Testimonies of the times those trees had gone through must have been deposited in the ridges between the grooves. We never think about it when we cut trees and use them to make boards for our floors. In the same way, Misha thought, he had never before tried to read what had been written in the wrinkles of Petro's forehead. And he had pulled Petro out of the roots from which his mother had sprung, and left him only with Misha's own roots, which Kostuna had brought from the faraway past of his people.

"Where is Parushka? Where is our little Nick?" Misha suddenly asked his mother when she entered in the room.

Nikolay was sleeping when his father saw him for the first time. Paroniya kissed Misha for both herself and their son and whispered:

"I do not know who he is like. Children change. And his forehead shows he will be an excellent human being. Look at him…"

"It does not matter who he is like, Parushka," Misha said, keeping his hand on Paroniya's forehead. "I want him to be a good man. To know no hatred. To be hardworking and to always have thirst for new knowledge. To be surrounded by love all his life. And to not have to run away before people as we have had to until now. My Nikolay," he continued in a low voice not to wake him up, "because you are a man your batya wants you to get rid of the instinct for isolation from other people. If your life path were that of distrust and discrimination against others, you would be persecuted. Even if they did not persecute you, you would think that you were in danger from others because you were different, so you would run away. All your life…"

"What's with you Mishka? What are you talking about?" Parusha asked him in a weak voice. "Do you think we were born with a curse to be different!? And that is why we have been persecuted…?"

Misha continued to look at his son's tiny face and followed the occasional spasms rising from Nick's stomach, through his throat, over his tiny round chin, to his still blue swollen lips. He realized it had been neither the time nor place for that sudden outburst of the feelings and philosophy swelling within him.

"I apologize to both of you. You have to bear with me, Parusha. Today my Kostuna died and my Nikolay was born. My feelings are mixed in me, and thoughts are crisscrossing in my head. Also, Nick does not understand my words, so he will not remember them," he said softly to his wife, whose pale face revealed she needed sleep. He patted Paroniya's forehead, pinched the tip of her nose, and stared at Nick's face.

"He looks like you, Parusha. Your forehead, your nose. Good luck to our Nikolay!"

Kostuna's grave was the second in the plot they had designated for the graveyard in the village of Spasovka. The granddaughter of the fat Stepko Dmitriyevitch Vasiliyev had died not long before him. She had just turned two and had left this world suddenly and without seeming to suffer. In the early evening she had been playing with the children in front of the house, and during the night her face had suddenly turned red and she had fallen asleep. She had spoken in her dream, whispered, and when her parents woke up she was already dead. The rumours were that maybe she had been attacked by some Aboriginal disease against which the people from faraway Russia had no immunity. Misha's medical explanations could not stop such rumours about this girl who had the night before run around with other children and had been found dead the following morning. While holding the body of his granddaughter, Stepka had tried to reach through her closed eyelids to the bluish irises more beautiful than the turquoise colour of the Swan River when calm during the summer dry weather, its beauty sparkling in the eyes of the people on its banks. Grandpa wanted to see what life images had been left frozen in the eyes of his granddaughter but, against his will, the tears blurring his vision prevented that.

Kostuna was an unassuming and unobtrusive man. He was thoughtful in making important decisions, and when offering advice, he would say that it seemed to him people should do this and that, but that everybody was the best judge of his own situation. He did not like leaders, and among friends he would say that the instinct to be above others ruled some people and that it did not bother him unless that ambition floundered in greedy egoism. The only Doukhobor leader he had never said anything against was Lukeriya Kalmikova, whom he personally considered wise and desirable. He believed the Doukhobors had accepted her as a leader because they saw that everything good after the death of their leader and her late husband, Peter Kalmikov, had been to her credit. When Kostuna was provoked to express his opinion about the leaders he blamed them for imposing themselves on the Doukhobors or for inheriting their position—sons from fathers, cousins from cousins. just like the Russian tsars of the Romanov dynasty—without demonstration of merit. Lukeriya herself had taken office because at his deathbed her husband Peter had pronounced her leader. Even their leader Peter Verigin had become the head of the movement because of his closeness to Lukeriya and his acceptance of her role in the development of the Doukhobor life philosophy. However, it had also been on account of the fact that the previous leader, Kapustin, was important in the Verigin family's roots. "We Doukhobors haven't chosen our leaders," Kostuna would say. "They have imposed themselves on us or have become leaders by inertia of family relations, just as lakes do not decide what water flows into them."

Pelagiya had always felt Kostuna to be a major part of her destiny because he had always protected her when she felt threatened. She did not like to see his gaze suddenly stop and melt on the breasts or hips of another woman, but as time passed she accepted that as part of the Almighty's mistake when He created men. She did not publicly accept the confessions of some of her friends who revealed they liked it when an attractive man looked longingly at them, but she recognized the same feelings in herself. In fact, she covered up her own secrets by saying she detested such looks because they betokened sexual fantasies and sacrilege against the morality of marriage.

Kostuna had gone on a journey of no return, and Pelagiya started to wrap herself in ever darker and heavier clothes in order to look older than she was. Her gaze had lost its freshness and she often noticed she failed to see a person standing in front of her but would instead see images far beyond that person, images from her memories. Inexplicable feelings were pushing her away from Misha, as if she understood she had no place in his life. Misha had early been weaned from her embrace because even as a child he had shown an extremely strong personality, and when he returned from Siberia she felt that his Boulisou had become closer to her than her son could ever be again. And since that experience with the mystical scenes with dolphins on the ship in the Mediterranean and then Boulisou's incredible departure from this world, she had started to notice on Misha's face, especially in his eyes, a strange glimmer and thoughtfulness which created an emotional barrier between the two of them. That was probably the reason she became even closer to Petro after Kostuna's death. Almost every moment she dedicated to her care for him and would move from one window to another when her grandson was away from home. She had an unnatural, restrained relationship with Paroniya, more official than intimate and friendly. She had been much closer to Boulisou. She also felt that little Nikolay was the sacrosanct property of Misha and Paroniya and was even afraid to hold him, who was so small in her arms, and to press him to her bosom as she used to do with Petro when he was Nick's age. All that new life they had been building since their arrival in Canada seemed to her unnatural and temporary, full of novelties for which she was not ready. When Kostuna was alive, everything was different. She had built most of her relationships with the outside world through her husband and preferred to be in his shadow than in front of him. Only now when he was no more did she realize that Kostuna had been the warm breath who had prevented the icy feelings of insecurity from forming around her. Pelagiya was quickly getting old and all her desire to live she linked to Petro. But Petro was growing out of childhood and every moment had a stronger need for the life and world beyond his home.

That year the summer was dry and hot. The inhabitants of Spasovka had planted the largest areas of fertile soil with grains, corn, beans and cabbage, and for days there was no cloud in the sky. People came to fear that their crops would die and started digging canals from the river to their fields and orchards. As a result, instead of dried-up crops, their fields were green the whole summer and promised a hefty harvest. Then at the end of August, representatives of the authorities in Regina visited them and presented their unequivocal position that the Doukhobors needed to be included in regular relationships with the state. The representative of Interior Affairs, a small man with a chubby stomach, Stephen Brown, briefly addressed the gathered villagers:

"First of all, all your names must be recorded in the census-book of the citizens of this country as those of all other Canadians have been recorded. The families must determine ownership rights; and the owners of the land you till, of the houses, and the cattle, must be recorded as such. They will become the taxpayers and will pay taxes to the state for the properties you own and for what you produce on your land, as all other Canadians do. Those who are under military service obligation will be recorded in the register of men available for militia recruitment as other Canadians are. The newborn must be recorded in the register of births, and the dead in the register of deaths. We need to record the names of the children of school age and before all that you need to swear an oath to the King that you will be loyal citizens of this country and that you will respect its laws."

"Wait a little, sir!" the voice of the sturdy Gresha Tarasov was heard. "We were promised that in this country we would be able to live according to our philosophy of life. And that's not what you are saying."

"I think you were not promised anything outside the laws of this country or beyond the rights of other citizens," the Interior representative hastened to explain. During a short pause following his words, he gestured for the tall official who accompanied him to stoop down so that he could whisper in his ear. The man obeyed his colleague's wish. After listening to the whispering, he shrugged his shoulders and straightened up his tall body as if he wanted to separate himself from Brown's discussion with the Doukhobors.

At that meeting the Doukhobors energetically confirmed that they would not accept the recording of land ownership in individual names, insisting that their property was of collective ownership; that none of them would ever accept military service; that their children would not go to schools where they would be taught to exploit other people or to be warriors; that they would not give oath of loyalty to any person since they had already give their oath to God. The representatives of the authorities carefully recorded everything that the Doukhobors had said and left the village. Soon the news reached the village that people who refused to give the oath to the King, to respect the laws of the country or to send their children to school, would have the land they had cultivated taken away from them, their right of stay in Canada revoked, and receive punishment accordingly for breaking the law regarding education. After that, the Canadian Doukhobors entered into open conflict with the authorities and suffered consequences similar to those they had suffered in Mother Russia.

One afternoon some years later, while Misha, along with Petro and Paroniya, was harvesting wood for the winter on the plots that the Doukhobors would clear in the spring to prepare them for planting, two boys came running from the village and before reaching Misha started shouting:

"Mishka, a man has come to the village and wants you to help some farmer!"

When they reached Misha, Petro, and Paroniya, they suddenly stopped as if they found themselves on the edge of a deep canyon; they breathed in heavily a few times and the one with curly fair hair said a bit more calmly:

"He has a moustache, and is yellowish and freckled. He came in a two-wheel horse carriage. His horse is the same as that of the hunched Matvey. He said that the Old Stewart from the farm, the one who has bisons' heads with thick horns on the posts of his fence, has asked you to come and help three of his workers. They have fallen ill and within a week have melted down as the last year's snow. He said that the doctor from Yorkton had fallen ill too and couldn't leave his bed."

"Mishka, this man says he has known you for a couple of years when you gave them advice how to save their oxen when a plague attacked them," added the other boy, who had until then only been looking at his companion, who for some reason had the privilege to address Misha first. "But to me that man with the moustache looks frightening! If I were you, I would not go to the farm with him. I noticed a big gun next to the seat of his carriage. And his eyes are frightening."

"Oh, my Zizka. I thought you were not even afraid of the coyotes who come to our village, and now it seems your teeth start clicking when you see a small mouse by the stream! Do not worry. I know that man with the moustache very well! It might be that his head looks frightening and he might look like somebody who could scare you in your dream. But he is like a dove…He feels safe only when in the middle of the village or on the farm with bisons' heads. He carries a gun to gain courage when riding through the prairie in the plain daylight."

Misha approached the boys and hugged them both and asked them if their father Seryoza had fixed the loose bridge over the irrigation canal, and then they all went to the village. Soon the moustached, yellowish and freckled George and Misha were riding in the carriage towards the farm with bisons' heads on the fence posts. The muscular Antisha Petrovitch Golubov transported them over the river on his raft, all the time telling them how since the last melting of the ice, some longish red fish had appeared in the river, the kind which not even the Aboriginals who rode their long, horned canoes ever remembered seeing.

"I have also heard about these fish in the river," George agreed and turned his gaze to search the depths of the water. "The Old Stewart believes they came from the Great Lakes because last year the river flooded the area down to the south, and right after that the cold weather came and formed ice on the surface of the floodwater, and thus enabled the fish to move under the ice even from the Great Lakes to this river."

The Old Stewart was born close to Newport in Wales. When he was ten, one morning his mother told him and his younger sister Elizabeth that their father had arrived on a ship late the previous night and had asked her to get ready because in about ten days they would move to Canada. The children were surprised at first, then started crying because from their father's stories they knew Canada was far away across the ocean and they also knew that the one who moves there never returns to his native soil. Stewart later asked his mother if another family was also moving to Canada with them, hoping his mother would mention the family of Stephen Buck. His mother shook her head, wiped her moist eyes with her apron and disappeared behind the kitchen door. Stewart stopped breathing for a moment, and his plump sister asked him if that meant he would never be able to see his Emily again, and without waiting for his answer, she ran in the direction where her mother had disappeared. After that, Stewart had exchanged letters with Emily for twelve years, and saved enough money to cross the Atlantic to Newport and ask for Emily's hand. He returned with his wife to Yorkton. They built a farm for raising beef cattle, gave birth to two sons and one daughter, and became one of the most amiable families in the Canadian Wild West.

Stewart was waiting for the carriage in which George and Misha arrived. He stood leaning against the porch railing of his huge house, built from thick tamarack logs. He accepted Misha's extended hand and hugged him.

"I must have interrupted your work in your village. But occasionally it is fine to accept somebody's offer for a break," the Old Stewart addressed Misha in his trembling creaky voice.

"Your interruption will be justified if am able to help you," Misha replied, smiling at the weathered old man.

"Let us have a drink, Doctor Chernov," Stewart suggested, but when he noticed Misha's wide open eyes, he added:

"I am not for alcohol either. Don't worry. I have other drinks," grinned the cattleman, whose age had not done any damage to his back.

"I would like first to see the young men," Misha suggested.

Stewart authoritatively pointed with his hand at a comfortable rocking chair and while Misha was making himself comfortable in one of two identical seats, the old man brought a wooden pitcher, a ladle and two big ceramic mugs.

"Such cranberry drink you cannot find on any other farm," the old man was bragging while pouring the red liquid into the mugs. "This one has a specific taste; it is bitter and is more like cider than juice, and you can mix it with yoghurt. As for the young lads, I owe you an apology. You will forgive me. I am much older than you and am not a skilled liar."

Misha raised his gaze from the red liquid, expecting Stewart's next words.

"There is somebody here whom you know very well, Doctor Chernov. If you promise that you will forgive me for my thoughtless lie and the circumstances of the meeting I have arranged, I'll…introduce…this gentleman," the Old Stewart stammered.

"What is this about, sir?" Misha asked, the tone of his voice more than a little curious. He knew that the old rancher was not capable of concocting any evil plan nor even a small trick that would bring harm to anybody.

"Doctor, can I bring in Mister Yakov Hasson?"

Misha instinctively rose from the armchair and in the doorway leading to the house he saw a man with thin grey hair and a long greyish beard. Even though it had been many years since their last meeting in the deep snow in Misha's village of Pokrovka, close to Kars on the foothills of the Wet Mountains, Misha immediately recognized Yakov's long bumpy nose and small blinking eyes, now sunk deeper inside their sockets with age. His clothes were similar to those of the entrepreneurs and merchants who had recently started visiting the Doukhobor villages, but his face was older and darker that the former face of his Boulisou's father. They had not been close friends before, but now Misha suddenly felt a warm feeling coming over him and he hurried towards Yakov, who also stepped forward, and they embraced each other. When they separated their eyes were moist and their cheeks red from the pressure of the blood rushing from their memories. Misha remembered Manidu's description of the man who had been asking about Petro a few years ago, the manner of dress and the bumpy nose, but in this moment it did not matter to Misha any longer. It was, nevertheless, unusual that Yakov hadn't asked Misha directly about Petro because he was, after all, Petro's *nono*. But in this moment Misha did not want to look for the reason for Yakov's behaviour.

"How come you are here?" Misha asked when they sat in the rocking chairs. The host, evidently pleased with the reunion of the two, hurried to pull up one more chair and to bring a mug for Yakov.

"Where do you live? How about the others?" Misha added while Yakov was thinking about where to start.

"We heard what had happened to our Boulisou," Yakov began, and reflectively touched the tip of his chin with the bony fingers of his left hand. "They told us how you had fought for her," he went on, and bent his head. "We heard about our Petro...My father died two years after you went to Canada. Rifka married Woskovs' Daniel. Soon after, they went to Boston, to America. In our region there had been rumours about a new war and we made a decision to immigrate to America too. My uncles and cousins from Turkey had been urging us to do that for a long time. We managed to get the immigration papers and moved to Boston. We sold everything we had back home and it was enough to start a merchant's business there. The Jewish communities have helped us a lot."

Misha felt that Yakov made a pause in order to hear news from Misha. Stewart excused himself, saying he had to give some orders to his cowboys, and left.

"You must have heard they had settled us in the uninhabited regions of Canada. The huge uninhabited spaces and uncultivated land whetted the appetites of the Doukhobor leaders and the promoters of our emigration from Russia. They believed that in this wilderness we

Doukhobors would be far away from the law and the authorities and that we would be able, without obstacles, to practise and develop our Doukhobor way of life. Our leaders hoped to build some kind of Doukhobor territory, immune from the customs and laws of Canada. The Doukhobors have organized themselves here as they did in Russia, built similar settlements, started a way of life similar to that over there. We thought the authorities would not make problems because of our philosophy of life, but…authorities are the same everywhere. Because of our stubbornness and the stubbornness of the Canadian authorities we lost a several years quarrelling about laws, oaths, ownership of property, education, military service. Even to this day I haven't received a licence to work as a doctor, but they unofficially accept that I practise in our settlements and occasionally outside of them when farmers or Aboriginals need me. Only recently have they officially given me a job at the railway construction because other doctors are not eager to accept work in such harsh conditions."

"How are the others? How is our Petro?"

"My father died when we moved into the new house. Petro is now a grown up man. He completed grade twelve and is now working in Genadiy's woodworking shop. I married Paroniya Strelayeva and we have a son, Nikolay. You will go with me and be our guest and see them all," Misha suggested at the end of his brief summary.

"Tell me about Petro," asked Yakov, and his gaze wandered to one of the darker corners of the room, dominated by a huge dining table made of roughly cut oak boards. "Rifka has two daughters. Petro is the only male descendant in our family."

Misha noticed a glimmer of tears forming in the corners of Yakov's eyes. Misha's thoughts were mixed. He assumed what was behind Yakov's latest words, and he remembered his own thinking about Petro and a possible injustice because the Chernovs had neglected his ties with the roots of his mother's family.

"You will see Petro, if you haven't decided to urgently go back to Boston. As I see him, he has a lot of his mother in him. He became a good man. And he is hardworking. You have to meet his younger brother, Nikolay!"

Yakov was searching for something in Misha's eyes. It seemed he was consolidating his feelings, as well as absorbing Misha's. He was looking for the best way to start the conversation about why he had arranged to meet Misha in such an unusual, even bizarre way. Misha was aware of Yakov's searching look. He made a pause, and decided to be direct.

"Why did you decide to find mediators to reach Petro and me? Why did you offer the Aboriginals money for information about Petro and me?"

Yakov raised his head towards the porch ceiling made of red engraved boards, swallowed saliva and looked Misha in the eyes.

"I was lost. I tried to get information about you and Petro from various sources and I often received terrifying information. Many North American newspapers have been writing about you as uncivilized Russians, who tyrannize their wives and children and make fun of the teachings in Christian books. I have to be honest with you. I heard—as you just said yourself—that you have organized yourselves here in the same way you organized yourselves back in Russia. You have built your villages, isolated yourselves from others, accepted aid from the state and from organizations and individuals, and then chosen complete civil disobedience. This has provoked the authorities and given wings to the enemies of your immigration to this continent. I was not sure what kind of welcome I could expect in your village, but I wanted to meet my grandson Petro. I was not even sure how he would accept me, even though our blood runs through his veins."

"I understand you," Misha helped him. "When they told me somebody had offered money for Petro, I did not think of you, but I also did not think it likely that anyone would pay to have something bad happen to Petro. Why should they? Yakov, is there anything beyond your desire to meet Petro that I should know before he sees you?"

"I am aware my grandson is a Chernov, and one of you, Russians. I had nothing against it even before. If my Boulisou had asked me before she left with you, I would not have given her my blessing. If a tree grows from an old root, and you pull it out and separate it from that root and then plant it in some other place, it is very uncertain how it will continue its life there. But once she was married to you and had your son, I had nothing against it. I have never hated Russians and in some way I loved and respected you. However, Petro is at the same time one of us. His roots are more branched, wider and deeper than yours or mine. And roots determine how the plant will look and how its parts above the ground will live," Yakov carefully explained.

"I am not of the opinion that Petro should choose one side," Misha replied. "To pick one identity and decide what he should be. I think he should be both. His identity should be more universal than our identities. If he is smart, he will choose what's good in each of us. Man is first of all born as man, and after his birth they pull the clothes of identity over him. But, Yakov, Petro has grown up among us. He is a Doukhobor. He has grown up in our culture following our relationship to God. It seems to me he is more of a Doukhobor than I am," Misha was merciless now.

Yakov did not show surprise while Misha spoke. He occasionally scratched behind his right ear and pressed his lips together.

"I know he is," Yakov agreed. "But you know it well, he is also Jewish. He is one of us Sephardic Jews. In his life he has been persecuted as we were persecuted in the past. I have nothing against the fact that he has grown up in the Doukhobor tradition. But with us Jews, the child is what his mother is. The father could be anything, but if the mother is Jewish, her children are too."

"But with us Doukhobors, Christians," Misha challenged him with a smile, "if the father is a Russian, a Doukhobor, the children are too, no mater who gave birth to them."

Only when they almost simultaneously reached for the mugs to refresh themselves with cranberry drink, did Misha and Yakov realize they were alone in the huge house of the old rancher.

"A good man, this Stewart…It is not hard to discern in the features of his face and in his gestures that he grew up in the wilderness of these prairies, and that with great skill he added to the tradition of his civilization, which he had brought from British soil, the freshness, pride and ability to survive which this harsh nature has now built into the genes of his future generations," Yakov praised the host.

"I do not know him that well. The few times I have met him is not enough for me form such an opinion about him. But I like him, and have heard some fine men of this region, especially the Chippewa, say that he is a man of strict character, fair and unconditional, like nature here. There is no false smile on his lips, nor is there superficial profiteerism in his relationship with people. They say he is a man who defends his own interests, but he does not make his fortune out of the misery of others. A just man. You can unconditionally count on his word," Misha detailed what he knew about the host's character.

Yakov became completely relaxed in this conversation with Misha and for the first time since they had known each other, he laid his cards on the table.

"We are now in North America. These societies are similar to those in Western Europe, but also very different," Petro's *nono* continued. "However, here almost everything is completely different from where the two of us came from, so far east in Europe it is almost Asia. Do you think it is good for Petro to live here according to what his Doukhobor tradition requires? In a sort of isolation, in some oasis of this society, in the best case? Doesn't this require a huge sacrifice from that young man? Misha, isn't it sacrilege against the basic principles of human life, of the ever-changing path of human civilization, which is, I am positive, the direct product of the desires of our Creator? A direct reflection of the laws of the entire universe? The Doukhobor tradition, to be honest with each other, is similar to our Jewish tradition. And now, if I even for a moment detached myself from all that, I would conclude that our Jewish tradition is also a sort of isolation. A reason that we are in some constant and difficult-to-explain conflict with other civilizations. That path carries lots of tragedy in itself. I can say I am proud that we have survived the successive holocausts originating long before Christ, but the extermination of my ancestors is a story full of suffering, terrible losses and never-ending uncertainty. Misha, isn't it similar with you Doukhobors? Man is not a plant and the Creator did not intend man to forever putter in one place. I find it closer to God's laws if one man, the human race through generations, cherishes the fundamental threads of humanity and strides through time like a

375

magnet attracting all the new values that the human mind discovers. Men should be slaves only to the universal values of humanity, brotherhood, and the revolutionary role of man in civilization," Yakov said, to Misha's growing admiration.

"If you are challenging me to talk about that, I'll tell you—not as Misha Chernov, but as a Doukhobor. We believe that our philosophy of life is pregnant with humanity. That it is worthy of man as God's creation. We do not hate anybody, and we teach our future generations to leave no space for hatred in their minds. We consider all people as brothers, and we unconditionally oppose any killing, especially that of people. In our understanding, war is never justified," Misha Kostunavitch Chernov stated very specifically.

"I beg your pardon, Misha, but these are slogans! You do not hate anybody, but your people isolate yourselves from others! They do not want to mix with others. Your case is an exception among the Doukhobors. Haven't recently all the male members of one of your families chased one of their girls who had had to run away with the man she loved because he is not a Doukhobor? If they had caught him, I am sure they would have demonstrated hatred against him. What you are saying is just a theory, Misha!"

"It was an exception, Yakov!" Misha smiled.

"Doukhobor theory is agreeable, it follows God's will, but as a people you are agreeable only as lions behind bars could be agreeable. We Jews are similar to you to a certain degree, but you Doukhobors are more orthodox. I have always been against your isolation. Against your physical corralling into enclaves, bristling with very visible nihilism towards others. Others do not force you into that. It is your decision. You have more of that in you than we do in us. Maybe because our tradition is much older than yours and the passing of time made us wiser. You do not want to accept novelties in civilization. You do not want to take part in the modern trends in society. That is one of the reasons they have launched serious attacks on you even here. What you have is a specific culture, closed in itself, and isolated from the influences of other cultures. Even though there are better shoes in the store, you wear only those you have worn for two hundred years. Life is difficult and unpredictable anyway. It is especially difficult for those whom others mark, or who mark themselves, with a specific colour or specific features to be different from everybody else. And who build a fence around themselves. Others will first pass by that fence, look at it, discover this or that about it, and then one day they will start throwing stones at it. And schools, Misha…Schools open people's eyes and provide them with the best tools for survival."

"Oh, Yakov! I did not know you in this light before. I like a lot of what you have just said. Now I know why it would be harmful if Petro lost the Jewish part of his roots."

Misha's last words expressed a lot of warmth and satisfaction. He got up from the chair, and Yakov instinctively did the same. They spontaneously embraced each other.

"If nothing else, what I have just said was the debt I have owed to my Boulisou from the time she chose you," Yakov whispered.

"I owe her that too," Misha whispered in reply. "You are going to be my guest in a Doukhobor village in Canada. There you will again get acquainted with your grandson, Petro."

"But wait, Misha! I haven't told you everything. I would like to take Petro with me to Boston and enrol him in university. Not because I want to make him an orthodox Jew but to help him obtain higher education, and be at least what his father is. And something else. Europe is boiling. The Balkan wars will transform into a war of huge proportions. The imperialistic powers will pull men from their colonies and send them to war. It will happen in Canada too. Our Petro won't be exempt regardless of the fact that you Doukhobors do not want to go to war. They will force him, will impose mandatory conscription on him, or will send him to prison as a war deserter and an enemy of the state. If he goes with me to America, to Boston, it will be easier to hide him there from trouble."

"Oh, ho…" Misha smiled. "That's why you wanted to steal him from me. To save his head and his Doukhobor honour. Eh, you are a real *nono*! I am sure that our Petro will love you."

377

They raised their mugs and toasted each other. At that moment the Old Stewart entered the room. He was breathless, his face red. Only his long flat nose was yellow, and he had blue swollen circles around his eyes.

"What happened, sir?" Misha asked him anxiously.

"You won't believe it," the old said angrily. "A group of my cowboys have just returned from the grassland we use for grazing beyond the west colony of the Doukhobor villages. They spotted a group of farmworkers from across the Whitesand River as they were trying to set fire to the prairie close to the Doukhobor land planted with grain. When they saw my men, they moved away towards their farms. I have to go to Kohren and O'Toole and warn them of the seriousness of such provocations. It could be bad for the Doukhobors and for all our farmers as well. Somebody might also start setting fires in the prairie close to our crops and herds. But we will first give a signal to my good cook Victoria to bring us food and drinks, and afterwards we will see what to do."

Misha asked the host to forgive them if they excused themselves this time, to allow them to leave for Spasovka right away so that they could reach the village before nightfall. The reasonable Stewart did not force them to stay, and left the house to organize transport for them.

33

Petro felt that the songs the Doukhobor choir sang had become part of his being. He was trying to imagine himself torn from that singing, from the socializing around singing, from that communication with God specific to the Doukhobors—and at the same time to look at himself in the mirror which Misha had brought from Regina for him. The first time he saw himself in the mirror, he had been genuinely surprised; then it became so normal to him that it seemed he was no longer looking at himself in the mirror but at somebody who was like him, had facial features similar to his but not the friendly twinkle in his eyes nor the noble shape of the lips. When he sang psalms with the choir, his thoughts wandered over time and space searching for the goodness of the Almighty and His Son on earth. The hymns excited his soul and he could not fall asleep for a long time, carried by the rhythm of their sensibility. The old Russian songs the Doukhobors had in their genes made Petro feel close not only to the tradition of these people but also to nature, which nothing could render better than those descriptive lyrics, which seemed to come from his own feelings.

That evening when he was expecting his father to return from Stewart's farm, Petro went to sing songs on the porch of Stepan Tarasov, the good-natured Stepko. Once Stepko had been cutting grass by the river when he suddenly heard children screaming and crying. He threw his scythe in the grass, rushed towards the sounds of screaming and saw two small heads by turns popping out and submerging into the water, which was deep and calm there. At that moment Stepka did not even think about the fact that he did not know how to swim; he took off his thick shirt and jumped into the blueness of the river. While still falling into the water, he grabbed the children by their hair with his strong hands. He submerged deep under the water, carrying the children along, and when he felt the firm, slippery bottom under his feet, he violently pushed himself toward the surface. He himself did not know how he managed to exert the strength to throw the children onto the bank, and then to start kicking his legs in the water so violently that he soon found himself next to the children. Later nobody could persuade him that it was not some supernatural power that had helped him save the children and reach the riverbank. He did not include any mystical elements in his story nor did he try to use this event to illustrate his spiritual connection with Jesus; but whenever he tried to explain to himself how it had happened that he, a non-swimmer, had saved the children, he always concluded that something stronger than man and the power of man's imagination had helped him. The two boys said that a school of some red fish had attracted them into the water. From then on they started calling Stepka Uncle Stepka.

Ivan Popov and Tanya Tarasova offered Petro a spot on the porch. While they were singing, Tanya held her hand in Petro's. She was a few years younger than he, but in Petro's opinion the most beautiful girl not only in Spasovka but also in all nearby Doukhobor villages. Even though she had long fair hair braided in two thick plaits, her eyes were black like those of a doe when, alerted by a nearby sound, it looks at the spaces among trees, bushes and rocks. Her face was as pale as those of the famed Petersburg girls, embellished by tiny freckles around her eyes. In the first days of their love, when they frequently sneaked into the tall bushes by Geese Stream, which flows into the river further down, Petro did not take their playing seriously. It was natural to him to have a girlfriend, for them to love each other, and for him to spend time with her and not daydreaming alone. Hidden in the tall bushes by the stream, they would stare at each other and suggest to their hearts that it would be normal to touch each other. At first they limited themselves to describing their feelings; Tanya took a step further and described why she found Petro attractive.

"You are the one I used to imagine while my mother was telling me the stories about Yegor Chelichny, but your lips are redder and fuller. You are more handsome than your father Misha because his eyelashes are not as beautiful nor are his ears as round and small as yours. It must have come from your mother. Your nose is more like our leader Verigin's than like anybody's in your family."

"It is not easy to describe you. There are no words as beautiful as you are. But, just do not compare my nose to Verigin's. I do not think I look like that man. I think we in my family are different," Petro was firm.

When Tanya found a similarity between his and Verigin's noses, Petro did not even try to think about whether it was true or not, but reacted spontaneously, affected by his feelings. He did not like Peter Verigin, at that time still leader of the Doukhobors. His Grandpa Kostuna had influenced Petro's feelings even when he was a little boy. He had formed his opinion of Verigin while listening to the stories about him before he actually saw him in the village of Terpeniye. He did not like Verigin's pompous posture, which he obviously affected to put himself above other Doukhobors, nor his practice of using conversation with the people for his own interests. When in Terpeniye he talked about his suffering in the Siberian exile, he emphasized that he had endured the suffering in good spirit, knowing that he was enduring it because of his love for the Doukhobors. From exile he had sent letters to his people and given them advice how to behave, as if he had been the only brain among them. Moreover, he had accepted the suggestion that a new village not far from Spasovka be named Veregin in his honour and be declared the Doukhobors' administrative centre. To Petro, it was the biggest proof that the man was not modest and that he used his role in the movement to feed his personal ambition. He would not be surprised if the leader proclaimed himself the descendant of Jesus Christ. He also heard rumours that Verigin would only support marriages in which the couple were both Doukhobors. Petro's mother was Jewish. He did not disclose it to anybody, but always felt pleasure when he remembered his Grandpa Kostuna's description of Verigin's visit to the Tartar Princess long ago. During the journey, Tartar riders had thrown Verigin and his horse to the dusty ground. As for Verigin's nose, Petro accepted a brilliant description he had also inherited from his grandpa: When Verigin lifted his head from the dust, above him he saw the huge heads of the Tartar's horses. His entire face and hair were covered in dust, and only his crooked nose—like that of an owl—was red as if all the vehemence he felt but didn't have the courage to show to Tartars had concentrated in his nose. Petro believed that the Chernovs' animosity towards Verigin originated in their understanding that the biggest flaw in their movement was allowing their leaders to place themselves above the other Doukhobors, to flaunt their power and give to themselves more rights than to others. Some leaders seemed to feel that they were all-powerful, a feeling uncharacteristic of Doukhobors. They acted from an extreme egoism bordering on the pathologically narcissistic.

At the time of the split in the Doukhobor Movement, Stepka Tarasov was undecided. For many nights, tormented, he sweated under the woven woollen cover. His strong attachment to the Doukhobor tradition—his conviction that their way of life and religion was purified of many evils that had pushed a great part of civilization into immorality and lies, into aggressive egoism and the bloodthirstiness of warring tribes—was quietly persuading him to join Verigin's branch of the Orthodox Doukhobors and make his family pack their stuff for the journey through the flatlands of Saskatchewan and Alberta to the mountainous south of British Columbia. On the other hand, the feeling that his Doukhobors had supposedly renounced orthodoxy for good and all at the time they decided to leave Mother Russia and emigrate to Canada—to that part of the planet Earth which had firmly established state and social regulations for the democratic organization of life—pushed him towards the decision to join the Independent Doukhobors. When he at last made the decision to stay and continue living among the Independents, he made it easier for himself by concluding that he could have been an Orthodox Doukhobor if Canada had decided to give one part of its territory to the Doukhobor community. There they could have formed their own state, where nobody would meddle in their internal affairs. But that wasn't the case.

From Stepka's extended family, two of his brothers and a sister left for British Columbia with their families. A couple of years after their departure for Grand Forks, on the very border of Canada and the United States, the railway system in that part of British Columbia was completed. Stepka decided to visit his brothers. On the long journey he was accompanied by Arhyp Samsonov, who was still undecided in which part of Canada to settle with his family. But when they arrived in Castlegar, a hundred kilometers away from Grand Forks, they were told at the railway station that they would not be able to visit their relatives because Verigin had forbidden all contact between his group and the Independent Doukhobors. The old Samsonov fumed in anger He shouted over the heads of the Orthodox delegation that had communicated Verigin's decision to them and had told them to return where they had come from:

"Who in this country could forbid me to visit my brother Ivan and the children of my sister Lukeshka? Tell Peter Verigin that this is not different from our suffering in Russia!"

Stepka did not abuse the others with his feelings, but he returned to Spasovka with a firm conviction that he would teach his children and grandchildren to love and respect the Doukhobor tradition but also to be proud citizens of Canada.

Misha and Yakov arrived in Spasovka at the moment when the day and the night met like a grandfather and his grandson meeting briefly and then sooner or later separating forever. At that moment the day was at its last breath and everything that represented it—the light and the daily activities of humans and animals, and optimism on the faces, the feeling of belonging to a much broader region, and the feeling of greater security—all that was slowly preparing for departure and for being replaced by everything that the night was bringing. The night first of all offered the Doukhobor village much more time for eating and drinking, for relaxation and songs. It entwined imagination into real life, dulled the blades of seriousness and the rules of behaviour and morality, and awakened challenges.

Yakov felt uncomfortable. A few times he reprimanded himself for having arranged a meeting with his grandson Petro and the Doukhobor part of his family in such a manner. He feared meeting the other

Doukhobors in the village and would rather something happened during the night so he and Petro could leave the village right away. If only George, who had provided transport, could stay with them that night, he would feel better. While walking along the central village road he noticed that some houses were empty. Misha explained they belonged to the Doukhobors who had moved to southern British Columbia with the others of Verigin's Community Doukhobors. When Yakov asked him why they had left, Misha briefly explained that they had refused to sign the state documents assigning property ownership to each family; as a consequence, they had lost their property. Verigin had enabled them to move far away to the southwest of Canada, to farmland among the huge continental mountain chains. When they reached Misha's house, George shook their hands saying goodbye, and apologized to Misha, saying that it was already late, so it was better if he returned to the ranch right away.

Pelagiya was genuinely happy to see Yakov, and Paroniya was as well; she had worked for the Hasson family in Kars and had always been welcome in their house. Yakov tickled little Nikolay's nose, took a white envelope out of his leather case and put it into the boy's hands.

"It is as if you had known you would meet our Nikolay, so you prepared a gift for him," Misha made a joke.

"I knew. Nikolay is not only yours. He is also ours. He is our Petro's brother," Yakov was quick to explain. "And where is Petro?"

"He is in the village. Probably at the Tarasovs. They are singing there," Paroniya replied.

During dinner Yakov was telling them what had happened in his family since the Doukhobors had left the Caucasus to go to Canada. Just when they were finishing dinner, Petro entered the room. Yakov instinctively rose from a heavy wooden chair and looked at the young man with open surprise. His eyes revealed admiration and tears. Petro was standing there surprised too; he realized looking at Yakov's clothes that he was not a Doukhobor. Misha got up, went to Petro, put his hand on his son's shoulder and said to him, while looking at Yakov:

"Try to remember, my son. You know this gentlemen."

Petro studied Yakov's face, smiled and spontaneously addressed him:

"My mother's face had female features, but if she were a man, she would have your eyes, eyebrows, and upper lip. Her features were like yours, but, no offence, more beautiful and charming. It is you, Nono! Since we left, I have dreamed about you a few times and connected with you in my dreams."

Yakov was happy. They stayed embraced for a long time and Yakov whispered to Petro as if hiding his words from the others:

"I did not imagine that you had inherited what is the best in both your mother and your father. You have brought together two diversities. Your eyes, ears, and chin are your mother's, and your eyebrows and nose are your father's, even his upright, proud gait, but your complexion comes from your mother's genes, from Spanish Andalusia.

They stayed up long into the night and recounted their memories. When Pelagiya, Paroniya, and Nikolay went to bed, Yakov explained to Misha and Petro that he would prefer it if Petro went with him to Boston right away, to prepare for school during the summer and to start university in the fall. Petro suddenly became silent, and Misha suggested they continue the conversation in the morning.

That night nobody slept well in the house of Misha Chernov in remote Spasovka. Not even the little Nikolay, who suffered from earache, and even Misha's drops of cactus juice did not help. When he had seen Petro, and especially when he embraced him, Yakov felt pride and gratitude to his Boulisou for having given birth to such an heir. During the night, while lying in Petro's bed in the attic of the house, he was for a long time making plans about the best direction for his grandson's education. He was happy that Misha had already given a sign that he accepted Petro's departure for Boston and now when Boulisou was no more, he felt Misha dear to him and closer than before.

Misha knew that it was best for Petro to go to school to America and to stay with his grandfather, even though it would be a hard blow for the feelings of all the Chernovs and for those of the others in the village as well. He was not afraid of criticism that would probably come from many Doukhobors, because he was aware that it was much better for Petro than to continue living in this Saskatchewan wilderness.

And Petro? He realized that his father had already silently agreed to his departure for Boston. Not because Nono had come with that idea from Boston, but because it had always been his batya's desire to send him to university. When the majority of the Doukhobors in their communities in Canada vehemently refused to send their children to school, Misha enrolled Petro in school with farmers' children from the other side of the river. At first, they were subject to a sort of isolation from the other Doukhobors, but they won. Petro completed the highest level of mandatory education in Canada at a time when a lot of the Doukhobors did not even send their children to school. Then came a period of repose. Petro did not show great interest in leaving home for a college or university in a bigger city, and after Kostuna's death the family needed Petro's presence because Misha was often away helping his patients, sometimes for a couple of days. However, Petro and his batya often talked about the continuation of Petro's education and waited for something to happen to realize that plan. Time was passing and Petro had become a good carpenter. He also skillfully crafted wooden figurines of animals; and, moreover, often helped Misha when there was a need to fix somebody's broken bone or to extract a tooth. Then he fell seriously in love with Tanya Tarasova. She was a beautiful, healthy girl, and Petro especially liked her naïve sincerity and reticent nature. Recently they had started talking seriously about marriage, but Petro had had a plan to go for a couple of years to work on the railway construction to make some money and then to settle in marriage and family life.

That night Petro suddenly faced a situation in which he needed to think about leaving with his Grandpa Yakov for school in Boston. He knew it meant a life change and he was not afraid of that challenge. He was certain Tanya would accept his decision and he even thought he might plan with her that she come to America soon after him. He felt pressure in his chest and throat when he realized it meant that he would go far away from his batya, Grandma Pelagiya, and Little Nick and Paroniya, from his Uncle Genadiy, Stepko, Mikhailo, Nadezhda and many others in the village whom he felt to be not only friends but part of his family. And yet, over there they were waiting for him too…Even though the pressure in his chest did not abate, an ever stronger desire came over him to get to know again his Nona Maribel, Aunt Rifka, and her daughters, and to see America. To become an expert there like his father and to come back to help the Doukhobors. He had always known that time was important but more important was to spend time in a useful way both for himself and for others.

When the following morning Misha took Yakov for a walk across Spasovka, they were both surprised. People spontaneously approached them and greeted Petro's grandfather, as they had done many years earlier in their homeland.

"They haven't changed," Yakov concluded. "We were happy when you built your village next to our houses, there close to Kars in Russia."

Misha, however, noticed unspoken sadness in Yakov's eyes.

"Is something wrong?" Misha asked.

"No, why? Everything is fine. I am happy for having come to Spasovka."

"You are not a good actor," Misha told him with a gentle smile on his lips.

"And you have good eyes," Yakov wryly shot back. "I am looking at these people and half expecting to see among them my Boulisou holding the hand of our Petro when he was tiny."

He turned his head away and stared somewhere beyond the Doukhobors' houses as if sending these messages that appeared deep in his eyes to the distant past, to a place of no return.

During breakfast it was decided that Petro would go with Grandpa Yakov to America. Afterwards, Petro got lost, but they all knew he was with Tanyushka. When he returned, he took Nikolay from Babuska Pelagiya's arms and rushed with him to the fields behind the village houses. There they chased butterflies but were careful not to step on ones that became so tired and thirsty from flying around that they landed on the grass. Nick noticed tears in Petro's eyes, and asked him:

"Why are you crying, Petrushka? You cannot hide your tears from me."

"It's nothing," Petro replied. He held him around his waist and lifted him so that they could look in each other's eyes. "It's nothing, but will you promise something to your Petrushka?"

Nick felt Petro had a reason for the tears in his eyes, and instead of a reply he stared at his brother's face.

"Will you promise me something, Nikolay? If your Petrushka goes to America, will you promise me that you will continue running around in these fields and playing with these butterflies?"

"I will, Petrushka. I'll run around and play with them. But you won't go anywhere…"

"And that you will look after our batya?"

"I will, I will look after him. But you won't go far away from us?!"

"I won't. Your Petrushka will come back."

Petro grabbed the already five-year-old Nick and pressed him against his chest, and Nick stared into Petro's eyes, trying to find there the answer he could not find in the words.

When Misha, Yakov, and Petro were leaving the village, a big group of men, women and children followed their light carriage to the last village houses. Pelagiya, Paroniya, Nick and Genadiy were at the head of the procession. Tanya was walking on the side, away from the group, and was for a long time holding her hand in the air bidding farewell to Petro. In Yorkton, when they had completed the formalities to obtain a passport for Petro, Misha handed his passengers into the care of a Doukhobor coachman who would give them a ride to Regina. From there they would catch a train to the east, and change direction in Toronto to head south towards Boston and New York.

Misha held Yakov and Petro in his embrace for a long time to bid them farewell. He stayed in one spot looking at the departing coach in which his son Petro was leaving for some other world, far from the Doukhobor villages in Canada and from their way of life and relationship with God and people. In the carriage on his trip back to Spasovka Misha almost constantly played his flute and with the sound of that magical instrument he dispelled the sadness and brought freshness to his thoughts and feelings.

After the departure of Petro Mikhailovitch Chernov to Boston, a dangerous storm came upon the Doukhobor villages in Saskatchewan and in the south of British Columbia. It was one of those storms that played with the lives and convictions of these people in Canada, similar to what had happened to them for centuries in Russia.

The First World War set the world on fire. They say it started in the Balkans, in Bosnia, when in Sarajevo the Bosnian patriotic—some say terrorist—organization Young Bosnia, using the hand of its member Gavrilo Princip, assassinated the Archduke Franz Ferdinand of Austria. If Princip's shots had not started the great war there in Sarajevo, some other shots in another part of the world would have done it, because people had brought their hatred and intolerance to a boiling stage, not knowing any longer how to communicate except by creating a massive human bloodbath. And for what reason? For the sake of somebody's interests. As a rule, these "interests" were those of unscrupulous individuals within the ruling caste. Interests of power and wealth. Interests of the ugliest emotion among the emotions of living creatures: hatred. And blood is a warm liquid, full of life juices, and to pour it over the fire of war makes that fire bigger, hotter and more merciless.

The great war also reached the Doukhobor villages in Canada, even though the Doukhobors were vehement opponents of war or any form of killing people. They taught their children that the worst human crime is to make profit at the expense of other people and to have man kill man. When the Canadian government announced mandatory conscription into the military and the formation of army units intended for the war in Europe, the enemies of the Doukhobors requested that these Canadian Russians be drafted as well, even though the whole world knew the Doukhobors did not want to participate in war.

Yakov Hasson had been right. The war cataclysm also came upon the Canadian Chernovs. The government lists included seven descendants of Evstafy Chernov. Petro avoided the trouble thanks to the love and devotion of his Nono Yakov, but his father Misha found himself in an unenviable situation. One day he received the news that he should appear at the Doukhobor Administrative Centre in Veregin on Thursday the eleventh day of August, 1915. There three officials of the Province of Saskatchewan faced him. After a brief conversation, he received an ultimatum: administer a medical examination of all Doukhobors listed in the army draft, or be permanently suspended from the medical profession. Misha faced the same destiny here in Canada as his distant ancestor Doctor Evstafy Chernov back in Russia.

"I do not want to offend you, gentlemen, but I need to use one comparison. You gave me a task for which I am not adequate. It is the same as if you decided to milk a mule instead of a cow. I have no power to order the Doukhobors on your list to line up so I can examine them and declare them fit for army service. What's more, how can I sign that they are fit when none of them is fit for war?" Misha explained, trying to stay calm and appear reasonable.

"What are you talking about, Doctor Chernov? How come no Russian in this country is fit for war?" asked one of the officials, a man with round glasses and longish moustaches, their tips turned upward. He was visibly agitated.

"I am talking about the Doukhobors. None of them is fit for war because none among us wants to use weapons to kill another man. You could send us to fight other people, but we would be of no use. We would not shoot at other people." Misha was attempting to choose reasonable arguments.

"You wouldn't even shoot at an enemy whose intention is to kill you?" the one with the glasses tried again.

"Even when you know the enemy is a monster who wants to conquer the world, and who would enslave and kill all people who do not follow its ideas and are not loyal to its leaders?" added one of the other officials, a neatly shaved fellow wearing a well-designed pale green tweed jacket.

"We are not children, gentlemen, to talk in that way about serious matters!" Misha raised the tone of his voice even though his intention was not to provoke them. He knew that would be neither in his nor in other Doukhobors' interests. "We believe, and it is our philosophy of life, that a man does not have the right to kill another man regardless of the nature and extent of disagreement between them. There are always other ways for people to come to an agreement. We believe God is in every person. How can you lay violent hands on God?! Finally, gentlemen, you know I am not the leader of the Doukhobors and I do not have any power to make them renounce their principles—especially since, as you know, their beliefs are deeply humane and reasonable to any good man."

The three officials were quiet and looked at Misha suspiciously, probably expecting him to continue his explanations. Since he said no more, the taller one, with the glasses, took a document from his briefcase and handed it to Misha:

"Doctor, we only execute the decisions of our government. You have to be aware that our country is at war. Please, sign this document."

Misha assumed what was written in the document and, without looking at the text, refused to sign it. Later he found out that Peter Verigin had also refused to offer the authorities any alternative that would draw the Doukhobors into the war. For Verigin, that refusal was like putting a king's crown on his own head as leader of the Doukhobors, while for Doctor Misha it meant revocation of his licence to practise medicine. In addition, like many Doukhobors considered by the authorities to be ringleaders of the resistance to war, he also faced the possibility of a prison sentence.

Stepka Tarasov had not wanted to discourage his daughter Tanyushka when he first learned from his wife that the girl was dating Petro. He believed that Misha would soon pull his family out of Spasovka to a place where he would have a better opportunity as a doctor and as a man because he was in many ways constrained by their way of life. He expected Misha to send his son Petro to university so that the boy could integrate into normal Canadian life. Misha had never seemed to him somebody who would putter in one place, satisfied with what he had inherited from his father and grandfathers. Misha could have become the leader of the Doukhobors a long time ago if he had only wanted it, and that would have been good luck for the Doukhobors because, Stepka believed, the thoughtful doctor would have directed them towards a revision of Doukhobor teachings about how to live and cooperate with others in the society in which they now lived. However, Misha stayed away from all important events in the Doukhobor communities and belonged to them only in a physical sense and as much as they needed his medical service. That was why Stepka thought Petro and Tanya's love would be short-lived, but refrained from telling Tanya that. He used an opportunity to talk to Misha about Petro and Tanya not long after Petro's departure for Boston.

After the meeting with the representatives of the provincial authorities in Verigin, Misha received the decision of the Ministry of Health from Regina that he was banned from practising medicine until further notice. He had known this would happen, but he never lamented over his destiny when it proved unfavourable. They banned him from practising medicine, but they did not send him to prison as he had expected. He took a greater part in the work of his community and decided to spend most of his time in the rafting of logs down the river to the construction site of a big settlement for workers who were building the new railway through Saskatchewan to Alberta. Stepka Tarasov, along with Gresha Feodorovitch Plotnikov and others, made up his team. Misha liked Stepka's stories about the universe, his reveries about the possibility of life outside Planet Earth, and his adding of details to the songs they sang. He liked that Stepka did not refrain from publicly relating his fantasies and would not be satisfied only with what he had received as his inheritance.

"Stepka," Misha confided in him on one occasion while they were resting apart from the others on a big raft of logs slowly moving down the river, "how come you have courage to talk about things you yourself are not certain about?"

"What do you mean, Mishka?"

"I mean your fantasies about changes in our Doukhobor communities and in relationships between men and women...About life on other planets, and about introducing melodies of other ethnic groups into our songs…Petro told me that your Tanyushka had given away your secrets."

"Eh, Mishka…I think Tanya was talking more about herself to Petro than about me. I am sure she was embarrassed to admit that she had thought about such things, so she credited me for a lot of that. Especially for the business about the relationships between men and women. My Tanyushka is an unusual human being. Her thoughts are sometimes so profound that I become afraid of what her brain engages in. She lectured me on how we Doukhobors need to liberate women. She thinks that it is our big drawback, keeping our women in their traditional place, and that maybe we keep our villages in isolation from the rest of the world just because our men are scared that that the liberation of our women would threaten their own position. She contended that soon women would start leaving the corrals she says we keep them in, go to school, and look for work beyond the borders of our communities. They will find that life more attractive and will lecture our men. They will start wearing clothes that women in other groups wear; they will start loving differently from how they used to and will demand to be loved differently. They will attack the fences around our villages more strongly than any Canadian policy has, or all the 'wisdom' of their newspapers and magazines. On one occasion she praised me for having decided to join the Independent Doukhobors, but right afterward she reprimanded me for not having said louder that Canada is an extraordinary country and that it would be normal if we helped it to become more extraordinary."

Misha listened to Stepka's talk about his Tanyushka and realized that the unusual Tarasov wanted to demonstrate that his daughter was as worthy as Petro and that they were both undoubtedly a match for the challenges that had already arrived in the Doukhobor settlements of Canada. That entire family was completely ready to bring their way of life even closer to the Canadian reality without compromising the basic principles of the Doukhobor way of life and of their religion.

"I still think, Stepka, that Peter Verigin is not as black as some try to paint him. He has offered a lot to us and has stayed loyal to the movement." To Misha and Stepka's surprise, Gresha Plotnikov had joined their conversation.

The current was becoming faster and faster as the river's bed became more uneven. The huge mass of logs started rocking and rippling so that the workers, about ten of them including Misha and Stepka, stopped sitting relaxed and grabbed hold of protruding knots to secure themselves. Some of them were moving around trying to find safer logs because they were rocking so hard that there was a danger they could be crushed. However, the river soon settled into a valley and the state of carelessness returned.

Stepka launched his rebuttal at Gresha Plotnikov. "I have never said that Verigin doesn't deserve that we shake his hand and give him credit. However, he has recently made a couple of mistakes that have torn the movement apart. I am sure it would have been better both for him and for us if he had asked at the last Great Sobraniye council that we choose a new leader, younger and less conservative. This way, I think he will try to continue being our leader until his death, and when he feels it coming, he will suggest that his son inherit his position. And, Gresha, it is the same as what the Romanovs in Russia have done for centuries," Stepka Tarasov concluded firmly. While he was talking, his face had become more serious and anxious, and the tips of his long narrow ears became more and more red. It seemed to Misha, observing him carefully, that his face also became strangely elongated and that his grey eyes turned even more grey and retreated into their sockets, as if suddenly facing a blazing fire.

"I still think, Stepka, that Verigin is a good man and smart enough to make wise and useful decisions for all of us. Whatever he did or advised us to do was in agreement with our way of life and belief. Do you think it was wrong that he advised us to keep together because the other way would lead us to assimilation with others, so there would be no more Douhobors? Our tradition, that we are so proud of, would be no more. He advised us not to marry into other ethnic groups and religions because it would thin our blood and drag many people away from our movement He advised us not to accept the more and more blatant avoidance of marriage by our young people because that leads to voraciousness and an unnatural way of life contradictory to God's laws. He advised us not to give the oath to the Queen because that would drag us into her wars all over the world..." Gresha was becoming excited. He looked in the direction where the river was slowly flowing through the flat land. His face did not reveal agitation— just as a bull when facing another bull seems so relaxed that nobody would guess that in the very next moment he will charge with full strength. The only signal of Gresha's turbulent feelings was his ever more frequent plucking at the hairs in his thick reddish beard and the occasional pursing of his upper lip, as if he were about to whistle. While he was talking, he did not even look at Misha even though it was obvious he reproached Misha for his unique life.

Not even then did Misha join the conversation between the two. He thought it was neither the time nor place for his intervention and that it would be malicious if he defended himself against the accusations of the normally benevolent Plotnikov. In fact, much of what he said about Misha was true, but Misha had never thought that this could create bad blood among the Doukhobors. He believed that the movement could survive only if it came out of its isolation and integrated into the flow of life of the others in the country.

But Stepka Tarasov definitely had more to say: "I also think Verigin is a good man. But have you forgotten that while still in Siberia and without knowing what circumstances, both positive and negative, we were facing here, he sent us his instructions how to build our relationships in this country, as if we were still in Russia, familiar to us all? It was not wise. He made fundamental mistakes, Gresha! Let me remind you that he suggested we do not sign any documents about individual ownership of the land. Many followed his advice, and what happened? They lost their land. He came here, brought the seeds of division into the movement, and now we have three branches. To save his face before those who followed his advice and refused to sign the state documents for ownership of the land, he decided to make them move to the south of British Columbia, so he definitely tore the movement apart. There he corralled them into communes and acts as our tsars did back in Russia. Luckily, we excluded ourselves from his control."

"We will see what's better, folks. I do not like it that we are divided and that we are distancing ourselves from each other," the stalwart ruddy Zupkov brought new interruption to the conversation in Misha's corner of the raft. But the others suddenly started singing a hymn to goodness, and the powerful male voices overwhelmed the discussion and the sounds of the river and poured into the prairie around it.

While the others were singing, Misha accompanied them with the sounds of his flute, his gaze travelling over their faces tanned by the sun. It was normal to him that people were talking about their leader, some approving of his actions, some not. He remembered that Verigin had sent him a message to meet him in Brilliant, in the south of British Columbia, the new headquarters of the Verigin branch of the Doukhobors. He knew the invitation meant that Verigin felt secure in his position and that the time had come for him to try to find a formula for the unification of the movement.

Misha's pondering over memories of his meeting with Verigin, before his exile to Siberia many years ago, was disrupted by an unusual noise from the direction of the artificial lake which supplied water for irrigation. At first, it sounded like an orchestra made only of bass voices imitating the howling of wind in a forest of tall trees. Two streams flowed into the lake, filling it as a reservoir for the irrigation of their fields during summer droughts. The others noticed Misha's anxiety and stopped singing.

The men on the raft became silent, and the noise Misha had heard became louder and closer. They looked in all directions to see if it was a wind approaching, but the sky was calm, the prairie grasses unruffled. Their gazes scanned the flat expanse to see if a big herd of cattle was stampeding in their direction, but could see nothing. Then, towards the west, they clearly saw a group of riders disappearing over a rise. However, in no way could they have created such a disharmony of ever more terrifying sounds that not only didn't abate as the riders vanished, but grew steadily louder and closer. The noise became so loud that some thought it was an earthquake, but realized that was not the case as soon as a huge mass of water appeared from the direction of the impounded lake. Towards them was rolling a massive wave, although their logs still calmly moved down the river. Even before they could try to decide what to do, the mountain of water crashed into the river with a roar like ocean surf. The previous stability and safety disappeared in a split second. The lashings of the big log raft sundered and the powerful surge of water toppled the people like kegels and their struggle for life began.

Misha was a skilled swimmer, but in these circumstances, with huge logs playing a death game, crashing together, jumping into the air and returning to dive into its depths, his skill was of no use. He tried to stay on the surface of the water, turning his head in all directions to avoid being smashed by the whirling logs. A few times he heard cries in that nightmare, then saw a huge thick log lunging at him from behind, throwing aside the smaller and more agile timber. With great effort, Misha flung himself from the path of the giant. Right at the moment when that colossus, with a fat burl at the stump of a thick branch, was passing by him, Misha thrust himself violently out of the water, got hold of the burl and landed on the log, as he had often thrown himself on the back of a horse which did not like to be ridden. The danger was similar. If Misha's huge log turned over, it would pull him under, and who knew what would happen then. In the same way, while throwing himself on the back of somebody's unruly horse in the Kars Valley, he had wondered if the animal, galloping at full speed, would turn its head, grab his hand with its big teeth and throw him to the ground, or suddenly stop and smile, watching Misha fly through the air to land on some rocks and thorny bushes.

Only when he managed to steady himself by getting hold of the branch itself did Misha see what disaster was happening among the long thick logs to the other men who had been using the river to quietly transport timber until that mountain of water from the impounded lake crashed into it. The wooden giants were still vigorously fighting for their place in the stream, and, at first, people were nowhere to be seen. Then Misha heard a new scream and in front of him saw a man holding onto a log, trying to keep his head above the water. Misha, following more screams that reached him, threw his gaze all around and discovered a frantic human struggle for survival. On the left bank of the river he saw a group of about a dozen Aboriginals rushing along the grassy riverbank at the same speed as the furious water. About a hundred meters behind them a group of people dressed as horsemen were doing the same. Misha understood that both groups were rushing to help the people in the river, but that they were waiting for the right moment.

The surge of water carrying logs and people in its waves was losing its strength, and because the terrain was flat the water started to calm down. Behind him Misha heard yet more screaming, turned around, and about ten meters away saw Gresha Plotnikov on a log. He was shouting in Misha's direction and pointing behind with his hand. Misha saw another man holding onto one end of a log with one hand, and with the other trying to pull his leg over the crest of the log, but, visibly weak and wounded, he hadn't the strength left to do that. It was Stepka Tarasov. Misha stood up on his own huge log and walked back along its length. Then he jumped to the log nearest him, steadied himself on it, and continued to the next one. He passed Gresha, who was not in danger, and soon reached the log Tarasov was holding onto. Misha had no time to evaluate Tarasov's condition. He jumped and started riding the log as he would ride a horse, and with his hands firmly grabbed Stepka's shoulders and pulled him up next to him. Only then did he see that Stepka's one arm was smashed and broken and that every second more and more blood was pumping out of the wound. One of his legs was seriously contused by logs and it dangled helplessly from his body.

Soon that cluttered mass of now calm logs entered the shallower and wider waters of the river, full of protruding rocks, and they stopped. The Aboriginals jumped from log to log to help the Doukhobors. The cowboys did the same and thanks to the eagerness and dedication of the rescuers, the survivors were pulled out of the water. Three workers were missing. After a few days, in the bushes growing on the riverbank, the Doukhobors who had organized the search found the body of Sergey Ivanovitch Samorodin. Hit by a log, his head was broken above his left ear. The other two, Dmitry Potapov and Stepan Perepolkin, were never found.

The group of Aboriginal men who rescued the Doukhobors from the furious river was from Manidu's tribe, and the cowboys were from the farm of Dorina O'Moor, the widow of Jacob O'Moor. There was never an official report about who the cowboys were that had galloped from the impounded lake to the west just before the huge mass of water had fallen into the river. Some powerful people did not want the truth behind the crime against the Doukhobor people to be discovered. There was a rumour, which more and more people believed, that the owners of the big cattle companies had organized the crime. They had vehemently opposed the decision of the Ministry of Immigration to settle the Doukhobors in that region. They were the same people who had contributed to the abandoning of the original plan to settle those Russian immigrants in ranchland near Fort Edmonton, Alberta. Misha did not follow some more radical Doukhobors who, after the failure of the authorities to find and punish the perpetrators of the crime, wanted to retaliate against the ranchers because he knew it was not all ranchers who had been involved, and furthermore such retaliation was absolutely not in accordance with the Doukhobor teaching about relationships among people. The law that regulates all relationships in the universe and on earth would find a way for justice to be served.

34

After Petro's departure for Boston the great war reached the Canadian prairies. At first it did not touch the Doukhobor villages, but when the news came about the many Canadians killed fighting with British war formations at the Somme, armed groups of horsemen started to pass by the villages, coming closer and closer. One day they started firing shots above the Doukhobors' roofs in Spasovka and set fire to a hay-barn in Veregin. The Doukhobors responded by singing psalms and old Russian songs day after day.

Misha found himself thinking about Petro more and more nervously. Eventually he heard about massive military drafts in the United States and about the imprisonment of those who tried to dodge the war laws. Misha hadn't heard a word from Petro except two letters right after his departure. Misha went to Stewart's farm to inquire, but they didn't know anything either. George told him that America and Canada had been sending German, Ukrainian, and Italian residents to special prisons, and that the Jewish community had started collecting money in both countries for the families of killed and wounded soldiers. This wise initiative increased sympathy towards Jews, so the national governments started increasingly to entrust them with military production and trade. This news lessened Misha's worries about Petro, but he still frequently went to a secluded place and, with the sounds of his flute, tried to make contact with his son. He believed in the power of music and was not surprised when the notes of his favourite instrument inspired him to write lyrics for entirely new songs.

One day right after lunch, Misha went with Nick to the field where Petro and Nick had said goodbye to each other. While Nick was running after the butterflies, Misha was playing the flute and observing his son's game. While running, Nick was careful not to step on the

400

fluttering butterflies. He laughed when one of them incited him to run after it then suddenly flew over Nick's head and started making circles as if expecting the boy to admit the butterfly's superiority. Misha was playing and singing in a low voice, the lyrics coming from deep in his heart:

> *Humans are made to create warmth with their smile*
> *When the sun hides in the darkness,*
> *And to love*
> *And with their love to breathe happiness*
> *Into the wings of colourful butterflies.*

Misha's verses represented his protest against the flames of war, against the mass killing of people, and it was his cry towards the realm of the being or force that creates and regulates relationships among living beings on earth. Misha was not naïve even as a boy. Now that the passing of time had created wrinkles on the face of his life, he rejected human nature, which had veered away from the concept of a creator of humans and their relationships. People had so many times in the history of civilization desecrated and wounded the concept of a benevolent creator that even the most humane deeds of good people could not achieve the absolution of so much cruelty. Many of the world's great minds, from Aristotle until now, had defended human brutality and hypocrisy by saying that criminal behaviour is part of human nature and that it is almost normal for people to practise lying, deception, killing, and living on the backs of others. Even after so many years, Misha very well remembered his studies in Kazan and his psychology professor, the grey-bearded Memishev, who had, with well-supported arguments, passionately defended cruelty in human relationships. These memories made Misha bitter and made his heart even more devoted to the Doukhobor teaching. If he could only meet that bony Memishev, now when Misha was not a student anymore and when his life did not any more depend on that vermin, he would hiss in his face that people are not beasts and that humanity would be happy if it followed the Doukhobor philosophy of life. And when he later became acquainted with the ideas and the social analysis of the humanist Karl Marx, the extraordinary Canadian psychologist Richard Buck, and the evolutionist Charles Darwin, Misha found indestructible support for the teachings of the movement he belonged to. When they came to Canada and organized themselves into closed enclaves, Misha became more and more angry because he believed that his small group of people had an extraordinary role in the social evolution of civilization. He was as angry as a teenager who cannot understand the mistakes of adults. Does any individual who has gained extraordinary insights have the right to be cocooned and narcissistically enjoy his achievements, or the right to escape in paranoid hallucinations in order to survive?

As he grew older, Misha increasingly favoured the Doukhobors taking an active role in human society. He had always respectfully criticized the great Tolstoy, when he, in the manner of a teacher, gave advice to his personal friend and admirer Peter V. Verigin, one of the greatest Doukhobor leaders since the beginning of that movement. Misha found them both guilty for leading the Doukhobors into enclosing themselves within unbending fences after their immigration to Canada.

"The light of our way of life, and our unique relationship with God and people, are great values of the human race and we have no right to shut them in some box and lose time that can never be made up, to isolate these values from the processes of human society. The Doukhobors need to scatter all through human society and tell people about themselves and their life, and only then will their teaching make sense and be useful for civilization," Misha was trying to convince himself. "We have to leave the riverbank, which only the nearby fertile fields have use of, and turn into drops of rain to freshen huge areas thirsty for that elixir of life."

His conviction that the Doukhobor Movement was of great civilizing value made him calculate that value for the human race. Then he clasped his head, realizing that value had retracted itself deep into the womb of the earth and tried to survive far from the mainstream of humanity. Doctor Chernov asked himself if they had the right to condemn themselves to isolation and temporary survival, when, according to the ancient Greek myth, Prometheus had given people the gift of limitless mind. Wasn't the Doukhobors' escape to isolation a form of egoism, unnatural for their philosophy of life? Aspects of that philosophy had for thousands of years crept through the crevices of civilization and survived all barbarities, which are natural to man but should eventually be erased from human instincts. Misha was aware of the accuracy of this thinking. The philosophy which the Doukhobors embraced and made possible in practice had not been born in their movement. It had been like a river disappearing inside the earth in one place just to bubble forth again in some other place in the form of a new stream or river.

Since the time when the Canadian Doukhobors at the big meeting in Veregin had faced their biggest challenge, Misha had found himself caught in their rupture. At the meeting, when he supported the recommendation of the group who was in favour of cooperating with the authorities, he realized he had become part of the wave of Doukhobor revisionism, which was the only way for his people to weave themselves into the Canadian social fabric and legislation without compromising the fundamental values of their way of life and beliefs.

"I know that acceptance of private property as a concept in law poses a great danger to our teaching about the equality of all people. But we will have to accept it if we or our next generation want to stay in this country. In our communities, we can continue to collectivize everything that individuals possess and in that manner cherish the principle of equality for all no matter what it says on the title deeds. We can join together in work and share the products of our work. I am aware that it is complicated, but it is possible. Regarding education, if we do not make a decision right away to send all our children to school, we are going to ruin the future of our movement. Our future generations will curse us. If our level of knowledge is not at the level of that of the other citizens of this country, we will lose the most powerful tools for our survival," Misha told the people gathered at the great meeting, while constantly looking at the face of Peter Verigin.

Verigin's face flushed darker and darker shades of red, and two yellow lines spread under his eyes, which bore witness to his psychological state. The great Doukhobor leader was facing a historical decision. However, he did not even think about choosing revisionism because he believed it represented inconsistency and weakness in their movement. Finally, that choice would look like an admission of the mistakes he had been making since the beginning of the Doukhobors' resettlement in Canada. Instead of revisionism, Verigin chose a new big migration for his people, searching yet again for a piece of our planet where the inhabitants would be friendlier to and more tolerant of the Doukhobors.

Instead of the great leader, it was the energetic Zubarev who confronted Misha and the group who had recommended prudence and the revision of some Doukhobor principles. "You, Misha, a long time ago betrayed many principles of our teaching. If you think you are so smart that you can offer us something better than what we have and what we do, why don't you do something about it right smartly! I think critics such as you pose a great danger to our movement. I suggest we talk about it openly today."

At that meeting, for the first time in the history of the Doukhobor Movement they raised aggressive and opposing voices about the present condition of the movement and its future. Misha felt sickness in his stomach and head and reprimanded himself for having taken part in the debate. Until then he had refrained from publicly expressing his thoughts about the movement; now he'd done it in a manner that kicked off an avalanche of ideas and suggestions. While he criticized himself, the words of Stepan Tarasov, who was sitting next to him on the left, gave him a start:

"Misha, I'll recommend that we choose a new leader, somebody who will lead us more successfully in this country, and not plan to drag us around the world again. If only you were willing to accept that role…"

"Stepka!" The word was almost a shout. "I do not want to be above others! Verigin is excellent…He only needs to correct certain things…I do not want…"

Misha got up, patted the surprised Stepan on the shoulder and slowly left the Orphanage. When he realized that the split among the Doukhobors about adaptation of the movement to new conditions of life had crystallized at that meeting, Misha felt weakness and sensed that some strange veil permeated by sadness covered his feelings. Soon came the official split in the Doukhobor Movement in Canada. Verigin decided to move like-minded Doukhobors to the south of British Columbia, and in Saskatchewan stayed those who believed that the movement needed revisions to its philosophy of life and its relationship with other people. They gave themselves the name of Independents. All the Chernovs, except the family of Misha's Uncle Nikolay, stayed in Saskatchewan.

One day Misha and little Nick took Uncle Genadiy to the field where they were accustomed to play with the butterflies. However, the butterflies were not there. Nick ran all over the place looking for them. Misha and Genadiy looked in the bushes, around the rocks, in the dried-up pond…But there were no butterflies. Nick was sad; he hid behind a bush of wild cranberries and became thoughtful. Suddenly, he saw the small eyes of one butterfly peering out from a knot of thin fibers. He looked around at the other bushes and saw dozens of such knots the butterflies were wrapped in. He realized it was the end of the summer's hot weather and felt relieved. Then he pulled himself out of the bushes and ran to his father and Genadiy without sadness in his face.

"Batya, the butterflies have wrapped themselves in some knots and they will spend the winter there. They felt the winter is coming before we did," Nick declared, proud of his conclusion.

"How come I didn't think of that! So you had to go to the bushes to find it out. To discover the secret of our butterflies," Misha praised him in his way.

"Batya, if you allow me, I'll make a birdhouse for the owls by our house," Nick suddenly proposed this unusual suggestion.

"What owls, Nikolay? What are you talking about? Where are the owls?" his father asked in surprise.

"It is our secret," Genadiy joined the conversation between father and son. "We have kept the secret until now when the owls are old enough. Nick and I found them last spring when they were fledglings. Their mother had disappeared and they were squeaking hungrily. They were in a hole in that old oak tree by my house. We fed them with worms and insects and gave them water, and now they are grown-up owls."

"We became friends, Batya. You might find them terrifying, but they like me and Uncle Genushka. If you want to see them, I'll bring them to the house," Nick prattled.

They decided to go together to that oak tree later at dusk, when owls wake up from their day of sleep.

When Misha and Nick returned home, the boy ran into the kitchen and threw himself in the arms of Paroniya. She bent over in the chair where she had been shelling peas, hugged him and asked in surprise:

"What happened, Nikolay? What have you and your batya decided to ask me?"

"Nothing," Nick replied. "We are both just hungry and thirsty. Oh, yeah…I want to tell you that I did not run after the butterflies because they had hid themselves in their houses where they will spend the winter. Uncle Genadiy was with us too. Batya was playing his flute for us on the way back."

"Did you recognize one of your butterflies in their houses?" the mother asked, getting up from her chair to bring them water.

"I could only see their eyes. They all have the same eyes. They are all mine. When I played with them the other day, some landed on my head and shoulders. They looked at me with their bulging eyes as if they wanted to tell me something. Maybe they wanted to tell me they were building the houses to sleep there till the spring comes. And that our Petro will come soon. Hey, I didn't think of that when I saw them in their winter houses. Only their eyes peered out from the wrappings they had made. They loved our Petrushka. They are peering out, so they can see my brother when he comes back from America. Mom, I miss Petro," Nick was chattering on and tearing small pieces from the loaf of dark bread on the shelf by the stove.

At that moment, Babushka Pelagiya entered the room. Her eyes were red. She did not try to hide her tears.

"What is it, mom?" Misha asked her. He went to her, looked at her eyes and embraced her.

"Stepka just came back from the store. He says that the Russian revolutionaries have condemned to death the whole family of our Tsar," Babushka said with difficulty and clasped her head in her hands. She was crying and trying to talk through tears.

Misha held her by the shoulders and pressed her head against his chest. Parushka approached as well, and Nick got up looking at his father in surprise.

"Wait, Mom. Calm down," Misha told her calmly. "I heard that Tsar Nikolay and the family are in Siberia and that many countries have offered the Bolshevik Government to give sanctuary to our Tsar and his family. Even Lenin has promised he would treat Nikolay II Alexandrovitch as the former Tsar of Russia."

"Stepka says they have shot them all, but they do not know what has happened to Prince Alexey. They haven't found his body among those who had been shot," Mother Pelagiya said a bit more calmly.

Paroniya screamed and took Nick into her arms. She hugged him, kissed his forehead, and cried. She looked at Misha and saw tears in his eyes and on his cheeks. Nick was also crying, looking in turn at his father, mother, and babushka. In these moments he did not understand why they were crying because of the Tsar and his family when until then they had always talked about "bloody Nikolay" who had brought so much evil upon them that they would never forget him.

Misha helped his mother to a wooden settee covered with a thick blanket made of wool.

"I am going to Stepka to hear what's going on," he told Parushka. He patted Nick's head and with his finger wiped a tear slowly running down his son's cheek.

In front of Stepka Tarasov's house were a lot of people and all eyes were wet from tears. When Stepka saw Misha, he shook his hand as if it was their own misfortune.

"It is true, Mishka. The news was in all papers in the world. They say they have killed them like rats. When they were hoping to hear the decision that would allow them to emigrate to another country, a group of Bolsheviks pointed their guns at them and shot them until the bodies of the Tsar and all his family stopped shaking. The Tsarina and the daughters were also killed. Some British newspapers reported that those who buried them secretly sent out rumours that the sick Prince Alexey was not among the dead.

"Later the news leaked from one of the Bolsheviks who had fired at the family of Tsar Nikolay that they had, before shooting them, asked the Tsar what his last wish was. With his bewildered eyes he looked at the Tsarina, their daughters, the son Alexey. He bent his head to the ground, and looked at the stormy sky, whispering. Then he crossed himself, looked at his daughters with his eyes full of tears and apology, and replied:

"'Our Alexey is ill. He cannot be Tsar. Take him to the hospital.' It surprised the executioners, but, nevertheless, the shots from the long army rifles flew towards the bodies of all the Romanovs. They threw themselves at each other and fell to the ground, in the country where Nikolay Romanov used to be Tsar."

"Barbarity!" said one of the gathered people. "The truth is he did not deserve the mercy of Russian people, but..."

"They were human too," the voice of the moustached Ilya Mikhailovitch Serafimov was heard. "Are the children guilty of the evil deeds that the Tsar committed?!"

Misha was sad and confused. When they had heard the news about the war that had fallen over Russia's people with all its force, Misha felt they should help the defence of Mother Russia in any way possible. When they learned that the new Bolshevik government had agreed to end Russia's participation in the war, he was happy and believed that the suffering of the people in that part of the world would soon stop. Then civil war started to rage in his Mother Russia. The news that the masses of the people had joined Lenin's Bolsheviks, who promised a people's government and justice, made Misha happy. Many things in the Bolshevik program looked to Misha like God's justice, even though there were rumours that Bolsheviks denied the existence of God. Now when he heard that they had barbarically executed one Russian family for being the family of the last Romanov, Misha was terribly surprised and felt the pulse in his blood vessels grow sluggish and confusion fill his head. His thoughts now were in favour of condemning this evil deed because no government has God's blessing to kill…

The news about the tragedy of the last Russian tsar and his family brought great sadness to the homes of the Doukhobors. For seven days in all their villages and on all their farms in Canada the Doukhobors stopped working and sang psalms and old Russian songs. Other Canadians were surprised at the reaction of the Doukhobors at the tragedy of the Tsar, who had mercilessly persecuted and killed them. They were also surprised because they believed the Doukhobors sympathized with the Russian Revolutionary Government, whose first steps in organizing life in that country were similar to the Doukhobor way of life.

On one of those politically hot Saskatchewan days when the Canadian authorities fought battles over deciding one more time their position on the Doukhobors, there was rumour in the Doukhobor villages that the conservative forces in the country were trying to associate the Doukhobors with the move of Russia to communism and to open animosity against the western capitalist world. Now more then ever, the authorities analyzed the Doukhobor way of life, their preferred engagement in collective land ownership and production, and equal distribution of the produced goods. It was easy to persuade the uninformed that Lenin's government was inspired by the Doukhobor Movement. Some even started to label the Doukhobors as "Red," the colour that soon became an anathema in the Western world so that even the producers of dyes put a temporary ban on making that colour. Soon again armed groups of enemies of the Russian immigrants started circling around Doukhobor settlements and threatened to attack these suspected enemies of Canada. The fact that the Doukhobors still mourned over the tragedy that had befallen the family of the last Russian tsar in March confused others. The Doukhobors continued their life as before, and when they gathered they sang and prayed for the happiness of all people.

Early one morning in Spasovka they heard that during the night the farm of Stephen MacKay, about ten miles from Spasovka, had caught fire. When they heard the news, more than half of the men and women of the village grabbed water buckets, picks and spades, and in five big horse wagons rushed to help the farmer. Misha Chernov was among them. When they arrived at the burning farm, they saw the owners and the nearby farmers fighting the fire, which had reached the big family house and the silos for grain. The farmers were surprised to see the Doukhobors, who pitched in right away. They created a line for the delivery of water in buckets, hand to hand, from a small lake to the main building on the farm, and soon a bigger part of the house was saved. Misha then suggested to the farm owner that they tear down the part of the house which could not be saved and to move any lumber still burning away in case of wind, because fire would quickly spread from the thick smouldering boards. The idea was accepted, and most of the Doukhobors joined those who were extinguishing the fire in the silos. These were full of grain because the harvest had been completed some time ago. The structures were close to the barns where the fire had started; two small silos were completely engulfed in flames and it was clear they could not be saved, but behind them were two big silos, thus far no more than scorched. Again the Doukhobors' strategy to sacrifice the small ones for the sake of the big ones was used. They tore them down and moved burning objects further away.

In fighting the fire, one farm worker sustained serious burns on the right side of his body while pulling valuables out of the burning house. Misha recommended that they tear off his clothes in the places where he was burnt and asked if they had oil of St. John's Wort, which was commonly used as a cure for cattle mange. They found some and Misha applied it to the burns, using soft lint cloths drenched in the oil.

When Misha and the others felt they were no more of great use to the farm owners, they decided to return to their village. MacKay and his wife approached and hugged each of them individually; then the Doukhobors climbed into their wagons and went into the prairie. The other people who had fought the fire watched as they were leaving.

When the Doukhobor wagons had crossed the valley and started moving uphill, MacKay and his wife raised their hands to bid them farewell. Misha raised his hand as well, and the others followed suit.

As soon as the defenders of the MacKay farm arrived at Spasovka, a few women rushed towards them with the news that Katya Goncharova, Gresha's eight-year-old daughter, was missing. Gresha was in the wagon with Misha. They all hurled themselves into the search for Katya, and after a long rushing around the village and across the village somebody shouted from a willow grove by the river:

"Katya is alive! Pavloosha has found her by the river!"

Almost everybody in the village rushed towards the willow grove, from which Pavloosha was coming with Katya in his arms. When they came close to each other, Pavloosha lifted the girl above his head so that all could see she was alive and healthy. When they returned to the village, they gathered in front of Gresha's house and listened to Pavel's report.

"To me this river has always been a danger for our children. As soon as I heard Katya was missing, I rushed to the river. I know that our children often gather in that willow grove, and I rushed through the grove to the water. I suddenly heard a child's voice singing. I stopped and heard it was a female child's voice coming from the riverbank. I knew it was Katya, but did not dare to shout, afraid that my voice might frighten her so she would slide down into the river. I was moving slowly through the bushes towards her, and Katya was singing:

They killed our Tsar and our Tsarina
And the little children, says Stepka,
They killed the children too.
But their souls hid
In the blooming flowers
And in the golden rays of sun.

"Katya was sitting on a mound above the river. I approached her from behind, and she was sitting there repeating the same verses and picking the petals of the flowers in the grass around her. She was

411

picking the petals and throwing bunches of them as far as possible into the river, so that the current could catch them. With her gaze she followed each one as the water took it somewhere into the distance."

Misha was listening to Pavloosha and looking at the rosy cheeks of Gresha's daughter. It crossed his mind that Katya did not know much about Tsar Nikolay II Romanov and even less about Tsarina Alexandra and their children. She probably did not even understand the meaning of the lyrics of the song about the killing, but she knew it was not good for the Tsar and his family, and that was the reason she needed to sing the song the adults had been singing in her house, with sadness in their chests. Katya did not know that in Bogdanovka the Tsar's cavalry had thrown into the Great Fire her Grandpa Semyon, whom she knew only from the stories of her batya. But she did know that over there in some faraway Russia her Grandpa had been burned to death because he had tossed his old gun and army saber into the fire so that he could not harm any human being. Katya did not know what her grandpa had looked like, but she believed he had been as handsome and strong as her batya, just a bit older. She knew nothing in particular about religious institutions and leaders, about politics and political machinations, and about why the powerful ones push people into nations and religions, why they label them with different colours and lead them into wars against those of a different colour. And why leaders force into people's heads that they belong to the packs they control and that the greatest crime is for anyone to dare to say that he belongs to all of human society.

When Katya turned around to see where the rustle came from, she did not interrupt her song, and held her hand in the air ready to throw another bunch of petals into the water. Pavloosha saw that tears had made two lines on her cheeks and that these two threads of divine liquid from her feelings shimmered in the sun. Her hand moved forward and the petals spread like butterflies in the air.

"What are you doing here all by yourself, Katya?" Pavloosha asked.

Katya recognized him and was not scared.

"Nothing," she replied, sadness in her voice.

"Why are your eyes teary?" Pavloosha asked as he sat next to her.

"I don't know," Katya replied and wiped her tears with the sleeve of her light yellow shirt. "Mamushka and Batya cry when they sing this song before we get up from our bed in the morning."

"I heard your mom calling you," Pavloosha told her, offered her his hand, and they both got up on the bank above the river. "Maybe she is looking for you to help her prepare dinner," he added.

Katya looked him in the eyes, shook her head as if saying she didn't believe it, and whispered:

"Mamushka does not ask me to help her prepare dinner yet. Anushka helps her."

She looked downstream as if checking where that last bunch of petals she had thrown in the river was.

"Why are you throwing flowers in the water?" Pavloosha asked.

The girl looked at him in surprise, turned her head towards the water and replied:

"Batya said they had died there far away in their country. This water will carry my flowers to them."

Pavloosha took Katya in his arms and carried her to the village.

35

Petro arrived at Spasovka after the news came from Europe that World War I was over. Canada ended the war alongside the victorious Allied Powers and Canadians celebrated for weeks. Petro came to the village in a bulky black Ford automobile, made especially for Canadian winter conditions. The black paint was visible only in the places which Petro touched with their fingers. The rest of the car was covered with a thick layer of dust.

On that day the Radio Regina weather program had forecast a storm in the afternoon hours, and all the villagers were in the fields to bring in the reaped grains and the dry hay for cattle. As soon as Petro passed the first houses, he realized that the adults were in the fields working and he decided to drive directly to his father's house. While driving, he met a group of children who lined up along the street as soon as they heard the sound of the engine. When he passed the children, he saw a group of young men by Stepko Tarasov's house, where young people often gathered. They were waiting for Stepko and his wagon so that they could transport the dry hay from the field where they were working. These fellows were standing away from the road and didn't move when they saw the car, as if they were not interested. Petro had a feeling that Nick could be among them; he stopped the car and opened the dusty window. He searched the faces of the young men, and by now they were looking at him and his car with curiosity. Suddenly one of them startled, pushed aside two guys standing in front of him, and reached the car in about two steps. He bent his head and stared at Petro. Petro's eyes were wide open and he whispered hesitantly:

"Nick?..."

"Petro! Brother!" the youth shouted.

They were beside themselves when they recognized each other. Petro opened the door in an instant, jumped out, and the two brothers firmly embraced each other. They held each other, smiling, but could not speak, could not control their tears. Petro pushed Nick away with his hands the better to see this sturdy adolescent who did not at all resemble the tiny Nick of more than five years ago. Only after studying his facial features a bit longer did he notice that Nick was looking more like his mother Paroniya than the father they shared. He had a handsome round face; his fair hair fell over his forehead down to his eyebrows and big eyes with their light-blue irises. He had a pert small nose, curved lips like their father Misha's, and his chin had a cute little dimple in the middle. Under his ears grew a beard of thin fair hairs as if he had come from the flatlands of Finland. Nick had changed a lot in five years. Petro had last seen him when he was a boy and now a sturdy youth was embracing him. He had recognized his brother only when he imagined this almost-man among the colourful butterflies, running after them in the field, and then realized it was his cheerful Nick.

When they'd had enough of looking at each other, they found their voices. Petro suggested that Nick introduce him to his friends. Some of the faces seemed familiar to Petro, but he did not want to risk making a mistake. They were Vasya, Ilya, Seryoza, Ivan, Kuzma, Alex and Peter. They were not surprised that Petro recognized only the scrawny Ivan because all the rest of them had changed a lot since Petro's departure.

Petro was a grown-up man, and his hairstyle and clothes looked like those of a businessman. He was bigger but as handsome as before. Only his voice was more rough, his eyes more serious, a bit tougher than the eyes of the gentle Petro of before. He had a barely noticeable bump on his nose right below the line of his eyes.

As soon as he saw him, Misha trembled as if Petro had appeared from thin air. While they were embracing each other, Misha noticed his son was a little bigger and taller than he and solid as a rock. Suddenly, he asked himself how Petro's Tanyushka would react at seeing him. She had been waiting for five years, fighting with time and working unbelievably hard; recently she had started avoiding Misha's gaze when she saw him. Misha was certain she had become embarrassed to always ask when Petro would finally come home. His letters to Tanya during the war had been brief and almost cryptic, as though fearing censorship, and in his letters he always mentioned that she could not reply to him because he did not have a permanent address. Very mysterious. On one occasion Misha told her that he was no longer certain if Petro would come soon, or where he really was. Tanya took it in her own way and said, blushing:

"I believe in destiny. Do not worry. I know my Petro. If necessary, I'll wait for him my whole life."

Petro and Paroniya greeted each other warmly, and when he embraced Babushka Pelagiya she reprimanded him saying:

"I feel you did not miss me, Petro."

"Oh, Babushka, how can you say that. You will always be my only Babushka."

Pelagiya looked at him suspiciously. He realized that she thought that Boulisou's mother had replaced her in his affection and he was quick to reassure her:

"The other one is not my Babushka. She is my Nona. And she is different from you. Her heart is different. She does not hug me as heartily as you. But, when I saw you, I was surprised not to see our Grandpa Kostuna next to you. I miss my Grandpa a lot...Oh how happy I would be if he were with us!"

Babushka hugged him even more and held him in her arms until Misha told them that somebody had come to see Petro.

At the wide-open door stood Tanya. She was not embarrassed to rise on her toes and almost jump into Petro's arms. He looked at her, pretending to be surprised, gathered her up and carried her outside. Then his face reappeared in the doorframe with a smile and nod of the head that made it plain the conversation would have to wait a bit because something was happening that couldn't be postponed, and he left with Tanyushka. They got into the car and drove toward the river. Tanya was a mature woman now, very open and cheerful, full of imaginative descriptions and stories, so daring that Petro was as surprised as he was glad. He immediately imagined her greeting him when he returned from work and transforming all the worries he brought with him to cheerfulness leading into the happy second part of the day.

Petro parked at the spot where the river often flooded during the rains in fall and spring, and vegetation became so abundant in summer that people avoided the place out of prudence. There they stepped out of the black Ford without speaking and fell into a passionate embrace.

"Petro, tell me openly where our relationship stands," Tanya insisted as she calmed down after their explosion of intimate touching in the depth of that small jungle by the river.

"What do you mean?" Petro asked her.

"The same as you, but you are avoiding that conversation. We have to be honest with each other," the girl replied.

"I still do not understand what you want to hear from me," Petro said, lowering his gaze to her breasts and waist. He moved closer again and put his hand on her shoulder. It was clear they'd both lost a lot of energy in their loveplay and needed a rest until the well of their energy refilled.

"What are your plans, Petro? Did you come home for good or are you going back to America?"

"I haven't completed my studies because I was in school and working at the same time. My Nono Yakov is frugal and prefers that I work and pay for my tuition instead of taking money from him. I will go back to Boston, finish what I started, and then see what's the best thing to do."

"What about me?" Tanya asked anxiously. "Do you see me in your plans?"

"You are a grown up, free person. Your life is in your hands. Do you want to reduce yourself to allowing me to plan your life?" Petro was playing nonchalant.

Tanya turned her head away, breathing heavily. Her face changed colour and the jugular vein was pulsing so strongly in her throat that Petro could feel it next to his hand.

"I have waited for you. You told me to wait for you...'

She became quiet, thinking fast. Petro had come with a different scenario, and suddenly that merciless and provocative scenario had imposed itself.

Tanya leaned on her elbow in the grass and started to get up. Petro wrapped his hands around her waist and pulled her onto the grass. She quickly faced him and her eyes became narrow slits sparking fire. Petro became afraid of the look on her face, laughed, and the girl said in a disappointed and angry tone:

"Let me go! I..."

"Why should I let you go? What do you...You did not understand me, Tanyushka. We made an agreement a long time ago. Why did you ask me what my plans are? You waited for me and I waited for you too. If you do not want to go with me of your own will, I'll force you!" he said, looking at her now more open and placid eyes; a smile started to appear on her lips from the depth of her feelings.

Tanyushka hurled herself on Petro, threw him to the ground and started beating him on the chest, laughing and crying; then she started kissing him passionately and vengefully, as if she wanted all the fear she had accumulated in the last few minutes to disappear into these kisses and give him a taste of it so that he realized how much he had frightened her. Petro responded to her and who knows where it would have gone if they hadn't started rolling down the small hill and bumped into a thorny bush that was on the path of their bodies.

The next day, right after breakfast, all the people of Spasovka gathered in the field by the village wearing festive traditional Russian costume from the region between Moscow and the Black Sea. The women formed a line facing the men. For a long time they sang the traditional songs for blessing newlyweds. Then two people stepped forward, one from each line, and stood between the male and female groups. Petro appeared, wearing the traditional Doukhobor suit, dominated by a long white shirt decorated with hand-worked designs and strapped around the waist with a broad belt embroidered in colourful wool; and Tanyushka, wearing the Doukhobor dress traditional to her family clan and wrapped in a long light-purple shawl. Petro's childhood friend Stevusha Plotnikov asked them if they wanted to join their lives and from now on live together and share the good and the bad. Then all the Doukhobors, one by one, blessed them and wished them a long and happy life. After the wedding ceremony, the Doukhobors for a long time sang the songs of apotheosis to family life and asked God and Jesus to give the couple happiness.

Petro gave his Ford to his father and asked him to take him and Tanyushka to Regina. From there they would continue their journey to Boston by train. On the way, he helped Misha to learn to drive the car properly and told him about his plans to take a more serious part in his Grandpa Yakov's commodities trading business and to develop the trade of grains and cattle with the Doukhobor rural communities and farmers.

"Does Yakov know that Tanyusha is coming?" Misha asked him when they stopped in front of a store close to Yorkton for Tanya to buy some souvenirs for Petro's family in Boston.

"They all know. I told them I would get married in Spasovka and come with my wife. Grandpa offered us the basement of their house until we find something better."

"What are your long-term plans, Petro?" Misha asked hesitantly.

"To come one day and take you, Nick, Babushka and Paroniya to Boston or Philadelphia. There are much better possibilities there than here in Saskatchewan."

"Who knows what time will bring," Misha smiled, and patted Petro on the shoulder. "Did you learn more about the tradition of your mother's people and their religion?"

"I learned a lot, Batya. They're not forcing that on me, but I think it is my duty. I know my mother would like it." He paused to look into the sky. "I have already seen many similarities between the destiny of the Jewish people and our own. From what I hear, Verigin is still looking for the right country for the Doukhobors, as if Canada were not good enough for him. It is the same with Jews. When you get into their soul, when they accept you and open the doors of their confidence to you, you realize they dream about some all-Jewish country and believe that would bring them eternal happiness. You taught me to be against manacles and to try to avoid them as much as I can. I think it would be better for both Jews and Doukhobors to fight for the idea that all people should be brothers and sisters and then it wouldn't matter what country one lives in. Maybe people would be happy if there were no countries. If human hatred disappeared, we would not need them."

Misha was very happy. He felt his Petro had become a good, solid person, which should be the goal of every human being.

"Petro, do not forget our Nick. He is becoming a good man too…" This slipped from Misha's tongue, as if he were the one leaving, and entrusting his younger son to the elder.

"Batya," Peter told his father with pride in his voice, "Nick is my brother. What are you trying to say?"

"Nothing special, Petro. I'm getting old, time is passing, and people are often very cruel. We are here on this continent without roots. It is not difficult for the wind to blow away plants that do not have developed roots firmly holding them to the ground."

In fact, Misha felt strongly the burden of his years, which had started to pass more quickly and more mercilessly. For a long time he had had a desire to say farewell to his life on that hill visible from Spasovka, there past the Aboriginal reserve and Kamsack to the east. The hill was no more than a hundred meters high, but it was above that endless Canadian flatland, which still reminded him of the vast ocean on his journey from Russia to Canada. Whenever he felt the tension of immigrant loneliness, from that hill he would creep with his gaze over their villages, streams and rivers, across the Doukhobors' grain fields growing ever longer and wider, and that would give back the weary breath of life to his spirit. He would drink the new energy and, much before the people at the foot of the hill, feel the breath of a gentle wind, often followed by weather change, rain or snow, and sometimes storm. On occasion he thought about how it would be best to sit on top of that Saskatchewan hill, take in everything his gaze could reach, and silently say goodbye to the world he lived in.

Suddenly Mother Pelagiya silently departed from their lives. Misha knew she would leave without much commotion, because she lived in that way too. One morning she stayed in bed longer than usual. She had normally risen first, as soon as the daylight replaced darkness. On that day Pelagiya departed along with the darkness of the night, a life having reached its end, inevitably retreating before what was being born. Babushka's death saddened Nick more than anybody else because in his youthful daydreams there was no place for death. When he was saying goodbye to his Babushka, with him was Katya, that same girl whom they had been looking for all over the village and around it after their return from rescuing MacKay's farm from fire. At that time she was the tiny daughter of Gresha Goncharov who at the riverbank had sung about her sadness for the tragedy of the last Russian Tsar and his family. Now she was not that tiny Katya any more. She was a beautiful girl, with whom Nick had fallen in love when he was still a little boy. He started to court her bashfully when thin fair hairs started growing above his lips. He had already seen her as his wife in the house of his father Misha, but Katya entered the house for the first time when Babushka Pelagiya died.

During the first autumn after Pelagiya's death the summer drought continued in that part of Canada. To the Doukhobor villages in Saskatchewan came alarming news from the south of British Columbia about renewed tensions in the relationship between the authorities in that part of the country and Peter Verigin's Community Doukhobors. The newly elected provincial government had insisted from the year 1914 that the Doukhobors consistently respect the Community Regulation Act. Now the government decided to definitively settle accounts with the Doukhobors who refused to send their children to the schools where young people were psychologically and practically being prepared for different occupations, but also indoctrinated to carry out the host society's militaristic and capitalist agenda. The Doukhobors found themselves under ever more dangerous attack in the authorities' campaign against the radical groups who insisted on continuing to follow the rules of traditional Doukhoborism, and demonstrated their refusal to cooperate in extreme ways. One more time the schools in the south of British Columbia were on fire and explosions were heard again in the region of the Doukhobor settlements and farms. The authorities started to crack down cruelly on the people who organized these protests.

There were a few families who had stayed in Spasovka but did not belong to the Independent branch of the Doukhobor Movement and who still respected Peter Verigin as their leader. Among them was the family of Gresha Goncharov. Whenever there were unrests in the south of British Columbia, Gresha became red in the face and could not hide the trembling of his hands. The segment of Saskatchewan Doukhobors who spiritually belonged to the orthodox group organized protests in the villages where they were most numerous, to warn the Canadian public about the Doukhobor problem and especially about the state laws that threatened the Doukhobor philosophy of life. Wherever there were protests, the state sent force to localize them. Then the Doukhobor radicals organized the protest of naked bodies.

As soon as he returned from a meeting of potential participants in the protest, Gresha informed his wife Svetlana, sister Yelisaveta and daughter Katya that the whole family would participate in the procession of naked protesters. When she heard her father's words, Katya jumped from a wooden bench covered with a woollen blanket and attacked her father with her gaze. Her face was red and she could not hide the trembling of her lips.

"I cannot participate naked in that, father! I cannot…"

"Why cannot you when we all can?" Gresha asked her, bitterness in his voice.

"I simply can't! I am ashamed to show myself naked to other people," Katya replied, and her voice expressed both determination and respect for her father. "I could—"

"We are all born naked," Gresha cut in resolutely. "We are created like that."

"I know father that we are created that way…That I was born like that. But it's been thirteen years since I was born…I look different now. And also, when I was born I had no power to say what I wanted and to do what I wanted."

Katya was surprised at her own daringness and at the tone she used to address her father. He was also surprised that his Katya so resolutely confronted him. But he made a judgement:

"We will all go, Katya! We have to...We have nothing to be ashamed of. We are all very much alike. We will warn the others, who will look at us and hear about our protest, and tell them that people are the same when they take their clothes off and that we must understand and help each other. We will all go, Katya!"

"But, father, people started to cover their bodies a long time ago and in that way became different from animals."

"Katya, people are different from animals only because of their mind, not because of their clothes. We will all participate in the protests." Gresha pronounced his last words in a tone that clearly indicated the conversation was over.

Katya turned away and fled to the window facing the street. Her mother went to her, embraced her, and whispered to her loud enough that Gresha and Yelisaveta could hear:

"You will hide behind me and Yelisaveta, and we will see to it that you are not in the last row."

Gresha and his family went to the protest in Veregin. Some other people from Spasovka went too, even though they did not want to participate in the protest because they thought the protest of naked bodies was not suitable for civilized people. They still went there, simply to try to prevent incidents from happening on any side. Among them was Nick Chernov. He knew Gresha was a good man, but he thought that Gresha's goodness should have prevented him from forcing his daughter to participate in the protest of the naked. But he also knew that Gresha was a follower of the radical Doukhobors and was afraid he would be firm with Katya too.

The participants in the protest of the naked bodies were taking their clothes off in the house of Evgeny Tihonov. A great mass of the Doukhobors who were not participating in the protest gathered around the Orphanage, while increased police activity was noticeable around the railway station. By the entrance to Evgeny's spacious house his father, the blind Timofey Ivanovitch Tihonov, was sitting on a low wooden stool. He was leaning against the beams of the house and staring somewhere into the darkness in which he had lived for the last twenty years, since that night when blindness had surprised him while he was sleeping. The old man would often turn his head away when he heard somebody coming close to him, as if he were ashamed of the motionless irises of his eyes. Sitting there, Timofey was travelling among the images which he jealously kept in his memory, and singing. He was singing about how the Doukhobors had left Mother Russia in the middle of the great winter, with a lot of bright snow reflecting the magical sunrays, sad because of their departure. His song had come to the new country far across the vast sea, again to deep snow and cold winter where some people's warm eyes welcomed them, and warm breath came out between their warm lips into the cold. Through the song of the blind Timofey into the hearts of the Doukhobors crept spring, which together with the thick layer of snow, melted and thinned their Doukhobor tradition.

Are we ever going to sing together in unison
Like when our song was in the hearts of all of us?

The last verses of the old man's song opened the door of the family Tihonov's house. From inside started coming the naked, first grown-up men, then young men, followed by women and young girls. The men came out with their hands spread between their legs and the women and young girls covered their breasts. Katya was among the last to come out. She was walking right behind the huge body of Miriana Samorodina, and at her sides were her mother and Aunt Yelisaveta, and behind her the tiny Agashka Borisenkova. Katya fixed her gaze at Miriana's nape and her face was red with yellow lines under her red ears. And her heart…Her heart was beating ever faster in the nightmarish storm lashing her brain. Katya was ashamed of her naked body and of her participation in that protesting procession. If those watching them were naked too, she would feel better. But this way, the young girl was thinking, her nakedness was washing away everything she had so far in her life learned to nourish and cherish. She felt the morals which her goodhearted father Gresha, now leading the procession, had instilled in her irrevocably leaving her spirit along with her female chastity, which had not allowed her to show her breasts to Nick, though he had begged her to see them through the eyelashes of one eye only, just for a moment. She felt that every moment of that exposure of her body pulled out of her everything she had learned about the richness of civilization in the human spirit, about her pride and dignity, and about her feeling of self-worth among other people. She did not want to take her gaze off Miriana's nape, not to mention looking at the faces of the people outside their procession.

Katya suddenly heard a man whose voice she did not recognize shouting they should stop their shameful politics of naked bodies. She felt their procession start to sway, and people around her were turning their heads in all directions. Then from the front of the procession she heard commotion and somebody's order:

"Tie them up and take them naked like that to Yorkton!"

The protesting procession scattered as if a swarm of aggressive bees had attacked them, and Katya rushed back to the house of the Tihonovs, towards her clothes. She ran past terrified and astonished faces and when she had almost reached the house she saw the face of her Nick. She stopped, exposing what she had so far covered with her hands, thinking in a split second what to do, then rushed again towards the house door. She had no time to wonder what Nick thought of her but she noticed astonishment and sadness in his eyes. She fell upon her clothes in the Tihonovs' house, and as if in a nightmare she put on the wide white dress with red and blue flowers which her mother had embroidered the pervious winter. She saw an empty corner of the room, threw herself at that emptiness and started to cry. She tried to free herself from her father and mother's hands, which were pulling her out of that corner, and through tears she cursed the people and the time she lived in. Deep in her mind she wrestled with the dilemma whether or not she should have allowed her already developed personality to be in anybody's service, even her family's.

Once she was home, Katya did not leave the house for a long time. She did not hear any news from Nick. One day when she saw him through the transparent curtains in the window as he was walking by her house with a group of friends and looking at her windows, she moved away so he could not see her. She soon managed to persuade her father to send her to Uncle Stepan in Kamsack. She later found out from her mother that Nick had a girlfriend.

36

The year when the Doukhobors in the south of British Columbia planned to build a big cultural centre named after Peter V. Verigin, Nikolay Nikolayevitch Chernov was thirty-one years old. He did not like the idea that the centre be named after the still living Doukhobor leader because he entertained the thought that a living man, even the wisest one, could make such a great mistake that his people would rather erase all traces of him and his deeds.

"I'll give every cent I need to give, but I suggest that the centre be named after the Doukhobors. It is important to build the centre, and the name could be changed whenever people decide to do that," Nikolay was firm while talking to a group of those who had proposed the building.

Nikolay was tall, with broad shoulders and a narrow waist. His hands were long and strong, his hair dark and straight, and many of his friends attributed his success in training horses to the suggestive twinkle in his dark eyes framed with bushy eyebrows. His nose was longer than the noses of his close Chernov relatives and it was gently curved in the middle. On the right side of his forehead and under the right ear he had a few deep scars; the biggest one was dark like his short-trimmed moustaches. His face revealed his strict character, almost hotheaded and even dangerous when confronted by a situation where he needed to use force. But his gait...His gait was recognizable even from afar. People remembered him by it. >From a distance he appeared very different from the Nikolay standing in front of you. He made everyone who saw him walking at a distance laugh. His gait was shambly as a bear's...He swayed while walking, as if he had one leg shorter than the other. And while running he also looked like a bear—

a bear that even the fastest caribou of the Canadian north could not escape.

Nikolay's father, Nikolay Dimitriyevitch Chernov, unlike most of the clan, had decided to stay with Peter Verigin at the time of the Doukhobors' split in Saskatchewan. He moved to the south of British Columbia in one of the biggest caravans in the Canadian Wild West. In that region it was much warmer than in Saskatchewan, and the climate was favourable for growing grains, fruit and vegetables, and for raising cattle. Nikolay chose horses. Soon he became "the king of the cowboys" and "Tsar Chernov" because nobody could train a horse as quickly and well as he could. Horses loved and obeyed him, and they trusted him when he whispered to them with his brow leaning on their long heads.

One day Peter Verigin asked him to bring the two horse herds he had bought in Alberta through the mountains to BC. Nikolay thought this over while sitting in the parlour of the Verigins' big house in Brilliant; then he got up on his long firm legs and decided:

"I accept if we hire our Doctor Misha."

"Why Misha Kostunavitch Chernov?" Peter asked him in surprise. He had expected Nikolay to ask for a veterinarian, but why this one? "Misha knows how to cure people and you are going to bring in horses. If you need a vet, we will pay the famous man from Saskatchewan, Doc Ballard, to come to Alberta."

Nikolay looked at the legendary Doukhobor leader with the eyes of a rough cowboy and answered briefly:

"I am sure you want all your horses to arrive at the farm. You paid for them. Misha knows about horses more than vets and I know. As soon as he looks a horse in the eyes, he knows if it is capable of travelling for ten days. If he sees a sick animal, he knows very well how to help it get better. And the vet Ballard? He is now in Vancouver and working more on building a factory to can food for dogs and cats than on curing animals."

Verigin looked at Nikolay's short-trimmed, thick moustaches and recalled his previous, memorable contacts with Misha. At that moment he felt pain and the pangs of bad conscience because of the way they had parted years ago. Nikolay's words interrupted Verigin's reminiscence:

"Yes, Peter. It is a pity that Misha did not move here with us."

"Nikolay! It was Misha's decision. I wasn't thinking about that now. It is a strange coincidence. I recently decided to send Misha a message that I would like to meet with him. I have asked him to be my guest for a few days. And now you are asking that Misha participate in the transport of the horses. You Chernovs are special people. If they sent you to opposite corners of the world and put a huge time distance between you, you would find some strange way to communicate," Verigin said as if talking to himself, far away from people, in some orchard, in the moonlight, when a man can talk to himself without fear of reality interfering.

"Is that bad or are you praising us?" asked Nikolay with a discreet smile on his lips.

"Well, it's not, Nikolay! You took my words too seriously. You remind me of myself when I went to California to check if it was a good place for us Doukhobors. There on one farm I met the Mexican foreman. He asked me why I wanted to move our folks to California when there was only hundred years till the end of the world. I was surprised, and he explained to me: 'The Mayan calendar ends with the year 2012, if you translate it into the Christian calendar. The scientists of the ancient Mexican people came from somewhere else in the universe and knew much more than human beings.' The Mexican tried to convince me of this, and I took it seriously. I owed him an answer. I remembered Tolstoy's words about Zarathustra and I said to the Mexican man:

"It might not mean the end of the world. It might rather mean that the Mayan scientists knew that two millenniums after the birth of Christ people would renew their existence. Until then, the calendar of civilization will be full of human blood and pain, and after that people will really become brothers, as our teaching says, and hatred among people will disappear. That's why there will be a need to start a new calendar. Because time is endless. Even if a tragedy happens on earth, time will go on as before.'"

"I do not think in that way," Nikolay said without hesitation. "I believe that our teaching is just and that one day people will realize they are brothers. Maybe a great tragedy will hit them on their heads and their brains will then start to function differently."

"I believe it will happen. The brain is the solution for the human race, not instincts and emotions. They are only decorations of human personality. The mind is human essence. The time will come when the brain will change the way it functions and it will take people into a new era, the era of brotherhood and love, when hatred and aggression will disappear with the disappearance of old calendars. When a heavy rain suddenly stops, the sky clears up and the sun starts shining as if wanting to show its splendour. And the Doukhobors? The Doukhobors will live to see the time when people renounce the beliefs that led them into hurting each other. Our beliefs are not time limited. We do not mystify God and Christ because mystification enables each man, even the most vile one, to interpret it in his own way," Verigin was speaking as if, instead of Nikolay Chernov, he were talking to that Mexican from California.

When Peter Verigin, at the suggestion of Lukeriya Kalmikova, accepted leadership of the Doukhobors after her, she gave him a strange cube with an orange-coloured sculpture of the human brain inside, and urged him to keep it in secrecy. For many years he thought about that sacred cube and came to the conclusion that it symbolized the power of the human brain and its final victory over evil. "The Lord gave people a very powerful brain and it should lead people through life, not any sacred books and religious dogmas," became a truism for the Doukhobor leader. In recent time he had often thought about who among the Doukhobors should take over and guard that secret, and he often remembered the face of Misha Chernov. Maybe he thought this way because he suffered more and more for having been the leader of the Doukhobors at the time of their split, and for having played the decisive role in that. Peter wanted to talk to Misha personally about the information he had received from a Doukhobor trader, Pavel Kirilovitch Kanyigin. On a train between Regina and Saskatoon, Pavel had met three burly men wearing the clothes of Russian Orthodox priests. They had told him they belonged to the Orthodox parish in Toronto, but avoided questions about where in Russia they had come from and where they were travelling. The three had shown great interest in the Doukhobors in British Columbia and had asked about the health of Peter Verigin and Misha Chernov. Verigin became worried after receiving that information and spontaneously made a connection between these three men and the three Antonovs on the ship *Lake Superior*. He knew from what Tolstoy's son Sergey had told him that the police had taken those men somewhere right after the ship reached Canada and nobody had thought about them since.

"I was not surprised when Misha decided not to go with us to British Columbia," Verigin returned to the previous topic. "I know Misha Chernov very well. Even when he scolds you, Misha will watch your back to help you if there is need. I know he blames me for my refusing to cooperate with the authorities for a long time and for my conviction that the life of the Doukhobors in communes is a recipe for the survival of the movement. Misha is against all extremism, he is of a gentle disposition, and life has taught him to be steady. Misha is not talkative and believes that those who spend their life in silence, those whose words are always weighed on the scale of usefulness, avoid making mistakes"

"So you agree that I hire Misha for the job with horses," Nikolay concluded.

"I have nothing against your contacting Misha. My message to him said that I would like him to be my guest during our festivities in the first half of May. I still haven't received his reply. I believe he will accept my offer because, even though he is not one of the official leaders of our movement, Misha feels responsible for all of us. He will come to our celebration. It will happen at the same time as the transport of horses. It is up to you now," Peter agreed, then added: "I forgot to tell you that you need to bring the horses to my farm in Grand Forks, not here to Brilliant."

During this conversation with Peter Verigin, Nikolay noticed the shadow of a man cast behind Verigin's back; from time to time it bent, as if the curtain that let the sunlight in had billowed. Nikolay's alert sense of hearing registered the creaking of wooden floorboards under somebody's feet and he saw the shadow hide behind something on the porch close to the window. Nikolay was certain that someone was out there, listening behind Verigin's back, but Verigin didn't once turn his head. It was obvious to Nikolay that the Doukhobor leader was not aware of the shadow Nikolay had spotted. In a flash he thought about what to do, but all the combinations he came up with seemed inappropriate, especially the thought that he should jump suddenly and rush onto the porch. He decided not to do anything unless he concluded that the man who was hiding was dangerous. He knew Verigin had two bodyguards, but he couldn't guess why one of them would want to listen to their conversation.

When Verigin and Nikolay left the house, they felt a strong gust of south wind. The blue of the sky was quickly retreating before heavy clouds whose orange colour surprised both of them.

"It is the beginning of a storm, Nikoshka! Look at these clouds!" Peter exclaimed.

"I have never seen anything like this," Nikolay agreed. "Even my black horse is scared. His eyes and nostrils are flaring as if he saw a bear, and his legs are dancing like when he gets nervous before a race. I have to hurry home. Good luck to you, Peter."

When he left Verigin, Nikolay spotted the broad shoulders of a man disappearing behind the corner of an auxiliary building on Verigin's property. It could be, Nikolay was thinking, the strong Prokofiev, one of the bodyguards, but also it could be another owner of shoulders similar to Prokofiev's. However, the shoulders could also belong to the one who had cast his shadow in Verigin's parlour. However, Nikolay had no time for thinking. The storm had already splattered the first big drops of orange rain and with each moment the wind was becoming stronger. People were scurrying around the houses, calling to each other and putting things that needed to be protected from the rain and wind under cover. Cows and sheep were running to shelter, dogs and cats were looking for safe places to hide, and chickens, ducks, geese and turkeys were scuttling in circles, letting out sounds of dismay. Crows huddled close to each other, clamping their claws into the branches of trees. A woman was calling her Ivan from a doorstep. Many women were running around, gathering the laundry from clothelines, calling their children, and disappearing into the houses. Three horses galloped in from some place and went to the open doors of Verigin's stable, stood on their hind legs, pawed at the void in front of them, and then, as if following a command, turned around with their front legs still in the air, sprung ahead and galloped to the valley that the river flowed through, and disappeared.

When Nikolay came running to his horse, tied in front of the Verigin's long cattle barn, the animal awaited him with visible fear in his eyes, expressing reproach because Nikolay had left him tied and unable to protect himself from the storm. His eyes urged Nikolay to do something immediately, and his ears, for reasons known only to him, were turned to the rocky ground that led up toward the mountain. As soon as Nikolay got hold of the rope he had used to tie the horse to a wooden rail in front of the barn, a gust of wind carried to him the cries of a woman hidden by the tall bushes covering that rocky ground. The woman was screaming for help. Nikolay stood still, turned his head towards the cries, looked his horse in the eyes as if apologizing, and rushed in the direction of the woman's screams. He crashed through the inhospitable brush, his eyes and ears alert to discern the direction where the sounds came from. He suddenly saw a woman pulling two bags with one hand; she had her other hand placed under her stomach and was fighting the wind. When he rushed to her from behind and grabbed her bags, she screamed in fear and turned her head towards him. Seeing it was a man not some monster, recognizing Nikolay, she dropped her bags and sat heavily onto the wet orange grass.

"Don't be afraid, Lushka! It's me. Why are you screaming and pulling these bags? Why are you pulling them in this storm?"

"I cannot run, Nikoshka," the woman replied and with her head pointed at her big stomach. "I do not want to leave the bags behind. All day I've been collecting spring grass for lambs and I can't leave it now in the wind...I cannot..."

Nikolay helped her up, hoisted the bags with one hand, and with the other supported Lushka's big stomach. They started to walk, pushing through the bushes, fighting the wind and rain, which was losing its unusual colour.

"You must have screamed because you are afraid of the storm," he said, almost shouting to be heard above the roaring of the storm.

"Oh, Nikolay. It is obvious you have no wife. My stomach started hurting when I began to run against the wind pulling these bags. The one inside got scared," looking down at her gravid belly, "and started kicking with its arms and legs and crying. Don't you hear?" the woman, also shouting, asked him completely seriously.

"I cannot hear anything except the storm," Nikolay shouted and pulled her and the bags more firmly. He was afraid that Lushka would give birth in that chaos; with both of her hands she tightly grabbed his shirt and looked at him as if apologizing...The storm had no mercy for either the two of them or the tiny creature in Lushka's womb.

When they reached Lushka's house, somebody opened the door a crack as if expecting them.

"Get in! Get in!"

When Nikolay dragged the woman and the bags to the door, the other one grabbed the woman from inside and pulled her into the house; then his hand grabbed the bags, his head appeared in the door, and he hissed:

"Oh, it is you, Nikoshka! How did she find you in this storm?"

Nikolay pushed the bags and the man's hand inside the house and slammed the door.

One week after that event, Misha was happy to welcome Nikolay to his house in Spasovka. It had been more than fifteen years since Nikolay's father and his family had moved to Brilliant, but Misha and Nikolay had met twice during that period. Nikolay quickly explained to Misha about the job with Verigin's horses and why he had come to Spasovka. Misha did not hesitate.

"I have already planned a trip to Verigin's kingdom," Misha started with a smile. "This is only an addition to that plan. I am happy to spend some time with you, to have a chance to be with horses, but also to see Peter again. Anyway, during the journey we will have enough time to talk about everything. Since we will collect the horses in Red Deer, it is best if we drive in my Ford to Regina and then take a train to Medicine Hat," Misha was thinking aloud.

"What should I do with my black horse in that case? I would not leave him for Verigin's entire herd. I need three days to get to Regina. I can leave tomorrow, and you can leave a day after in your Ford. We will meet in Regina. You leave your car there, and I will put my horse on the train. That's how we came here. We will take a train to Alberta, all three of us."

At dusk Misha and Nikolay joined those who had gathered in front of the Orphanage. They started hugging Nikolay as if they had never been separated nor taken different paths of the Doukhobor tradition. They wanted to know about the newspaper stories from the south of British Columbia. Then they all started to sing. The song of that mighty Doukhobor choir was full of different voices and often-dissonant intonations, but it proudly spread over the valley around the village, reaching to the thickets that hindered approach to the river as if consciously protecting that precious beauty in the bosom of the prairie. While they were singing, Misha remembered the words he had used aboard the steamer *Lake Superior* to explain to Captain Taylor why the Doukhobors sang a few times a day and all together.

"With our singing we sustain our collective psyche and include each individual in a community of different people. Through singing we express our beliefs about man and his role on earth," Misha had told Taylor. "In that way, we join our individual goodness into one great goodness and with that great goodness we again and again communicate with God, who is in the spirit of each of us. With our songs we want to help the world wake up from its ugly dream, and each individual to realize that all people are brothers and sisters."

When darkness enveloped the village, the song from the Orphanage could not be heard anymore.

As soon as they bid Nikolay goodnight, Paroniya put her arms around Misha's waist and pulled him closer to her, as long before when they burned with the passion that Parushka had cherished for so many years before the prairie fire, before they started to live together. Misha was surprised when his wife embraced him tightly and tenderly put her lips on his Adam's apple. She held his head in her hands, then pushed it away to see her husband's face more clearly. She did not wait for him to ask what the good news was.

"Mishka, you have decided to go to the celebration in Brilliant. I do not want to give you advice because you did not ask for my opinion. But I have to tell you that I would be much happier if the celebration were here in Saskatchewan. Since the days when we found out the Lordly Verigin had settled there in Brilliant, I have felt that place is cold to me. I have never been to our communities in British Columbia, but recently strange things have happened there. Schools and houses have burnt; there have been explosions in and around Peter Vasiliyevitch's place..." Paroniya was almost whispering.

Maybe she spoke in such a low voice so that Nikolay could not hear, or maybe so that Misha would pay more attention to her words than to the way she spoke. She knew her husband very well. He was quiet when many others in similar situations would be noisy; he thought that noisy words affect emotions more than a call for reason and cooperation. A few times he had said that words spoken under the influence of emotion are like an angry wind when it breaks branches and trees in orchards. Wind is the most useful in spring when it silently creeps through woods and flowerbeds and helps buds to develop and bloom. That is why Parushka now whispered to him, even though she felt like screaming that he should not to go to Brilliant. Even then Misha would not have raised his voice but would have calmly explained to her that it was not useful to let herself be guided by instincts, which are often tools of paranoia and of uncontrolled anger.

"That is why I am going there, Parushka," Misha now held her head in his hands. "I feel Verigin needs help. He is a wise man. Very intelligent. But he is hot-tempered. His emotions are too close to his tongue. Between the tongue and the feelings there is no space for wisdom. Not always. Parushka, in a situation that requires crucial decisions to be made, emotions get stirred and it is difficult to control them. Often they do what the mind never would."

"What is happening now, Mishka? What decisions does Peter need to make?"

"He has in the last years become very flexible. He made some good moves to improve the Doukhobors' production in that part of Canada. He has established good relationships with the authorities. Finally, he heartily accepted public schooling once he realized that isolation is like the case of Troy when the Trojan Horse was infiltrated to make an end of them. I think Peter wants to make new threads to create some connection among the divided Doukhobors. He is now against radicalism in our feelings because that is the biggest enemy of our philosophy of life," Misha explained what influenced his decision to visit Verigin in his capital.

Paroniya took a deep breath.

"I think Peter is more worn out than old. A lot of things are out of his control now. But he is still thirsty for glory and in some sense extreme. He will still make moves by which people will remember him. And now, Mishka, we should do what my father has been telling us since we came to Canada—we should lie low and see what direction the winds blow before we do anything that might be dangerous."

Paroniya took a deeper breath and tried to keep her eyes calm.

"I will see, Parushka. You could tell me all this even in bed. I am not one of those who say that two heads on one pillow can only think about one thing—the caresses of their bodies," Misha smiled, and pulled Parushka into the bedroom. There, above their heavy wooden bed covered with a spread made of white wool, was hanging a painting, also embroidered in wool, of a bluish water over which flew a strange bird the colour of overripe rays of sunlight. Nobody had ever seen such a bird, either in the homeland of their fathers nor here in Canada.

Misha and Nikolay belonged to different groups of the Canadian Doukhobors, but, in fact, they were very similar. On the journey by train from Lethbridge to Castlegar they had a lot of time to talk like brothers about many things that were important in their lives, in the Doukhobors' philosophy, and in the world in general. During a pause in their conversation about the rebellion of the Aboriginal people on the reserves in eastern Washington State in America and about their fear that this rebellion could easily spread across the border to the south of British Columbia, Misha suddenly asked Nikolay:

"Tell me Nikoshka, why you are not married. Do you maybe think that it is crazy to get married in youth because youth is craziness, so two crazy youths at once would be too much?"

"Eh, Mishka! You do not expect that I will tell you how you are not happier than me because you got married twice? Or that I have a quieter and easier life than you? No! You experience the happiness and suffering that the making of a family brings. I also experience happiness and suffering, in the things that the life of an unmarried man brings. I could have gotten married a long time ago if that girl had not imagined that I preferred horses to her and disappeared from my life. She was jealous of horses! And she did not realize that it was not smart to compare herself to them. Because these are two different types of love. It would be the same as to compare a chimney on a house with a grain mill. You need both but you cannot hug them both at the same time. I admit, I am the happiest when I am with horses. Not because they cannot speak our language. Or, to say better, they cannot talk to us in our language. It is because their eyes are so clear that they remind me of the early morning in this vast prairie. And because their eyes become teary when they feel your sadness. And because they snort and turn their head away from you when they are annoyed. In their behaviour there is no politics, Misha."

Every twenty minutes or so Nikolay would go to the two livestock cars in which Verigin's horses were being transported. And he always returned with new impressions about them. He did not know them and was surprised by their behaviour towards him and towards each other.

"Somebody has filled the heads of these horses with that Biblical saying: 'Love thy neighbour'," he was quick to inform Misha upon his return from one of his visits to the animals.

"Where did you get this, Nikoshka? What do horses have to do with that saying in the Bible?" Misha said, looking at him thoughtfully.

"They are looking around patiently, those ones. They even lean on one another. And they snort at those farther away and show their teeth as if they hate them," Nikolay explained.

Misha smiled and stared out the compartment window, as though at something far away. It did not even bother him that a group of people looking for better seats passed between him and the window. "You've discovered something I hadn't thought of. It is good that we have found our different place in Christianity. Horses have a lot to teach us, if we learn how to listen," Misha told him, still gazing at something far away from the train.

"Now you explain to me what I said that you did not know," said Nikolay.

"What else could that Bible saying you mentioned mean if not that you should love your neighbour, but it's okay to hate those not close to you? Isn't it, Nikoshka, an open call for hatred and warmongering? Those who thought of that and recorded it in the Bible, and those who remind people to follow God's will and behave like that, should kneel down and ask God for forgiveness of their sins as long as they live."

"And not to get up from their knees until God summons them to account for their deeds," Nikoshka added gaily. Then he suddenly asked:

"What will become of your Petro?"

Misha asked himself the same question every time he thought about his older son. When Petro decided to go to Boston, Misha believed he would return quickly because life there was certainly very different from the Doukhobor life in which Petro grew up. But Petro did not return. To tell the truth, it was during the world war and it was not advisable to travel back and forth. Especially if you could easily be caught by those who were after deserters and men dodging the draft. But the war ended, and Petro came to Spasovka for only a couple of days and took Tanya back with him. Misha was sad because of his son, but in some secret compartment of his mind he believed it was good for all of them to have Petro somewhere in the outside, free world. Then a letter had come from Petro, accompanied by a picture of Misha's grandson Igor, and an invitation for all who wanted to visit them to come and see the beauty of Boston and New York.

Misha had gone by himself and returned with confusion in his head, which would stay with him forever. Occasionally, with the power of his mind, he could step back from that state of confusion for a moment. In such moments he concluded that the doors of the outside world were open to the Doukhobors without danger of losing their Doukhobor philosophy of life. Tanya and Petro had managed to incorporate into their traditional way of life that which they liked in the life they encountered in America. There is no danger, Misha thought, if you put on clothes different from the traditional ones, if you eat different food, if you teach your child to be familiar with both, if you go to see movies, if you listen to different music, and if your spirit absorbs what is good in the outside world but is not part of your tradition. There is no danger, Misha thought, in sending children to university, including them in any new life that offers people happiness, because a well-educated Doukhobor will always find a way to respect the great values of his tradition…But one does not have to pursue higher education, as long as he does not get stuck in fanaticism and permanent isolation. If some facet of the tradition is not in accordance with the positive values that other people have achieved, it is not sinful to remove that facet from one's practice. Misha's confusion was attached to a door: the door that any material or spiritual value has; the door designed to protect and keep separate what is behind. However, a door is a door, and it makes sense only if it can be opened so that what is inside can come out and what is outside can come in, in order for them to mingle and compete with each other so that people can choose the ideas that will more securely lead them into a happier future.

When he returned from Boston to Spasovka, Misha went with Nick to the riverbank and told him about Petro's family and their life in the big American city. In the end he entreated him to send his children to university or college and not to turn his head away from anything that is valuable regardless of whose house that value came from.

"I will, Batya! I will! I am of the same opinion. But I do not have children yet, and you are making plans with them," Nick smiled, looking at his father's grey hair.

"You will have them, Nikoshka! You will not permit yourself to abstain from creating humans whom you will orient to the good path in life."

Misha concluded his memories about the journey to Boston and briefly answered Nikolay's question:

"What will become of my Petro? He is a grown man. He knows how to discern what is good and useful, and I don't worry that he might live in a bad way. I advised him to keep from our Doukhobor tradition whatever he can offer to all people in the world, and to keep from the tradition of his mother's people the grace of survival. If he manages to bring the two together, civilization will gain a new quality and people will be able to have a future with more dignity."

"What about isolation, Misha? They say you were the most reasonable one in confronting Peter Verigin with regard to the isolation of our people," Nikolay provoked him.

At that moment something violently hit a window toward the rear of the coach, and people jumped from their seats to rush there. When after a few moments Nikolay returned and took his place, he explained what had happened.

"A bird...It hit the widow and fell in the bushes by the tracks. One of the trappers says he saw a hawk was chasing this bird, a meadowlark, towards the train and when its claws were ready to clamp into the meadowlark's back, the bird quickly changed its path and hit the window. It seems that it preferred such a death to the one waiting for it in the claws of the hawk."

Nikolay's description was dramatic, but Misha chose to change the subject. "Shall we have a bite of this cheese from Regina?" he asked, opening his bag. He cut a big piece of the white cheese for them, sighed, and decided nevertheless to explain his opinion about isolation to Nikolay.

"I think people are entering an era of great changes. So far isolation has been one of the ways to survive. Today people have telephones, radios, newspapers…News travels quickly. People on our planet are erasing the borders between nations. They are offering each other what they have achieved. More and more the destinies of individual groups will be tied to the destiny of all people. And that will change philosophies of life."

"I don't understand you, Misha. What does it mean for us?" Nikolay interrupted him.

"It means a lot. Our movement has become a tradition, and a tradition is always a thing of the past. In the present it is part of the philosophy of the descendants of those who created it, and in the future its value will depend on how much others in civilization accept it. At that big meeting of the Doukhobors before the world war, they criticized me when I opposed those who do not respect time. Everything appears and disappears in time. Nothing is permanent. I said then that it would be deadly for us if our leaders did not separate tradition from identity. Tradition is inheritance, while identity comprises some percentage of traditional beliefs mingled with a lot that is created individually and absorbed from others. Identity is a personal, not collective thing because the identity of the father in most cases, except instances of fanaticism, is not the identity of the son."

Misha felt the need to explain things to Nikolay because he was not sure how much the Chernovs who had followed Verigin knew about his own understanding of the paths of the Doukhobor people.

"I am afraid that we have started to quarrel seriously among ourselves and to separate from each other, and I believe it is the fault of the most respected ones in our movement," Nikolay aired thoughts he usually kept to himself.

"Maybe it is good that it happened. When coming to Canada we should have expected that our movement would be a target of many influences from this society. Even if we had stayed in Russia, time has brought changes there too. It seems to me that we will have to accept the fact that the Doukhobors in North America are getting closer to the time when they will disappear as a homogenous and isolated movement."

"What then Mishka? Then the others will assimilate us." Nikolay had stated the common fear, but only as though he were curious.

"The values of our tradition will stay," Misha continued. "The time has come when nobody can any longer hide verities from the whole world. Many learned people as well as lot of the common people all over the world have become familiar with our teaching. Every one of them who is an honest person knows that our philosophy of life is humane…That all people are brothers and sisters, that we do not hate anybody, that a man has no right to kill another, or to exploit him in any way. That our understanding of the relationship with God is in the domain of each individual's spirit, and that nobody has the right to make politics or profit out of it…In time the Doukhobors will take part in the life and the social organizations of other civilized people, but in our spirit we will preserve the values of our philosophy. Our people and the verities of our philosophy of life will induce other people to evaluate these principles and to accept what they also find valuable."

"Oh, ho, ho…" somebody's husky voice coming from behind their back surprised them. "Nikolay Chernov!…A Doukhobor cowboy! I know you, but I do not know your clever companion. If I accurately followed your conversation, I should not be afraid that I will have a bad lunch, provided I use the recipe of this honey-mouthed one…Maybe I do know him…" in an ugly tone the newcomer squeezed out the words between his teeth.

Nikolay slowly turned his head, and slowly rose to his feet. His eyes suddenly met the big brown eyes of a man taller by a head than Nikolay himself, but whose stylish green jacket and spotless hands made clear that he did not plough the fields or raise cattle. He spoke the English language with a heavy Russian accent.

"I do not know you, but I know those who interrupt the conversation of others in such a manner," Nikolay's words hit directly at the communication style of that arrogant, sixtyish old man. Age had diminished neither his apparent physical strength nor his grating self-confidence.

"Maybe it would be better if I did not interrupt you, but I could not stand any more of that smarmy extolling of the apostates from the normal Christian world. It would have been better if you had kept quiet. Silence is a godly way of communication and keeping everything in eternal order. If you want your house to be warm, keep the door closed. And you, obviously, don't know about that," the man told them, while his face revealed nothing of his intentions. He had adopted the mien of a bully.

Nikolay did not like either that giant or his words. He moved to the aisle to get closer to the bully, and by looking at the movement of Nikolay's feet and the changing colours on his face, Misha realized that his cousin had become annoyed enough to react explosively to the big man's clear provocation. Misha got up with the intention of pulling Nikolay back to his seat, but another man, also burly, of like age, and dressed similarly, approached the provocateur. He put his hand on the provocateur's shoulder and whispered something to him that others could not hear. The provocateur became thoughtful, shook his head like a bull when not allowed to charge at another bull, and walked away without saying anything more, but casting a few belligerent looks at Nikolay and Misha.

When they approached the town of Brilliant they noticed that the train slowed down even though it was not scheduled to stop before Castlegar. They did stop, however, and the engine and the first two cars were detached from the other nine and backed onto the siding in the train station. There awaited a railway coach with the faces of a few men and women visible at its windows. Nikolay recognized the face of Peter Verigin in the company of some other people. Both Nikolay and Misha were surprised and thought that the famous Doukhobor leader, long since nicknamed Lordly, was taking the train to go to Grand Forks for some important business meeting before the celebration planned for the following weekend. They did not think that he would want to greet the two of them and the horses as a surprise at the railway siding. That is why when that coach was added to the train they decided it would be better not to disturb Verigin and his company during the journey.

The train approached Farron. A few farms, with the main buildings made of logs, announced the outskirts of the village. The midday sunrays reflected on the metal roofs of the train cars and lazily bounced back to the sky, with only a few clouds of different shapes crowded together. Nikolay opened the window next to their seat and poked his head out. He could hear the snorting of horses from the livestock cars and also sporadic snorting from some others on the farm by the rails. Two children were standing in front of a house with their palms spread above their foreheads to protect their eyes from the sun, calmly looking at the passing train. The engine was breathing slowly and noisily, working to overcome the inertia of the train cars as it slowed to enter the station yard. A group of people was standing close to the rails, facing the engine as it lumbered toward them billowing smoke from its two black chimneys. The train slowed down, but it appeared that the engineer did not intend to stop in the village. While the first cars were passing by the group of people standing in front of the long station building, also made of logs, two men wearing backpacks jumped off train, joined the waiting group, and together they all went into the station.

The train was now crawling up a steep grade towards a long bend beyond which the rails entered a forest of tall evergreen trees. Suddenly a cloud of dust appeared behind the shoulder of the hill they were climbing, and from the cloud shot a car without a roof. The car sped up the dusty road towards the rail bend as if the driver wanted to reach the intersection with the train tracks before the engine. And they managed to come first; the car stopped just short of the level crossing, the two passengers got out, put heavy packs on their backs and stood right beside the tracks. While the engine was passing them, the engineer leaned from his platform and explained something to them. At the moment when Verigin's coach was passing by, one after another they held onto the metal rails of its stairs and jumped into the train.

"Mishka, something is wrong in Verigin's car," said Nikolay, pulling his head back in the window as the train came out of the bend and headed into the forest.

"What's wrong?" asked Misha getting up from the wooden bench.

Having heard Nikolay's words, other folks got up from their seats and started opening windows. They poked their heads out and looked at the front of the train.

"I could hear quarrelling in the car. It seems there is a big fight, shouting and screaming," Nikolay explained and again poked his head outside. Misha did the same. The sounds of raised human voices came from the direction of Verigin's coach, as if they were competing with the roaring of the locomotive. The horses were silent. The shouting from Verigin's coach, which was three cars ahead, was reaching them in waves and occasionally turned into violent shouts. Suddenly a man was thrown out of the car and while he was rolling down the hill, another was thrown out in the same manner. The two were rolling down the rock-strewn hill, and the noise could still be heard from Verigin's car. Misha and Nikolay instinctively moved away from the window and rushed to the compartment door. The passengers in the other cars were also alarmed. When the two Chernovs got through the door of the coach where the incident was occurring, they saw the commotion in a group of people, Verigin among them. It was obvious that the majority were restraining two men, whom they held on the floor of the compartment, pressing down on them with their arms and bodies but unable to completely subdue them. A few women were crowded on a bench fearfully awaiting the outcome of the fight. Verigin turned his head towards Misha and Nikolay, signalling them to help.

At that moment the blast of an explosion blinded Misha and simultaneously a wave of a devastating sound and terrible pressure hit him with a mighty force. He felt pain in his head and chest and lost consciousness. When he again opened his eyes, the pain in his chest was agonizing. He tried to concentrate, he remembered the blast and the explosion in the compartment, turned his head around to see where he was and realized what had happened. All around him on the hillside was the debris of the train; further down he saw overturned railcars and people in different positions. Some were standing, some were trying to get up, some were sitting trying to make sure they were still alive, but many were lying motionless, stretched out or curled up on the slope below the rails. Up there, as if surprised at what had happened, stood the engine, sending clouds of dark smoke into the sky. Misha suddenly saw the giant grumpy man from their compartment approaching him and saw blood on his face. His clothes were no longer tidy and clean.

"Are you in one piece, Doctor?" the man asked in his baritone voice and knelt next to Misha. Misha tried to move his body, but it refused to obey. He made a final effort to see that man better, and from his memory there emerged at last the image of the three burly brothers on the ship *Lake Superior*. The man looked like one of them, but older, and with a neater beard.

"I am Antonov, Doctor," the man next to him said in a low voice.

"What do you want from me now?" Misha asked, in fear because he was in mortal pain, unable to move.

"Just that cube in your hand," said Antonov in an even lower voice. He bent down to Misha, reaching toward the cube grasped in Misha's fist. He held his hand above Misha, waiting for his reaction.

Misha saw, moving his head by huge effort, the cube with the sculpture of the human brain inside.

"I do not know how this object came into my hand," Misha whispered, realizing he might never be able to move his body again.

"Lordly placed it there before he passed away," Antonov explained.

"Verigin?..." Misha was amazed.

"Verigin, Doctor...Here he is, above your head, dead, "Antonov told him, pointing to the place where Peter Vasiliyevitch Verigin lay motionless.

"Why?...Why do you need it?..." Misha spoke slowly. It dawned on him that this was the mysterious object from Pandora's Box which people secretly talked about. The idea occurred to him to try to create an illusion for Antonov that it was not that cube but an apple. But it didn't work. He concentrated with what little energy he had to make his mind affect the mind of this man above him, but again to no avail. He only felt sickness rushing from his brain into his lungs and his vision became blurred.

"It is a sacred cube. It belongs to our Church. That big apostate of the Holy Church, Samuilo, took it from our church in Constantinople. It does not mean anything for you Doukhobors. It only brings you misfortunes. I have to take it to the treasury of our Holy Synod…" The words were now coming out faster from Antonov's lips.

Misha understood everything, all that had happened before, from the abduction of his Boulisou, to the events on the ocean, the sinister interest in Petro, and now these events on the train before and after the explosion.

"What is the truth about my Boulisou?" he asked Antonov, his voice betraying his plea for an end to lies.

Antonov looked at him apologetically and told him, as if taking his words out of some unguessed depth, from some secret treasury:

"Our Synod had discovered that destiny would bring the Sacred Cube to your hands. In its mystery is the divine recipe for the liberation of the human race from the evils that Satan bequeathed us. We paid ransom to the bandits for your wife to get to you. She herself disfigured her face so you would not recognize her anymore; in that way we could not blackmail you. Maybe she did it also that no man would desire her anymore. Then on the ship, we wanted to abduct your son to use him for blackmail."

Misha cast his gaze to the ground and noticed that Nikolay was approaching them. He came at Antonov from the back, and suddenly like a cougar threw himself at him. He knocked him to the ground and squeezed his throat with his hands. Antonov was startled and did not try to defend himself.

"Don't, Nikoshka!" Misha tried to speak loudly; Nikolay managed to hear his feeble voice. He flicked his eyes from Misha's face to Antonov's head, back and forth, his hands still squeezing Antonov's thick throat.

"Leave him alone, Nikoshka! You are a Doukhobor! It is not his fault…" Misha begged his voice to be more powerful and that Nikolay obey him.

Nikolay, still not understanding what it was about, lessened his grip on Antonov's throat and stood away from him. Nor did Antonov understand Misha.

"Take this from my hand," Misha told Antonov, pulses of powerlessness visible on his face. "We do not need this. We already have this message inbuilt in our philosophy of life. Your Church needs it."

Antonov took the object from Misha's hand, and while Antonov was straightening up next to the unsatisfied Nikolay, he and Misha saw a small dark cross hanging on a thin silver chain around Antonov's neck.

The explosion close to Farron killed Peter Vasiliyevitch "Lordly" Verigin, his loyal woman companion, both of Peter's bodyguards and a few of Peter's business friends. The Sacred Cube disappeared with the big Antonov. Misha remained unable to move of his own volition, and the desire to live seeped slowly from his mind. While Nikolay was transporting him by truck to the train in Castlegar, Misha asked him several times not to tell anybody what he had learned about the magic cube from Pandora's Box.

Newspapers all over the world published accounts of the explosion of the train in the south of British Columbia and the death of the great Doukhobor leader and teacher. Vancouver's daily newspaper published the report of a farmer who was at the scene of the tragedy right after the explosion. The readers were amazed the most by his description of the suffering of the horses on the train:

Two cars with horses rolled a few times down the slope to its bottom where there is the dry bed of a stream that disappeared long ago. The horses were screaming and whinnying in the dust raised by the cars as they rolled down. Those that could slowly pulled their bodies out of the wreck. The less injured rushed to a field near that streambed as if running away from the jaws of hell. There they huddled close together in two groups and stared back with fear and astonishment at the hillside covered with the debris of the train. Those more seriously injured tried to stand on their legs; they staggered and fell back on the rocks and bushes. Some managed to stay upright and slowly walked to the field. Those very seriously hurt were whinnying for help, and all the horses in the field and some moving uphill answered back. In that whinnying of the horses there was also happiness that they had stayed alive and fear of what had happened, and sadness because of those seriously injured and those who lay motionless among the wreckage of the train. All these horses came together in the field by the streambed and stayed there for a long time; they came close to each other and snorted and whickered in a strange way. It was clear they were telling each other how they felt and asking each other what had happened to the dear ones they could not see among them.

The dust above the broken cars had not even settled when a flock of pigeons flew in high above the place of the disaster. They first circled in one spot in the air; then like a mighty waterfall they tumbled down and stopped above the very scene where the screams and cries of the people and horses were heard; then they flew vertically into the air, as if scared of something. Then they stopped at a height where they did not feel fear any more. One more time they dropped down into the depths as if wanting to check something one more time; then they soared back up into the air and made a commotion as if not knowing what to do anymore and suddenly dispersed in all directions, as if something exploded in the midst of their flock. Or as if they agreed to fly to all corners of the world to spread the news to people about what humans did to each other in a place close to a small village called Farron in Canadian British Columbia.

Perhaps inspired by the example of the birds, the horses in the field below the rails suddenly became more animated, started to amble around each other, and looked toward those whom the explosion had mercilessly dragged into death. Then, as if following an order, they started whinnying and rushed up the hillside and across the rails into the fields above the dead canyon of the mountain stream; they separated into a few groups and galloped without stopping as far as the human eye could reach.

37

With a pensive gaze Paroniya said goodbye to Nick, Mavroona, and their two sons, Kuzma and Misha. When they came to the frame of the wide glass doors of the Old Friends' Home in Calgary, they stopped and turned to raise their hands, waving to the old woman with short grey hair who, unable to walk, stayed in her wheelchair by the hallway window of the visitors' room. Nick felt sadness as always at leaving his mother behind, and a new, fearful poignancy because he was not sure how many more times he would stand in the frame of this door waiting while his mother gathered enough strength to raise her hand and slowly wave to bid them farewell until the next visit. In the last two years they had been coming the first Saturday of each month to see Mamushka and Babushka Paroniya. Every time as soon as they opened those wide glass doors, the dark complexioned and smiling Ivanka would walk swaying towards them and in a few sentences give them the news of the old woman since their previous visit.

"A few days ago she asked me why I was sad," Ivanka was proud to say while she was leading them down a long corridor to the visitors' room. "I confided to her that I had received sad news from my country. Your mother told me that my sadness adds to the sadness of the news and that it would help if I could find something in that news that would cheer me up. I did not understand her right away, but now I see her logic."

"My mother has a lot of life experience and it is good sometimes to follow her advice," Nick commented. That day Nick had come to his mother with a suggestion that she go with them to Kamsack to visit the grave of their Misha on the tenth anniversary of his death. Paroniya turned her head away from him. For a few moments her gaze wandered over the ceiling of the spacious room where the patients met with their families and friends, and then she replied in a low voice:

"How can it be that you decided to mark the date of the death of our Mishka? What is in the grave in Kamsack is not he. Mishka is here. He is with us now; it's just that you maybe cannot see him. I cannot see him either, but I can feel him."

Paroniya truly felt Misha's presence and to her it was strange to think that he could be there in Kamsack, under that modest stone bearing his name. While her gaze followed Nick and his family as they departed, she sensed that Hans Fluger, a chubby old man with thick fair eyebrows and completely bald head, had parked his wheelchair next to her. Lately she had been spending a lot of time with him, going over the pages of their memories. They talked spontaneously but only about pleasant memories. This time she greeted him with a slow movement of her head and with the look she had learned from Misha, the one he had when somebody quietly approached him from behind while he had not yet finished an intimate encounter with somebody, or had not yet finished thinking about something deep in the spaces of his mind.

"How did you part today?" Hans asked her.

"It was different from before. I was rude to my Nick. But he provoked my rudeness," Paroniya replied.

"I cannot believe that you parted with them in that manner when a journey home of a thousand kilometers awaited them!" the old man stated frankly.

"I did. I was egoistic. For a moment I forgot that Mishka is theirs too. I told them that our Mishka is with me. That he is not there in the graveyard. That I feel him here close to me. They had invited me to visit his grave with them at the tenth anniversary of his death. I do not want to mark Misha's death."

"Oh, Paroniya! I understand what happened. Nick won't blame you for your rudeness. How did your grandsons, Kuzka and Mishka, react? Every time I see them they are bigger and more serious."

"Kuzka looks more and more like my father, and Mishka has the goodhearted shape of face and the searching eyes of our Misha," Paroniya explained in a melancholy voice.

"There are two more hours until dinner. If you have that sort of feeling, tell me what happened in your family after the explosion of the train close to Castlegar. It is warm outside. We can find shade in the garden, so you can tell me," Hans suggested.

The nurse Ivanka, a big, easy-moving girl, followed them unobtrusively as they moved in their wheelchairs towards the lane of evergreen trees at the bottom of the park. She strictly followed the rules of the institution that service personnel should know in each moment where their patients were in case they required urgent medical help. Ivanka had established a strange connection with Paroniya Chernov, maybe because the old woman reminded her of her grandmother Luisa, from the small island Guadeloupe in the Caribbean Sea. And maybe because she admired Paroniya's stories about the philosophy of life and beliefs of the Doukhobors. Lately, since the unusually high temperatures had settled on southern Alberta, Paroniya and Hans would often go out for a morning ride in their wheelchairs. Ivanka had noticed the bald man's desire to hold Paroniya's hand while they sat side by side. Paroniya was quite aware of his intentions and discreetly kept her hand out of his reach. Since childhood she'd known that bodily touches disturbed her spiritual state and that it would be impossible for her to give somebody even the least important part of her body to hold unless she'd previously prepared her spirit. Ivanka explained the old woman's restraint as a consequence of her unbroken connection with the long-departed Misha.

Hans Fluger had finished his working years at the University of Alberta in Edmonton a few years before the regular retirement age. His former friends, the professors of mathematics in the department, forced him to retire. He had come up with a thesis that astonished all the mathematicians who heard about it. He maintained that the inventors of modern mathematics, the great Greek philosophers, had made an amateur's mistake in establishing one of the basic postulates of mathematical functions—that two minuses equal plus. They made such a mistake, Fluger argued, because they lived in a class-based society and because their philosophy was dominated by aggression. This argument frightened his colleagues, who protected themselves by saying he was losing his reason. "Two minuses can only produce one bigger minus. If we measure each minus with some determination of its specific weight, then numerically the negative mass will only increase. Because," Hans was explaining to Paroniya in the manner of a teacher, "on the scale of values, from a zero point the negative values go in one direction and the positive values in the other. Following that logic in humaneness, it could never happen that negative values have the sign of plus in front of them. The ancient Greeks their logic from the politics of the human race based on power and aggression where there is the assertion that a crime instigated by another crime could lead to a positive result. If these inventors of mathematical logic had been pacifists like your Doukhobors—"teacher Flugel paused for effect— "then a crime instigated by another crime could not have a positive result, nor could two minuses in the scale of values produce a plus because between minuses and pluses there is a zero point, the impenetrable membrane that does not allow their mixing."

"My Misha and I had a professor of mathematics named Demidovitch, and I am sure that we would not have received a passing mark if we had come up with your thesis! Do you know why? Because he was not a Doukhobor. And even if he had been, he would have considered the rules of mathematics an untouchable dogma, as the teachings of great religions are considered to be permanent values. As long as human society is controlled by the system of power and aggression, the system of mathematics where two minuses equal plus will be applied. When human society accepts the philosophy of the Doukhobors or some similar pacifist philosophy, mathematicians will have to change some fundamental postulates and axioms and understand that minuses are negative values and that they are separated from pluses by the zero point on the axis of values, as you have explained to me. My husband Misha would say that even the great Aristotle fell into that trap and on that built his philosophical, political, and even mathematical rules," Paroniya said to Hans. Then in the shade of a branchy spruce tree she told him her story, inspiringly and in a voice revealing her desire to speak what was in her memory before some sudden storm of time mercilessly closed the possibility of anyone reaching into her memories any more.

Misha survived the explosion of the train close to Castlegar. His cousin Nikolay, by some strange miracle not hurt in that terrible blast, brought him home. When Paroniya saw motionless Misha lying among hay bales in the truck of the farmer whom Nikolay had found at the railway station in Veregin, Misha smiled at her, shook his head as if to say "I was lucky," and quickly comforted her:

"I am not anymore that young man you saw in your imagination. Now, you will need your imagination more than ever. Maybe you will be able to love me as I am now."

Paroniya slowly put her hands on his chest, searching for something in his face, and started caressing his still resilient grey hair. Her gaze stopped at the chipped-off tip of Misha's ear, that scar from the goose bites in his childhood. Doubtlessly, he was still her Mishka but misfortune had hit him hard this time. She tried to reply in the jesty way he had used.

"Since I finally caught you in my trap, I have always worried a bit that you would run away, just as our Nick was afraid that his young owls would fly away. And now…Now you are mine forever. I will try to offer you my best pharmaceutical knowledge, and you won't be able to run away when I come to you with a medicine," she said smiling but with a touch of the sadness rising within her.

Despite his jesting words, Misha's desire to live soon started melting away even faster than it had on the painful journey home. When he realized that he was irrevocably losing touch with nature, with everything alive around him, and that he had become a burden for his loved ones, would not ever again be able to run at the pace of wind when it rushes between trees, never again feel the impulse to climb up the rays of sun when they sent shafts through the openings among clouds, Misha thought it would be best to leave forever. But in a quiet, dignified way, without spasms of pain and no ability to take care of himself, which would leave his dear ones with the memory of him in a miserable state.

As time went on, Misha's life was visibly passing away. Paroniya made great efforts to keep his mind fresh, but she understood more and more that she was not equal to her task. When Petro, *Tanya*, and their son Igor, a boy with fair hair, blue irises, and a happy freckled face, visited them, Misha was quiet, few words laboriously pushing out between his lips. He kept his gaze on Petro. To make his dispirited father happy, Petro told him that Nono Yakov had handed over to him the management of their big trading company and that he was satisfied with the work.

"How about your studies?" Misha asked.

"I slowed down on schooling. I work and travel a lot," Petro shrugged.

"Only when you finish university will you be secure. Business could go well but also badly," his father replied in a monitory tone. "It can load you with gold but also kick you into the street. In this world, competition is merciless. Good education will never put you under somebody's feet."

Misha felt he had said enough and that maybe he should not have talked that way to his elder son, who for the first time looked to him more like a Jewish man obsessed with business than like a modest Doukhobor. Without a lot of explanation he refused Petro's suggestion to transport him to Boston to undergo medical treatment. When they parted, he tightly pressed Petro to his bosom and patted *Tanya* and the little Igor gently on their hair.

Not long after that visit, Misha abruptly started to lose concentration, his face acquired a hue of grey, and then one morning he did not wake up. He breathed slowly and quietly. Paroniya sent Nick to Kamsack to fetch Doctor Marki. When the good doctor came and checked Misha's pulse and lungs, he was thoughtful for a short time standing by Misha's head, and with condolence in his voice he told Paroniya:

"My colleague Misha is sleeping now. If he wakes up, give him my greetings. Try to wet his lips and give him some water with a teaspoon if he'll take it."

Misha started to talk in his sleep, but Paroniya could understand only a few words. Nick was with them whenever the work in the fields allowed. One morning Misha surprised them. While they were trying to pour some milk through his lips, he opened his eyes, red from the long sleep, and said:

"I cannot drink. I am not thirsty, not even hungry. Nick, you need to cut your hair. I had a dream that you married Mavroona Popova. They are good people, my son. Are you still with her?"

"I am, Batya," Nick replied, his eyes and voice surprised.

"Then get married. Time will not wait," Misha was very clear.

Paroniya's face revealed puzzlement at what was happening with her husband. But she tried not to show concern. One day a group of villagers came to visit Misha. They talked to him, made jokes, quietly sang old Russian songs and some verses from religious hymns. They told him that his old friend Manidu had died and that the Chippewa had burned his body in a boat on Quill Lake. When they were leaving, Misha signalled with his eyes to Stepka Tarasov to stay a bit longer.

"Nick will ask Mavroona to marry him, but I cannot go with Paroniya to the Popovs in Nadezhda. Maybe you could go instead of me?" Misha asked Stepka.

"There is no need to ask, Mishka! I'll go to the Popovs." He paused, and added, "Maybe old Genadiy could go with us, too."

"Oh, the Uncle is weak. Why do you need a hundred-year-old man with you? It is better not to mention that to him," Misha suggested.

"I am glad you decided to talk to me," Stepka changed the topic. "I agree with you that somebody is lying…"

Misha's look bespoke his perplexity. He liked Stepka, especially because of his healthy reasoning and free mind. But what lie is he talking about now? Misha was thinking.

"I do not understand what lie you are talking about," Misha finally said.

"I am talking about your dilemma with regard to God and Herod."

"Oh, that…" Misha understood. "It is not my dilemma anymore. Somebody lied, but to me lying is so base that I cannot see why it would be in anybody's interest to do so. I am sure God could not have hurt

457

Joseph by fathering Jesus, the child of Joseph's wife Maria. It is even more unreasonable to believe that he whispered to Joseph only to save the newborn Jesus, but allowed King Herod to kill all other male babies in the kingdom because he feared the prophecy that a newborn boy in his kingdom would one day seize his crown."

"I do not believe in that either, Mishka. God is a symbol of good and he could not have committed such a crime."

"The one who invented that story must have been shortsighted and thoughtless," said Misha.

"God in Herod's spirit could not have allowed that frightened and cruel king to commit such a crime while saving only Jesus," Stepka concluded. His voice was low and trembling as if he were frightened by his words.

"But above that human lie rose Prometheus. He had made sure that lie could not have deep roots," Misha continued.

"What do you mean?" asked Stepka and tried to straighten up, but felt pain in the upper part of his back, bent by the burden of his age and life.

"Along with Zeus's deceptions for the human race he sneaked into Pandora's Box the cube with the sculpture of the human brain inside, the mystery whose solution is that the human race is capable of discovering any truth, truth as a banner to lead humanity. To lead it into the time when all people will realize they are brothers and sisters and will refuse hatred and aggression. It is very similar to our teaching, Stepka."

Stepka went home and while walking he was trying to figure out why Misha had told him about the forces beyond human knowledge. And why had his friend the doctor become concerned with this old cube legend after the explosion near Castlegar? Stepka was more inclined to believe that man is part of life's processes on earth and that he is not the only intelligent creature in the universe. However, he, like Misha, believed that the human brain is limitless but that something had programmed it sequentially so that in each new era a new possibility is discovered within it. As though the brain were maturing in stages and nobody knew when it would finally grow up.

Nick got married before Misha's departure on the journey of no return. When he and Mavroona came to hug the father and ask for his blessing of their marriage, they heard the shouting of a woman through a half-open window. She announced over and over that Ivan's mare had given birth to twins.

"Live in peace, and teach your children to be always thirsty for new knowledge. Ignorance is blindness and keeps people enslaved. A blind man cannot easily walk through blooming meadows, not to mention over rocky ground in stormy weather," Misha told them. Then ever more energetically he expressed his desire that they sell everything they had in Spasovka and buy a farm near Kamsack, a town that was quickly growing and becoming a city. Mavroona strongly approved of Misha's desire and they all moved to Kamsack the following spring. Hearing that news, Petro came from Boston. He and Nick chose a farm, and Petro helped his brother to pay it off right away and to buy modern agricultural equipment.

For reasons known only to him—as if leaving Spasovka was his farewell to everything dear to him in his life—in the middle of the second month after resettling on the farm near Kamsack Misha Chernov, without saying goodbye, plunged into the permanent sleep. When she was putting clean clothes on his body, Paroniya was surprised to see that Misha's legs were swollen above the knees and that they had blue circles on them. She took his face in her hands, looked at his closed lids and whispered to him, afraid that Nick or Mavroona could hear her words:

"Why didn't you tell me, Mishka?! You did not want to tell me that you were dying from poison. This on your legs is from poison, Mishka. You knew that better than I. You wanted to go into your peace but you had to suffer pain. Why Mishka? If you could only tell me why you left me in such a way..."

She lifted her hands from his face, looking at him with disapproval. There was no sign on his body that would bring her closer to an answer. She breathed heavily, and strange pressure accumulated in her chest, something difficult to define, something close to pain: could it be that her Misha had betrayed her in some way and left as he did because he felt guilt? With her hand she instinctively touched his eye and opened its lid, feeling that she would discover the secret there. Then she winced as if having touched boiling water. She looked at the closing eye in disbelief and moved backwards.

"Why a tear in your eye, Mishka?" she whispered and rushed her gaze through the window into the orchard as if expecting to find the answer there. It seemed to her that Misha replied through the blowing wind, saying he could not return anymore from the place he had gone to. The old woman became frightened of these words, instinctively closed her ears not to hear any more, but deep in her brain there was a wild storm and Misha's voice was leaving with the wind and she could no longer understand his words.

It had not been long since the death of Misha Kostunavitch Chernov when Paroniya suddenly stopped visiting his grave. She explained to the astonished Nick that she felt her Misha close to her always, and Nick believed he understood her brief explanation:

"Our Misha never liked graveyards."

A few more times Nick tried to ask his mother to visit their Misha's grave, and on one occasion she forced him to sit on a bench in the kitchen, spread her fingers wide in the space between their faces, and firmly explained to him:

"You make me wonder, son! I told you Misha did not like graveyards. He always said that a dead body is not a being; it is not what it was before death. He was a doctor, Nikoshka! You want to force me to accept that Misha has died! If he had died, I would have died too. I know he did not die and that's why I live. I will live as long as I feel him close to me. I feel his blood in my blood, Nick, just as I felt it in my youth when Misha was not mine. When all of you plunge into your sleep, I am with Misha. Our common blood starts rushing through my body and I feel his touches. We are one, my son! And do not try to force me anymore to believe that my Mishka has died!"

Nick hugged his mother, feeling he was hugging both of them, at the same time: his mother and his father.

Years passed, the Doukhobors became more and more independent and integrated into the society in which they lived, but they did not forget their fundamental Doukhobor beliefs. Nick had changed his profession, as if he'd grown bored with being a farmer. He worked in the grain trade, built silos, became a merchant and a butcher, and when his sons were born he firmly decided to support them and push them to go to college or university.

Paroniya started to change. In the beginning of her mourning for Misha it had been obvious that she used all her psychical strength not to forget how to be happy. But then she gradually retreated into solitude and more whispered to herself than talked to others. And when the news from Europe came that Hitler had started a new war, she stayed in her room most of the time. She was no longer firm on her legs. First, she'd started to drag her left leg, not being able to lift it and step out. Then her other leg started to shake, and she realized she was condemned to sitting and lying down. One spring morning she called her daughter-in-law Mavroona and asked her if Nick had gone to work. Mavroona realized that Mamushka had something important in her mind and ran outside to fetch Nick, who was putting his stuff in his long black Chevrolet.

"I want to go to a home for old people, my son!" she told him in a voice that did not allow any negotiation. "And not here in Kamsack, nor Regina. I want to go to Calgary."

"You want to run away from us, Mama," Nick confronted her nevertheless.

"Even if I wanted, I would not be able to run away from you. But you need to have your life, and not live to make me comfortable. I will have my own company in the home and I will be fine. And I will always be happy to see you when you come to visit. I need help, somebody who will feed me, change my clothes, and I would be ashamed if you did that. Please, Nikolay, do not oppose my desire. Convince Mavroona, Kuzka and little Mishka that you will be happy whenever coming to visit me. And I will be enormously happy to see you."

461

When they took her to the Old Friends' Home on the banks of the Bow River in Calgary, she tried hard not to cry when parting with them. And she did not. Not even when they shed tears turning their heads to see her all their way to the exit door.

Paroniya lived two years in that home. At first, she felt blessed in the company of old people, ready to accept everybody and to help if needed. Then she felt proud for having decided to come and live in the environment where she belonged. But, as time passed, she felt more and more lonely surrounded by people who were daily losing hope. The more she got to know them the more she realized that each was an individual, difficult to know, each with memories that didn't belong to others. And finally, that all of them were on The List With No Consecutive Numbers, a list on which somebody crossed out each name at the moment when that person left this world. All of them were on the list for dying…That realization made her feel hopeless, useless, and condemned to departing life without a chance to press the hands of those who would have been happy if she had continued to live with them. And she would no longer be able to communicate with Misha. One of them needed to be alive to carry their shared blood. Suddenly she grew fearful of the old faces around her, with all the changes she could notice on them unstoppably leading to misery and the end.

In that home Paroniya felt comfortable only in the company of Ivanka and Hans. The nurse had a warm heart, her eyes emanated a desire to help, and she liked it when Paroniya occasionally embraced her. And Hans? She felt that she reminded him of someone and that her company was the best antidote for the sclerosis afflicting his brain functions with ever more terrible forgetfulness. She liked his company but only when she talked to him about her Misha, and only after discovering that her stories did not upset him.

Every time Nick and his family visited her, she became more restless. Nikolay was her son and it was enough in their relationship. Mavroona? In her eyes Paroniya discovered firmness and the capability to find seeds of content and faith even in the most difficult situations. But Kuzka and Mishka…At first she criticized herself for searching in their faces, in their behaviour and gestures, for similarities to her Misha. Why could she not accept them the way they were? On one occasion when they visited her, Kuzka noticed her looking intently at his face and passing her gaze across his body. When they were parting with her by the window of the visitors' room in the Old Friends' Home, he asked:

"Babushka, who are you looking for behind my back? We are all here, in front of you. There is nobody behind me."

Paroniya did not reply, but that daring boy became convinced that Babushka had better eyes than he and was able to see somebody else among them.

The next spring came early, warm temperatures rushed from the south, and the snow melted overnight. Paroniya went to sleep right after dinner and in her dream some people visited her; their faces reminded her of pears when they spend winter in grass under a thick layer of snow. Then she heard a rumble, as of a herd of bison approaching chased by a furious grizzly across the prairie. Fear made her wake up. She tried to compose herself and separate reality from dream; her pillow was wet and her hair wet and flattened on her forehead. Around her was the darkness of the night diluted with a breath of early morning. The faces from her dream were not even in the corners of her room, but through the window came the roar she had imagined as the thunder of stampeded bison. She went to the window, opened it a bit more, poked her head outside and found a surprise. Outside there was no more snow, and the roar was coming from the river. She realized that the snow had suddenly melted and the river had risen. The water was rushing in its bed and the noise of the river woke people up, demonstrating its might. As soon as the morning sun pushed the darkness of the night to the west, Parushka noticed that the Bow was no longer crystal green but had turned dark and so rough that it was no longer beautiful or gentle. For the first time since she settled at the bank of this river, Paroniya became afraid of it. The river is like people, she thought, looking with suspicion at the powerful current rushing with desire to terrify and destroy. It is beautiful when it flows gently in its bed and brings blessings. As soon as it becomes immensely powerful, it becomes wild, loses its beautiful colour and roars, pulling in everything it can reach on its banks. It instigates fear and mercilessness. The old Paroniya felt better when she remembered that Nick would come at noon to take her home to Kamsack.

When Nick arrived around lunchtime and knocked on the door of Paroniya's room in the Old Friends' Home, he heard some unintelligible words. He recognized the voice of his mother and entered the room. She was sitting on the bed, dressed for a trip.

"Oh, finally, my son!" she greeted him with impatience in her voice.

"What happened, Mamushka? Are you ill?" Nick hastened with questions while holding her in his embrace.

"Nothing special, Nick. I want to go home!"

"That's good news! I was afraid something bad had happened." Nick was overjoyed, but took a moment to think about the trip. "Would you be able to travel in my car or should we take the train? The roads are still not good for the long journey to Kamsack," he asked and explained.

"I'll go in your car. It's boring on the train. I cannot avoid boredom and I also do not like it when people I do not know address me and start a conversation. I want peace, son."

Paroniya had already packed her belongings into two big suitcases and a few bags. While saying goodbye to Hans, she allowed him to embrace her and kiss her neck a few times. She gave Ivanka a big colourful woollen shawl, a present from her daughter-in-law Mavroona when she visited their house for the first time before marrying Nick. They were soon on the dusty road through Alberta towards the east. She was surprised when she realized that, after parting with Hans, she had not cleaned the places on her neck where he had kissed her.

"Many of our people complain that this endless flatland is killing them, but I don't mind," Paroniya said when, in the distance in front of them on the road without any bends, they both saw a small cloud of dust from another car. The cloud was so far away that it only symbolically appeared to become bigger even though the car was getting closer.

"I do not like the prairie in winter, but in summer it is full of life: people plant grains, then they harvest and transport them; plants grow, give fruit, and then get ready for winter; animals take care of their young and teach them to live independently…" the old woman continued.

"I don't mind this flat land either, Mamushka. But I would prefer the summers to be less hot, mosquitoes and flies more afraid of humans, and winters less cold—or at least without those winds that carry the cold through clothes and accumulate it in your bones, so you can't get rid of it until midsummer," Nick agreed.

On the way home they spent the night in a new motel at the entrance to Moose Jaw, about eighty kilometers before Regina. When they arrived at the farm the next day in the afternoon, there was Mavroona's cousin Ilya Alexeyevitch Popov from Grand Forks. Nick put his hands on Ilya's shoulders, pushed him away a bit to see him better, and looked at him searchingly a few minutes; then he embraced him tightly.

"Mavroona has been praising you for years, even though we knew you only by letters. You look the way we imagined you would, but we thought your hair was fairer and less wavy, your nose more prominent and we did not think that your eyes would reveal an intellectual and artist. For a long time we have been planning to visit you, but life is unpredictable. Something always came up and we postponed the trip to some better time. You have become our sons' idol, especially Kuzka's. As soon as he was able to write, he started to brag among his friends that he could describe his owls as you would describe them," Nick was chattering on. Then he realized he should give his mother a chance to greet Ilya.

During dinner they encouraged Ilya to tell them about life in British Columbia. His warm recollections emanated love for the old Doukhobor ways. Kuzka found Ilya's story strange and he was all the time thinking about how it was possible they were cousins when their lives were so different.

"As I hear it, many things have changed in your way of life too," Nick stated. "Time never sleeps. Here, among us, that way of life disappeared with the generation of my father. Do you think, Ilya, that your life in British Columbia will also change more radically? Here we live pretty much like other Canadians. Only their weddings and funerals are different from ours. And we do not go to church or pay priests," he explained.

Kuzka was interested in the discussion, while Babushka's sudden falling asleep and then returning to the conversation attracted Mishka's attention. Whenever Paroniya closed her eyes, he expected she would fall off her chair, but Babushka continued to sit firmly.

"With us too, every year brings something new, except that we have a stronger organization and are closer to each other. We pay special attention not to forget the things we consider exceptionally valuable in our heritage, left to us by our fathers and mothers," said Ilya. There was a lot of nobility in the posture of that twenty-year-old man, and his manner of speaking was quiet and edifying.

"What do you think Ilya, until when? How long will the young resist the influences of the modern time and keep to their tradition?" Mavroona asked.

"I don't know. I do not think I could be a prophet. I personally love our tradition. It is my spiritual wealth. It is like a river; it belongs to nature, but is still different from all other rivers and from the surrounding banks. Our movement originated in the same way as the river. It is like what happens when stormy weather hits and frightens the living things in nature. Drops of rain start falling in the storm, then torrents of them that come together and create streams. The streams then come together and create a river; it flows through fields and waters everything thirsty for that precious liquid of life. Our Doukhobor Movement is like that. It originated in storms of time and was formed in them. Each new storm has brought new streams and freshness to it."

"For how long?" Mavroona asked again. "Do you think, Ilya, that river could disappear: flow and flow and then eventually disappear?"

"I do not know," Ilya became thoughtful. "But even if it disappears, dries out, its bed will stay. A trace of it will stay in civilization. A trace of the river which watered and nourished the spirits of many human beings."

"Oh, Ilya! Ilya!…" Nick got up and moved his chair closer to Ilya's. "You are a poet! You are blessed with the ability to talk nobly. And me? I do not like prison even if the most fragrant flowers grow in it."

"What do you like, Kuzka?" Ilya asked, putting his hand on Kuzka's shoulder.

"I like our owls."

"I like hockey," little Mishka said suddenly. "I played hockey on the small lake last winter. I'll play in Kamsack. In the big arena…"

Mishka made them all laugh; Paroniya, when she woke up from a short slumber and realized they were still sitting and talking, started the song her Misha used to like:

I wanted to plunge into forgetfulness,
Springs and winters, my happy moments…
Burning eyes of young girls…
But now when moonlight wakes me
I feel the whisper of your wind in my heart,
In my hair.

Next morning, right after a breakfast of fried bread with cottage cheese and apple jam, Kuzka and Mishka introduced Ilya to their two owls.

During the day, the owls slept in a grain silo and dreamed a quiet night full of moonlight and a field full of tiny mice playing far from their holes. They felt comfortable and safe in Kuzka and Mishka's arms, but their eyes rolled strangely trying to identify Ilya in the daylight.

"How come they are so gentle with you?" Ilya wondered. "As if they did not have such sharp claws on their feet."

"They do not have them for us. When they see a mouse at night their claws wake up. Maybe they would also wake up if you tried to take them in your arms," Kuzka teased him.

"Why don't you write about the owls, their dreams and maybe how they decide not to eat mice but to feed on grass, apples and plums," Ilya suggested to Kuzka.

"Good idea. I will write about it to see what our teacher 'Mosquito' will say," agreed Kuzka in a serious manner.

"I know you will become a writer," Ilya added. "Write about us Doukhobors too. The more we write about ourselves the more people will have the use of what is good in our tradition. I write about us, the Popovs, and you write about you, the Chernovs. And do not forget to add your Russian name next to the Canadian when you sign your work. I sign my name as Don, but I always add my Russian name, Ilya. What are your real names?" Ilya asked them.

"My Canadian name is Charlie," said Kuzka. "My Russian name is Kuzma, but my babushka Paroniya gave me the nickname Kuzka, and it stuck."

"My name is Mikhail, and my friends call me Mike. At home they call me Mishka," the younger of Nick and Mavroona's sons quickly said and stood in front of Ilya so he could see him better.

"Now you only need to stand on you toes so that we could see how big a boy you are," Mavroona interrupted their conversation. She brought them a warm strudel filled with cranberry jam.

When after a few days Ilya left for Grand Forks, Kuzka and Mishka bid him goodbye at the railway station.

Paroniya spent most of her time in her room by the window, reclining in the armchair that Nick had bought for her in a big store for furniture and construction materials in Yorkton. When she saw it, she was happy as if receiving a gift for which she had waited all her life. She had him place it by the window, pulled a thin embroidered curtain across to screen herself from view and thanked her son, explaining that only now would she be able to follow the life of Kamsack and the changes in the sky in case there was a storm coming. And read the *Regina Sun* whenever he brought it from Praskoviya's general store. After she got the armchair and her permanent place by the window facing the town, she less often used her wheelchair and left her room. Nick and Mavroona realized that Paroniya enjoyed solitude and did not bother her, but Kuzka and Mishka often knocked on her door, rushing into the room with news of equal interest to themselves and Babushka.

On one hot and stuffy day, during the grain harvest in the fields of the farms all around Kamsack, somebody knocked on Paroniya's door a few times and entered without waiting to be invited. Two heads became still in the doorframe, waiting for Paroniya's reaction. She moved her face away from the windowpane, turned her head towards the door and gestured to the boys that they were allowed to come closer. They reached her armchair in a few jumps and Kuzka, as soon as he caught his breath, reported to her:

"Babushka, Gypsies have come to Kamsack! We saw many of their cars and their slim horses when we went with Batya to town. Batya says they will stay in Kamsack for a long time."

"They have a lot of children," Mishka added.

Later Nick explained that about a hundred Gypsies had come to their region. They had arrived in Halifax on a ship from Europe. They said they were from the Soviet Union and that they had come to the East Coast in a cargo ship transporting food for Canadian troops in the Mediterranean. They were seeking any available farm work, at much lower wages than the going rate.

"How did they come from Russia to the Mediterranean in that terrible war?" Paroniya asked him.

"I do not know, Mamushka. I am thinking of hiring some of their men to help us bring in the harvest, and we can ask them about that. It is certain they are from the Soviet Union because they speak good Russian."

A few days later, when the dust from Nick's second long Chevrolet settled, through the window Paroniya saw a horse-drawn omnibus approaching the farm. When it reached the house and people started getting out of the bus, the old woman wondered why Nick had brought so many of them when he had said he needed only a few men for the summer work. In addition to three young men, four children and three women came out of the vehicle. They crowded in a group in front of the two horses, which differed in both size and age. The people were waiting for Nick to approach them. Paroniya estimated that the old woman was of like age to herself, but her back was straight as that of a young girl, and her movements like those of the two young women.

Nick housed the newcomers in the outbuilding that served as a summer kitchen with a dining room. Later he took them out and showed them the farm and explained what their job would be. Through the half-open window Paroniya enjoyed listening to them speak in their Russian language, which was faster and fresher than what the Doukhobors used. Later Paroniya got to know the whole family, and when Mavroona brought the old woman to her room, Paroniya stared at her face, closed her eyes to prevent the sense of sight from interfering with her memories, and then searched again for something in the old woman's visage.

"Do you have a chair for our guest?" Paroniya asked Mavroona. Not waiting for the old woman to sit, Paroniya asked her:

"Where are you from?"

While the woman, surprised at the question, was thinking about an answer, Paroniya continued searching her face.

"From Georgia," the old woman replied at last. "From Tbilisi."

"What is your name?"

"Svetlana."

Paroniya bent her head towards the old woman and held her breath in her chest.

The old woman knitted her brows and stared at Paroniya's irises. They stared at each other fearing the words that were to come. They were both quiet, but their eyes revealed their tension. After a long uncomfortable silence, Svetlana took the initiative.

"Many Gypsy women have the name Svetlana. Do you want me to look in your palm and guess your name?" The Gypsy woman asked.

"You are not a Gypsy," Paroniya whispered. "You are Svetlana."

Svetlana was quiet for a few moments.

"If I am not a Gypsy but Svetlana, you are Parushka…"

Paroniya's head dropped to the soft back of the armchair but her eyes stayed fixed on Svetlana's clear-green irises. Svetlana got up from the chair Mavroona had brought, stooped and held Paroniya's head in her arms for a long time.

"How did you find me?" Paroniya asked her when they separated.

"I did not look for you. I did not even know where you were. It did not matter to me where life would take me. Without any desire for men, I married the father of those three young men and now I have a big family. When Hitler attacked the Soviet Union, only Gypsies and Jewish people had permission to leave. My Alex and I decided to try to take the family out into the new world. One group of Gypsies, moving towards Turkey, accepted us as theirs and enabled us to run away with them. My husband was killed when the Turks joined the Germans and Gestapo men came to our small town of Malazgirt in old Armenia. Many Gypsies were killed at that time. Now we have arrived at the end of the world. I never thought that the two of us would meet again."

As soon as Nick found out that the old Svetlana was his Mamushka's friend from the time of her and his Batya's exile in Siberia, he prepared a special room for her in the basement of his big farmhouse. When Svetlana entered the room, her pointed chin started to tremble in her bony face. She exited the room walking backward and shook her head.

"I beg you, Nikolay. I cannot accept to live here. I want to be there where you housed my family. I thank you very much for your kindness, but I cannot. My grandchildren have been sleeping in my bed since they were born, and I am the happiest when at night I feel their kicking me with their legs in their sleep."

"But here you would be closer to my Mamushka and you could talk to her about the events of the time you spent together."

"Maybe you will not be able to understand me, but the two of us have talked so much that we would have had enough of talking even if we'd lived several lives. And when we have a desire to see each other, we will easily find each other on your beautiful ranch."

And that is how it was settled. Paroniya was happy to observe her Kuzka and Mishka playing with Svetlana's grandchildren, and the two of them would occasionally get together on the porch at the front the house.

That year, the third year of the second Great War on earth in the twentieth century after the birth of Christ, the harvest was abundant on the farms in the Canadian prairies. The fall was dry and warm, full of those nights lit with moonlight when even the most eager sleepers do not feel like sleeping. The life of people reigned during the day in the villages, in the fields, and on the rivers. Human voices and their machines, people of different ages, wearing different clothes…At night reigned that part of nature that was not far from people but that did not want to have any part of them. Birds were singing, solo or in choirs, verses only they could understand; coyotes enjoyed their strange conversations, cattle called each other from well-locked barns, horses occasionally neighed to complement that noisy recitative with their shrill horse sopranos, geese honked in protest with their necks stretched towards the sky, bats squeaked to signal each other which corridor they were moving through in their rush to hunt. Only occasionally would a western sleepy wind blow through the orchards and woods to announce that the part of nature whose life we do not understand was planning its changes.

On the farm of Nick Chernov the fall brought gifts to Svetlana's family. For their great help in harvesting and the transport of the yield from one farm to another, Nick paid them as they had agreed, and above that gave them a herd of sheep and two young cows; he also gave them the farthest corner of the farm towards the hilly valley by the river, so, if they wanted, in the spring they could start building their own house and buildings for grain and cattle. Svetlana hid for a few days, not finding the right way to express her gratitude for the benefaction by Paroniya's son. When one early morning she saw Svetlana exiting on tiptoe from the building where her family was sleeping, Paroniya called out to her.

She looked at Svetlana's surprised irises and gently whispered: "Why haven't you dropped by these days? I did not ask my son for any favour to your family. It was his own decision. And I am happy you will stay close to my family."

Winter suddenly fell upon the prairie with all its might. For a few days light, unhurried snowflakes drifted endlessly from a featureless blanket of grey and covered everything they could reach; then stunning cold enveloped everything so that people and all the life around them became still in uncertainty. The first sounds to wake this sleeping world arrived one night on the icy breath of the northern wind. First, it was the sudden throaty cry of a wolf from the side of the farm bordering a stand of tall maple trees. The howl of another beast came as a reply from somewhere by the river. They were howling from time to time, and moving, as if conferring about their manoeuvres. Then a few faster barks joined them, obviously from the younger and more impatient wolves.

Svetlana listened to the wolves conferring and realized they were getting closer to the main buildings of the farm. She dressed quietly, trying not to wake her grandchildren, and went out into the frigid dark night. The wind was blowing from the northwest and froze everything it touched in its path. The old woman heard the long bark of a wolf from the direction the wind was blowing toward and realized that the beast was much closer than she might have thought because the wind made the distance seem greater. Another wolf replied, also from the east. She knew the beasts were coming from downwind, so that the people on the farm would not notice them. The wolves were getting closer to the large shed on the farm where Nick's sheep were spending the winter. The old woman knocked on the door of Nick's big house. Soon he got up, and Svetlana's sons as well. Armed with clubs and lanterns they went in the direction from which the wolves were howling.

Paroniya did not insist that Svetlana stay with her till the morning because the old woman convinced her that her grandchildren might need her in case the wolves decide to attack the farm buildings. Mavroona supported Svetlana and saw her off, advising her to keep the two lanterns lit in front of the building where her family was.

That night, near the very beginning of the harsh Canadian winter, at the meeting of the years 1943 and '44, the old woman Svetlana did not have luck at the doorstep of the house where the friend from her youth lived…In the same unusual way that they had met in the long-ago time, they now parted from each other. Svetlana was just a few moments late entering the building which Paroniya's son Nick had given her family to use. As she stretched her arm to open the door, she heard a terrible howl from Nick's huge shepherd dog, Sharov, then the sounds of a fight behind the sheep shed and more painful howls from the domesticated dog. The old woman cried for help a few times and hastened toward the fighting animals. On her way she saw a bunch of trimmed branches piled against the wall of the shed; she grabbed the first branch her hand reached and quickly continued toward the back of the sheep shed. In the darkness she saw a pack of animals fighting frantically, a mass that curled and changed shape like swelling waves on the ocean; she heard the sounds of fighting and pain. She understood that their Sharov needed help and without thinking she approached that mass and started hitting it with the pole. The mass suddenly became still; dozens of burning eyes faced her and like a swarm of bees rushed at her. The old woman had enough strength to strike out several times at what was flying toward her; she felt the weight of the animals upon her and she fell in the snow. Svetlana lashed out with her arms and legs, instinctively pulled her head between her shoulders, but felt pain after pain in her legs, arms, shoulders, back, and chest. Only for a moment her eyes dispersed the darkness in front of her and she saw the huge jaws of the wolves spitting bloody foam that sprayed all over the place and covered her face and eyes...

Svetlana's daughters-in-law were first to come to her, then Mavroona and Nick and Svetlana's sons. Mavroona chased the wolves away from the curled up old woman in the snow by waving with two burning lanterns in front of her. When the men rushed in with clubs and more lanterns, the wolves realized they had lost the battle and ran away; at the place of the unequal battle the old woman lay still, and a few steps away from her lay Sharov, flattened on the snow permeated with blood. Svetlana's eyes were wide open, while the dog signalled its last moments by the spasmodic stretching and curling of its hind legs.

Paroniya did not want to see dead Svetlana's body nor did she go to her funeral at the Doukhobor cemetery in Kamsack. After that event, she completely retreated into her room. Kuzka, Mishka and all four of Svetlana's grandchildren attended the funeral of the good dog Sharov. Kuzka wrote his first newspaper report about that event and took it to the editorial office of the local newspaper.

The winter lasted for months. As if it had decided to mock the official calendar, it lasted long into the spring. And even when spells of warm wind from the south announced the new season for days and the sun rose high above people's heads at noon, as soon as night came the mass of cold air from the north returned over the prairies and made fresh ice on the edges of the lake and lit fires in the houses. There were still no flocks of migrating birds overhead, and the smoke shooting from the chimneys towards the sky adorned with fluffy clouds bent in the morning gently towards the north and in the evening changed its direction, bending towards the south.

Everybody on the farm became worried about Paroniya's health. Mavroona spent most of the time with her, and the old woman even allowed her to help her bathe. At first she apologized repeatedly for her wrinkled and sagging body, for the long and thick grey hairs on her chest and face, but then she got used to having Mavroona help her keep her body clean and change her clothes. When two women who worked for the magazine *Prairie* came from Regina to talk to her about the position of Doukhobor women in Canada, she told them that in some cultures women are like precious stones and men guard and hide them so that nobody can take them. In some cultures they always walk a few steps behind their husbands because the husbands are much older than they are so it is a normal task for a woman to help her husband if he staggers and falls. Among the Doukhobors, Paroniya explained, and among those whose roots are in the Doukhobor Movement, women are different from men; nature gave them different functions and the biggest transgression against nature is to associate emancipation of the female gender with making women and men equal.

"I would never like to become a man, nor instead of mine to see on me their bony shoulders and muscular arms. I would always rather be a gentle pharmacist or a cook than a lumberjack or a miner. I am for the emancipation of the spirit and the social status of women, but not for the equalization of women and men in rope pulling or boxing."

"How about the Doukhobors?" asked the journalists. "Do you still believe in the Doukhobor philosophy of life?"

"I do not know how much you know about this philosophy because I am aware it is considered by some a type of extremism. But our extremism is not harmful to people. On the contrary, it offers hope that eventually people will understand that every person should erase from his brain the segment which creates feelings of aggression and egoism and makes harmful plans against other human beings. I am not sure how long the Doukhobor Movement will prevail. I think that the development of civilization will integrate it into a universal philosophy of life and the need for the movement will cease. For me, such pacifism and philanthropy is a universal human need, and people will find ways to satisfy that need. Because even this war raging now in the human race will help people understand that the biggest step back in the development of humanity is killing people. Pacifism will neutralize the need for patriotism because patriotism is belligerent and keeps people inside divided communities."

The magazine published Paroniya's answers and called her the last Russian woman of the clan of the Evstafy Chernovs in Canada. They said she gave precedence to pacifism over patriotism at a time when this world was in the midst of World War II, with bitter battles being fought for the destruction of Nazism and Fascism, among the darkest monsters in the history of human philosophy; when in the Balkans, where some of the distant Doukhobor roots developed in the beliefs of the Bosnian heretic Bogumils, Tito's partisans were resisting the ferocious armadas of the enemies of freedom and brotherhood among people; when deep in the bosom of the Soviet Union and Russia, where the clan of the Evstafy Chernovs came from to Canada, Hitler's armies, inculcated with the philosophy of bloodthirsty expansionism, were being stopped in their invasion and enslavement of Europe, which had followed in reverse the path of the former conqueror and destroyer of Asia and Europe, the schizophrenic butcher Genghis Khan.

"They did not understand me," whispered Paroniya when she read the text in the magazine. "I have never liked to be promoted. I told them about my belief, and they turned it into politics. I feel you, my Misha, looking at me in a strange way and asking why I allowed them to push me around and move me away from your spirit. Even what happened to

Svetlana was not my fault. Maybe she found me in order to be with me, thinking that you were no more, as she had been with me while I was waiting for you. I only want to be with you forever. I feel sometimes that I will also free myself from this desecrated body and I am happy that we will be undisturbed and together. Then I become afraid that maybe I will lose you entirely, so I try to live ever longer."

Nick and Mavroona, hidden behind some tree or building, often observed Paroniya sitting behind the transparent curtain and moving her lips and arms as if talking to somebody. Mishka and Kuzka saw their grandmother only when accompanied by one of the parents because they were uncomfortable that she, while they were talking to her, was looking through them at somebody behind or beside them. When Nick brought another issue of that same magazine from Regina and showed her Mavroona's picture in their garden in front of the house and the text announcing she had won the award for the most beautiful garden in the province, Paroniya's gaze cleared and she asked why he did not bring Mavroona along, so she could embrace her; she also said she was happy her daughter-in-law had disproved the statements of some politicians and conservative journalists that Russians in Canada were a historical mistake and that Canadian society should cherish only the Anglo-Saxon culture.

"We have learned a lot from them, but we also did not climb down from the trees the day before," Paroniya told him and her gaze wandered through the window and her thoughts into the company of somebody she felt comfortable with. Nick had long ago accepted her belief that their Misha had not died, that she felt his abiding presence close to her.

AFTERWORDS

FAMILY HISTORY, HISTORICAL FACTS AND A MODERN
DOUKHOBOR PHILOSOPHY OF LIFE ACCORDING TO
ONE RESEARCHER OF DOUKHOBORISM,
CHARLIE KOOZKA CHERNOFF

EVSTAFY CHERNOV'S CLAN

Deepest Roots

Chernovs' Toil and Peace was born out of Rifet Bahtijaragic's acquaintance with Michael Chernoff, who showed him an account of the family history written by his brother, Charlie. These Afterwords, based on writings by and about Charlie, present the actual background upon which the fiction of the novel is based. (Among the Doukhobor people, the extended family is known as a clan. The Russian family name Chernov was transcribed as Chernoff in Canada, to preserve the pronunciation of the original. The suffix *-ov* or *-off* would translate as *-son* in English.)

Charlie Koozka Chernoff, in searching out his distant ancestors, reached back five generations to Evstafy Chernov in the first decades of the 18th century. Beyond that time, Charlie could find no usable trace of his deeper roots. It is difficult to research the Chernov family tree because written records were not kept of births, deaths and marriages in Russia once people left the Orthodox Church and began the Doukhobor Way-of-Life. In the Doukhobor society of those days, it was convenient to keep family histories oral so that the prying eyes of the government and military would be unable to discern actual facts and circumstances.

In contrast to searches by Jonathan J. Kalmakoff and Fred J. Chernoff, Charlie's study focused largely on family members and relationships following the arrival of the Chernovs in Canada. With some percentage of uncertainty, he can accept the opinions of the two mentioned researchers that Evstafy Chernov had two brothers, Nikolenka and Makei, that they lived in the first part of 18th century and that from each descended one clan of Chernovs: Nikolenka's Clan, Makeiv's Clan and Evstafy's (or Kars) Clan.

All three branches of Chernovs came to the Milky Waters region (Tavrida province of Russia at that time) from the northern Tambov province. When all the Doukhobors who would not renounce Doukhoborism and return to the folds of the Orthodox Church were expelled to the Caucasus regions, the three Chernov clans became separated. The three family groups lost touch with each other because of expulsion to different regions and the lack of communications.

The Chain Across Generations

Charlie believes that he has enough relevant historical proof to summarize the senior male members of his clan in direct lineage from Evstafy Chernov in Russia and Canada. In the deeper past, the year of birth is estimated on the basis of life stories and anecdotes about them passed down through the generations.

The originator of the Clan, **Evstafy CHERNOV,** was born between 1730 and 1740, somewhere in Tambov province in the southern part of Russia. We have been unable to determine his patronymic.

Evstavy's son, **Vasily Evstafyevich CHERNOV,** was born in the year 1765, also somewhere in Tambov province.

Vasily's son, **Stepan Vasilyevich CHERNOV,** was born in the year 1805, in the village of Radionovka, Tavrida province, Milky Waters region, South part of Russia.

His son, **Vasily Stepanovich CHERNOV** (Chernoff in Canada), was born in the year 1830, also in the village of Radionovka.

His son, **Kostuna Vasilyevich CHERNOV** (Chernoff in Canada), was born in the year 1858, in the village of Ormasheny, Tiflis (today

Tbilisi) province, Trans-Caucasian region of Russia (today Georgia). Kostuna emigrated to Canada in 1899, together with his family.

Kostuna's son, **Misha Kostunavich CHERNOV** (Chernoff in Canada), was born in the year 1879, also in the village of Ormasheny. After their departure from the Kars region, he married Paronia Hancherov, nee Streliov (in Canada, Hancheroff, nee Strelioff) and adopted her young son Petro, who had been born in Russia. Misha settled in with the greater family group in Prokuratova village (earlier Pokrovka) and moved in 1907 to Spasovka village. These villages were in the South Doukhobor Colony of Assiniboia Territory (now Saskatchewan Province), Canada. Misha and Paronia had two children, a daughter Tanya and a son Nick. Tanya chose to move to British Columbia when Peter Verigin relocated his followers there. Unfortunately, Charlie Chernoff knows little about the move, her family, or other circumstances concerning her life. Misha himself died young, at the age of 48, from blood poisoning. He was digging a well on his farm wearing tall rubber boots. He developed a blood blister that broke. Misha neglected to seek medical attention until the foot was turning black, which was too late and the blood poisoning claimed him the next day.

His son, **Nick Mikalayevich CHERNOFF**, was born on December 6, 1909, in Spasovka village. For the first few years he attended the old Tolstoy school, which was about five miles distant. When he was in grade three that school burned down and he concluded grade eight at Whitesand Valley School, closer to his village. After his father Misha died, he took over the family farm. He married Maud (Mavroona) Popoff of Nadezhda village.

The Chernoff family had undertaken the responsibility of running a threshing outfit for the community farmers. They owned the largest threshing machine in the area, a 36-inch Minneapolis Moline thresher. That size of machine required a large crew to feed it. Ten teams, each consisting of a pair of horses and their driver drawing a rack, gathered sheaves and carried them to the thresher. Two field pitchers helped with the loading of the wagon racks in the field to keep up with the thresher. The thresher gobbled up the sheaves as fast as two men could empty their wagonloads from either side of the long feeder. That thresher was powered by a steam engine. In 1940 the steamer was dissected into manageable chunks with an acetylene torch and the booty hauled off and loaded onto a railroad car destined for a smelter in Ontario. In that year there was an active "war effort" to gather all scrap iron and turn it into new steel for military tanks. There was a cleanup also of all the old bone piles remainig from cattle and horses that had died and been dragged off the farmyards,the bones left to bleach in the sun. These bones were used for making glue needed for aeroplanes that were being manufactured in Canada. A couple of planes were made of wood glued and bolted together. The wood was spruce and the glue came from animal bones. The Mosquito fighter/bomber was made mostly of wood, as was the Anson Mk V trainer used in the Commonwealth Air Training Plan.

Later, Nick was the designated community butcher who traveled from farmyard to farmyard to perform the butchering. Many Independent Doukhobors eat meat. He was of the mind that since it was acceptable to eat meat it was acceptable to butcher livestock, but he did insist that animals be dispatched humanely by placing a bullet in the brain of the selected animal. One might think that Nick's acceptance of butchering animals might have compromised the non-violence central to his pacifism. Not so. Nick was adamantly against warfare. He was not an outspoken pacifist but he could not tolerate leaders who seemed to embrace war making little or no attempt to sidestep warfare through negotiations. He believed in negotiations and compromise.

Nick and Maud had two boys born on the family farm. In an attempt to provide a better education for the boys, he accepted a grain buyer's position in the village of Veregin, Saskatchewan. He fared extremely well out-buying the Pool elevator a couple of years after moving to the W.J. Anderson Grain company house in 1944. Unfortunately, the grain dust irritated the lining of his nasal passage and the doctor recommended that he leave the elevator business. In 1946 Nick purchased a general store on Railway Street in Veregin. Veregin began shrinking in size and people began to use Kamsack as their shopping headquarters, so in 1949 Nick and Maud sold their store, bought a section of land near Nottingham, Saskatchewan, and moved their family to Kamsack. Eventually, Nick came back to Veregin, buying and grain farming 240 acres close to the village.

Nick was never afraid of challenges. He was president of the Whitesand School board, he sponsored a baseball team in Verigin, he curled and was icemaker for the curling club in Kamsack. Nick was obsessed with education and convinced both his sons to attend university. He was proud to have all four of his grand children graduate from university. Nick died of a massive stroke in 1996 in the Kamsack hospital.

Nick's wife, **Maud (Mavroona), nee Kuzmova Popova, Chernoff,** was born in Canada in 1908. When she was still a child her father Kuzma home taught Russian to her and her two brothers. They learned to read and write Russian and Maud in her adult years preferred to write in Russian because she could think more lucidly in Russian. She started school knowing no English but caught on fast and she received better grades than English speaking students. Maud was indeed a genius who could have done anything she may have chosen had she had an opportunity to continue her education. As it was, she excelled in the following: raising a family, her cooking was superb—worthy of any Chef in the restaurant business; she was her own architect when she designed the house and green house in Kamsack, she was her own interior decorator, she sewed well from patterns and even made blouses without a pattern; she knitted, she crocheted, she raised the earliest maturing vegetables in Kamsack; her flower garden was the envy of Kamsack and she found a way to protect roses that were not expected to survive the severe months of that temperature zone. She had little patience for the rest of us who were not as intelligent. She was stern, demanding and a bit vain, which showed when she refused to go "uptown" unless she was in her dress clothes and her hair was coifed.

Nick's sons and their families:

Charlie (Kuzma, Koozka) Nikolayevich CHERNOFF, was born on April 25, 1932, on the farm in the SE of section #35, near Kamsack, Saskatchewan, Canada. That event made the doctor's trek from Kamsack to the farm on muddy roads an adventure. Charlie attended an eight grade, single room, one teacher school at Whitesand Valley then three grades per room at Veregin to complete elementary school. Two years of high school in a four grade school in Veregin, and on to Kamsack to complete grades eleven and twelve in separate grade rooms. Charlie was ambivalent about attending university but his dad, Nick, had no doubts that he was going to attend. With intention to escape, Charlie suggested that he did not know what to study but, after father's suggestion of Dentistry, Charlie quickly decided on Engineering. After three years of Engineering with emphasis on mining, Charlie went mapping hard rocks in the Pre-Cambrian shield of Saskatchewan. At the end of the mapping season he had an opportunity to visit underground at the Flin Flon mine. This type of work had no appeal whatever so Charlie decided to take soft rock geology in graduate school after earning his engineering degree. He talked the department into letting him take a two year course in one year, which was a mistake. The courses required a lot of work so there was no time to enjoy the University experience and the thesis required late evenings in Calgary to get it done. In his writings about his life Philosophy, he suggested to new generations: *"I do not recommend rushing through graduate school to anybody. Take your time and get it done right."*

Charlie did geological surface mapping in the McKenzie and Rocky Mountains of Canada for four years then transferred to Geophysics for training. It turned out that the combination of Engineering plus Geology fit a niche with Chevron Geophysical and he stayed on past his training assignment to teach and work on special technical projects. More years of special technical projects and supervising the software development programmers led to a position of

Chief Geophysicist with Chevron Geosciences. Charlie retired from that position in 1992 and decided to remain in the USA in the warm climate, where he could play softball the year round. Seventeen years after that time softball is still Charlie's game. He played some hockey in high school but the game did not come easy for him. Charlie played a lot of baseball and fast pitch softball and at these games he was a "natural".

After Charlie retired, he started to research Doukhobor History and Philosophy and his works inspired Canadian/Bosnian writer Rifet Bahtijaragic to write this book. As the descendant of an Independent Doukhobor father and grandfather, Charlie decided to implant the best values of the Doukhobor philosophy of life and religion into the modern capabilities and achievements of civilisation.

His interpretations of the Gospels of the New Testament may be in conflict with churches that cling to a literal interpretation of the Gospels. He still attends their services at times. Charlie enjoys mingling with people who have the "Spirit," are caring and loving.

Charlie Chernoff married Helen Bojechko of High Prairie, Alberta, in 1959, and they have two daughters, Cheryl Teresa Chernoff and Carlotta Bridget Chernoff.

Helen (nee Bojechko) Chernoff was born in a Canadian Northern railroad section house at Joussard, Alberta. She excelled in elementary and high school and went on to the University of Alberta at Edmonton to earn her teaching degree. When her father fell ill she withdrew from teaching in Calgary and helped him recover at their home in High Prairie, where her parents had cabins for rent. Helen was brought up in the Ukrainian Orthodox Church but in her teen years she transferred to the Catholic Church. To get this sanctioned officially by both churches she had to get permission in writing from her father, from the Orthodox priest and from the Roman Catholic priest. Subsequently she returned to Calgary and got a job in the oil industry, where she met Charlie. Helen was a dedicated mother who made certain that her daughters took advantage of all the opportunities she did not have in a small town. She was busy every day driving them to and from parochial school, driving them to dance classes, driving them to art classes and driving them to piano classes.

Helen's parents came from the Kiev region in the Ukraine. Her father, John Bojechko, served in the Ukrainian Cossacks to fulfill his military conscription obligation. He became tired of being coerced into extending his service in the Cossacks and decided to emigrate to another country. John left his pregnant wife Rose in the Ukraine and made his way to Canada in 1922. In Alberta he was employed by the Canadian Northern Railway and, after several pretty miserable, toil intensive jobs, he saved enough money to bring Rose and their newborn son Mike to Canada. Later he and his boy began building cabins for rent in High Prairie.

Charlie's and Helen's daughter, **Cheryl Teresa Chernoff,** was born in Calgary, Alberta, on January 14, 1960, but completed her elementary and high school in Houston, Texas, USA. She earned an undergraduate degree in Architecture at the University of Texas at Austin. She equalled Charlie's feat of completing the Master's program in one year, at Berkley. After very successful architectural jobs, she opened an independent architectural business in San Francisco. Her specialty is remodelling, refurbishing, earthquake proofing and decorating and furnishing older structures.

Charlie's and Helen's second daughter, **Carlotta Bridget Chernoff,** was born on December 22, 1967 in Houston, Texas. In high school she was the primary player in their annual singing, dancing and acting group for three years. Carlotta went on to college at the University of Texas, and the Sugar Land Rotarians sent her to Australia for study at the Australian National University at Canberra. She participated in a travelling university choral group who traveled Australia on weekends, giving performances in local towns while being billeted in private homes. She learned to appreciate the warmth and hospitality of the Australian people. Upon completion of her undergraduate geophysics degree at Austin, Carlotta spent a semester at Academgaradok, Siberia, Russia, studying Russian in an immersion-type atmosphere. She then completed courses at the

University of Texas leading to a graduate degree in geology. After that Carlotta went to the University of Arizona at Tucson and earned a doctorate degree in geology and started to work for ConocoPhillips as an exploration geologist.

Charlie's brother, **Michael (Misha, Mishka) Nikolayevich CHERNOFF,** was born on December 21, 1936, on the family farm NW of Kamsack, Saskatchewan, Canada. An oral history relates that the doctor's fees were paid by granting him a pig carcass.

After high school, Michael studied Geological Engineering at Queen's University at Kingston, Ontario, Canada with full GMC Scholarship support. He started his career with the Canadian subsidiary of Chevron in 1959. In 1967 Michael left Chevron and worked for two junior oil companies until 1970. In 1970, Michael resigned to accept a new position with a start-up but the job never materialized and Michael was unemployed. This was the start of a long career as an independent consulting and exploration geologist,. From 1971 until the present (2010) he partnered with son Bruce to develop a major oil field in Ecuador (sold to Alberta Energy Co., which later became EnCana Corporation). At various times he performed surface geological field studies in Canada, from the U.S. border to the Arctic Ocean and beyond (Arctic Islands). In his search for oil Michael is tireless and untameable. Even today, fifty years after his career start, he is still looking for the "big one".

All his life he has been physically active. Michael was a Canadian Curling Champion in 1978 (Lukowich rink out of Medicine Hat, Alberta). He is an avid recreational golfer who has shot his age at 68, 69, 70 and 72…

Michael's passion is altruistic financial help to schools and students: he and his wife Dorine have funded major scholarships for university students at Queen's, Brandon University, the University of Saskatchewan and the University of British Columbia (UBC baseball), and provide support for British Columbia 4H members pursuing further education and for students at two Saskatchewan high schools. He and his son, Bruce, partnered to kick start the Chemistry Building at Queen's University, which is now known as "Chernoff Hall".

When he was asked did he ever in his life experience any kind of oppression on the freedom of his spirit and mind, from father's or mother's tradition or from contemporary philosophical and theological systems, Michael Chernoff wrote in his E-mailed answer:

"When growing up, I never was instructed in the ways of the Doukhobors. Our parents did not participate in Doukhobor celebrations other than weddings and funerals. They did not attend the local prayer hall and neither did we, my brother and I. I was aware that I was in Doukhobor country but I had no feeling of belonging. I was like every other prairie boy, playing hockey and trying to make it to the NHL. My parents were both born in Canada and although raised as Doukhobor children, they drifted away at adulthood and became people of the 'prairie sod'."

Michael's philosophy on life is not complicated. It is one of pragmatism and avowed scepticism with one exception: his rules do not apply to the search for oil where he assumes excessive risks, dreams a lot and is the classic wildcatter. He is non-religious but is tolerant of other people's faiths. After experimenting with several faiths at University, Michael concluded that their rituals and formality were silly and they were out of touch with reality. Rather than providing clarity on the subject, it was confusing and Michael withdrew to simply try and be a "good person".

Michael married Dorine Dennison on April 6, 1962.

Dorine, nee Denisson, Chernoff was born in Brandon, Manitoba, Canada, on August 18, 1930 to Agnes (nee Dalgleish) and Roland Dennison. She acquired all of her schooling in Brandon including a B.A. degree from Brandon College. After college, she went to work for the California Standard Company in Brandon and thereafter she worked in the oil industry in Regina, Calgary and Edmonton where she met and married Michael. In 1971, she suffered a massive brain aneurism which required two operations within a period of a few days. The incident was a huge setback since she was unable to walk and talk. It took several years of therapy to regain these abilities; however, this never deterred her from seeing her children through primary and secondary school.

Michael's and Dorine's daughter, **Catherine Anne Chernoff**, was born on October 24, 1962, in Edmonton, Alberta, Canada. She received a Bachelor of Architecture degree from the University of Texas, Austin, USA. She has her own independent architectural firm in Calgary, Alberta. Her firm concentrates on residential, commercial and industrial projects. Besides providing professional services, she is also a developer. Catherine has two children: **Reid Foose and Brooke Foose.** With her characteristics (tenaciousness, toughness and stubbornness), she reminds her dad of her grandmother, Maud (Mavroona). Catherine is divorced and has two children.

Michael's and Dorine's son, **Michael Bruce Chernoff,** was born on June 12, 1965, in Calgary, Alberta, Canada. He studied Chemical Engineering at Queen's University at Kingston, Ontario, Canada. He partnered with his father, Michael, to grow a small oil company into a firm with substantial oil reserves in Ecuador. After the sale of this company in 1999, Bruce struck out on his own to become a highly successful entrepreneur in the Canadian energy industry based in Calgary. He has large ranch holdings in British Columbia (Stump Lake) and Alberta (D. Ranch). He has become an accomplished "team roper" competing in British Columbia and Alberta events.

Bruce's wife, **Dina (nee Abdel-Barr) Chernoff,** was born in England (Egyptian father, English mother) and she was raised in West Vancouver, British Columbia, Canada. She has an undergraduate degree from the University of British Columbia and a Masters in Business Administration from the University of Western Ontario. Dina and Bruce have three children: **Michael Lucas, Nyah Anne** and **Stella Jane Maud.**

Nick's sons, Charlie (Koozka) and Michael (Mishka), are the last Evstafy Chernovs exposed to Doukhobor tradition. The generations after them, Charlie's and Michael's children and grandchildren, are North Americans, born in multicultural settings, cognizant of their mixed traditions only when they think about their roots.

THE DOUKHOBOR RELIGION

A Historical Sketch

The roots of the Doukhobor religion began to take form in the later 1600s, when the Spiritual Christians appeared in the Russ. Half a century later the Spiritual Christians evolved into the pacifist Doukhobors, who forsook the Bible. They preferred to recite the stories of the Gospels orally, having lost confidence in the Orthodoxy for keeping the Bible untainted.

The Doukhobor Movement itself began in the early 1700s, when an unknown retired military man in Har'kov (in today's Ukraine) began teaching that all external forms of the church (edifices, icons, crosses) ought to be rejected. He introduced the idea that each individual has the reasoning power within him to make the choice of right and wrong. It is the belief of the immanence of God, in the presence within each individual of the spirit of God or Christ. This not only renders priesthood unnecessary, since each man can choose to be his own priest in direct contact with the divine, but it makes the Bible a story book rather than a rule book, since every man can be morally guided by self, if only he will listen to the voice within. These premises pretty well negated the need for a church and priests. This religious movement grew and embraced pacifism, love of all human beings, while rejecting idols and excluding priests as intermediaries between men and God.

At the start of the Doukhobor Movement, they called themselves "People of God" or merely "Christians," possibly implying that adherents of other sects or churches were only "false" Christians. The name "Doukhobor," like other names treasured afterwards, was first used in anger and derision by one of their opponents, Archbishop Avrosij Serebrennikov of the Ekaterinoslav region. It means "Spirit Wrestlers," to suggest that they were fighting against the Holy Ghost. In adopting it, the Doukhobors changed its negative connotation to a positive spiritual connotation, claiming that they fought alongside the spirit of God, which they believed to dwell within them.

They differed from the traditional Christian churches in having no liturgy and no icons, no fasts, no festivals, no churches and no priests. They did have appointed, sometimes makeshift, meeting places to praise God, pay homage to neighbours, friends and relatives, and to sing hymns of praise to God or verses of tribulation dwelling often on the harshness of life. They often met in residential homes to conduct prayer meetings. In some communities they had prayer homes, where prayer services and a capella singing of hymns was performed. The prayer homes were of a plain design and architecture with no religious sacraments save the ever present cellar of salt, loaf of bread and pitcher of water. They acknowledge no sacraments and in denying the importance of baptism, by immersion or aspersion, they are more radical than the Anabaptists (Mennonites, Huttterites and Molakons). >From the Quakers they differ in rejecting the doctrine of redemption.

Doukhobors believe *heaven* and *hell* to be states of mind, and for that reason they bury their dead with little ceremony. They regard marriages as free unions between individuals, not contracts bound by laws of church or state. However, most often the consent of parents of both bride and groom was sought and secured before marriage.

They believe in one God and interpret the Holy Trinity to mean: God is manifest in the human soul thus: in memory (Father), reason (Son) and will (Holy Spirit).

Doukhobors believe that Christ lived, was an intelligent holy man who brought many inspiring messages to mankind. They do not necessarily believe in immaculate conception nor in the resurrection of the flesh. They believe that Christ preached in parables and that the Bible stories are most often metaphors and need not be interpreted literally.

The only visible symbols of their faith are the loaf of bread, the cellar of salt and the jug of water that all stand on the table in the middle of their meeting houses, symbolizing the basic elements of existence. In Doukhobor parlance, bread is the staff of life, water is the spirit of life and salt is the essence of life.

The Doukhobors believe and practice the equality of men and women. A woman can as easily be elevated to be elder or leader in the community as any man. Children are revered and all take a responsibility in seeing them grow up, particularly close relatives.

The Doukhobor Seven Virtues and Seven Sins: Every Doukhobor was encouraged to know the seven virtues and the seven deadly sins. The seven virtues are: **humility, generosity, chastity, patience, fasting, brotherly love** and **spiritual vigil.** The seven deadly sins are: **pride, greed, lust, anger, sorcery, envy** and **despondency.**

The most enduring and oft quoted Doukhobor proverb is: **Write it in your heart, proclaim it with your mouth!**

Doukhobors have many mottoes which guide their lives, but the most prominent are: Toil and Peaceful Life, and The welfare of the whole world is not worth the life of one child. Their motto *Sons of Freedom cannot be slaves of corruption* has a couple of different explanations but it was created from the deep of reaches of Doukhobor morality.

STRUGGLE ACROSS THE CENTURIES

Doukhobor Leaders and Russian Sovereigns

Historically, the Doukhobor Movement had its roots in the reforms of Nikon, Patriarch of the Russian Orthodox Church, in 1652. Those reforms caused a split in the powerful Russian Christianism and produced several Christian factions. From some of them born on the left wing of that split, the Doukhobors borrowed their first basis for a new teaching: God exists in spirit and truth and man needs no priests to worship God; a person does not need an intermediary nor a formal church structure in order to attain God's grace. Governments are unnecessary, as are church clergy and churches, as are official registration of marriage, birth, death and divorce.

The new teaching was professed by an unknown retired military man in the village of Okhochem in the Har'kov district, between Moscow and the Black Sea. He articulated the new movement's beliefs in three basic propositions:

• Each individual has the reasoning power within him to make a choice of right or wrong;

• External forms of the church are rejected, such as the cross, sacramental rituals, sacred relics, icons;

• The spirit of God is in every person but is not equally welcomed...

The first acknowledged leader of the Doukhobors was **Sylvan Kalesnikov** (1750s), from Nikoloskya village of the Ekaterinoslav Gubernia. He espoused simple brotherly living and he used the New Testament in his teachings. He introduced the use of bread, salt and water during meetings as symbols of basic needs and hospitality.

The official church proclaimed the new movement as a heresy and the first persecutions of Doukhobors started at the time of **Catherine the Great.** Some residents of Tavrida Gubernia (on the north coast of the Black Sea) convicted of Doukhobor heresy, were put in restraints and exiled to work in the mines of Yekaterinburg and others from Ekaterinoslav were exiled to Azov to labour on fortifications.

When leader Kolesnikov died (1775), he was succeeded by **Ilarion Pobirokhin,** a wool dealer from Goreloe village, Tambov Gubernia, in the same region of Russia. He proclaimed that the "Spirit of God" resided not in material structures or icons but within the hearts and souls of human beings. He denounced violence and professed that love and goodness are the true guiding principles for every human being. He implored that truth is not in the books but in the spirit, not in the Bible but in the "living book" in the "living memory" (through oral communication amongst the devout). He rejected the use of the Bible. Ilarion Pobirokhin set up an untraditional village commune (compared to existing Slav villages) dominated by religious teachings and with punishment meted out for transgressions of current teachings. He composed many Doukhobor psalms, often condemning ritualistic and dogmatic practices of the Orthodox Church. Unfortunately, Ilarion repudiated equality concepts and declared himself a divine leader.

During the time of Ilarion Pobirokhin appeared the first separation in the Doukhobor Movement. His son-in-law, Semen Uklein, became disenchanted with the Doukhobor teachings of his father-in-law and created Molokonye as an offshoot of the Doukhobors (1780). The main difference between the Molokonye and the Doukhobors is that the Molokonye believed in an after life and used the Bible, both New and Old Testaments. The Molokonye drank milk (moloko) during the Lenten Fast; this is how they derived their name.

In 1785, Catherine the Great's regime exiled several groups of Doukhobors to Azov, others to Archangelsk, some to Finland, others to Tobolsk in central Siberia and others to Irkutsk in western Siberia. Doukhobors were conscripted to bear arms. Members of exiled groups formed communities in exile, which survived into the 1900's as Amur Doukhobors.

Ilarion Pobirokhin was brought to trial for his teachings around 1785. During that process, for the first time the official church named them "Doukhobors". Ilarion was exiled to the Amur region in Siberia (1790s) and never returned.

After his exile, Pobirokhin was replaced by **Seveli Kapustin** (1792), purportedly the son of Ilarion Pobirokhin. Kapustin departed from the traditional Slav village organization by establishing an Orphans' Home, an edifice where households who had lost their heads resided as well as orphans and the infirm and aged, where travelers were put up, where government officials were entertained and where the common treasury was kept. He and the Elders set up a Communal Structure. Towards the last days of Kapustin's leadership the communal system was being slowly abandoned in favour of private ownership. He composed or edited many of the Doukhobor Psalms.

During much of Catherine the Great's reign, the Doukhobors lived mostly unmolested lives and grew unimpeded in numbers in several gubernias of Russia and adjoining territories. Towards the conclusion of her reign, however, the government decided to clear the land of Doukhobors to stop the spread of Doukhobor beliefs throughout all of Russia, in particular areas around Moscow. The widely used penalty was to exile them to remote areas of the Russian Empire. More Doukhobors were exiled to places like Finland, Yekaterinburg, Archangelsk, Tobolsk and Irkutsk.

After the death of Catherine the Great (1796), the new **Tsar Paul** issued an Edict (Ukaze): *Everybody who shall be convicted of belonging to the Doukhobor sect shall be condemned to a life of long labour!* The new Tsar fully annexed Georgia in 1801 and exiled to that part of his empire, to the Caucasus, a group of Doukhobors. This was the beginning of the Trans-Caucasian exile.

Tsar Paul was killed in an organized conspiracy later in 1801 and his son, **Alexander I Pavlovich Romanov,** was crowned Tsar. He decided to rectify the injustice made to the Doukhobors and issued an Edict allowing all Doukhobors throughout the Russian Empire to resettle in the Milky Waters (Molochnji Vodi) area of Tavrida Gubernia, north of the Black Sea. Each returning family received from the Russian government a land grant of 45 acres with tax exemption for five years and each was eligible for a 100-ruble loan. That looked like an act of kindness of the new Tsar but it was a clever way of concentrating and isolating the Doukhobors in one part of the Empire to protect other parts of Russia from the influence of their new teachings.

Seveli Kapustin died in 1817 and **Vasily Kalmykov** (son to Kapustin) became the new Doukhobor leader. With him the Kalmykov dynasty assumed the Doukhobor leadership. Unfortunately, Vasily Kalmykov was dull-witted, self-indulgent and a drunkard. The next year, Tsar Alexander the First visited the Doukhobor settlements in Milky Waters and he was duly impressed with their lifestyle and agricultural progress. He opened doors for new moves for Doukhobors from other parts of Russia to that region. At this time the Don River Doukhobors were resettled to the Caucasus Alkhalkalak and Elizavetpol regions.

The golden time of the Doukhobors was under Tsar Alexander I but the new Tsar, his son, **Nikolai I Alexandrovich Romanov** (from 1825), had a different opinion. On February 6th, 1826, he issued his first decree against the Doukhobors: 1) Doukhobor peasants of Orthodox Landlords could be recruited for life; 2) Travel passports and work permits would not be issued to Doukhobors; 3) Doukhobor teachings and services in public no longer permitted; 4) The Orthodoxy were to begin a vigorous program of Doukhobor conversion and dispersal including the taking of children of Doukhobor parents. This was a huge distractible wave of that time against Doukhobors and their Way-of-Life. That wasn't enough! Three years later, Tsar Nikolai I issued a new Edict that all Doukhobors in the Milky Waters region either rejoin the Orthodox Church or be banished (at their own expense) to the Wet

Mountains district of the Trans-Caucasia, near the Ottoman Empire. Approximately 4000 Doukhobors were deported to this new location in the period from 1841 to 1845. In that region they found everything different: the Georgian Language was totally different from Russian, worse climate and no cultivated soil, different oppressed ethnic groups...The Doukhobors had been expelled from the north shore of Black Sea and forced to move to the Caucasus during 1841—45, to avoid conscription for the Crimean War between Russia and Turky, France, Great Britain and Sardinia.

Vasily Kalmykov died before the Doukhobors were sent to the Caucasian Mountains. His son Ilarion assumed leadership but Ilarion was effeminate in appearance and habit as well as being a confused, impotent alcoholic. Ilarion died shortly after arriving in the Wet Mountains of the Caucasus. The decision was made to designate his son, Peter Kalmykov, to succeed Ilarion (1841). But, since Peter was still a child, a temporary leader, **Levusha,** was chosen. Soon, mysteriously, Levusha was exiled to Siberia. **Peter Kalmykov** finally became leader of the Doukhobors in 1845. His lack of the necessary qualities rendered his leadership an empty one. Peter's most profound contribution to the Doukhobor movement was his marriage in 1856 to Lukerya Gubanova. He named Lukerya to succeed him as leader of the Doukhobors just before he died in 1864.

Lukerya (Gubanova) Kalmykova was one of the most charismatic and beloved Doukhobor leaders and the first woman in that role. During the Russo-Turkish War, following an ultimatum by Grand Duke Michael Romanov, brother of the Tsar, **Alexander II Nikolayevich Romanov**, leader Lukerya allowed Doukhobors to transport supplies for the Russian army. In this way she escaped pushing Doukhobors into direct war operations. For their help to the Russian army, the Russian government paid the Doukhobors one and a half million rubles and invited them to colonize the war-occupied Kars region. Between 1879 and 1883, 5,000 Doukhobors moved to the new Russian territory from the other side of the Caucasus. During Lukerya's time Doukhobors showed compromise and moral laxness; many of her followers began to drink vodka during their time with the army, and came back to extravagant weddings and began to carry rifles to defend themselves. During Lukerya's leadership the Doukhobor population swelled to 20,000.

After the assassination of Alexander the Second, his son, **Alexander the Third, came to the Russian throne**. The new Tsar revived autocracy and started with the decision to clean out any kind of opposition to the Imperial laws and the official Church.

Five years before she died in 1887, Lukerya Kalmykova chose the first cousin of her deceased husband, **Peter Vasilevich Verigin,** to succeed her, and started to teach and prepare him for Doukhobor leadership. This training took place in the Orphans' Home, tradtionally used for meetings and other community purposes. Thus, although her choice was public knowledge, she unfortunately left no documentation of this succession in leadership. That produced a split in the Doukhobor movement: the followers of Peter V. Verigin (great-grandson of former leader Kapustin) formed the Large Party and the **Gubanov brothers**, Mikhail and Ivan, created the Small Party of Doukhobors. Very soon the Russian regime sentenced Peter Verigin to five years in exile and sent him to Shenkursk in the far northern gubernia of Archangelsk. From exile he issued a decree to his followers to abstain from tobacco, alcohol and meat.

In 1887 the Russian government introduced in the Trans-Caucasus mandatory Military Service. As a revolt, in Doukhobor villages and areas pacifism again became the central theme of Doukhobor spiritual re-awakening. At the same time communal ownership of property was rekindled and sharing re-introduced.

Because of his big influence on the Doukhobor movement, Peter Verigin was re-sentenced and exiled to northern Siberia, near the village of Obdorsk, by the River Ob, and contact with his followers curtailed (1894). He sent instructions to the Trans-Caucasian Doukhobors to organize a Burning of Arms in three villages as a protest against militarism (June 29, 1895). Many arms were privately owned. Some were obsolete muskets issued to Doukhobor families during their move from Milky Waters to the Wet Mountains of the Cacasus, ostensibly to ward off the pagan Tartars and Hill People. The arms were never used and lay rusting away in attics. Military and local police officials did not intervene in the communities of Kars and Elizavetpol. Cossacks charged the singing choir in Wet Mountains, flailing whips as they feared for their own welfare.

Three months later, the Governor of Tiflis, Commander-in-Chief of the Civilian Sector in the Caucasus, Prince Shervashidze, sent his report about Doukhobors burning arms to the State authorities and made a proposal: "In view of the above, I suggest it would be advisable to send the Doukhobor fasters (Postniki) out of the Province altogether, it would be best of all to send them out of the country into neighbouring Turkey, where, according to rumours, they have been trying to go themselves.... The Kars Doukhobors are by comparison with all others, in all respects the most rebellious and dangerous of anarchists in continuing anti-government ferment.... The Elizavetpol Doukhobors are compliant in all respects except conscription".

Lev Tolstoy reinforced his activities in Russia and in the Western world to obtain the permission of Russian authorities for Doukhobors to emigrate abroad. Tolstoy's letter drawing attention to the plight of the Doukhobors (translated by John Coleman Kenworthy) was published in the *Times* of London, under the Title: "A Russian Religious Sect". From many sides of the world pressure grew on Russian authorities to give Doukhobors permission to emigrate. And finally, the Russian Ministry of Internal Affairs issued such a permission in principle. This decree was delivered during a visit by the wife of new **Tsar Nikolai II Alexandrovich Romanov**, Dowager Empress Alexandra Feodorovna, to her son in the Caucasus (December 31, 1897).

Lev Tolstoy issued an appeal in London's *Daily Chronicle* of the 29th of April, 1898, for contribution of funds for the relocation of the Doukhobors.

Early in 1898 the Doukhobors received official authorisation to leave the country—but with the condition that, having emigrated, they would lose the right to return to Russia and they would leave at their own expense.

DOUKHOBORS IN THE NEW WORLD

The first group of Doukhobors (1126 souls) left Russia for Cypress on the French ship Duran, on August 6th, 1898. But the soil and weather proved inhospitable, and the Doukhobors were unable to cope. The relocation to Cypress was a dismal failure and many Doukhobors died of fever. Some of them returned to Kars while most of them left Cypress for Canada in May of 1899.

In August 1898, James Mavor, a political economist at the University of Toronto, received a letter from the Russian anarchist Prince Peter Kropotkin, drawing attention to Tolstoy's plea for assistance to the Doukhobors. Mavor contacted Tolstoy and Clifford Sifton, Canadian Minister of Interior, and pursued negotiations with the Canadian Government for the Doukhobors' emigration to Canada.

Very soon, in September 1898, two Doukhobor families accompanied by Tolstoy associates Aylmer Maude and Prince D.A. Khilkov arrived in Canada and travelled west in search of suitable land for settlement, available free through the Dominion Land Act. Canadian authorities moved a step forward to prevent eventual discontent of Doukhobor emigrants and on December 6th, 1898, with an Order-in-Council, exempted Doukhobors from military service on Quaker-Mennonite-Tunker precedence. Other pacifist individuals and groups were accorded the same privilege.

At the end of 1898, Tolstoy contributed $17,000 for the Doukhobor move to Canada. The money come from selling his novel *Resurrection*. He collected an additional $17,000 from friends.

The first shipload of 2,134 Doukhobors, from the Tiflis area, and exiles from scattered villages along Kura River, boarded the vessel *Lake Huron* and sailed for Canada out of the Batum, east side of Black Sea, on December 22nd, 1898. With that shipload, an ethnographer, Vladimir Bonch-Bruevich, came to Canada. He worked out of the village of Mikhaelovka recording Doukhobor psalms and hymns. He returned to Russia in 1900 and published in 1909 a collection of Doukhobor oral tradition *Zhivotnaia Kniga Dukhobortsev* (*Doukhobor Book of Life*). The first shipload arrived at the port of Halifax on January 23rd, 1899. They spent the winter at Brandon, Manitoba.

The second shipload of Doukhobors, from the Kars and Elizavetpol regions, arrived in Canada on the vessel *Lake Superior*, which docked at Saint John, New Brunswick, after a three-week quarantine at Lawlor Island. This ship brought to Canada 1,342 Doukhobors from Elizavetpol, 647 from Kars and 8 from Tiflis. They proceed to Yorkton, Saskatchewan.

The third shipload of Doukhobor emigrants (1,036 passengers) arrived at the Port of Quebec on *Lake Superior*, on May 9th, 1899. The fourth shipload, with 2,286 Doukhobors on the steamer *Lake Huron*, docked at the Port of Quebec on July 3rd, 1899. The fifth shipload of 670 Doukhobors on the *Lake Superior* came to Canada on July 20th, 1899. This one carried the families of Doukhobor military personnel detained in Russia until their terms of military service had expired.

During the summer of 1899, the Doukhobors established 57 villages in the Assiniboia District—24 in the South Colony, 10 in the Good Spirit Lake annex, plus 10 near Blaine Lake in the Saskatchewan District (north of present day Saskatoon). About 5,800 Doukhobors established themselves in Assiniboia and about 1,700 residents in Saskatchewan.

The first couple of years of Doukhobor life in Canada passed under huge pressure and influence on the Doukhobor Way-of-Life. Tolstoy praises Doukhobors in a letter for remaining cool to government regulations, refusing to take the oath, condemning private property, abstaining from eating meat and using tobacco and intoxicants. He asserts, "The Christian teaching cannot be taken piecemeal; it is all or nothing at all." Under the pretext of furnishing the Doukhobors with a "Handbook For Learning English," Vladimir G. Tchertkov seeded and stimulated radical ideas such as: "All governments are based on violence", "Do not take the oath", "Oppose private property", and "A Man must be free." Alexander Bodyansky, an anarchist, circulated amongst the Doukhobors and around the world petitions on behalf of the Doukhobors, complaining about government treatment of the sect concerning regulations of land ownership and registration of vital statistics. He objected to the Canadian government that the recording of individual homestead entries contradicts Doukhobor beliefs, as does the registration of births.

The Canadian government reiterated that Doukhobors must abide by Canadian law which includes recording vital statistics (births, marriages, deaths) and laws governing homesteads (1901).

Peter V. Verigin played one-upmanship with the likes of idealists like Tolstoy and wrote letters meant to outdo them. Verigin praised vegetarianism and the simple life, condemned ownership of land, use of metals, wearing of dressy clothes and use of animals. He professed that cultivation may be evil. He preached that the Garden of Eden is the ideal state. Verigin's letters were not meant for the Doukhobors but they heard about the contents and the radicals began a movement to follow all these ideals. The letters were written while Verigin was still in exile in Siberia but they were used by extremists in the community to justify extreme and radical beliefs (December 1901).

Awakened by government calls for registration of vital statistics and a call for individual entry for homestead land, and by the propaganda of Tolstoy, Tchertkov, Bodyansky and Verigin, a few radical Doukhobor seekers of freedom released cattle and horses, began pulling wagons by human power, dispensed with money and objected to tillage of soil with advanced machinery (October 1902).

In October, 1902, extremist Doukhobors aroused by calls for simplification joined a maniacal trek (1,700 souls) to express their displeasure with materialism.

After 15 years in exile Peter Vasiljevich Verigin was released in the Autumn of 1902 and instructed to proceed directly from Russia to

Canada to join the Doukhobors. He laid the foundation of the CCUB (Christian Community of Universal Brotherhood) in Canada (1903). Verigin began consolidation of the Doukhobors by moving 200 young Prince Albert Doukhobors to the North and South Colonies area (Swan River and Kamsack) in April 1903. A Doukhobor Committee paid half the required fees and registered about 2,000 Doukhobors by proxy as land (~320,000 acres) homesteaders. Independent Doukhobors continued to depart from CCUB.

Initially the Doukhobors had come to Canada as a single group, at least so considered by the Canadian Government.

However, the first shipload carried the most extreme believers who had been moved by the Russian Government out of their Caucasus villages and dispersed amongst Georgian inhabitants along the flatlands neighbouring the Kira River near the Greater Caucusus Mountains. These Doukhobor souls had no money, chattels or animals and could not speak the local Georgian language. They were mainly sustained by monetary contributions from less strident Doukhobors who continued to live in the villages. Almost all of these displaced Doukhobors were vegetarians or even vegans (Posniki), whereas most in the Caucasus villages ate meat (they were called masniki). In Canada the first-shipload people were settled in the North Colony, so the North Colony was where the more extreme believers were located. It is mostly out of this group that the militant Sons of Freedom grew.

The Doukhobors next to arrive were settled in the South Colony. These were not extremists but were dedicated followers of Peter Verigin.

Both the North and South Colonies became united in a cooperative.

As the years progressed it became apparent to some Doukhobors that a few members were not contributing to the farming effort that was expected of them. So dissension began to grow in the cooperative.

Many began to become totally disenchanted with the cooperative and also with Peter Verigin because he began to espouse ideas that suggested he had divine authority.

Now there became two groups of individual Doukhobors, the Cooperatives ("Community Doukhobors") and the Independents.

Eventually the extreme believers in the cooperative group felt that the Cooperatives were becoming too wealthy and too materialistic so a further split occurred and they became the Sons of Freedom. Initially their protests against materialism and schooling were passive but extremist leaders emerged who guided them to "terrorist" acts like burning schools, burning houses of the wealthy and dynamiting power lines. They also desecrated cemeteries because they believed headstones were Icons and not memorial stones.

In May 1903, Sons of Freedom released Peter "The Lordly" Verigin's horse and set fire to the wood and canvas of the village reaping machine in Otrodnoe. This was the first act of arson and depredation by that radical group of Doukhobors. They continued to Nadezhda, where they were confronted, whipped and driven off. Some of them went on to Yorkton, where they disrobed in protest against materialism. A group of 52 Doukhobor nudists, Sons of Freedom, wandered about the villages of Smyrrenia, Otradnaya and Nadezhda and were beaten back with switches for fear that they would torch property. They too continued on to Yorkton, where they are jailed for indecent exposure. They made a pact to be martyrs for the cause of religion.

The Canadian Northern Railway (later to become the Canadian National Railway) mainline reached Kamsack and Veregin in the South Colony (1903). Right after that Pete Verigin moved his headquarters to village of Veregin from the village of Otrodnoe. On February 10th, 1903, at the village of Terpenia, government officials Crerar and Harley presented the oath of allegiance to the Crown. This caused great consternation and misunderstanding amongst Doukhobors.

In 1904, the Railroad mainline reached Buchanan in the Good Spirit Lake Annex of the South Colony. On December 15th, 1904, the Doukhobor Land Reserve status was terminated; this amounted to over 500,000 acres of the original areas reserved for Doukhobors which had not yet been "legally taken up". The village of Kamsack was incorporated on May 15th, 1905, and later became a Doukhobor centre. In the same year, two districts of the North-West Territories,

Assiniboia and Saskatchewan, were absorbed into the new province of Saskatchewan.

Big changes for Doukhobor conditions of life started when Frank Oliver succeeded Clifford Sifton as Minister of Interior of Canada (1905). The administration rejected the Hamlet Clause provisions and became rigid in applying the rules of the Dominion Land Act homestead regulations. Oliver, a man of little conscience, believed that the only good way in Canada was the Anglo-Saxon way. In 1906 Minister Oliver re-interpreted the Hamlet Clause. The Clause was an addendum to the Dominion Land Act regulations meant to accommodate the Mennonites and later the Doukhobors. The Hamlet Clause interpretation in 1899 was: "If a number of homestead settlers, embracing at least twenty families with a view to greater convenience in the establishment of schools and churches, and the obtainment of social advantages of like character, are to be allowed to settle together in a hamlet or village, the Minister may, in his discretion, vary or dispense with the forgoing requirements as to residence, but not as to cultivation of each separate quarter section entered as a homestead."

Community Doukhobors (followers of Peter V. Verigin) purchased nearly 15,000 acres near the town of Veregin (1905). One hundred eighty-two Doukhobors released from Yakutsk exile (Russia) were settled in the South Colony. The exiles were released following a Manifesto of Merciful Pardon issued by Tsar Nikolai II Alexandrovich Romanov after his wife gave birth to their son, Peter V. Verigin travelled to Russia in October 1906, supposedly seeking land for emigration for those who wished to return. Suspicion is that he left to avoid confrontation with the new Land Regulations in Canada and let the Doukhobors make an independent decision.

In 1907, the Canadian government declared that Doukhobors could no longer own large parcels of land communally; Doukhobors could apply for individual improved homesteads but were required to sign the oath of allegiance to the King. All land title deeds held by Community Doukhobors were cancelled. In Yorkton and Prince Albert 1,600 Doukhobor homesteads were made available for new filing by the general public. This constituted nearly 260,000 acres of improved and semi-improved land and this action became legal with the cancellation of the Hamlet Act in 1907. Protesting the land issues, about 70 Doukhobors trekked to Fort William (July 1st, 1907). In April, 1908, the government rounded them up and shipped them back home.

In June, 1907, the Doukhobor community purchased about 10 acres of land near Yorkton and built a large modern brick factory. This was the second brick factory in Doukhobor community proprietorship; the first was built in Veregin. On the northern boundary of the North Colony in 1907 and 1908, Doukhobors established three new villages. Community Doukhobors from Blaine Lake and Good Spirit were relocated to these villages. Shortly many moved back to their old villages, while some relocated to British Columbia. Improved Doukhobor lands were offered to homesteaders on a first-come, first-served basis. Doukhobors had the opportunity to apply for homesteads but were required to sign the oath of allegiance to the Queen.

At a Doukhobor meeting in Nadezhda (December 15th, 1908), Peter V. Verigin proposed abandoning customs such as bowing to the ground and reading and singing of psalms. This proposal was rejected by conservative followers. An austerity program was imposed to pay off community debt.

In the year 1908 Doukhobors from the Canadian Prairies began moving to British Columbia. They were mostly Peter "The Lordly" Verigin followers organised as Communal (CCUB) and Sons of Freedom Doukhobors. They purchased 15,000 acres in B.C., thus avoiding the pledge of allegiance. In the next five years, over 5,000 Doukhobors moved to the Kootenays region in British Columbia. Almost all Independents and some Community Doukhobors remained in Saskatchewan.

Saskatchewan Doukhobors and the Provincial government started to recognize each other: Doukhobor marriage rites were acceptable to the government as long as a vital statistics report was submitted. The Saskatchewan Doukhobors were required to report births and deaths.

On the November 20th, 1910, Lev Nikolayevich Tolstoy died at Yasnaya Polyana, Russia.

The Canadian Northern Railway reached Pelly, Arran and Benito in the North Colony (1911).

In British Columbia public schools Militia training and rifle training were introduced (1912). This action precipitated alienation of Doukhobors and they started to boycott public schools until a compromise agreement was reached in 1915.

Doukhobors constructed the Brilliant, B.C., suspension bridge at Ooteshenya in 1913.

Community Doukhobors in British Columbia accepted public schools for the teaching of their children (1915). At the same time all vestiges of military training at public schools were erased. In Saskatchewan all Doukhobor children from the age 8 years to 14 years had the obligation to attend public schools (1916). The first Doukhobor graduated from the University of Saskatchewan was Peter G. Makaroff (1916).

Independent Doukhobors sent delegates to Ottawa to discuss their objection to National Military Service. The Solicitor General affirmed exemption from service for this group of Doukhobors on January 17th, 1917. In October Peter V. Verigin attempted to deny them this right but his objection met with no success.

On April 9th, 1917, the CCUB (Christian Community Of Universal Brotherhood) was incorporated with $1 million total capital. It had 5800 Doukhobor members with 14 directors, including Peter V. Verigin as president. The Central Office was in Veregin, Saskatchewan until 1931, when it was moved to Brilliant, B.C.

On April 9th, 1917, the first St. Peter's Day was held on the farm of N. G. Makaroff. This is a two-day celebration commemorating the burning of arms in Russia and asks people to become proactive in the mission of non-violence and universal peace.

By 1918 many community villages had been abandoned. In the same year a new colony of Doukhobors was established at Kylemore, Saskatchewan.

On June 9th, 1919, Canadian Parliament passed Order-in-Council P.C. 1204, prohibiting the landing in Canada of any Doukhobor, Hutterite or Mennonite because of their "peculiar habits, modes of life and resistance to secularization". This Act was rescinded in 1921 for Mennonites and Hutterites, and in 1925 for Doukhobors.

Community and Zealot Doukhobors again opposed public education in 1922. Soon after that, in 1923, the first case of arson surfaced in the Kootenay region as a protest measure. The B.C. Government levied a fine against communal property in retaliation for Doukhobor parents not sending eligible children to public schools.

In October 29, 1924, Peter "The Lordly" Verigin died in a railroad coach explosion between Grand Forks and Brilliant, British Columbia. In the same misfortune fourteen others were killed. The cause of the explosion has never been determined.

A new Doukhobor leader was named in September, 1927—Peter P. (Chistiakov) Verigin, who was living with his family in the Soviet Union. Accepting the nomination, he left his wife Anastasia and son Peter in the Soviet Union and sailed for Canada. He arrived in New York on September 16th, 1927. The new Doukhobor leader arranged to have his grandson, John Voykin, emigrate to Canada (1928). John changed his name to John J. Verigin. Peter P. (Chistiakov) Verigin collected over $500,000 for an emigration scheme but nothing ever came of the migration. Most of the money disappeared (1929).

CCUB Central Office transferred from Veregin, Saskatchewan, to Brilliant, British Columbia (1931). In the same year all Doukhobors in British Columbia were barred from voting and The Dominion Government prevented all British Columbia Doukhobors from voting in federal elections (1934). Dissolution of the B.C. cooperative began when two major creditors launched foreclosure proceedings on their properties. They served eviction notices to the B.C. cooperative in 1939.

In 1937, the Independent Doukhobors disassociated themselves publicly from Peter P. (Chistiakov) Verigin and stated that they no longer recognized the Verigin dynasty. One year later, a large flour mill in Veregin was destroyed by fire.

Peter P. (Chistiakov) Verigin died in a Saskatoon hospital on February 11th, 1939.

At the six-week commemoration, the followers elected Peter Iastrebov Verigin as their new leader. Since his whereabouts in the Soviet Union were not known, John (Voykin) Verigin was chosen to lead the Doukhobors temporarily. Peter Iastrebov Verigin died in Soviet Union before assuming any leadership role in Canada.

At the time of conscripting troops for the Second World War, the Canadian authorities mailed a notice to Doukhobor eligible males (over age 18) who refused military service (1941). They were offered three alternatives: join the military, join the alternative service work brigade for not more then four months, or go to jail for one year with time off for good behaviour. Alternative service camp concluded forced work internment at the Prince Albert site (October 29, 1941). Men disbanded and went home.

Doukhobor marriages in British Columbia were recognized by Government in 1950.

In the period from 1953 to 1959, many B.C. Zealot parents were jailed for failing to send their eligible children to public schools. Children of jailed parents were taken away and imprisoned in a detention camp at New Denver, B.C.

The Federal government amended the criminal code to delete penalty of three years of prison for participation in nude parading (1955). That was, of course, an unreasonably stiff penalty and totally unjustified to begin with.

On November 14th, 1957, the Orthodox Doukhobors received word of the death of Peter P. (Iastrebov) Verigin (the son of Peter Chistiakov) Verigin, in the Soviet Union.

The restoration of federal and provincial franchise regarding elections came in 1957. All B.C. adults were allowed to vote in both federal and provincial elections. This was in response to a study commissioned by the Federal Government in trying to deal with the "Doukhobor Problem". The B.C. Provincial Government began recognizing Doukhobor marriages on May 13th, 1959.

John J. Verigin (original last name Voykin), grandson of Peter Chistiakov Verigin, was named Honorary Chairman of the USCC (Union of Spiritual Communities of Christ) on August 16th, 1960.

On December 7th, 1975, an arson blaze destroyed the USCC headquarters in Grand Forks, B.C.; store, publication facilities, library and many archived rare photos and documents were destroyed.

On June 29th, 1980, the National Doukhobor Heritage Village in Veregin, in the Canadian Province of Saskatchewan, was officially opened.

In his later years, Charlie has put the Doukhobor Way-of-Life under the prism of his very serious research. He believes, wholeheartedly, in the basic early creeds established by the faithful. Other practices did not work out too well. The Doukhobors' communal system was established by Doukhobor leader Savely Kapustin, early in the development of the faith. However, the community enterprise was not a success and was being dismantled and replaced by Independents late in Kapustin's leadership prior to his death. The communal enterprise that began a resurgence in 1893 under the guidance of Peter V. Verigin and the elders succeeded in Russia, because there were so many exiled Doukhobor brothers and sisters in desperate need of assistance just to subsist. But this unrestricted, mandatory sharing was not popular once the Doukhobors moved to Canada where no Doukhobors who chose to pull their load were starving or suffering from maladies caused by malnutrition. The second communal experiment which began in Russia in 1893 failed in Canada in 1940 when the Community of Christian Universal Brotherhood (CCUB) declared bankruptcy.

Charlie is all for sharing if the help is for a good cause and gets to the recipient with little or no skimming. He is for giving to charities that help the poor, the sick, the homeless and those deprived of complete families. He is for giving to medical research institutions if they are not adequately funded by government. He is all for giving to educational facilities that use the money to improve the education system so that a larger numbers of students (poor, minority, without family) can receive a proper education and become contributing citizens who participate in society by casting a knowledgeable vote. He is not for turning over one's wealth to a leader or committee who may use a portion of the

512

proceeds for personal gain. Unfortunately, there were persistent rumors of Doukhobor leadership excesses. One story has it that Peter P. Verigin would have volunteers travel about the villages to collect cash for one enterprise or another. Part of the money would be siphoned off into the leader's valises who would make a secretive trip to Winnipeg. The undisclosed purpose of the trip was for personal pleasure; Winnipeg business leaders were invited to a hotel room where poker playing ensued night and day. The interlude would end when leader Verigin headed home with two empty valises. The rumour may be without merit but Charlie has found that such tales are not usually fabricated out of wisps of fog.

Charlie likewise has no quarrel with the suppression of intoxicants and smoking. Smoking has proven to be more than a luxury, it is also a destroyer of health. On the issue of alcohol, he would prefer that the creed stated that spirits could be used in moderation. Wine has proven to be a healthful stimulant. Drinking to excess is not acceptable and some, who have a decided weakness for alcohol, are better off as total abstainers. Drunkenness is not a virtue.

Regarding meat, Charlie is not in agreement with the restriction on meat consumption or the experiments that also rejected fish, eggs and dairy products. He has absolutely no argument with persons who wish to abstain from eating meat or any of the other foods just mentioned or any foods for that matter. There is nothing wrong with vegetarianism or veganism as long as the choice is left up the individual. There is absolutely no evolutionary excuse for introducing vegetarianism or veganism into the Doukhobor creed.

Charlie is in agreement with the creeds that resist the adoration of idols. He contends that he can get along without intermediaries (deacons, priests, bishops, cardinals and the pope). He cannot believe in immaculate conception nor the resurrection of the flesh. Neither of these are necessary to the recognition that Jesus was a man of unparalleled goodness with no prejudice against women or colour or race. Yes we should all try to be as good and as forgiving and as caring and as loving as Jesus.

Charlie does not believe that heaven and hell are places (especially up there in the sky or firmament, or down below). He will go with the Doukhobor belief that they are states of mind because he cannot think of a superior metaphor. If we do good, share, are forgiving, caring and loving, our mind will be in a state of euphoria which is our heaven. The Buddhists use the term bliss for this state of mind. They reach this state of mind through meditation. Charlie believes it is better to reach this state of mind through good acts, sharing, caring and loving as was/is the custom of the Doukhobors.

The most prominent of Charlie Koozka Chernoff's works are the **questions and answers** in his

Thinnest Book in the World on Spirituality

Charlie (Koozka Nikolayevich) Chernoff started this little book with the question—*How should I live*—and with the answer—*I should strive to be good and kind and treat others as I would have them treat me.*

His explanation of those words is full of pacifism: *Good and kind means respecting others for what they are; intellectual giants or average folks. If they need assistance then I should offer assistance or I should look for individuals who may be able to help them and try to convince these folk to assist them. And, do not be quick to judge! Evaluate, discuss…Be kind and do not impose one's own philosophy or will on anyone. Be gentle in conversation. There is never any excuse for shouting or cursing. Often listening and empathizing is all that is required.*

And in this smallest book Charlie writes that: *The Win/Lose situation is not satisfactory. Let us say the husband is domineering, is a control freak, will not listen to alternatives. This may not have been too big a problem during courtship where the couple spent only part of a 24-hour day together. It can be a big, big problem when the married couple has to spend many hours together every day, every week, every month, every year. This marriage cannot survive.*

If I were the woman in this relationship, I could be meek and totally submissive and let the other party always control the situation; let them play the role of all-powerful. I do not care for this solution because while it may make them content, it will make me miserable. I do not believe even Tolstoy would subscribe to this practice. I think this is shallow and foolish thinking and is only meant for public consumption. That is no satisfactory Win/Lose situation.

In the Lose/Win situation the husband is always being submissive to please his wife. He shops when she wants him to, he stops when she wants him to, he watches her TV shows; well you get the idea. This marriage will not last. The husband will begin turning to a female that will be more compliant and before long there is an outside relationship and the marriage is on the rocks.

Now we go to the Win/Win situation. In this case the couple takes turns at giving in and sharing. Maybe George does not like broccoli while Laura does. It will not kill George to eat some broccoli once in a while; in fact it may save him from prostate cancer. Laura may not like fish but George does. It will not kill Laura to eat fish once in a while; in fact it might sharpen her mind. This marriage has big chances to survive, because nobody gets their way all the time and in a spirit of sharing and giving and getting both should be spiritually satisfied.

Having established the proper, spiritual lifestyle, let us proceed to three questions that many beg to have answered. I must admit that it took me a long time to come to a solid consensus in my own mind on my answers.

Do I believe in **Heaven?** I do not believe in Heaven in the traditional sense that Heaven is up there somewhere in the firmament. I believe that heaven is a state of mind. If we live a good life as we have outlined earlier then we will be content and satisfied and our mind will be at peace and in a state of bliss. The Buddhists speak of bliss but they achieve it through meditation. I cannot subscribe to this. I believe bliss must be achieved through living a good life and doing good works and interacting in a friendly, neighbourly fashion with people.

*Do I believe in **Hell?** I do not believe in Hell as down there somewhere; as a place where people or souls go. I believe that hell is* *a state of mind. If we do not live a good life as outlined above, if we disrespect our friends and neighbours, if we do not treat animals gently, if we do not protect the environment, then our mind will be in turmoil and never satisfied. We will be experiencing torment and anguish and dissatisfaction in our mind. It will be hell! The Hellish state of mind is just the opposite to the Heavenly state of mind.*

Do I believe in **immortality?** This is the toughest question of all. But after many years of reflection I conclude that this question cannot be answered. And indeed there is no need to answer this question. If we try to use mathematics to derive whether immortality exists, we will find that there is no formula that can be used for such a computation. Science likewise is no help. If we hypothesize that immortality does exist, then we must be able to devise experiments which will either support or deny this hypothesis. It turns out that experiments of this type cannot be devised. We are left with a conundrum for which there is no answer. And indeed there is no need to answer this question. However, in accepting that Heaven and Hell are states of mind and that either state can be achieved in our normal life on Earth, then it is easy to conclude that if we live a good normal life on Earth, we can continue on that track if there is immortality. If we live a life of oppression and immorality in our normal earthly life, then its consequences will continue into forever. The answer then is that we do not know if immortality exists, because there are some things we are not meant to know, but that if we live the good and generous life on Earth, we can continue to experience heaven for eternity if immortality does indeed exist.

CHARLIE'S RELIGIOUS AND SPIRITUAL PROGRESSION

As a result of his lifelong quest, researching his roots and the history of the evolutionary processes of contemporary philosophy which are creating humane ways leading to a state of global pacifism and philanthropy, Charlie Koozka Chernoff wrote this acknowledgment and confession:

I can finally say, with unabashed honesty, that I have completed my lifelong search for a sense of religion that I could live with and spiritual enlightenment that is totally fulfilling.

It was not easy; it took a long time.

The journey started when my dear mother began teaching me the fundamentals of the Doukhobor Way-of-Life. I learned about the Spirit of God within me and within every other human individual. I learned that because we were all brothers and sisters (since we all shared the spirit of God) we must not kill and must treat others as we want them to treat us.

These basic precepts allowed me to accept, without shame, the pacifist stance of the Doukhobors during World War II.

Further discussions with mother exposed me to the notion that since the scribes of the Gospels had manipulated the message in the

517

biographies to suit their own intentions and since the Church authorities continued to rephrase the texts every few centuries, it was best to embrace the Doukhobor tradition of passing the teachings of Christ on orally rather than relying on the text of the biographies in the Bible. Although I must admit that mother did study the Russian language version of the King James Last Testament.

When, in early high school, I became totally confused by the Christians' claim that Jesus Christ was born of a virgin, making Mary both a mother and a virgin, I again turned to my mother for clarification.She said that she earnestly believed that Christ was a mere mortal of uncommon goodness.

After that my belief in a non-virgin birth and a resurrection that did not involve the raising of the flesh were not discussed with devout Christians, especially the fundamentalist kind, because I feared being scorned. Indeed, I was a bit ashamed to harbour these beliefs since so many of my erudite friends were so convinced of a virgin birth and resurrection of the flesh.

The Doukhobor belief that one could worship and pray to God without having to go through an intermediary (priest) appealed to me and seemed always so sensible. The idea that one need not go into a church to appeal to God also made sense to me although I did go to the United Church on Sundays during my two senior high school years. I simply enjoyed the company of the congregation.

During my adult life I have attended Catholic Church with my wife, who is a devout Catholic. During services I have often been perplexed by the adherence of educated clergy to the exact Gospel wording and to accept and teach, in a literal sense, some rather preposterous "historical happenings".

I was always haunted, though, by the fact that I was so much unlike other Christians in my beliefs; and were they so right and I so wrong? Why was it clear to me that the Bible stories ought not be taken literally? Was I alone?

After I retired and had more time to think about religion and spirituality and had more time to read theological books that introduced new information about the early years of the Christian faith,

I began to see that I was not the only one who believed that Bible stories and historical Gospels were not to be interpreted literally. I also met people of faith, Baptists and Jews, who believed as I.

Elaine Pagels was the first to bolster my self-confidence, with her books *Beyond Belief* and *Gnostic Gospels,* that it was I who was correct and the literalists who were on the wrong track.

Bishop John Shelby Spong reinforced all my beliefs about Christ and the Gospels in his book *Why Christianity Must Change or Die.* However, I must admit that I was not fulfilled, my soul not fully nourished, by his attempts to introduce a substitute course to traditional Christianity.

By this time I had enough confidence in my own ideas about religion and spirituality that I wrote a short essay titled "The World's Thinnest Book on Spirituality". I do go back periodically and update the text as my perceptions become clearer and more stable.

Now along comes Tom Harpur, a one time Anglican priest and professor of Greek and New Testament at the University of Toronto, with his book *The Pagan Christ—Recovering the Lost Light.* He presents an absolutely convincing argument in a most straightforward language and manner (quoting many earlier works that are in difficult prose) that the stories of the Bible date back to ancient Egypt; that the Egyptian's treated these stories as myths or allegories and never were they meant to be taken literally. He explains how the early Gospel scribes and proponents of Christianity (which he refers to as Christianism, after Kuhn) turned myths into historical biographies of Jesus Christ. He exposes, delicately, albeit forcefully, how we totally garble the message when we try to interpret the Gospel literally. He also questions that there ever was a historical Jesus but sets that question aside with the message that it really makes no difference to the meaning of the story, or mythos, for our time (see page 178 of the book). "What next?" Was the question that still lingered after I had read Elaine Pagels and Bishop Spong. Then Tom Harpur makes a case for the indwelling presence of the divine (Incarnation) in the life and soul of every human being. The message is that if one recognizes the divine presence in another person, one cannot harm them or suffer them to endure pain, suffering or any injustice for that matter (see last chapter, page 184) since they are your brother/sister. He asserts that if all religions can be persuaded to believe in the divine spirit within every individual then we can achieve world harmony amongst all peoples, all religions.

So where has my religious and spiritual journey taken me? I have come full circle. **I am back where I started because as a fledgling Doukhobor that was what I was taught to believe.** The spirit of God lives in every human being. We are all brothers and sisters. We must, therefore treat everyone else as we ourselves would like to be treated. And the Doukhobors always believed that the Bible stories were myths, allegories or metaphorical parables.

Since the early Doukhobors had called themselves Christians (implying possibly that Orthodox Christians were inferior in spirituality and belief) it is quite possible that they were referring to gnosis (knowledge) gained from adherence to the mystical spiritual message interpretation of the Gospels; rather than the literal and historical message interpretation propounded by the Orthodox Church. The Doukhobor Way-of-Life then was merely the continuation of the Mystery Religions that were suppressed and brutally stamped out by the unforgiving, power hungry Christians of the fourth, fifth and sixth centuries.

The Doukhobor faith is sound because it is built on a solid rock foundation.
AMEN!

ABOUT THE AUTHOR

Rifet Bahtijaragic originated in the Balkan Peninsula. Here cultures of East and West mixed, and here also the sectarian politics of power and predominance bred confrontation and ignited destructive wars at least twice during one human's life. Running from that destructive Balkan syndrome, Bahtijaragic has spent the course of his life searching for paths throughout narrow nationalistic and intolerant religious societies close to home and far away and tried to grow into an earthling with the sensibility of cosmic belonging. In the last war of bloodthirsty nationalisms in Bosnia, he could very easily have been murdered because of his pacifist orientation.

He was born on 7 January 1946 in the small mountain town of Bosanski Petrovac, Bosnia and Herzegovina. He finished his university studies fourteen years before the Sarajevo Winter Olympic Games, and during those years worked in two separate fields: as a specialist in economic development for state banks and companies, to make his daily bread; and as a writer of journalism, poetry, stories, essays and novels, to earn sustenance for his soul.

In the time of peace and happiness during Tito's Yugoslavia, Bahtijaragic did not succumb to the challenging temptations of the international metropolis. (He served as governor of the Centre of *Privredna banka Sarajevo,* the Bosnian state bank service for Francophone countries, headquartered in Paris.) He could have stayed in this role while remaining out of Yugoslavia, but, during the last Balkan Wars, at the end of the second millennium, he emigrated with his family from Bosnia to Germany, and then in 1994 to Vancouver, in

Canada. He is a member of The Writers' Union of Canada and The British Columbia Federation of Writers.

Rifet Bahtijaragic is known also in the world of UFO-logists. His sightings of the unidentified objects over Ukraine, Bosnia and British Columbia in Canada are very important pruf that our civilisation is not alone in the cosmos.

He is active in the Canadian Multiculturalism Movement (Interview under the title "The politics of Identity").

ABOUT THE ARTIST

Born in West Germany in 1951, Bill Hoopes grew up in both the United States and Europe. He immigrated to Canada in 1981, and currently lives and works on Bowen Island, near Vancouver, British Columbia.

Hoopes' formal training in Fine Arts includes an Associate of Fine Arts degree from Parkland Junior College (1974-1976), a Bachelor of Fine Arts degree from the University of Illinois (1976-1979), and graduate studies in Fine Arts at the University of Wisconsin (1979-1980) and Illinois State University (1980-1981). Since that time, Hoopes has worked as a professional artist in Canada.

Over the past 20 years, Hoopes has participated in numerous national and international juried and solo exhibitions, with paintings displayed in both public and commercial galleries and used as illustrations in various publications. Much of his work portrays the delicate balance that exists between humanity and the environment, reflecting the earth's precarious ecological and political situation. Some paintings depict the peaceful co-existence that can occur between humans and nature; others emphasize the consequences of failure to recognize our contributions to environmental and social imbalance.

As one artist observed, Hoopes' interpretation of nature are like "looking through to the other side of a mirror". His idyllic scenes evoke a soothing, romanticized vision that conveys a feeling of familiarity while at the same time evoking the sense of a place waiting to be discovered. Bill's stylistic approach to handling form, combined with a subtle tweaking of space result in a greater sense of compositional movement and an attempt to reveal the fragile soul and precarious nature of his environments.

CPSIA information can be obtained at www.ICGtesting.com
Printed in the USA
LVOW071520171111

255452LV00004B/9/P